GLORY GROVE

A NOVEL

GARY BYE

Glory Grove: A Novel
Published by Granite Point Publishing
Pomeroy, WA

Copyright ©2022 by Gary Bye. All rights reserved.

No part of this book may be reproduced in any form or by any mechanical means, including information storage and retrieval systems without permission in writing from the publisher/author, except by a reviewer who may quote passages in a review.

All images, logos, quotes, and trademarks included in this book are subject to use according to trademark and copyright laws of the United States of America.

ISBN: 979-8-9867002-0-5 (paperback)
ISBN: 979-8-9867002-1-2 (ebook)
FICTION / Literary

This is a work of fiction. Names, characters, businesses, places, events, locales, and incidents are either the products of the author's imagination or used in a fictitious manner. Any resemblance to actual persons, living or dead, or actual events is purely coincidental.

Cover photograph by Eric Argyle.
Cover design by Natasha Brown. Interior design by Victoria Wolf, wolfdesignandmarketing.com. Copyrights owned by Gary Bye.

QUANTITY PURCHASES: Schools, companies, professional groups, clubs, and other organizations may qualify for special terms when ordering quantities of this title. For information, email garywbye@gmail.com.

All rights reserved by Gary Bye and Granite Point Publishing.
Printed in the United States of America.

To my wife, Kayleen, who loves me, close families, farm life, small towns, good books, and football.

"In the great cities we see so little of the world, we drift into our minority. In little towns and villages there are no minorities. People are not numerous enough. You must see the world there, perforce. Every man is himself a class." —W.B. Yeats

CHAPTER 1

LEAVING

IT WASN'T EXCESSIVE SPEED that left hair on the grill of Brock Gallagher's car. Instead, given the slow pace on this rural backroad, he let his mind wander to the meeting he'd called a few days earlier with his football team in Seattle. He couldn't forget the look on the boys' faces. But the sudden glint from branched antlers and the flash of a copper-colored hide yanked his mind back into focus.

A massive bull elk burst from the hawthorn trees shouldered up to the two-lane blacktop. The thousand-pound brute, nostrils flared and tongue flopping side to side, swung his massive rack toward the auto as he sprinted across the road. Gallagher dropped his coffee, stomped on the brake, and yanked the steering wheel hard, veering into the opposite lane. He instinctively braced for impact. But as quickly as it appeared, the animal vanished. Heart pounding, Brock slid out of the car to survey the damage.

It wasn't a mirage, he thought, as his fingers lifted the brown tufts of hair from the grill. He watched them drift away on the puffs of a hot June breeze. As a teenager, he often hunted for such a trophy animal with his father, but they'd never seen an elk as regal as this one.

Brock climbed back in the car and retrieved the coffee mug, one of the hundreds given to boosters of the football team he coached at Brighton High School. He mopped up the pooling black liquid at his feet. Any evidence of the spill would annoy Celia, his wife of thirteen years, who prized the new black Lexus as yet another status symbol.

As a teacher in Seattle, Brock became accustomed to freeway driving, but this incident on a country road reminded him of his life before Celia and the city.

A few days earlier, Brock handed his resignation papers to the athletic director at Brighton, then called his football team together to give them the news. The young men were expecting a rousing speech about working hard over the summer to finally bring home a state championship. When Brock was hired as the head coach, he promised the players the sky was the limit. He believed it then and now. They had the potential to go both undefeated and take the state crown. He'd wanted it for them and to be a part of it himself.

When the young men gathered—some sat while others stood—they were in the same locker room where, before each home game, Brock attempted to inspire them with his words. Now he was finding it difficult to come up with any. He fumbled with his papers while summoning the necessary courage to deliver the news the team was not expecting to hear.

He saw a smiling Joe Nelson, the star quarterback, playfully joking with Yancey Washington and Brian Crayton, his top receivers. Bill Blessinger, the running back who'd been named first team All-State as a junior, was wearing his usual grin while chatting excitedly with two linemen, John Felts, all six feet five, 260 pounds of him, and Evin Johnson, nearly his identical twin, weighing in at 270 pounds. These players were destined to play at the college level. A few might eventually play on Sunday. He took one last look at the entire group of young men, held up his hand, and began to speak.

"Gentlemen, you may be one of the finest groups of high school football players in the state of Washington. You've worked hard to achieve that goal. But when the season ends, I hope you haven't settled for being a runner-up. Work to be a state champion."

There was loud cheering at the mention of a state championship. Brock held up his hand again. "Try to be champions and teammates on and off the field. I expect that of you. Football is a team sport. It takes a dedicated group effort to deliver a memorable season. Keep that in mind during the summer as you prepare. And next fall when you're facing adversity, remember it isn't a single player who will put the ball over for the score. It's the entire team. As a member of that team, you have a responsibility to your teammates to leave nothing behind. Your effort needs to be one hundred percent. That's how you will win the trophy."

Again, the players let out a cheer, this time louder than the last. Brock took a deep breath before delivering what he didn't want to say and what he knew would shock the team. But he'd delayed long enough. "Sadly, I have to tell you I won't be able to be with you on your journey. I have resigned from my teaching job and as your coach."

He saw the shocked faces as he continued. "My mother is very sick and doesn't have a good prognosis. I'm moving across the state to be with her. It means I'll have to leave it to you to inspire each other in the season ahead."

He heard the gasps and saw the tears of the toughened teenagers as he fought back his own. Brock's voice cracked as he delivered his final thought. "I'll be with you in spirit, but remember it's your job to listen to your new head coach, whoever that might be. Rely on yourselves and each other to make your dreams come true. Now bring it in here, and let me lead one last cheer for the Brighton High Bulldogs."

The team gathered around, and he led the cheer in a group hug, mixed with tears and stifled emotions, as the young men said farewell to their coach. They'd followed him with undying loyalty. To some, he was a father figure. Now he was walking out of their lives.

The parting was just as difficult for Brock. Leaving everything he'd worked for at Brighton was like an artist slaving over an easel, creating a masterpiece, only to give it away. He'd spent a decade turning a perennial losing high school football program into one the city admired and opponents feared. At Brighton, one of the state's largest schools, he'd guided his teams to five playoff runs and a state championship appearance. With each year's improvement, the booster club sent a bigger check to sweeten his salary. He and Celia used them to help buy a fashionable home by the lake and their luxury automobile.

Before dawn the following morning, Brock eased his six-foot-two frame into his car and brushed the shock of unruly brown hair from his eyes. He was going home to a town called Glory Grove. He'd left Seattle early to avoid the worst of the traffic, but as he hit the on-ramp to the freeway, it was already bumper to bumper.

Eventually, the great migration heading toward downtown broke away, and the remaining vehicles relaxed into an orderly flow. When he reached the summit of the Cascade Range, the highway became a two-lane affair. Passing through one of the small towns on his route, he pulled over at a convenience store for fresh coffee. It was one of the few active businesses in a downtown dominated by abandoned storefronts. "Pretty quiet this morning," he said to the gray-haired woman with bright orange fingernails at the counter.

"Always is," she shrugged. He dropped change into a can placed at the counter for donations to a local athletic team. "For football camp," the woman said, noting his contribution. "We should have a good team this year."

"Yes ma'am." Brock smiled. He knew her words were often spoken in every community, on every college campus, and even in the professional ranks leading up to the season opener. *Hope springs eternal*, he thought.

Brock stepped outside and let his eyes take in the little main street. The morning was already heating up, but there was little movement in the town. His journey would take him to a place like this—once a thriving community, grown old, struggling to hold onto its earlier identity. On the surface, it seemed the communities had little to offer the youngsters in their sphere.

But Brock appreciated the hidden strength of small towns. He had fond memories of his own years in Glory Grove, where he'd grown to manhood. Of course, he'd been away so long; perhaps he couldn't comprehend the effects of the downward spiral the town was experiencing. Would the boys there still understand hard work and sacrifice and still carry the banner of optimism for the people of their community? Did their success on the athletic fields or courts still bring pride to the small crowds who came to watch them play?

When he'd played high school ball, the people in his town adored their Grizzlies sports teams, especially football. For over a century, the final days of wheat harvest quickened the pulse of the locals anticipating the first Friday night game. Even as the threshing machines gathered the last bushels of wheat in the upper elevations of the hill country, the serious beginnings of a new football season were unfolding in the settlement down below.

As a teenager, Brock joined his teammates, shirtless young men sprinting up and down the track bordering the gridiron, preparing to impress their coaches. At the school, the doors were locked for the summer except the one leading to the dark basement, which housed the weightlifting equipment. The evening ritual of pumping iron attracted even the bashful boys wanting to become part of a popular group.

At practice before the season started, the teenage girls gathered at the edge of the field in their cut-off jeans and spaghetti-strapped tops—some dressed a little too daring for the church ladies—to witness the reshaping of the team for the upcoming season. There, they'd scope out a potential date for the annual homecoming dance just months away.

Those days in Glory Grove were a springboard for his own bit of fame and wealth. Brock had lived a wonderful life—a seamless arc of open opportunity and good fortune. He routinely returned to the family farm to visit with his mother, but for personal reasons, he avoided spending much time in the town where he'd led his high school football team. Now, his mother's cancer diagnosis was bringing him back to his hometown. As her only child, Brock would care for her until the end. It was a promise he'd keep. It also meant reacquainting himself with the town and the people who helped launch his career.

After the near miss with the elk, Brock steadied himself and resumed his drive. He was on the outskirts of Glory Grove when he spied the sign. *Welcome back, Brock.* Fashioned out of a cardboard box with letters neatly drawn in black magic marker, it was nailed to the old locust tree marking the city limits. He nearly missed it as his heart picked up its pace. He didn't expect the greeting and wondered who would go to the trouble. He didn't want it, hoping to slip into town unnoticed. But there it was. Word was out. He was back in Glory Grove.

CHAPTER 2

IRENE

BROCK DROVE DOWN THE MAIN STREET; seeing the familiar road sign, he turned left off the pavement onto Kirby Road. Another twelve miles on a gravel surface and he reached the family's silver mailbox still bearing his father's name. A right turn took him up their private lane to the two-story, white farmhouse. He pulled himself out of his car, stretched his legs, and slipped silently into his boyhood home.

When he found his mom asleep, lying on the couch, he caressed her hand. She was recovering from another round of chemotherapy, and her arm was bruised from the IVs she'd received. Her blue eyes opened slowly, but they sparkled with the sudden recognition that her son had finally come home.

"Hi, sweetheart," Irene whispered.

"Hi, Mom."

"Is Celia with you?" Irene knew Brock's wife probably wouldn't be there. Celia almost never came to the farm.

Brock rocked back in the chair he'd pulled up next to his mom. "No, she stayed in Seattle … had a lot of odds and ends to finish before the renters move into our house."

"I see. It's going to be a bit of a shock for her, coming here."

"She'll get used to it," Brock said, although he half-wondered if his wife would ever accept living in Glory Grove. Celia loved the people in her art world, especially those who frequented the gallery where she worked. Celia's work was in a different universe than Brock's. But they'd always met halfway and were comfortable in their marriage.

In Glory Grove, there wasn't much of an art world. A small gallery on the north side of Main Street displayed the works of local artists, but it only opened on special occasions. Still, it filled up the space of an empty storefront and helped make it look like the town had some life.

"Maybe Celia can start a painting class," Irene offered. "The young folks in this town could use it. I'm sure there might be some budding artists among them who just need some encouragement. Most of the kids here just do one or two sports in school or raise animals for the fair. It would be nice if they had some other opportunities. Besides, our teams haven't done very well recently. The football team has really fallen on hard times."

"So I've heard," Brock said. "It'll cycle back. These small schools have their ups and downs. It takes Jimmys and Joes to perform the x's and o's."

The response he gave his mother embarrassed him. The 'coach-speak' had bubbled up instinctively. It came from talking to sports reporters. As a coach, he learned early in his career how to give a reporter a quote without really saying anything. At least not anything with enough meat on it to hang on an opponent's bulletin board or that could irritate a frustrated parent with a bone to pick. His mom deserved better.

Although it had caught him off guard, Brock had gotten wind of the controversy in Glory Grove the year before. A Facebook post came midsummer when the school board made a decision that many thought impossible.

The exact wording of the press release was straightforward. "*Due to the unexpectedly low turnout for varsity football, the decision has been made to cancel the upcoming season.*" It went viral among the alumni on social media. The response was instantaneous.

"What the hell is that about?" one post said. "Has the school board lost its mind?"

Another post was more to the point. "Football too tough for the snowflakes? Do they need a safe space and a teddy bear?"

Dozens of former players jumped into the conversation. Most were stunned. Others derisive. Many downright accusatory. How could the young men of the school abandon the gridiron tradition?

Locals were less antagonistic, endeavoring not to ruffle the feathers of their friends and neighbors while still trying their best to get the teenagers to rethink their decisions. "It's a choice you'll regret later," noted one of the former star players, who ran the local farm implement dealership. "Playing on a football team with your friends will give you memories you will cherish forever."

Of course, there were a sympathetic few who had never liked the power football held in the community and were quick to find a reason to tear it down. "I can fully understand any decision these boys make not to damage their brains for the rest of their lives. The sport should have been outlawed years ago," said one especially vocal critic. The woman finished by stating, "There are too many men out there suffering from the abuse of their bodies as teenagers."

Brock had stayed out of the conversation. He knew people would want to know his opinion on the subject because of his high profile in the sport, but he didn't want to stir the pot.

Irene was fully awake now, her glasses firmly fixed on her slender face. She was propped up with two yellow pillows behind her back.

"You know the town is going to start asking you questions," she said, trying to prepare him for the inevitable. "Even before the season was canceled, they weren't real happy with Coach Newton and the way the program had struggled."

"Figured that might happen," Brock said. "Well, I hope they can put together a team for this year, but I'm not here to help fix a broken program. I'm here to help you get better." He wondered if she also knew the true reason for his return—to help her in the dying process. "I'm just going to lie low and let things work themselves out," he said. "Football has always been a part of what made this town tick. Just because they didn't have a team for one year doesn't mean it's the end."

Irene sat upright. "It's going to be pretty hard for you to stay out of the public eye now, with the Derby Daze Festival coming up. People already know you're back in town. They will expect to see you."

Brock had almost forgotten about Derby Daze. The event was officially called The Glory Grove Combine Demolition Derby Daze Celebration. The community gathering marked the beginning of summer and served as a long weekend full of class reunions, picnics, a Main Street parade, classic car show, and a country dance. And to top off the action … the combine demolition derby.

Farmers and their mechanic friends spent days fixing up retired, junkyard threshing machines, decorating them with spray paint to resemble small-track stock cars. Each of the entries had its own moniker reflecting the owner's particular sense of humor or allegiance to a brand of farm machinery. *Deere Killer, Red Dawn Destroyer, Machine*

Mayhem, and *Litening McGrain* were a few of the community's favorites.

Most of the crews entered for fun. But a few took the competition seriously and worked long nights to ready their machines to challenge the perennial winners or to hold onto their dominance. In a series of heats, the roaring grain gatherers would run headlong into one another until smoke and steam poured from their metal hulks, and only a single combine was left moving under its own power.

The weekend was the community's biggest social gathering. By the end of it, nearly everyone had run into old friends or neighbors with an opportunity to renew friendships or stir up old rivalries. For Brock, it would be a weekend full of harmless handshakes and inquisitive looks as he attempted to discern someone's identity created by a nineteen-year absence.

"I suppose you'll want me to go," Brock said with a knowing smile.

"Yes, and I want you to take me with you, so people realize I'm still alive and kicking."

When she appeared in public, Irene always made a point of masking her pain. Even at the funeral for Brock's father, Max, who had perished in a freak farm accident the summer before Brock's senior year of high school, she'd appeared composed and attentive to the hundreds of mourners who came to his funeral.

Max had been one of the community's most well-respected citizens—he'd held every organization's leadership role—and didn't seem to have a single enemy. And if there was any friction between him and his wife, Irene, it was over Max's younger brother, Richard, who spent a little too much time at the local tavern and squandered some of the farm's money at the gambling tables.

Still, after Max's death, Irene and Richard had developed a working relationship that kept the farm from being sold. Irene ran the business, and Richard—who admitted he couldn't safely handle the money—would do the day-to-day work of running the farm.

Even when Richard, on a whim, started up a swine-raising business, Irene knew enough to let him go with it. They would market the little pigs to the local 4-H and FFA members as show animals for the local fair. Besides, she loved watching the white and black piglets romping around the barnyard. And she took pride in watching the young kids displaying their grown animals. And, for the most part, the extra effort the pigs required detoured Richard from his weekend benders.

"Okay, Mom, if you're up to it, we'll go to Derby Daze," Brock agreed but wondered if his mother could summon enough energy to make it through the whole affair.

CHAPTER 3

TIM

BROCK AWOKE WITH A START. He wanted to be up before the sun, but now it was shining through the curtains into his eyes. Bothered by the utter stillness of the farm, he'd tossed and turned throughout the night. When he finally collapsed into a near catatonic state at two o'clock in the morning, his dreams were intense, with odd visions of football and Glory Grove. Old friends and enemies filed through the ether of his dream world.

He was in his old bedroom. The walls still displayed his football jerseys ... one from his days on the Glory Grove High School team and another from the state All-Star game, where he'd led his Eastside team to victory with three touchdown passes. Hung most prominently was the jersey he'd worn for the four years at the state university.

But now, he could smell the fresh coffee and bacon his mother was preparing; he hurried down the stairs. She was excited for the day ahead, especially to be on the arm of her son.

"Good morning, Mom," Brock said, rubbing his eyes as he slid onto a chair at the kitchen table. "I forgot how quiet it is out here in the country."

"Except when the wind is whipping," Irene smiled. "Some say it will either give you peace or drive you mad." She was anxious to get to town for the celebration and was dressed in comfortable jeans and a frilled turquoise blouse. Her makeup covered the spots brought on by the cancer treatments.

She laid out four strips of bacon and two pieces of toast for Brock with orange juice on the side. While in high school, he'd eaten the same breakfast every morning and was happy to resume the tradition.

Back in the city, his wife, Celia, was still in bed with the curtains pulled tight as she always was when he left for school. When teaching at Brighton, his breakfast was cold cereal and a waffle in the toaster. At school, he'd grab a cup of coffee from the cafeteria. He and the cooks were friendly, and as loyal supporters of the football team, they hung a Bulldog pennant from the kitchen wall. Some days they would have a cinnamon roll waiting for him.

"Your uncle Richard is coming by to pick us up," Irene said. "He wants to see you and bend your ear about the Grizzlies football decision last year."

"I guess it's probably better coming from my uncle than from some of the others." He knew how much Richard loved football and how upset he'd been about the cancellation of last year's season. To satisfy his football fetish, he'd begun betting on college games. Still, he loved the high school game best.

"Not so many instant replays. Professional and college games take forever. It's all business," Richard liked to grumble. "The kids in high school play for pride and to represent the town. It's real emotion, win or lose."

Brock ate quickly, put on a pair of tight Wrangler jeans, and slipped into the cowboy boots he still favored when he wasn't coaching or teaching. As he finished dressing, he could hear the rumble of the jacked-up late 90s Ford pickup Richard doted on and saved for trips to town. Rolling to a stop in the gravel driveway, Richard let the truck idle for a few seconds, then revved the engine to announce his arrival.

"Hey, Rocket," Richard warbled as he stepped into the kitchen. The nickname had been dropped on Brock years ago in the lead-up to his first game of high school football. Coach Sullivan claimed his new freshman phenom had a rocket for an arm. Brock never missed a start in his four years of high school. The name stuck.

"Hello, Uncle Ricky," Brock shot back in mock exaggeration. He loved his uncle even with all his faults. Although not as tall or as handsome or as ambitious, Richard reminded him of his father. With his thinning hair, rosy cheeks, and wire-rimmed glasses, he might have passed for a high school social studies teacher.

Richard was flushed and happy. Brock wondered if it was the weekend festivities that lay ahead or if his uncle had a few nips on the bottle for breakfast. His uncle had no competition when it came to socializing—always ready with a joke or tease for anyone who wandered by. Usually, he was surrounded by friends who absorbed his glow just by standing, listening, and laughing.

"So, are you ready to greet your throng of admirers? They're all looking for guidance from the all-knowing, wise one."

Brock rolled his eyes. "They won't get any advice from me. I'm just going to watch the parade, eat country food, and cheer on the combines." He wished he had his uncle's outgoing personality. Even when speaking to football boosters or at an award banquet, he found he couldn't tell a good joke. But he ultimately realized if his teams kept winning, the fans would forgive his lack of glibness.

"Then saddle up. Brock, you're going to have to boost your mother into my big truck."

"Maybe you should buy a smaller pickup," Irene said. "How many little pigs would you have to sell to buy a little pickup?"

"Hey, this little piggy is going to go wee-wee-wee all the way home, if you don't stop talking and get into the truck," Richard said as he lifted Irene up into the seat.

As he watched his mom climb into the rig, Brock noticed how much weight she'd lost. She'd always been slender, but now there was a certain fragility to her frame.

"Still don't lock the house when you leave?" Brock asked.

"This isn't the city, son. We haven't had any trouble since those neighbor boys raided the watermelon patch and left their beer cans scattered by the side of the road. Poor boys got a little too juiced up for their own good. Of course, by noon hour the next day at school, everyone knew who the culprits were. We got a good day's work out of them and a promise to never do that again."

Marveling at the trust his mother had for her neighbors, Brock compared it to the precautions he had to take in the city. There, packages would be stolen off his front steps and Christmas decorations pilfered. His house in the city had two locks and an alarm system.

They headed south, down the rutted gravel road to Glory Grove. On the trip, Richard broached the subject Brock knew was coming.

"So, can you believe they canceled the football season last year in the Grove? It has a lot of people wondering what's happening to this country when boys don't even have the gumption to play football anymore."

Brock took the bait, knowing he might as well find out as much as he could before the rest of the town came asking his opinion. "So, what's the story? Not enough kids left in the high school?"

"There are plenty to field a team. And a few kids were really upset they couldn't play last year. But I guess the seniors just said no, and once they laid their marker down, they got stubborn and wouldn't change their minds."

"Afraid they'd get hurt or just not very good athletes?"

"No, that's part of the rub," Richard said. He took his foot off the throttle to round a particularly sharp corner with loose gravel. "They had some good athletes. Might have even made a playoff run."

As they entered the fringes of the little town, Brock stared out the window of the big Ford. Richard slowed to ten miles per hour over the speed limit, knowing the town's one policeman would be busy directing parade traffic. There were a few well-kept houses with American flags hoisted high on front yard flagpoles. But some houses sat empty as a testament to the exodus from a wealthier period in the town's history—before the farm economy had slowed and the population began its steady decline.

Brock struggled to understand local boys not wanting to play football. In his own high school era, all the boys tried to play every sport. And if anyone chose to skip a sport, it wasn't football.

"Yep, and the brain thing," Richard mumbled. "Too much being made of the concussion deal. Every time a kid gets knocked in the head, he thinks he has dementia."

In his own recent coaching experience, Brock had dealt with that subject. There was a danger; he could admit that but didn't want to think it could spell the end of the sport he loved. "We've made football a lot safer," he said. "We hit less, hardly ever scrimmage, and we've altered our tackling techniques. But we can't do away with all contact sports, or the kids will just sit and vegetate. Video games are making kids soft, and that's dangerous too."

He'd made his argument. He knew of former players in their eighties who were still as mentally sharp as they were in their twenties. Most of them loved to relive their glory years on the gridiron and attend football games on Friday nights. Granted, a few had developed dementia, but how was one to know if it was from football or genetics?

"Where does Coach Newton live?" Brock asked, changing the subject. Richard pointed to a single-story yellow house on the right side of the street.

"He's lived there since he moved here seven years ago to take over the football program," Irene said. "The place is a mess."

"Yep, and football has been going downhill ever since he arrived," Richard said, glancing over at the house.

Brock had met Conrad Newton at a few coaching clinics. Short and thick with close-cropped hair, his loud, deep voice told anyone who'd listen how he'd played linebacker at a small college and what a great player he'd been. Brock had chatted with him briefly but was immediately put off by his determination to let others know how smart he was.

"Our offense can't be stopped if it's run well," Newton insisted, although when he failed to win games, he would point the fingers at the boys for lack of effort or their bad attitude.

Brock stayed away from the brash man and hoped for the Grove's sake they could win despite their coach's flaws. *My hometown deserves a better coach*, he'd thought.

"Doesn't do much to make himself popular," said Irene. "Guess he thinks being a football coach is all he has to do. When he isn't coaching football, he is off hunting or fishing. Look at the garbage around his house. I feel sorry for his wife. He even makes her mow their lawn."

Rumbling up the main drag, Richard slowed the pickup to a crawl. The sidewalks were heavy with pedestrian traffic. Many of those on foot turned to stare at the noise and the Gallagher trio sitting high in their truck. Smiling and waving broadly, Richard acted as if he were already in the parade. Irene was pleased that people could see she was still alive. And Brock wished his uncle would turn onto a back street and avoid all the unnecessary stares.

Finally, they turned left by the fire station with the washed and polished red engines parked outside, waiting for the parade. They drove past the Baptist Church, which had been shuttered for over a decade, and found a spot in front of Tim Palmer's house. Palmer was a family friend and an old teammate of Brock's.

"How's Tim doing?" Brock asked. A smile crept across his face.

"Good as can be expected," Richard said. "He's still not quite right in the head, though. I think bull riding knocked a few brain cells loose." He killed the engine and relaxed his hands.

"He always wanted to be the toughest guy in the room," Brock said. "Hell of a football player. Never would have made it to the state championship our senior year if he hadn't been looking out for me."

Suddenly the door of the green two-story house flew open. "Rocket, you ugly lop-eared nose of a horny toad. 'Bout time you came a-callin'." It was Tim in full throat; a misshapen cowboy hat pulled tight down over his shiny head, a chew in his mouth, and a half-buttoned red flannel shirt exposing his chest and still muscular body.

Brock could never be serious around Tim. Even in the state championship game years ago, he convulsed with laughter when Tim, agitated to the hilt with excitement, led their pregame cheer. The juxtaposed words were still in Brock's head.

"What are we here for?" Tim had screamed in the huddle, his eyes bugging out of his head. "I'll tell you what. We're here to smell the ass and kick some grass."

When he was hyperventilating, Tim could never quite get the words in order. Even now, as he remembered the moment, Brock couldn't help but smile.

"So, you've returned to God's country." Tim punched Brock on the shoulder.

"Yep, figured you were missing me." Brock grabbed his old friend by the hand and squeezed it as hard as he could.

"Sure been quiet around here without you, Rocket. Now we can get this town back on the right track. Can I get you a beer?"

Irene shot a dirty look at Tim. "Don't you dare," she scolded. "You three men need to stay on your best behavior. People don't need to see the worst in you fellows."

"Okay, Mom," said Tim sarcastically. "We always do what you say."

Irene had a soft spot for Tim and had come to his defense more than once when he was in the doghouse in Glory Grove. After his parents divorced, he was often left to his own resources. Irene had been like a second mother to him.

Since Tim was scheduled to ride his horse in the parade, he promised to catch up with the family later and headed for the staging area. But before leaving, he pulled Brock aside and dropped his voice so Irene and Richard couldn't hear.

"Cort Jepson wasn't very happy to hear you were coming home," he whispered. "Started drinking heavy again, and you know how crazy he gets when he gets a snoot full."

"What's that have to do with me?"

"He's got a jealous streak and thinks maybe Ronnie still has a soft spot for you."

Brock stepped back and shook his head. "Ronnie and I haven't spoken for years. I probably wouldn't even recognize her if I saw her."

"You'll know her. She still makes fellows turn their heads. Maybe not like your city women but she looks good in a pair of jeans. For sure, she could have done better than Cort Jepson, that SOB."

"What's he doing with himself other than causing you heartburn?"

"Mostly bouncing from job to job and creating turmoil in Ronnie's life and for their son, Justin. The boy's a good athlete, and Cort has this idea he can go Division I and get a full ride to some college. He was furious when the high school canceled the season last year. Threatened to move to Timbertown, but everyone knew they couldn't afford that."

"Glad you keep up on the town gossip," Brock said. "Anyway, thanks for the heads-up. I'll stay away from Cort. We haven't spoken since the state championship game anyway. Blames me for his turn of bad luck, I guess. I wish he could get over it."

"Gotta go, Rocket. My horse is waiting." Tim whirled around and limped away, favoring the knee that the Brahman bull at the Pendleton Rodeo had shredded. The incident had put an end to his dream of making it to the National Finals Rodeo. It had been a long shot anyway.

As Brock watched his friend walk away, he turned to his mom. "Okay, let's go watch the parade," he said, raising his voice so he could be heard over the sound of the trumpets and trombones of the local high school band warming up with the Grizzlies' fight song. He still knew every word.

CHAPTER 4

PARADE

BROCK'S INFREQUENT VISITS to Glory Grove hadn't included the community parade. He was quick to notice; it hadn't really changed in his absence. Even the order of parade entries was the same. Veterans led, carrying the American flag. Everyone watching from the sidewalks stood silently, with hats off and hands firmly planted over their hearts. Parents quieted their children and scolded those who fidgeted.

Next came the mounted posse on their horses, waving at the crowd and throwing pieces of candy to the children. Tim Palmer, on his bay gelding, made a point of waving to Brock and Irene. A hard spearmint jawbreaker went zinging by Brock, barely missing his left ear. Even over the noise of the parade, Brock could hear Tim's laughter.

Homemade floats followed. Each high school class had its own theme, as did the sports teams. Clearly absent was the football float. Coach Newton wasn't there either. "He's on a fishing trip in Canada," someone said.

"Maybe he should stay there," another man added.

Inching their way down the street were kids on crepe-paper-covered tricycles and moms pushing strollers with the community's newest babies. Parents and grandparents raised their cameras in unison to capture the image. Each year someone would comment how the number of babies seemed to get smaller. But the shrinking numbers made each one of the infants more precious to the remaining citizens.

Close behind the babies rolled one of the derby combines that had been hammered together for Sunday's demolition event. An old John Deere, wearing a coat of blue paint and named the *Blue Goose,* was driven by a red-cheeked farmer, who also served as a county commissioner. A favorite among the derby fans, he raced his engine and sounded the air horn affixed to the handrail. Black smoke roared out of the exhaust. Women pointed, men smiled, and children covered their ears.

Bringing up the rear were firefighters on the county's newest fire engine. Every few hundred feet, the captain would sound the siren. Babies in their strollers, already startled by the noisy combine, shrieked with fear and began to cry.

They should put the babies in front of the horses, Brock thought, but he knew better than to express the thought out loud. The people in charge of the parade weren't especially receptive to new ideas. There was a strict pecking order among the parade officials, and despite his celebrity, Brock, even if he were on the committee, would be near the bottom of that list.

"I need to sit down," Irene whispered to Brock. The color had gone from her cheeks. "Let's go over to the park and join the picnic. Maybe we can beat the crowd."

"It's a bit of a walk," Brock said, but she was already pacing down the sidewalk as if she was heading to the barn to check on the baby pigs.

Grabbing her arm, Brock held the weekend program of events over her head with his other hand to shade her from the noonday sun.

At the park, they picked a spot under a large oak tree, and Brock pulled one of the picnic tables closer to the tree. "Sit down, Mom. Let me get you something to eat."

"I'm not very hungry. Just some water and a pretzel."

When Brock picked out one of the concession booths, he recognized the folks from one of the local church groups inside the plywood shack. Some of these church ladies never seem to change—pleasant women with stiff hair and noses for gossip.

"Brock Gallagher, good to see you," said one of the older women. "What can we do for you … something for you and your mom?" They'd spied them under the tree.

"Two waters and a couple of pretzels, please," Brock said, using his best manners. Even after all these years, he still stiffened up around women of the church.

"If you're in town for a while, it would be nice to see you on Sunday. And bring your mom; she hasn't been in church for a while."

"She's been sick, but when she's better, I'm sure she'd like to be there."

"And I hope, while you're here, you can do something about our football team."

There it was. Even though he hadn't expected the first public grilling about the Grizzly football program to come from a church lady, he was prepared, just the same. "I wish I could help," he said politely, "but I'm just here for my mom. I'm not getting involved in football in the Grove."

After paying for the food, he returned to Irene's side. They were soon joined by his uncle, who seemed a bit more flushed than before, and by Tim, who'd ridden his horse to the park. The rest of the afternoon they spent together. A soft, westerly breeze made the leaves on the oak trees dance over their heads. Irene watched the children play. Brock and Richard talked about the farm while Tim continually interrupted with questions about football. "What was college football like on the big stage? Did he get a ring for his Copper Bowl victory? Why couldn't he make it in the pros?"

Brock tried to answer all Tim's questions. He knew if his old friend had better grades and a little more foot speed, he could have made a terrific college football player. With his passion for the game, Tim was fearless. If the other twenty-one starters on his college team had possessed Tim's drive, they might have won a national championship.

Tim had followed every step of Brock's football career. After watching the Copper Bowl on television, when Brock led a last-minute drive to steal a victory from a Big Ten opponent, Tim had been the first one to call his old friend. "I was screaming my freaking lungs out at the television," he said. "And got really drunk that night just for you."

As they watched the picnic crowd drift over to the adjacent playground to watch some of the relay events, Brock asked Tim about the football situation in the Grove. "Why didn't you try to help with the high school team?"

Tim shook his head. "Well, I'll tell you why. When Newton took over, he let everyone know he didn't want any of the old guard hanging around. He was all about turning the page … installing his new offense. Instead of us good old boys, he hired the new business teacher who didn't know squat."

"I'm guessing it didn't work out."

"Well the first couple of years, they won a few, but that was just because some of the holdover players remembered what it was like to win. But after those kids graduated, the Grizzlies started losing more often, and the kids got turned off by his attitude. Pretty soon, they could barely field a team. And then last year, nothing. Damned shameful if you ask me. The guy's a piece of shit—no offense, Irene." Tim suddenly realized she'd been listening to his rant.

"None taken." She agreed with everything Tim had said.

"Nobody is stepping in to get things changed?" Brock asked.

"It's complicated," Irene said. "The school principal says the kids at the Grove are behind in their studies. If he had his way, they'd do away with sports entirely. I think he likes the fact the football program is failing."

"What about the parents? Don't they want to see their kids compete?"

Irene thought for a second. "A lot of them do. The older folks like me would like to see things back the way they used to be. But times have changed. Folks are beginning to think we'll never see good times again."

By now, the summer heat was beginning to take a toll on Irene. Brock looked around for his uncle but couldn't see him anywhere. Probably wandered over to the beer garden.

"Hey, Tim, any chance you could take us back to the farm?"

"Yessir, it would be my pleasure." He removed his floppy hat and tipped it to Irene. "You wait here. I'll go get my pickup. I'll bring my horse, and when we get to the farm, you and I are going to take a ride out to Piney Ridge."

"Okay," Brock said, glancing over at his mother. "Might as well see if I still know how to ride."

CHAPTER 5

DANCE

WITH TIM'S PICKUP pulling his horse trailer, the trio headed back to the farm. Wheat fields along the gravel road were in the period of ripening, caught between dark shimmering green and the golden hues that signal harvest.

The fields belonging to the Gallagher's neighbor looked thick and heavy with promise. But after passing the property line fence, Brock could see his mom's crop looked a bit thinner. His father had always admired the neighbor's ability to produce top yields every year. A pioneer family, the neighbors had homesteaded the best ground in the valley. Gallaghers were latecomers who had to settle for the rockier soils that edged up toward the mountain ridges. Their land, along the timbered hills, wasn't as fertile but did provide pasture for a few cows and, today, a place to ride their horses.

When they arrived at the house, Irene made a beeline for the couch for a nap. Brock quickly caught and saddled the family's only horse,

Dolly, a little-used pet kept around for company. After Tim unloaded his bay gelding, the two friends started for the timber. It was a long climb up a steep slope through the trees to reach the crest of the ridge. They dismounted and walked to the edge of the drop-off. From there, they could look down into the valley and see the winding stream named Cold Creek.

"We had some good times down there," Tim said with a grin as he took in the view. "Our personal hideout when we were in high school. You remember the night we brought the girls up here with our sleeping bags? Would've been the end of us if their parents had found out."

Tim shook his head as he thought of his ex-wife, Peggy. "First time for both of us. Lucky, we didn't get pregnant that night, but it happened eventually anyway. We thought we were in love, and I guess we were, but it kinda fizzled out when we both started drinking too much." He swatted at a fly. "Problem was, I could quit, and she couldn't. She crawled inside that bottle and never came out."

"What's she doing now?" Brock asked.

"After her second try at rehab, she got pissed at me and walked out. Moved to Denver with her sister. Took our son with her. I don't get equal visitation rights. The judge thought I was too much a liability when I was chasing the rodeo." He stared down at his feet.

"How old is your boy now?"

"Luke turns sixteen in September. We talk every couple of months. He's a big boy. Likes sports, like his dad. Shitty grades just like his dad too."

"You could have been a pretty good dad if you hadn't started so young," Brock said without looking at his friend. He knew how much Tim had loved Peggy and how tough their life was when her drinking got out of control.

"What about you?" Tim asked. "Any regrets?"

"Well, my high school romance didn't turn out all that well either," Brock confessed, thinking of the years he'd dated Veronica O'Malley. "We got pretty serious for a while but it fizzled out when I went to college."

Tim turned and looked straight into Brock's eyes. "Ronnie never got over you. She thought you'd forgotten about her when you left and became a football star. And Cort Jepson couldn't wait to step in. No girl wants to go to the homecoming dance by herself." He spit part of his chew against a rock. "And he wanted to shove it in your face 'cause he was still pissed at you from the state championship game. Gave him pleasure stealing your girlfriend."

Brock looked away from the canyon as if he could shake away the memories of the night he and Ronnie spent in the valley talking for hours under the stars. "Those days are gone, my friend. Long gone. History. He got Ronnie, and I married one of the most beautiful women who ever walked on our college campus. The benefits of being a college quarterback, I guess."

"So, when will Celia show up in the Grove? We're all waiting for the grand entrance."

"In a couple of weeks. She called and said some special artist was having a showing in their gallery, and she can't leave. Once that's done, she'll head over."

With the sun setting behind the ridgetop and the evening temperature dropping rapidly, the two old friends headed their horses back to the farmhouse. Tim was bent on convincing Brock they should return to town for the big dance. "Just like old times," he said. "Two studs checking out the local talent."

"I think these old studs were turned out to pasture years ago."

DANCE

"Come on, Rocket. I hate to go alone. I know you're married, but I need a wingman to protect me from all those beautiful Glory Grove cougars."

"Okay, I'll go with you, but I'm not going to protect you from anything. Remember, I'm the quarterback. Not my role to protect you. It's the other way around. 'You gotta get low and stick your helmet between their numbers,' Coach Sullivan used to say. Then, I'd run like the wind."

Tim laughed, remembering all the times he made that one block springing his quarterback for some long run. Brock got all the ink in the newspaper while Tim got the pain in his neck. Still, he loved every minute of every single game. He'd do it again in a heartbeat.

After Tim left for town to clean up for the dance, Brock checked in on his mom. She was sleeping soundly. He straightened the afghan she'd curled up in and turned off the television. She looked worn out but happy. *She enjoyed today*, Brock thought. He was sad to think it might be the last Derby Daze parade she'd ever see. They would know more in the coming weeks after a scheduled visit to the oncologist.

With his limited wardrobe, Brock dressed in jeans and a plaid shirt. He dug out his old straw cowboy hat and checked himself in the mirror. *Bad idea*, he thought. He opted instead for the team cap from his Brighton High Bulldogs … navy blue with a yellow cursive B on the crown. The blue matched his eyes. He wasn't quite sure why he cared about his appearance. *It's not about Ronnie*, he assured himself. He wished Tim hadn't stirred those memories.

A crowd had already gathered at the fairgrounds when Brock and Tim arrived at the Palladium Dance Hall. Grove folks loved to dance, especially the night before the derby. Young and old alike would kick up their heels to the Barbed Wire Bandits, a local country band that for years had been a staple of community revelry. Their music was reflective of what the town itself once was, raucous, loud, and full of spirit.

The evening was warm, and the early high steppers were already sweating. Standing near the cattle watering troughs, filled with ice and beer, was a group of young men, checking out the available women—mostly girls back from college or local divorcées. Across the hall, Brock could hear his uncle entertaining the younger set with a series of off-color jokes.

Without warning, Cort Jepson and Ronnie burst into the dance hall from the back door directly across from Brock and Tim. Trying to act like everyone's best friend, Cort wore his usual look-at-me grin. "Let's get this party started," he whooped to no one in particular. His big Stetson was tipped back on his head, framing his rugged good looks. Standing six feet, two inches tall, he still maintained his athletic build from high school. Tousled blond hair hung past his ears, and now he was sporting a goatee, making him more menacing looking than Brock remembered. With a vice-like grip on Ronnie's arm, Cort pulled her to the middle of the dance floor.

She's still a picture, thought Brock. He could feel the blood rushing to his face. He stepped back into the shadows by the wall, hoping the couple wouldn't notice him.

Cort and Ronnie began to do the Western swing as if they'd practiced the scene every night—perfectly synchronized and rhythmic, spinning and dipping in a kind of cowboy Olympic performance. Rough and physical. Soon all eyes in the building were following their movement, especially her feminine form. Her tight jeans had just the right number of rhinestones attached to the back pockets; her top was yellow with short sleeves, a scoop neck, and frills around the collar. Loop earrings shimmered through her auburn hair. Her green eyes sparkled as she hung on to survive the whipping motion.

They finished with a flourish. Cort dipped Ronnie deep to the floor and planted a hard kiss on her mouth when he pulled her back into his arms. The crowd murmured at the spectacle. Cort Jepson always had to put on a show.

Suddenly, Ronnie's eyes met Brock's. She stared, fixated on his face until tears welled up. Cort, clearly enjoying all the attention he had garnered, followed her gaze. His demeanor changed immediately. Bowing his head, he walked straight over to Brock and Tim, leaving his wife standing alone in the center of the dance floor.

"So, the big star has returned to his humble roots," Cort snarled. "And still hanging around with his misfit friend."

Brock could smell the alcohol on his breath. "Good to see you, Cort. It's been a long time."

"I hope it's not too hard on you hanging out with the common folk," Cort said. His eyes were focused on Brock. "Too bad you won't be able to strut around our football field with the high school team this fall and hand out autographs, seeing we don't have a team here anymore."

"I heard about that; that's too bad. But I'm just here to care for my mother. So, you can stop worrying."

"I ain't worried about you. But since we don't have football, you might want to take in the derby tomorrow. It's a man's sport. It don't take a good knee to drive a combine, so you can't take that away from me." Cort took one step closer to Brock and lowered his voice to a growl. "Ronnie will be in the pits with our son. Stay away from her. She don't want to see you."

"No problem," Brock said, smiling in defiance. "You know I'm married. But good luck in the derby."

"Sure, a married man with a fancy wife who's too good to even visit the Grove. Don't push it, Rocket. Stay out of my way and away from my wife."

Tim had heard enough. He stepped between the two men. "Go squirm up a greasy pole, you sorry son of a bitch," he spewed. His eyes were bulging. "You're still carrying a nineteen-year-old grudge. Grow up. Hell, we were all hurting after that game. It's not like you're special. Only you won't get over it."

"Damned right I won't. Your golden boy here cost me my career. Hung me out to dry so he could score one more meaningless touchdown. Got himself a scholarship and left me on crutches. Never played another game of football." Cort bared his teeth as if emphasizing his pain. "You better believe I'm bitter. But at least I got the girl in the end. Your loss," he said, his face twisting into an artificial grin. "She's a fine piece."

Ronnie was still waiting in the middle of the dance floor, looking embarrassed and confused. She knew she couldn't go to the men. And if she left, Cort would launch into another one of his physical rages. She'd learned when not to cross her husband. So, she waited, not daring to look again at Brock.

CHAPTER 6

DEMOLITION

THE SUNDAY MORNING SUNRISE blazed red. Blood red.

"Red sky in the morning, sailors take warning," Brock said under his breath. His father had taught him a handful of old farmer warnings about the weather. Most of them proved true.

After a long sleep, Irene was anxious to go to the derby. Even after her husband's death, she never wavered from her routine. Up early. Eat a big breakfast. Have a list of things to do and go after them. On Sundays, she would take time for church, but she'd stopped going after being diagnosed with cancer. "I don't want those ladies praying over me all the time," she said.

"Good morning, sunshine," she said to Brock as he eased his long legs under the kitchen table with its red-checkered tablecloth. "Did you stay out of trouble last night?"

"No bruises to show. I had Tim to keep me out of trouble."

"Tim was usually the one who got you into trouble," she said as she set his coffee in front of him.

"We've mellowed with age." He laughed and blew on his coffee. "Although, we did run into Cort Jepson. He wasn't too happy to see me. The guy's got a lot of anger. Told me to stay away from Ronnie."

Irene paused before speaking. "Word on the street is he can be pretty rough with her. Won't let her out of his sight. I think she'd leave him if she could get away. But she loves their boy, Justin, so much she wouldn't want to hurt him. He's good-looking like his dad, although he takes her personality. Justin was the best hope for a good football team until the board shut it down. I felt bad for him."

"That's rough," Brock said. "I guess Cort is driving a derby combine today. I can only imagine the kind of driver he is."

"He does well until he gets banged around a little and loses his temper. Starts chasing the other machines around like a mad man until his combine falls apart. But it's probably a good way to get some anger out of his system. You'll see what I mean today."

Breakfast over, Brock wandered outside to feed the horse and the pets. To keep her spirits up, Irene had taken in a new border collie pup, black and white with cocked ears. A typical stock dog, she was smart as a whip and full of ambition.

"A dog like that needs a job," Tim had said the day before. They'd allowed her to follow them on their trail ride. Even after all the exercise, during the night the pup managed to drag several empty feed sacks out of the barn and tear them into pieces no bigger than a handkerchief. Despite the mess, Brock knew the pup's antics were helping his mom keep her mind off her cancer. Between the dog and the little pigs, she was thinking about life … not death.

When it was time to leave for the derby, Brock persuaded his mom to ride in his car. It might be more comfortable than the old farm pickup. But when they started down the gravel road, every rut bounced her to the ceiling.

"It's a pretty nice car for a high school teacher," Irene said as she hung on. "None of our teachers can match this. But it's kind of a city car, I think. A black car shows every speck of dirt from a country road. Lets everyone know you're a visitor."

Brock explained how most of the coaches of his caliber in the big schools got a hefty stipend from their booster groups. Football had made the down payment on his Lexus.

As they drove through town, they were caught up in the congestion of people exiting church and others heading to the derby. They followed the derby traffic to the fairgrounds. The county posse was in charge of parking. Blurry-eyed cowboys waved from their horses and guided the cars in the modified cow pasture. Brock's low-slung sedan drug through the bumps but found its way to their spot.

Looking down at them, a cowboy yelled from his horse, "Hey, Brock, if you want, you can drive on up to the gate and let your mom out so she doesn't have to walk."

Brock glanced over at his mom, but she was shaking her head no. She wouldn't want people to think she was weak. "Thanks, but we're okay," he said. He was struck by the family-like kindness of the gesture.

"Okay, don't say I didn't offer." He pushed the hat back on his head. "Irene, I could hoist you up here and ride you up to the front," he teased, "but people might tell my wife, and I'd have some explaining to do."

They found seats under the shaded grandstand and watched as the combines received their last-minute preparations. Sixteen machines were entered, with four in each heat. The top two survivors of each heat would return for the semifinals, and the routine was followed until there were only four left for the championship round.

The group of men tending each combine worked like the pit crews at a NASCAR race. After each heat, they scurried around with a cutting torch or welder along with a sledgehammer to repair the damage. Leaking radiators were quickly filled with a leak stopper. Air wrenches ratcheted through the afternoon air, sounding like a group of aggravated woodpeckers.

Each driver had his own strategy. Those who liked the adrenaline rush of combat rammed their combine headlong into the opponent's tires or backed their machine at full speed into the propulsion system of the enemy. Other drivers, especially those new to the sport, ran like scared rabbits, hoping the others might disable themselves. The crowd would boo at those avoiding contact, and though disgraced, the runners sometimes survived longer.

Before the action began, the announcer addressed the crowd, reminding them the proceeds from the event would help fund the school's sports and the FFA for another year. "It's all to help the kids of Glory Grove," he said. "Let's hope this fall we might even have a football team to cheer for." Brock could hear the groan from the crowd.

"If we can find enough brave boys to suit up," shouted one lady dressed in a jean jacket and cowboy boots. She yelled loudly enough for those around her to hear, including the mother of one of the boys who had refused to play.

"Watch your mouth, Laurie," said the offended mother.

"You watch yours," said the first woman. "Your boy and his friends spoiled it for everyone."

The women, who had once been good friends, glared at each other until their husbands shushed them, and one of the couples moved to another part of the grandstand.

Thankfully at that moment, the first four combines entered the ring, circling one another like lions ready to pounce. A man with a green flag stood in the center of the field. The announcer spurred the crowd into a countdown.

"Ready," he hollered. "With me now—ten, nine, eight, seven, six" … the children were screaming … "five, four, three, two, one." The man with the flag waved it furiously over his head and made a mad dash to get out of the combat zone.

At his signal, the drivers, perched high on the old machines, jammed their throttles forward. Smoke belched from their exhausts. Mufflers had been removed to add to the noise, and the crowd reached to cover their ears.

At the first of many collisions, the audience cheered. The impact echoed off the fair buildings nearby. When an especially vicious hit buffeted the driver against his steering wheel, it became clear why the drivers were belted onto their seats and wearing helmets.

An older model New Holland suffered a punctured drive tire and, while limping along, was an easy target for a bigger International Harvester. After some rear ramming of the engine compartment, steam roiled from the engine block. The day was over for the *Little Dutch Boy*.

The three remaining machines rammed, parried, and dodged until the Harvester, which had inflicted the first casualty, was crippled when a rear steering tie rod snapped on impact, letting the back wheel spin at a perpendicular angle to the rest of the frame. It left the old red machine dead in its tracks. Declared winners of the heat, the two remaining combines headed back to the pits for repairs. A tow truck from Rex's Wrecking Yard pulled the disabled machines from the arena like lifeless bovine carcasses pulled from a Spanish bullfight arena.

As round one was finishing, Brock offered to get his mother a cold drink from the refreshment stand. But she demurred. "Don't you want to stay and watch your old friend, Cort? He's in the next round."

"Okay, it'll be fun to see him get knocked around a little. Maybe his day will end quickly."

"I doubt that will happen. He's got a good team and spends what little money his family has trying to build a winner."

The next four contestants entered the arena. Piloting a newer model John Deere named *Destructo Deere*, Cort was dressed in a bright yellow pair of overalls. He caught everyone's eye. The metallic silver helmet he was wearing was like a beacon. Flying a Glory Grove Grizzly flag, with the bear claw logo in red and white, the combine looked imposing.

"At least he's loyal to his old school," Brock said under his breath. In the distance, in the pit area, Brock could see the auburn hair of his old girlfriend, as she hung on the fence, watching the excitement. Next to her was a big boy Brock suspected was her son, Justin, already a foot taller than his mom.

As the announcer introduced the drivers, he made a special note that Cort Jepson had made an appearance in the final round in each of the last three years. "Maybe this will be his year to win it all," the man said.

When the green flag flew, it was clear why Cort was usually one of the last drivers eliminated. He charged the other combines, picking on the weakest first, spinning at the last minute to crash the rear of his machine into the vulnerable parts of the opponent's combine.

Taken out first was an older Gleaner thresher named the *Silver Streak*. Battered with a powerful blow, fuel poured from the bottom of its tank. For fear of fire, the driver quickly dismounted and scurried for the fence. A fire truck, on hand for just this kind of emergency, raced out and pelted the silver hulk with foam.

Cort was delirious with laughter; you could see it from the grandstand. "Who's next?" he hollered. The crowd could read his lips. They were cheering the spectacle.

Cort's next victim was an older model John Deere. Its crew had put little time into preparation. No special paint, simply a number 666 painted on its side. Taking aim, Cort acted as the angel of death, driving his machine straight into the numbers. The machine's torque tube, on which the entire combine centered, buckled, causing it to collapse like an animal with a broken back. It slithered around in circles until the arena referee waved a red flag, declaring it dead. Cort moved on to the semifinal round.

The final two heats were just as exciting. When the top eight machines had been identified, the announcer called a short intermission to allow for repairs. Brock headed for the refreshment stand. When he got there, he saw the same two figures in line he'd identified earlier hanging on the fence. With his heart racing unexpectedly, he cautiously walked up behind Ronnie and her son. He thought about Cort's warning to stay away from his wife.

"Hi, Ronnie," Brock said casually, as if he'd spoken to her every day. She turned and drew back, nearly dropping the handbag tucked under her arm.

"Hello," she said, forcing a smile. Her eyes gave away her surprise at seeing him standing behind her.

Searching for words, Brock settled on the derby. "Cort had a good run. He might win the whole thing."

"That would make him happy," she said with little joy in her voice. She put her arm around the boy next to her. "Brock, I want you to meet my son, Justin. He's sixteen years old and will be a junior in high school next fall."

The boy was well over six feet tall, thick, strong, and athletic looking. He bore a strong resemblance to his father. Flashing an innocent smile, he stuck out his hand. His grip was powerful. "Pleasure to meet you, sir. I've seen your picture in the trophy case at the high school. You and my dad played on the only team from the Grove to play in a state championship."

"That's right," Brock said, releasing his grip on the boy's hand. "We had a good team with talented players. And a pretty girl on the sidelines cheering us on." He winked at Ronnie.

They locked eyes for a moment. "Still the same big flirt," Ronnie said. She relaxed her posture. "It's nice to see you back in the Grove after all these years. Bet your mom is glad to see you. Why didn't you bring your wife with you? Everyone in town wants to see her."

"She'll be here in a few days; she had some last-minute things to attend to."

When the line moved up to the counter, Ronnie turned to order. With her back to him, Brock could admire how well she'd aged. Still lissome and fit. And then something else hit him. The fragrance. *Tigress.* It was the same perfume she'd worn in high school. He'd given it to her for Valentine's Day.

With their food in hand, Ronnie knew they should head back to the pits and began to step away, but her son hung back for an instant and leaned over to Brock. "We're going to try and get a football team back together this fall. If you're still here, it'd be nice if you could help. My dad thinks Coach Newton is clueless."

Brock floundered for a response. "I don't know, Justin. It might not be the right time."

"I thought it couldn't hurt to ask. I think my dad would like that," he said, obviously unaware of the friction between the two old teammates.

Ronnie bit down on the paper cup she was drinking from. "Justin, we'd better get back to the pits. Your dad's waiting. Nice seeing you, Brock." She touched his hand for a second, then turned and walked away, keeping pace with her son. Her fragrance hung in the air.

All throughout the afternoon, the action continued. As the semifinals narrowed the field, threatening clouds began to build in the east. Wind whipped through the arena, and folks shielded their eyes from the dust—while cheering for the last four combines running. Cort Jepson on his John Deere was one of them. An old International Harvester named *Rust Bucket* also managed to play enough cat and mouse to avoid elimination. The *Blue Goose*, which had been driven in the parade the previous day, had come through the first two rounds unscathed, along with the mangled-up, but still running, Gleaner named *Litening McGrain*.

When the finals commenced, Cort was fully lit up—face flushed, frantically waving at the crowd and shaking his fist at his opponents. Catching a glimpse of Ronnie and Brock together at the concession stand fueled his desperate determination to win the derby. When the final green flag dropped, he was a man possessed, taking no pity on his combine. He didn't approach his opponents carefully or with clever strategy but rammed into them with all the speed he could force out of the machine.

Clouds swirling over the fairgrounds began to cut loose, gradually at first but then with sudden ferocity. Large splatters made the crowd sitting on the lawn run to whatever shelter they could find. Folks in the covered grandstand squeezed together like a welcoming family to make room for the others. But their hospitality was testing the weight limit of the old wooden bleachers. Irene, sandwiched by the crowd, sat still, determined to see the finish.

Going down first was the rusting International. There was no place to hide with all three opponents teaming up to pick on their weakest foe. The remaining machines were now slipping and spinning. Flying mud chunks threatened the spectators nearest the fence. The drivers wiped their goggles to clear their vision in the maelstrom. Cort rammed the little Gleaner, breaking the rear steering rams away from the wheels. The silver machine could only move in a straight line, so Cort and the county commissioner driving the *Blue Goose* took turns ramming her from either side until both tires were flat. With the mud getting deeper, eventually, the *Litening* couldn't strike anymore.

"Hang on, folks, there are only two combines left running," pleaded the announcer. "We should have a winner very soon."

As he spoke, a lightning bolt crashed down on a nearby hillside, exploding a tall pine tree that had stood over the fairgrounds for decades. Not wanting to take a chance on becoming a statistic, the people were now running for their automobiles. Pounding rain on the metal roof covering the grandstand created a thunderous cacophony rivaling the real thing.

The remaining two drivers on their machines, now dripping with mud and oil, were determined to end the contest. Eyeing one another, they backed to the edges of the arena. As if on cue, they hammered down their throttle handles, and the tattered beasts lumbered toward one another. The metallic impact signaled the inevitable final notes to the orchestrated violence.

The *Blue Goose* was lifted into the air. Momentum from both machines came to a sudden stop. Neither moved as if locked in a fateful embrace. The drivers tried reversing but to no avail. Cort pounded his steering wheel and slammed his gear shift from forward to reverse repeatedly out of frustration. In a departure from his usual politician-like behavior, the county commissioner yelled a profanity and shook his fist at Cort, mocking his opponent's wild antics.

Sensing the futility of the situation, the announcer wisely put an end to the contest. "Folks, it looks like a draw."

"Bullshit." Everyone within earshot could hear Cort yelling at the top of his lungs. "It's not over."

But it was. Thunder rumbled. People packed up their things, covered their heads with whatever they could find, and made their way out of the fairgrounds. A cloud had burst over Glory Grove, and it wasn't just the weather that was angry.

CHAPTER 7

CELIA AND JIMMY

CELIA WAS ON THE PHONE. "Hi, hon," Brock said.

"One of your players came to our house this morning," Celia said, without greeting her husband. "He wanted to talk to you. Seemed pretty distraught over something but didn't want to tell me."

"Who was it?"

"I don't know, never saw him before." After Brock's first years at Brighton High, Celia had stopped going to football games. She didn't understand the rules, and even though she'd been on the dance squad for football games at the university, she seldom watched the contest. So, it wasn't a surprise to Brock that she didn't recognize one of his players.

"What did he look like ... old or young, black or white, big or little?"

"He looked like an underclassman, black or mixed, but pretty small for a football player. Seemed uncomfortable being in this neighborhood. He must have walked over from the Hill District. He was pretty troubled about something."

"You didn't get a name?"

"No, but I told him you were in Glory Grove and gave him your mom's phone number. I'm going to get things wrapped up here in the next week, so I can head your way. How's your mom?"

"She's okay but has been overdoing a bit. We're going to stay home for a few days and let her recuperate."

"See you soon," Celia said.

"Love you, babe," Brock said and hung up the phone.

Brock guessed Celia's visitor was probably Jimmy Ivory, the sophomore running back most upset by his recent resignation at Brighton. Jimmy was small, but Brock had seen his potential and thought he would eventually find a place in the Brighton offense if he could keep his family life on track and not turn to the streets. With the new coaches at Brighton, there was no guarantee Jimmy wouldn't drop out and end up in trouble. The street gangs were an attraction for boys without direction.

The phone in the kitchen rang again. Irene picked it up.

"Yes, he's here," she said. "Just a moment." She stretched the cord from the old landline over to Brock and handed him the receiver.

"Brock Gallagher here," he said.

"Coach, this is Jimmy Ivory from Brighton; remember me?"

"Of course, Jimmy. What's up?"

"My mom died."

Brock could hear the trembling in his voice. "God, Jimmy. I am so sorry. What happened? When?"

"Right after you left … from a drug overdose. They took her body to the cemetery. I didn't have money for a funeral."

"What are you going to do? Do you have anybody you can stay with? Are you still in your house?"

"It was just me and my mom in the apartment. Now I don't want to be there by myself. I've been kind of hanging with friends. The football team started lifting weights for the summer, but I don't like the new coach. And he don't seem to like me either. Coach, when are you gonna be back?"

"Not for a while. I gave up my coaching job at Brighton. So, I won't be the coach there anymore. I'm here with my mom, trying to help her out." He couldn't explain in detail because Irene was sitting next to him, listening.

"Jimmy, I'll make some calls and see if I can find someone to help."

"Coach, can I come and see you?"

"It's a long way. How would you get here? Can you afford a bus ticket?"

"I could probably sell some of my mom's stuff. I just need someone to talk to."

How could he say no to this boy? He preached to his players how the football team was like a family. How could he turn his back on Jimmy now when he really needed a family? "Jimmy, I'll be in touch. You take care of yourself. Don't start hanging with those gang bangers." He hung up the phone.

"What are you going to do?" Irene had heard Brock's half of the conversation.

"I'm not sure, but someone needs to take care of that young man," he said. "I think the only real family he had was the football team. He was always there first thing in the morning when I opened the weight room and the last to leave at night. He's a good kid."

"We've got an extra room," she said, looking up at her son.

Not surprised, Brock remembered how his dad would scold Irene for bringing home every stray cat or dog she would find and making them part of the family. But this was different. She was sick. He was without a job. And the town of Glory Grove had seen very few black people inside the city limits. Not that they'd harbor any ill will toward the boy. The few minorities who'd settled in the town in recent years were welcomed with open arms. If for no other reason, as the population declined, any new body was a push back against the inevitable demise of the old town.

"That would be an awfully big step, Mom," he warned. "It's too much a burden for you, and I'm not sure he could ever fit in here."

"But you said he had no family. How will that end up, living by himself in that big city? You can't just write him off. You said he was a good kid. Give him a chance. If he's already in high school, he'll be done with school in a couple of years anyway."

She'd made up her mind and what she said made some sense. Still, Brock wasn't sure Jimmy would want to move to the country. He said all he wanted to do was talk. Perhaps after visiting Glory Grove, he'd want to go back home. In a few days Celia was coming. He could hitch a ride with her, although the image of his sophisticated wife spending six hours in a car with a street kid made him shake his head. He would ask and see what she said. Her position at the gallery had her rubbing shoulders with all kinds of different cultures; it might be all right.

Brock notified the state's Child Protective Services, and four days later Celia and Jimmy arrived in the Grove. As they drove up the main street during the noon hour on Wednesday, curious heads turned. The license plate on Celia's bright-red SUV spelled out *ILUVART*. What the people in town saw was a beautiful woman with shoulder-length blond hair at the wheel and a teenage African American boy sitting in the passenger seat. It seemed out of place in the little farm town. And when Celia pulled into the town's only filling station to ask directions, the fuse on the grapevine was lit.

As she stepped out of the SUV, the men in the station could see her long legs covered by black yoga pants and a short gray skirt. Her pink pullover top was snug but covered with a white lace sweater. Long earrings bobbed along her neck. Inside the building, the overhead fan hummed, dispersing the fragrance she was wearing.

"Can I help you?" the star-struck attendant asked. "Are you lost?"

"Just need directions to the Gallagher farm; seems my phone won't work here," she said, aware of looks she was getting from the two men dressed in grease-stained overalls in the bay next door. She ignored the giant pinup calendar of a nearly naked woman hanging on the wall behind the old pickup truck they were working on.

Pleased to be the first one in town to see her, the attendant gave directions for the twelve-mile journey, writing detailed instructions. As she bent to follow his pen, he could take in more of her beauty. The men paid little attention to her teenage passenger, who was reluctant to leave the safety of the vehicle.

"Thanks," Celia said as she ducked out of the station and climbed back into the SUV. She drove east, away from the onlookers.

"Good god," said the attendant to the others. "I've never seen anything like that in the Grove. She looked like a movie star. You don't suppose that's Brock Gallagher's wife, do you? If it is, I wouldn't leave her side for a minute. And why was that black fellow with her?"

The other two men hadn't even noticed the boy in the car.

Celia's first introduction to Glory Grove happened shortly after she and Brock were married. She didn't like it much. Too few people. No shopping. No real art. The old family home out on the farm made her anxious, since the police were half an hour away. And the coyotes howling at night gave her the willies. She always found an excuse to stay in Seattle when Brock went home to see his mom.

She didn't like the idea of moving, even if it was only temporary. She knew moving to Glory Grove meant sacrificing her sophisticated lifestyle for her husband. She was giving up her role as assistant to the gallery owner, Alan Pinford. She was going to miss the beautiful collection of contemporary, impressionist, and Native American art. She'd miss helping in the classrooms where transformative learning took place. She'd even miss the charming little café tucked into a corner of the building. But most of all, she'd miss the hundreds of guests who visited each day.

Despite the respect and love they showed for one another, Brock and Celia found little in common these days. She didn't like football, and he didn't understand art or her artistic friends. One of the few things she enjoyed about football was the times she and Brock hosted college coaches who came recruiting the top talent from Brighton High. On those occasions, she could use her looks and personality to help her husband make them feel welcome. The recruiters often seemed more interested in her than in Brock's players.

The journey with Jimmy had been easy. He didn't talk for the first three hours, disoriented by her beauty and the fanciest automobile he'd ever sat in. Eventually, he started talking and for the next two hundred miles didn't stop. Celia learned about his love of football and his fondness for Coach Brock. She listened to his description of the night his mom passed away and learned about life in the Hill District.

She, in turn, talked about her romance with Brock, a college quarterback. How she caught his attention at a college dance—he was a sophomore, and she was a freshman—and made him dance with her until the band stopped playing. She talked about growing up in Los Angeles, being married in Las Vegas, and their move to Seattle so that Brock could help with a struggling high school football program.

When she saw the sign, she turned onto Kirby Road. About halfway to their destination, they came to a sudden sharp corner next to a steep drop-off. Peering into the canyon, her breath left her body, and she instinctively slowed the car to a crawl. How would it feel if one lost control in the loose gravel and plunged hundreds of feet to the bottom of the tree-lined ravine?

"Damn, I ain't never seen a road like this before," Jimmy whispered. His eyes were open in amazement at the expansive landscape in front of him. Back on a straightaway, they relaxed and bumped along like old friends; Jimmy hummed quietly to a Jay-Z song he'd found on the car's radio.

As they approached their destination, Celia asked, "What are your plans for the future?"

"To get away from our old apartment mostly," he replied. "I can't stop thinking of my mom lying there. She was cold and blue." He blinked hard. "You know, she was my best friend. She might have done some bad things, but she always looked out for me."

"I'm sorry, Jimmy. You know that's why Coach came here, to be with his mom—because she was always looking out for him. She was his best friend, and he wanted to be with her until the end too."

"Coach's mom is dying?"

"Not right away, I hope, but she has cancer and is getting treatment. We don't know how much time she has, but Brock wants to make her happy until she passes."

"Coach is a good man, isn't he, ma'am?"

"Yes, he is. That's why he said you could come visit. He cares about you too."

Jimmy was silent for the remainder of the drive until they approached the white farmhouse with the red barn. "Is this where Coach grew up?"

"Yes," Celia said. "He really loves it here. He's a farm boy at heart."

"You like it too, Mrs. Gallagher?"

She hesitated for a moment. "I'm more of a city girl, but I'm going to try this for a while. Maybe you can help me adjust. A couple of city people out on the farm." She inhaled deeply at the thought.

"We're here." Celia pulled the SUV into the driveway and watched as a little black and white border collie pup came bounding from under the house's front porch. As Jimmy opened the car door, the bundle of energy leaped up, trying to reach his lap, but fell back, wriggling and tumbling in a vain attempt to gain her feet again. Laughing, Jimmy bent over to pick her up and felt the dog's little tongue splash across his face. He wrapped his arms around her and lifted her up to his chest while she continued to lick and shimmy and expend her energy on this newfound companion.

"It looks like you've found a friend." It was Irene, who'd stepped out from the screen door and was laughing at the sight of Jimmy trying to hold the wiggling pup.

"What's her name?" Jimmy asked.

"We just call her Pup," Irene said. "We haven't come up with a name yet."

Brock sauntered out from the back of the house where he'd been washing his overshoes after a trip to the swine barn. "Well, look who's here." There was a bounce in his step as he walked to the car. "Did you have a nice trip?"

"I forgot what a long drive it was," Celia said, giving Brock a perfunctory kiss on the cheek. "But I learned a lot about football and a little about hip-hop music. And I got to know a nice young man." She said it loud enough for Jimmy to hear.

"Hi, Coach," Jimmy said as he gently set the pup on the ground and gave Brock a fist bump. "Thanks for letting me visit."

"Jimmy, I want you to meet my mom. Her name is Irene. She won't bite. And I'll bet she could find you something to eat in the kitchen."

Irene extended her hand. "Nice to meet you, Jimmy. I've heard good things about you. I'm glad you could come. Looks like you've already made one friend," she said, motioning toward the pup. "Maybe you could think of a name for her."

"Yes ma'am. I'd like that. Maybe Wiggles or something like that. I'll think of one for sure," he said. He reached down to rub the pup's ears. Just petting the little dog relieved his nervousness.

"Well then, come on in and have some cookies. I made a fresh batch this morning," she said, leading him into the kitchen.

Brock and Celia stood for a while in the driveway. He smelled a bit like the swine barn, but she didn't comment. She looked like the same beautiful woman he'd left in the city, and he was glad she'd arrived. They studied each other as if they had been apart for months instead of days.

"Is your mom all right hosting our visitor?" Celia asked.

"She couldn't wait to meet him. She rallies anytime there is something more to live for. I hope it wasn't too awkward for you, driving all this way with him."

"No, it was great once he started talking. It made the trip go faster. I can see why you decided to let him visit. He's a nice kid but a bit traumatized by his mother's death. I have to say, though, we turned a few heads when we drove through Glory Grove. I hope your little town is ready for us."

"Our little town will do just fine," he said. "Maybe the people here are a little quick to judge. But given time, they'll come to the right decision about somebody. And once they do, they'll fight for them every time. When they get to know Jimmy, they'll make him one of their own."

"You sound like you think he'll stay."

"I don't know. My mom seems to think it's a good idea. We'll have to let it play out."

Brock had already asked himself the obvious questions. His mother was terminally ill. How could Jimmy stay with them while she was dying? And what if she passed away quickly? Brock had no reason to stay in the Grove. Celia had every right to expect him to return to Seattle. With two years of high school left before graduation, where would Jimmy go then? Was that too much to put on the young man's shoulders?

"Let's go inside," Brock said. "I'm sure you're tired from the trip." He took her suitcases full of clothes from the trunk and grabbed Jimmy's travel bag. Together, he and Celia walked into the pleasant old farmhouse.

CHAPTER 8

COLQUIT

LESTER COLQUIT, the principal of Glory Grove High School, wasn't well-liked. It was only because he was the lone applicant for the job that he'd been hired. He'd gone to a liberal arts college and considered himself a cerebral thinker, above the level of the people he served in the Grove. He didn't socialize with the townsfolk and wasn't a regular churchgoer. He avoided the high school's sporting events. And he didn't hide the fact he found athletics unnecessary in the education of young people.

"They are a drain on the resources of the school," he was fond of saying. Still, he was wise enough not to buck a century of tradition and try to diminish the importance the town gave to sports. However, he'd secretly celebrated the cancellation of the previous year's football season.

His distaste for the games stemmed from his own school experiences, where he was routinely the last boy picked for a team. A particularly nasty incident took place his freshman year of high school when he turned out for the football team only to be duct-taped to the goal post in his underwear by some especially cruel upperclassmen. The embarrassment haunted him even now.

The loathing he had for football carried over to the face of the Grizzly football program. Coach Conrad Newton reminded him of the characters who'd tormented him as a boy—mean, cocky, and vain. He performed poorly in the classroom and was disliked by other faculty members. Colquit wanted to terminate Newton's employment. But the man did just enough to keep his job.

With Newton in Canada on a fishing trip, the principal decided to inspect the coach's office, adjacent to the locker rooms. He was appalled by the area's appearance. School supplies were strewn around in random piles. A video camera lay on top of grass-stained football jerseys. As he was about to exit the messiness, Colquit noticed a wooden desk in the corner of the room. He tried to open the drawer. It was locked. He took out his master keys and tried several of them. Finally, the drawer opened, and the principal gazed into the clutter.

Inside, a coach's silver whistle leaned up against a starter's pistol used by the track team. There was a pile of player rosters. But what eventually caught the principal's eye was a flash drive in a plastic bag marked only with the words "girls basketball" and the date. Colquit had given in to the idea of his daughter participating in sports at the behest of his wife. Now, as the father of a player on the girls team, he was curious. Taking the bag, he closed the drawer and returned to his office, where he inserted the drive into his computer.

A film flickered to life. The video was disturbing. At first, Colquit was confused. *Cheap pornography*, he thought. But as he sat and watched, he recognized images of the schoolgirls from Glory Grove High School. They were showering after a sporting event, probably a basketball game.

He surmised the tape had been recorded secretly in the boys' locker room where the girls from the Grove were required to shower to allow the visiting team use of the girls' facility. He'd seen all these girls in the hallway but now was seeing them naked. His heart pounded. He felt outraged watching his female students innocently laughing, unaware of the voyeurism taking place, but needed to watch the entire film to see which of his students had been violated.

When he saw his own daughter emerge from the shower, her small breasts in direct view of the camera's hidden lens, he became incensed. He slammed his hand on the desk and stopped the video. He removed the drive, put it in his pocket, and vowed to confront the man who had done this.

A week later, when Conrad Newton returned from Canada, the principal went to see him. Colquit walked the five blocks from the school through the city park, under the shade of the giant oak trees planted by the Ladies Auxiliary after the First World War. He needed to clear his head, calm his nerves, and steady his demeanor. He was about to confront a disgusting bully and, in the eyes of the law, a criminal. As he took a dozen deliberate steps up the crumbling sidewalk to Newton's house, he took a deep breath and knocked on the coach's door.

"Hello, Mrs. Newton," he said when the door opened. She looked, as usual, tired and worn. "I'd like a word with Conrad."

When the burly coach appeared, sleepy-eyed and unshaven, Colquit asked him to step outside for a moment so they could speak privately. He wasted no time with conversation. He'd practiced exactly what he was going to say. Pulling the thumb drive from his coat pocket, he waved it under Newton's nose.

"Conrad, this came out of your desk. It's got your writing on it. I don't need to tell you; you know what it is. I made a copy of it, so don't get any ideas of wrestling it away from me. Here's the deal. I want your resignation immediately. I want you out of the school immediately and gone from this town within two weeks."

Colquit paused before his final threat. "If you aren't gone within that time, I'm going to the police. I'd rather not do that for the sake of the girls on this video. Resign now and move on. And by the way, you'd better find a new occupation. If you pursue another teaching position, I will alert the authorities."

Newton dropped his head and stared at the ground.

With that, the principal, who'd been bullied by boys just like Conrad Newton, turned and walked away. He'd made a stand. He felt manlier than he'd ever felt in his life. He straightened his spine, lengthened his stride, and walked slowly back toward the high school through the grove of trees. Now his senses were truly alive. The breeze felt good on his face. He noticed the shimmering leaves dancing over his head. And he smelled the fresh-cut grass.

At the gazebo, he skipped up the steps to the upper level of its platform. Instinctively, he clapped his hands together, raised his arms over his head, and exhaled deeply. *Life*, he thought, *has a way of eventually making things right.*

CHAPTER 9

WEIGHT

NEWS OF COACH NEWTON'S resignation came to Brock via his old friend. Tim's words stumbled over each other in his excitement. "That worthless piece of shit finally figured out he wasn't wanted here," he said.

It got Brock's attention. "Slow down, partner," he said, chuckling at his friend's giddiness. "What the heck are you talking about?"

"Coach Newton. He's resigned and is leaving town, going back to where he came from, wherever that is. Rumor is that when he was in Canada, he had a midlife crisis and decided he was tired of dealing with kids. If you ask me, he finally might've figured out he was a lousy coach."

"What's the school going to do now?"

"Nobody knows for sure, but I know one thing, maybe now we can get a coach in here who can put together a football team. Somebody who can take them to the top." Brock had seen this smile on his friend's face many times. "That's you, old friend."

Brock shook his head chuckling to himself. "I'm not going down that road, Tim. Besides, it'd be hard to build a team out of a group of kids who don't want to play. You and I love the game. Maybe these kids don't care."

But the conversation with Tim wouldn't be the last. The phone in the farmhouse was suddenly ringing off the hook. People in the Grove knew there was an opportunity to get one of the best coaches in the state—one of their own—to bring the town some success on the gridiron. There was the chance to revive their favorite game—to turn the lights back on at Grizzly's Sullivan Field. The people wanted Brock Gallagher and were going to work every angle they could to make it happen.

Brock knew the timing was all wrong. Celia had only been there a few days. And Jimmy was starting to feel homesick, missing his friends. The one thing the boy seemed happiest about was the little border collie. He spent hours sitting with her stroking her long black hair. And when he found out she liked to chase, he'd lace up his sneakers and sprint across the pasture behind the house with the little dog nipping at his heels.

Irene watched Jimmy's interaction with the dog for a few days and knew a bonding was taking place between the boy and the pup. One afternoon, after the two friends had tired of their game, she walked out and sat down in the wicker chair on the front porch next to them.

"So, Jimmy, have you come up with a name for the pup yet?" she asked.

"Yes, ma'am," he said. "Would it be okay if I named her after my mom?" His eyes glistened.

"What was her name, Jimmy?"

"Her real name was Saphire. But people called her Sassy. Could I call the dog Sassy?"

"That'd be perfect," said Irene. "It fits her personality. It shows spunk. I'll bet your mom was spunky. What do you know about her? Did she have family anywhere?"

"She told me she grew up in South Carolina. People said she talked funny, like people in the south. Met my dad when he was in the army back there and followed him out here, but then he left. I don't know why. I never knew him, really, but I've seen pictures. I look like him."

"He must have been a handsome fellow," Irene said as she reached over to rub the dog's ears. "I'm sorry you never got to know him."

"No problem. There were other men around, but most of them I didn't like. That's kind of why I hung out with the football team. The team was like fam. That's what Coach always told us. We all just looked out for each other, you know, had each other's back."

"You know Brock cares about you. He didn't want to leave the Bulldogs. I think he just felt guilty about me getting old and staying on the farm."

"Well, I'm glad I got to come see him. I like it here, and I've never had a dog before. Sassy and I get along real good," he said, proud to be using the dog's name in front of her for the first time. The pup's cocked ears perked up. She licked Jimmy's hand and stared up at him, waiting for another pat on the head.

"How long do you think you will stay?" Irene asked.

"You want me to go now?" Jimmy bit his lip and looked away.

"We want you to do what you think is best," she said. She placed a hand on his shoulder. "You're welcome to stay here as long as you want. Sassy needs someone to keep her out of trouble. But if you want to get back to Seattle, we understand."

"Do they have a football team here? I still really want to play football."

"Last year, we didn't have one. Folks here were disappointed, so we hope maybe they'll have one this year. But the old coach left town, so I'm not sure what they'll do. People have been calling Brock, asking him to do it, but he wasn't planning on coaching again right away."

Jimmy's eyes widened. "He's a really good coach. I'd stay here if I knew he would be the coach. But they're mostly white boys here, I think," he said. "I don't know if they'd like me." His first trip through Glory Grove had been his only visit to the town, and he remembered the curious stares.

"People here would just have to get to know you. You'll have time to figure all this out. It's a couple of months until school starts, so let's give it some time."

"Mrs. Gallagher, if I'm gonna play football, I need to get stronger. I should be lifting weights. Can I find something heavy to lift around here?" He'd worked hard his years at Brighton to become strong enough to survive a football season.

"Jimmy, if you're going to live here for a while, you need to stop calling me Mrs. Gallagher. Just call me Irene. And there are a lot of heavy things to lift in the old boneyard behind the farm shop. Help yourself. And if you really want to get strong, hay season starts soon, and Brock's uncle will have some bales to stack. It's hard work, but we can pay you."

His curiosity roused, Jimmy walked out behind the shop to see about the 'boneyard.' The pile of scrap iron was impressive. Old car axles and block weights littered the field. There were weeder rods and steel wheels from discarded field implements. And there were lengths of broken chain and wire cable. While Jimmy's mind was engaged trying to fashion a crude system of weights, Sassy was by his side, sniffing under the piles and digging at the mouse holes. Once the pup let out a yelp when she stuck her nose into a hornet nest and disturbed their sleep. Engrossed in his search, Jimmy didn't hear the sputtering exhaust of an old farm pickup.

Irene had told Jimmy about Brock's uncle Richard, but he hadn't met him yet. He was about to. Through his bug-splattered windshield, Richard spied the youngster. He slid out of the little half-ton Ford, being careful not to let the empty beer cans from the weekend fall out the door. As he walked around behind the shop, he made sure to create enough noise to warn the boy of his presence.

"Hey there, kid," Richard said. "Are you looking for treasure out here? Well, if you find one, you're going to have to split it with me."

Jimmy looked at Richard, a man in his sixties with a wrinkled face, round bulbous nose, and a short neck. His eyes twinkled when he smiled. Even without a white beard, he looked a little like a department store Santa. He seemed friendly enough.

"Hi, I'm Jimmy," he said. "I'm visiting Coach Gallagher."

Richard stuck out his hand and shook it hard. "Yep, Brock's my nephew. I'm Richard. I help run the farm with Irene. So how are you getting along in this dried-up neck of the woods? Not like the city, is it?"

Jimmy kept his left hand on the dog's neck. "I'm getting used to it," he said. "It's a long way from Seattle, but I don't have much left back there."

"So, what are you finding in the boneyard?"

"I'm just looking for some heavy stuff to lift. I wanna stay in shape for football."

"Did you play for Brock's team at Brighton?" Richard propped his foot up on an old cultivator.

"I was on the junior varsity, but I was hoping for varsity next year. But then Coach left, so I'm not sure now. Irene said maybe they'd have a team here next year."

WEIGHT

Richard's pulse quickened. Jimmy playing for the Grizzlies. Just by looking at the youngster, he knew how valuable he would be if the Grove could field a team. But, of course, the team didn't have a coach, and no one knew for sure if there would even be enough boys who wanted to play.

"You and Irene getting along okay?" Richard asked, knowing Irene had taken a liking to the young man.

"She treats me real special," said Jimmy. "And she's a great cook. I think I'm getting a little chubby. Kind of feels like maybe what a grandma might've been like. I never had one."

"Then be good to her. Help out when you can because she's been a bit under the weather. You can do that, can't you?"

"Yes sir, I'll do whatever she wants. I know I can't live here without paying back."

When Irene first told him about a teenage boy from the city living with her, Richard had reservations. But on first impressions, the youngster seemed okay. He told Jimmy a few of the corniest jokes he could remember. And they both laughed, Jimmy shaking his head at the punch lines. Richard was happy to find a new audience to try out his standard list of dumb jokes. Everyone else in town had heard most of them.

"So now, what are we going to do here with this junk?" Richard asked. "Do you need some dumbbells or something?"

Jimmy explained, and he and Richard spent the afternoon picking out the pieces they might assemble into weightlifting equipment. After they drug things into the cluttered shop, Richard showed Jimmy how an acetylene torch could cut metal. And how a grinder could make sparks fly and round the ragged edges of metal into smooth surfaces.

Finally, after adjusting an arc welding helmet onto Jimmy's head to protect his eyes, Richard demonstrated how to strike an arc and lay down a perfect bead to attach the chunks of metal into one solid piece. "It might have been quicker to run to a sporting goods store and buy a set of barbells," Richard said as he stood back and stared at their creation. But Jimmy seemed to fill with pride as his imagined project took shape.

When the iron cooled, they stood back and appraised the results. "Well, go ahead, give it a try," Richard said, patting Jimmy on the shoulder. Jimmy picked up the barbell and did several repetitions, straining hard to do the final lift.

"Yessir, this will work real good," Jimmy said after he caught his breath.

The long June day had come to an end. As the sun was setting, the yard light in front of the house flickered on automatically. "After all that work, I think we deserve something to eat," Richard said. Illuminated by the light, Jimmy and Richard, with Sassy by their side, walked to the house to tell Irene about their accomplishment and to see about supper.

CHAPTER 10

CHURCH

CELIA MISSED HER TIME AT WORK. There was a void without the everyday interaction she had with creative people, the kind who studied each new painting or sculpture that came to the gallery, discussing the interpretation of the artist's motives—the use of light, color, and shape to describe an inner feeling or emotion.

Hoping to find something on the farm to fill that void, she had brought along paints and an easel and tried to capture scenes from the area. She knew she wasn't a great artist but liked trying. In the evenings, as the family gathered for dinner, they'd praise her work. But she could have done a paint-by-number, and they would have said it was wonderful.

It was during one of her down days that the phone rang. When Irene answered and handed the phone to Celia, she was pleased. "Hello. Oh, Alan, it's good to hear from you." It was the head of the gallery, calling about a famous sculptor from New York who'd agreed to a showing in their gallery. It was a once-in-a-lifetime opportunity for the exhibition hall. Alan wanted her to help with the event.

"That's wonderful news, but I don't know if that's possible," she said. "I would love to come; you know that. When would you need me, and where would I stay? We've already rented our house."

Alan assured her there was plenty of room at his place, and if she could just come for three or four days, she'd be a great help to him. "I need your creative hand," he said. "It's an opportunity to work with one of the top artists in the country."

As Celia hung up the phone, she worried about Brock's reaction. But he'd always supported her in her work, especially after the crisis they experienced when a pregnancy ended in a miscarriage. She'd sunk into a deep depression. It was only when she returned to the museum that she pulled herself out of the darkness. She refused to try to get pregnant again. And even though he yearned for a family, Brock agreed they would stop trying for children.

"I'd like to go back," Celia told Brock that evening. "It would only be for a short time." He wasn't surprised by her willingness to leave, just dismayed by how quickly it happened. Not wanting her to sink into another depression, he put his arms around her and gave his blessing.

They'd been happy to see one another when she arrived. On her first few nights on the farm, after they were sure everyone in the house was asleep, they'd wake in the darkness and make love. Her long smooth legs, the same beautiful legs that first caught his attention as he watched her on the college dance squad, wrapped around his. Upon reaching climax, they laughed as they cupped their hands over one another's mouths to stifle any noise, aware of the old home's thin walls. Their bedroom rendezvous were wonderful, but in their daily lives, they were growing apart. He feared her pending departure would only add to the predicament.

CHURCH

Before Celia was to leave, Brock had a request, something he'd thought about since the church lady peppered him with guilt at the Derby Daze Picnic. "Celia, I'd like to take my mom to church," he said. "And I'd like you to go too." Brock also invited Jimmy. The community was curious about the goings-on at the Gallagher farm; why not show their faces to everyone at once. Celia agreed to go the next Sunday, and Irene also said she would go if they would protect her from "a couple of those busybodies who want to hurry me along to be with the Lord." Jimmy said he'd go if he could sit with Irene.

So, on the last Sunday in June, they went to the Glory Grove Methodist Church, which once boasted the largest attendance in the county. It now barely drew fifty people for regular service. The number of people in the pews would swell on Easter and Christmas, but those were the exceptions.

When Brock dressed for the service, he slipped on the one sport coat he'd brought to the farm. When he did, he found a note in a front pocket left from his last football banquet at Brighton High. He smiled, remembering the young men he'd addressed, then folded it up and laid it on top of the dresser like he was handling a sacred script.

Celia, wanting to make a good first impression on the people in church, wore a bright yellow summer dress with a gold bracelet and a necklace of pearls. A black ribbon in her hair matched her stacked heel shoes.

Irene, having lost so much weight from chemotherapy, couldn't find anything that fit but didn't really care. She was going to church to pray—for Brock and Celia, Richard, and Jimmy. She also wanted to pray for Sassy but didn't know if it was right to pray for a dog. She would anyway.

The four climbed into Celia's SUV. Heading to the ten o'clock service, they left early enough to preclude people from staring at them if they walked in late. The beautiful old church, sitting on top of the only rise in town, brought some bittersweet memories to Brock. He'd been baptized there and years later had his church confirmation training done by the old white-haired Norwegian pastor. To conclude his training, at the age of twelve, he recited the Apostles' Creed by memory in front of the entire congregation, stumbling through his nervousness.

Then at the age of seventeen, in the summer before his senior year of high school, he helped carry the casket bearing his father's body from the church. Walking up the center aisle in stride with his uncle, Brock led the procession. All eyes were on him. The pallbearers carefully lifted the casket into the hearse for the short drive to the county cemetery. That was his lasting memory of the sanctuary.

The church, its high vaulted ceiling and hardwood floor sloping toward the pulpit, was akin to a cathedral with its classic architecture. Stained glass windows bordered each side of the sanctuary, and a larger one was located high above the altar, so the morning sun shone through the image of Jesus as a young boy teaching in the temple.

Brock and his mother had memories of the place, but for Celia and Jimmy, their introduction to the building was happening now. Walking slowly up the concrete steps, Brock and Celia led the family, with Irene and Jimmy following close behind. Jimmy had a firm grip on Irene's arm. He was strong and nervous. She was weak and confident.

Meeting them at the top of the stairs was one of the church elders who recognized Brock. "Good to see you, and thanks for bringing Irene. We've missed her."

"It's good to be back. Mom has wanted to come but has been down a little. I don't think you've met my wife, Celia. And this is Jimmy Ivory, a friend of the family."

CHURCH

The elder stepped back, and Brock wasn't sure if it was due to Celia's beauty or the sight of a young black man on Irene's arm. Either way, the introduction disrupted the man's usual mechanically performed greeting.

They made their way down the center aisle and found seats about halfway to the front of the church. Brock let the others into the pew first. As people drifted in, the foursome could feel the stares. Hushed conversations were floating through the air. Often, the greeter would nod his head toward them and explain in whispered tones who they were.

The few men in church that day—there were mostly women worshippers—didn't hesitate to come down the aisle and shake the coach's hand. A few even asked him if he was thinking about taking over the Grizzly football program. When they did, Celia would stare down at her feet and rub her hands together ever so slightly, suddenly becoming aware of the pressure being put on her husband to take over the local football program.

When the organ player concluded her pre-service music, silence filled the church. The young woman minister, who'd only been with the church for a few years, stepped forward and welcomed them. After making the usual announcements, she gestured to the Gallaghers and, in a friendly tone, said, "It looks like we have some visitors with us today. Can you tell us where you're from and what brings you here?"

Despite being uncomfortable with the attention, Brock smiled and replied politely. "We're actually members of the church. We've just been away for a while. I'm Brock Gallagher. I'm here with my wife, Celia, my mother, Irene, and our friend Jimmy Ivory."

As the service continued, Brock could see his mother was enjoying the routine repetition of the standard Methodist protocol. And it was comforting to feel some continuity in a fast-changing world. The sermon was uplifting. From Proverbs, Chapter 13, it dealt with pride and Brock felt as if it was written for him. The minister's final fitting summation, spoken with her eyes directed squarely on him, was *He who walks with the wise grows wise*. Brock glanced knowingly at his ailing mother, who also caught the irony in the words.

The quaintness of the morning service was in stark contrast to what he and Celia had attended in the city, in one of the giant megachurches with its massive choir and ebullient speakers. Those services, attended by hundreds, were part revival and part entertainment. All the most recognized people of the community attended. Brock wondered if the Lord suddenly reappeared, would he choose a little church like the one in Glory Grove or the glitz and glamour of the megachurch? The question tickled his imagination, and he could picture Jesus walking down the aisle of his old church wearing blue jeans and cowboy boots, followed by a dozen of his friends.

When the service ended, people quickly surrounded them. Everyone wanted to meet Celia. The men, even the oldest of them, couldn't take their eyes off her. The elderly ladies hurried over to welcome Irene back. And a few came to shake hands with Jimmy.

The service had been rewarding, but Brock was ready to head home. "Let's skip the coffee hour," he said. The family agreed. They'd enjoyed the service, and Irene was comforted by being back in her house of worship. Jimmy was anxious to exit the stuffy confines of the building and to breathe air not saturated with the heavy doses of perfume some of the older women were wearing. And Celia wanted to have a serious word with her husband.

As they filed out of the building, Brock caught sight of Ronnie and her son, Justin, standing toward the rear of the sanctuary. When Ronnie turned, for just an instant, her eyes met his, and he could see her blush behind her auburn curls. She promptly looked away and pretended not to notice Brock and his beautiful wife.

"Who was that?" Celia asked.

"She's an old friend of mine," Brock said. "We went to high school together."

"She's very pretty. Did you two ever date?"

Brock stammered a bit, searching for the right words. "She was in a class behind me, and I took her to a few dances," he said, trying to minimize what their relationship had been. "Her husband and I played on the same team. That was their son with her."

Satisfied, Celia quickly changed the subject. "What's all this about you coaching football in Glory Grove?" She'd been so focused on the research needed to promote her gallery's newest client that she'd somehow been oblivious to all the phone calls Brock had been receiving.

"It's just talk," Brock said. "The high school coach resigned, so people want me to step in and take it on."

"You're not seriously thinking about it, are you?"

"I wasn't at first, but it would give me something to do while I'm here. It sounds like they need some leadership."

"That wasn't in our plans," she said. "You should have let me in on this discussion." Somehow, her husband seemed to be falling under the influence of his old friends and the town itself.

As they walked down the concrete steps in front of the church, Brock noticed a dust-covered automobile across the street, an older model silver Chevrolet Impala with dents in its rear fender. Behind the steering wheel, a man was reading the Sunday paper, a cup of coffee in his hand, presumably waiting for some family member who'd gone to the service.

The man lowered his paper, raised his eyes, and stared at Brock and his group. His gaze narrowed, and his jaw tightened. Cort Jepsen realized his Ronnie and Brock had been together again. He knew it was innocent. But he still didn't like it.

CHAPTER 11

HAY

JUNE LEFT. July came rushing in with intense heat. Local ranchers were cutting hay to bale, hoping the weather would hold. Understanding their financial existence depended on Mother Nature, they scurried to take advantage of the near-perfect conditions.

"I love the sound of those machines running," Irene said one night as she sat at the kitchen table. "It means work is getting done." Swathers were running from sunup to sundown. The hum of their engines could be heard late into the evening. Lights could be seen crisscrossing the bottom ground next to Cold Creek, which ran through the valley. Days later, the same men and women would begin baling as the sun set. Working through the night, they would use the evening dew to hold the tiny leaves together, letting the big machines sweep the foliage up into the desired shape.

The Gallagher farm produced enough hay to feed their small herd of cattle through the winter and, of course, the pet mare, Babe, in the corral. They owned a small baler, and for a full week, they gathered the hundred-pound bales onto one of their single-axle trucks and moved them to the barn for stacking.

For Jimmy, his first few weeks on the farm were an adventure. He enjoyed exploring the tree grove, looking through the old buildings, and doing his weightlifting routine. But most of all, he enjoyed the little dog. She could learn commands after only a few days of instruction. And they ran, with Jimmy sprinting through the fields, preparing for some imagined football team—he still didn't know where he might be—and Sassy following close behind. They'd become a team. It was the best therapy Jimmy could have asked for after the trauma he'd lived through.

"Are you ready to go to work?" Richard asked Jimmy after the hay was baled. Earlier, he'd invited Jimmy to take part in the labor of the farm, and Jimmy had agreed, knowing he needed to repay the Gallaghers for their hospitality. The time had come to prove his worth.

"If you're going to make hay, you're going to need these," Richard said as he tossed Jimmy a new pair of leather gloves.

"I'll be okay." Jimmy said, "My hands are tough."

"Kiddo, your hands will be bleeding by the end of the day without these. You might get blisters even with them, so put 'em on and work them a little."

Then, pulling a straw hat from the back seat of the pickup, he offered it to Jimmy. "And this is for the sun." Jimmy hesitated for a moment, thought about how silly he might look in a cowboy hat, and turned down the offer.

When they reached the field, Richard parked the old 1978 Ford two-ton truck in the center of the bales and demonstrated to Jimmy how to stack a load. By laying the bales one layer at a time on the truck bed, in an alternating fashion, the load was secure, so it wouldn't tumble into the middle of the road on their way to the barn.

With a small wheel tractor, Richard hoisted the bales onto the truck, and Jimmy tried his best to wrestle them into place. To the rookie hay hauler, it seemed like they'd been working for at least ten hours when Richard cut the tractor engine and said, "It's ten o'clock; do you want to take a break?"

Dumbstruck, Jimmy thought he'd never worked harder, and it had only been three hours. Practicing for football and lifting weights was a grind, but he'd never used these muscles before, inhaled this much dust and pollen, or tried to keep his balance on the top of a five-tiered stack of hay on a moving truck.

"Yes sir," he said. "I'm ready for a break." He wiped the sweat from his forehead and shook the hay from inside his gloves.

They sat in the shade of the loaded hay truck to cool down. While they rested, Jimmy rattled off a series of questions. "Why did Celia leave? I miss her. How sick is Irene? Do you think Brock will stay and coach the team in this town? Can I ride Babe? Do you have a wife and kids? What do people around here do for fun? Do you like hip-hop music? Do Methodists ever dance in church?"

Richard laughed. "Slow down, kid, we'll be at this hay hauling business for a while, so maybe by the end, I can get all your questions answered."

Jimmy adjusted to the work. Along with getting stronger, he knew his balance should be improving from his work on the truck. Eventually, he even decided the straw hat wasn't such a bad idea as the sun beating down made his eyes tired from the glare. And now, he was a contributing member of the farm operation.

On the third day, Richard said it was time for Jimmy to learn how to drive the truck. "It's easy," he said, "four gears forward and one for reverse." The gear shift pattern was inked in pen on the dash of the old Ford.

"You're kidding? Me drive? I've never driven anything before," Jimmy said. He pushed his hat back on his head.

"High time you learned. Here, slide under the wheel, and I'll show you." After some basic instruction and a couple of hippity-hop tries at using the clutch, Jimmy was driving with a big smile on his face.

As the week wore on, the number of bales stacked in the barn outnumbered the ones still lying in the field. Jimmy found the rhythm of the day to his liking. Up early, big breakfast, work hard, lunch break with a short nap in the shade, corny jokes at every dull moment from Richard, more practice driving, a big supper on the table by Irene, and exhaustion and sound sleep in a soft bed in the countryside. The dog was always with them—in the hayfield, in the barn, there for their breaks, and lying by his bed each night, waiting patiently for Jimmy to crawl out from under his covers in the morning.

On Saturday morning, Richard was late. "Slept through my alarm," he said. But Jimmy could smell beer on his breath when he came in for breakfast. He was bleary-eyed but still pleasant to him and Irene. He picked at his pancakes while Jimmy devoured his. Then they headed out for another day's work. The July temperature was getting warmer each day, and Jimmy could tell Sassy was feeling it too. Her panting was harder, and she would seek shade whenever the truck was parked.

They'd stacked one load in the barn by ten o'clock and, after a quick water break, were going to try to get one more in before lunch. "Take the wheel," Richard told Jimmy as he crawled into the passenger seat. He closed his eyes and leaned his head back against the rear of the cab.

Jimmy put the truck in first gear, eased out on the clutch, like he'd been taught, and gently depressed the foot throttle. It was now becoming routine. But this time, something felt wrong. As the truck began to move, a gut-wrenching howl came from under the rear duals. Jimmy's skin crawled, and there was a pounding in his head. "Sassy," he groaned. He didn't want to believe it. God was too cruel. First his mother and now his little friend.

He quickly killed the engine. He pounded his hand on the steering wheel in a fit of anger, then reached across the cab and slapped a still dozing Richard hard on his chest. The older man's eyes popped wide open. "What the…? What happened?"

"I killed Sassy," Jimmy wailed. "I killed her; I know it. I killed her. Damn you. Damn this truck. Damn everything."

CHAPTER 12

CLINIC

WHILE HAY WAS BEING GATHERED on the farm, Brock was attending the state's annual coaches clinic. It was a chance for high school football coaches throughout the state to rub shoulders. As they learned of rule changes, they could exchange game strategies or pass along word of possible coaching vacancies. For ambitious young coaches, it was a chance to network with hopes of eventually finding employment at one of the premier schools.

Out of habit, Brock was attending. "I just don't want to lose touch," he said, trying to explain to his family. He didn't have a team but wanted to visit with his peers and share in the brotherhood between coaches. Since he began his coaching career, after his short stint in the professional league, he hadn't missed one of these clinics.

His own transition into the coaching profession was unplanned. After college, he'd signed a free agent contract with one of the West Coast NFL teams and found himself standing behind two other quality quarterbacks. In his second season with the team, he was let go. Despite his accurate arm and stellar college career, he lacked the speed and mobility to compete in the league. His playing days were over.

Still loving the game, Brock looked to the one avenue open to him—coaching. With his name recognition in the state, he landed an assistant position at an urban high school—a job few others wanted. Brighton High was a perennial bottom rung finisher. After two seasons with the program, he became the head man. With a lot of hard work, he turned the program around. Due to his rapid rise to the top, he became a bit of a celebrity, once named the state's coach of the year, when his team nearly won the state championship. Other coaches began seeking his advice.

This year was different. Rumors swirled among the ranks about Brock's sudden departure from Brighton. Had there been some sort of scandal? The assemblage of men loved to gossip. During the day, they'd attend forums and listen to speeches by top drawer college coaches. In the evening, they'd crowd into the hotel bar and revel in their camaraderie. Some would brag. Others would complain. But there was a hierarchy of status, and Brock had once been at the top.

"My mom has cancer, and I needed to move back home to be with her," Brock repeatedly answered those who quizzed him about his exit from Brighton. After a time, the rumors died away. What replaced them was the question, what next? Brock couldn't answer. He didn't know, but he felt the tug of football. The more he was around his peers, the more he began toying with the idea of taking on a new challenge.

He had pushed back against the pressure to coach at Glory Grove, but the vitality of the coaching fraternity seeped into his subconscious. His mind was engaged on the possibility. He sought out coaches from the small school divisions to explore their feelings about the Grizzly program.

"It's a shame what's happened over there," one said. "That program was always solid with old Coach Sullivan. He could never win the big one, but he was always in the hunt. They came close once a dozen years ago but couldn't bring the trophy home. Now the school doesn't even have a team."

Brock knew the man was talking about his year when the Grizzlies went into the playoffs undefeated, looking for their first state championship. They'd won a quarterfinal contest in a slugfest. He'd thrown three touchdowns, two of those to Cort Jepson. But it wasn't until Tim Palmer broke the leg of the opposing quarterback in the fourth quarter that Glory Grove was able to send the opponent home with a 28–27 loss.

Thinking his boys hadn't played with enough toughness, Coach Sullivan pulled out his best Bear Bryant impression and decided a week of hard practice was what the boys needed. He put them through a "hell week" to toughen them up. They scrimmaged for three days before the semifinal tilt. It worked. Even though they were beat up and exhausted for the game and played on a snow-covered field in freezing conditions, they still took home the win. However, the weeklong ordeal exacted a heavy physical toll with injuries.

That was history. Brock was more interested in the recent past. "What went wrong at Glory Grove? Could the program be revived? Was there hope?"

Most coaches just shook their heads. It'd be a tough task. It seemed both the football program and the little town were slowly dying. All agreed Coach Conrad Newton hadn't been a good fit. And it seemed the school administration was trying to kill the sports programs. "I feel sorry for anyone who would take on that job. Probably a hopeless situation," one respected elder said.

CLINIC

Brock had heard enough. It could take years to resurrect the Glory Grove program, and he wasn't sure what his own timeline was. But he would know more in a week. He was taking Irene to Seattle for a complete diagnosis from an oncologist who specialized in her rare form of cancer. When they had those results, he might be able to plan.

On Saturday, the clinic ended. As Brock drove home, he revisited all the conversations he'd had with the other coaches. He was deep in thought as he turned into the driveway but immediately caught sight of the commotion behind the barn. Jimmy was in the driver's seat of the old truck with his head on the steering wheel. Richard was kneeling behind the rear duals.

Jumping out of his car, Brock jogged toward the truck. When his uncle looked up with an anxious expression on his face, Brock saw the reason. The little border collie was pinned beneath the tires, her face stretched in a painful pose, her eyes pleading for help.

"Let's move the truck ahead," Richard said. "We need to get the weight off. Jimmy's going to need some help. He's lost it."

Running to the driver's side door, Brock yanked it open. "Get out, Jimmy," he yelled. He was in his coaching mode, the man in charge, giving orders, making decisions.

Jimmy was sobbing. "I killed her, Coach. I'm so sorry. I named her after my mom. I jinxed her. She's for sure going to die. It's my fault."

Brock grabbed Jimmy by the arm. "Stop that. She's not dead yet. We've got to move the truck to see how bad it is. Get out now," Brock ordered.

With his head bowed and shoulders slumped, Jimmy slid out of the driver's seat. He couldn't look at Sassy. To look at death was too fresh in his mind. He could still picture his mother, lying contorted on the apartment couch, a needle stuck in her arm, her face with no expression, her skin sallow and sunken. He'd tried to forget, but now it was all coming back to him.

When Brock pulled the truck ahead, Richard examined the dog. Her rear leg was cocked in an unnatural angle, clearly broken. But she was still breathing, frightened but not angry. "Jimmy, come here," Brock said in a calm but stern voice. "She's your friend; get over here and take care of her. She needs to see you now."

"She's not dead? I thought she was dead. She's still going to die, isn't she?"

Brock put his hands on Jimmy's shoulders. "Won't know for a while. We need to get her to the veterinarian. The sooner we get her there, the better the chances are. Carry her to the car. I'll lay a blanket in the back seat. Be gentle." Turning to his uncle, he said, "Call the clinic and tell them we're coming."

With tears still streaming down his face, Jimmy knelt and slid his arms under the pup's belly. She didn't squirm or fight. He lay her down on the old blue blanket with the Brighton logo on it and slid in beside her with her head on his lap.

With that, the fancy auto became an animal ambulance. Gunning his prized sedan down the straight stretches, Brock could hear the gravel rattling against the car's fenders as he slid around the corners. The trip took less than ten minutes. Sassy lay still, staring up at the boy while he stroked her head with trembling fingers, praying for her survival. "Please don't die," he pleaded softly.

Richard called the clinic from the farm kitchen, then sat at the table with Irene, his throbbing head cradled in his hands. "For that boy's sake, I hope the dog can pull through, but animal docs don't come cheap."

"You know Brock won't spare any expense. He loves animals as much as youngsters like Jimmy," Irene said.

Richard grew serious and philosophical. He rubbed his calloused hands together. "Growing up on a farm can be hard," he said. "Things die. It hurts. But somehow it prepares you a little better for life. I think if more young people grew up out here in the country, we'd all be better off."

Irene, her head bowed, thought of the hard lessons her own son had faced as a teenager. She knew Jimmy was going to be hurting from what had just taken place, and she hoped he could pull through it. She raised her head and brushed back her hair. "You know, Richard, if more of today's kids could grow up on a farm, we'd have more men like Brock," she said.

CHAPTER 13

VET

AS BROCK AND JIMMY WATCHED, the young woman veterinarian administered the anesthetic to ease Sassy into a gentle sleep. "We'll give her a few minutes to make sure she's under, and then we can set the leg. We'll have to put a rod in to secure it. She won't be able to run on it for several weeks, but if everything goes okay, she should still have use of the leg. She might limp a little, but you can live with that, can't you?" she asked, directing the question toward Jimmy. She could still see traces of the dried tears that had streamed down his face.

"Yes, ma'am," Jimmy said. His prayers were being answered. The pup would live. He was overwhelmed with gratitude toward the doctor who was putting his little friend back together and even more appreciation for Brock, Richard, and Irene. He knew now that he wouldn't go back to the city. Even if Glory Grove didn't have a football team, this was where he belonged.

After the surgery, Brock checked his watch. "You want to get something to eat?" he smiled over at the teenager.

"Sure, I'm hungry," Jimmy said, finally relaxing from the turmoil of the morning.

There were only two places to eat in the Grove. One was a drive-in named the Cozy Corner that had been serving burgers since the 1950s. There was also a little steak house on Main Street that served a full meal, mostly hot beef sandwiches and chicken fried steaks.

Each establishment hosted a morning coffee crew, all men, divided philosophically between working-class farmers and laborers and the town's businesspeople. Both groups gathered early in the morning, often brewing the coffee themselves before the owners arrived. The coffee klatches had their own distinct personality. Every morning the men gathered around the tables, took their personal cups off the rack, poured a bit of the steaming black liquid, and settled in their usual chairs, waiting for the conversation to begin.

The drive-in crew, dressed in overalls or blue jeans, was the conservative group. The farmers and laborers were accustomed to the early morning hours. There was occasionally a little one-upmanship to see who could be the first one to arrive. Eventually the matter was settled, and the early bird would be given his own key to the restaurant. Then it was his responsibility to have the coffee brewed and the place open for the rest.

Since it played such a big role in their lives, the farmer group talked about the weather. For years it had determined their daily schedule. Mother Nature dictated how abundant the crops would be and accordingly, how healthy their finances were. Those who ran cattle understood how a good rain could stretch the grazing season for a few more weeks. Or that a cold snap would mean sleepless nights protecting newborn calves from the elements. For both farmers and ranchers, there were sporadic periods when lack of good weather led to heartbreak when hard work wasn't enough.

The steak house attracted the more liberal group—retired teachers, salesmen, and some of the ministers from the town's five churches. Their discussions centered on the plight of their little community—how another business seemed to be on the verge of closing. The school was also a favorite topic. The recent talk had been of the quick exit of Conrad Newton.

But the one conversation each breakfast group would come back to was the plight of the football program. When word circulated the year before that the season would be canceled, none of the men in either group could believe it. Football in the town had always marked the beginning of another sports year. Without football, the men around the tables had one less thing to talk about.

Some blamed the boys. Others blamed the school administration. No one had respect for Coach Newton and the downward spiral he'd initiated. All the men seated around the morning coffee tables understood the current concern for head injuries, and some questioned whether the lights dimming in the eyes of some of their companions might have been accelerated by the vicious hits they'd taken on the local football field decades ago. "Maybe the sport is finished," someone would say, but none of them wanted to believe that could happen.

"What do you want to eat?" Brock asked Jimmy.

Considering his appearance—he was covered with alfalfa dust and dirty sweat from the morning's hay hauling—Jimmy opted for a burger at the drive-in.

"Sounds good," Brock said and drove to the opposite end of town and pulled up to the Cozy Corner. Jimmy brushed off as much dust as he could and rubbed the tear stains from his eyes. When they entered the establishment, the morning crowd had left, but a few of the older gentlemen were still nursing their coffee and reading the Saturday morning newspaper.

"Morning," one man said as he lifted his eyes to stare at Brock and Jimmy. He had the sports section tipped so he could read the fine print of the box scores. The man studied them as they sat down at a table across the room. After a long silence, he said, "Brock Gallagher, is that you?" Brock was stilled dressed as he was when he left the coaching clinic.

"Yes sir," Brock said. He didn't recognize the silver-haired man.

"Well, I heard you were home. You don't remember me, do you?"

"I'm sorry. I guess I don't. Help me out. I've been away for a while."

"Don Baker," the old man said as he reached over to shake Brock's hand. "I helped Coach Sullivan with the football team your senior year. We almost won the state championship. I remember it like it was yesterday. You had quite a game."

"Not quite good enough, I guess," Brock said, embarrassed he hadn't remembered the veteran coach. Baker had spent most of his time with the younger players, but Brock remembered him as a good man and a coach who always treated his players with respect.

"You're bringing back a lot of memories," Brock said. "I wish we could talk about how great it was to win a state championship, but it didn't quite work out, did it?" He closed the menu he'd been holding in his hands.

"You did everything you could," Baker said. "I think after that frozen tundra game up north in the semifinals, and with Sullivan putting you through hell-week, you were just worn down too far. And Northfork had a couple of college-bound guys on their team that were hard hitters, especially the linebacker who took out Cort Jepson's knee."

As Baker spoke, he lowered his voice and looked around to make sure no one could hear, even though the place was almost empty now. "Anyway, it's great to see you. You know there's a spot open for a football coach with Newton gone. Why don't you do us a favor and bring your talents back to the Grove? I'd even come out of retirement to help you out."

Brock laughed, but he could see Baker was serious.

"I've tracked these boys since they were in grade school. I could tell you which finger they scratch their head with. They have talent. Some of the younger kids are itching for the chance to get back on the field. Give it some thought."

Jimmy had been listening. When Baker finished, Jimmy leaned over close to Brock and quietly spoke. "Coach, I decided this morning I want to stay here, even if they don't have a football team. But I want to play ball. I know I don't count for much, but it would be great if you'd coach here."

Baker overheard the boy's comments and winked. "How can you argue with that, Brock? I think the young man is on to something. And son," he said, looking at Jimmy, "we could really use you on the Grizzly team. If you're ready for Glory Grove, I'm pretty sure the Grove is ready for you."

CHAPTER 14

SEATTLE

EARLY MONDAY MORNING Brock and Irene left the farm for her oncologist appointment in Seattle. It had been a year since her first diagnosis, and the trip to the specialist was to measure the progress of her treatment. At first, it was thought surgery would be required, but after chemotherapy her cancer count had dropped dramatically.

Before leaving, Brock sat down with Jimmy. "You can ride over with us if you want," he offered. But with the dog recovering from her surgery, the teenager wanted to stay on the farm, and there were still two days of hay hauling before they were done. Rain showers were in the forecast, and Richard wanted to get the last of the hay in the barn before it got wet. Irene prepared enough food to last Jimmy during her absence. Richard would be there to check on him and the dog every day.

With Jimmy deciding to stay on the farm, Brock agreed to settle up with the boy's landlord and bring Jimmy's personal possessions back to the Grove. He'd rent a small U-Haul trailer for their return trip. While in Seattle, Brock wanted to make a surprise visit for the opening of the new exhibit at Celia's gallery. "Don't you think you should let her know you're coming?" scolded Irene. But Brock thought it best not to bother his wife in advance of her big day.

Irene didn't particularly relish the busyness of the city. She was nervous about her visit to the huge hospital and the new set of health professionals. For Brock, his return to Seattle made him realize how little he missed it. He'd adjusted when he lived there, but now the high-speed travel, the constant vigilance for traffic hazards, and the anxiety of making quick decisions wore on him. "Nice move, you dummy," he grumbled at a driver who cut him off in traffic.

"Easy, son," Irene warned. "I'm here to get well, not get into an accident." At the hospital, they checked in and were surprised how quickly they were ushered into the doctor's office.

"Hello, Irene," the young physician said. Irene wondered how he could be old enough to have graduated from medical school. But he was polite and friendly. "You are in a special class of people," he said. "There aren't many others who suffer from cholangiocarcinoma. It's one of the rarer forms of cancer."

"That figures. I can never do anything with the big group," Irene said. Her blue eyes lit up. "I kind of like being out there on the fringes."

"It's a pretty serious thing. But you're responding well to treatment. I have your CAT scan results. There are still a couple of little spots on your liver, but if they stay small, we'll hold off on surgery. If they grow at all, we'll have to look at other options. Anyway, so far, you're doing great. And you seem to be in good spirits. Is your home life good?"

Irene told him about her son returning home, her little dog, and the new visitor they'd taken in. And she told him how she loved being on the farm. "It gives me peace," she said.

The doctor was impressed. "A lot of people don't have your attitude. It sounds like you've been blessed," he said as he bid them goodbye and hurried off to his next case. Irene felt she'd put him in a better mood. *How stressful it must be*, she thought, *for a young doctor to deal with cancer patients every day.*

After checking out, Brock decided they still had time to visit Jimmy's apartment. The Hill District was in a rough part of town, but the middle of the day would make it relatively safe. As they maneuvered through the city, he eased onto a familiar street. His and Celia's home was in the same section of the city, but the difference between their trendy new neighborhood and the one where Jimmy and his mother lived was enormous.

They passed through several intersections before Brock turned down a one-way avenue that took them to their destination. It was a section of town filled with the outcasts of society. Low rents gave the unemployed and the out of luck a roof over their head but offered little else. They passed by block after block of austere brick buildings devoid of lawns or adornment. Unkempt men lounged on porch steps. They stared uncaring at Brock and Irene. Aged autos sat abandoned on side streets. Some were on cinder blocks; others had their hoods half open, waiting for mechanical first aid that would never arrive.

 Brock slowed, counting down the house numbers until he spied the one he was looking for … 2643 Buchanan Street. The building was a two-story brick structure with bars on the windows, framed by weathered wooden shutters. He could imagine Jimmy coming home to this dwelling each day after football practice. He parked next to the curb, his black auto out of place on the street.

Jimmy said the landlord lived on the bottom floor and he and his mother, Saphire, on the second. With one eye on his mom in the car, Brock climbed a few steps to the apartment door. After knocking, Brock could hear someone rustling around inside. Eventually, the door opened with the safety chain still attached. A man, probably in his late sixties, looked through the crack. "What do you want?" he grumbled.

"I'm a friend of Jimmy Ivory," Brock said deliberately, understanding the landlord's suspicion.

"I ain't seen him for a month," the man, dressed in sweatpants and a worn t-shirt, said. His thinning white hair was protruding in a dozen different directions like a storybook wizard. "He owes me a month's rent. His mom died, you know."

"I know. He's been living with me. We've come for his things and to settle up with you. May we see the apartment?"

"Ain't much to see," the man said, softening his tone. "They was good people. She just got messed up with drugs and couldn't get clean. But she loved that boy. I feel bad for him. How's he doing?"

"He's okay. Still troubled by the loss of his mother, but that's to be expected. Do you know anything about what happened? It might help us understand what he's going through."

"Heroin. Jimmy'd been going over to Brighton to lift weights with the football team. Left early an' stayed all day. Come back late. I think some dealer came over. She got a bad fix, and when Jimmy come home, he found her. It wasn't pretty with her being dead for a couple of hours. He comes runnin' down here, so I called the cops, and they checked it out. Boy was freaking out. He ain't got no family, so I sat with him for a while, but he didn't want to stay in that apartment after they took her away."

Brock thanked the man for sharing the information, then asked for the key to the apartment. "We'll take a look and come back tomorrow to move stuff out," he said.

SEATTLE

As they climbed the stairs, Brock had to help Irene. When they opened the door, they could tell the place had been shut up for too long. "Let's try to open a window and let it air out," Brock said. When he cracked the window, a breeze pushed through the single room.

A double bed was pushed up against the wall, and there was a cot in the corner. A few dishes were stacked in the sink. Several dresses filled the closet, and a chest of drawers held jeans and shirts. "A little U-Haul trailer will hold all of this," Brock said to his mom.

In the corner, they found a box with Jimmy's name on it. "This is what we really came for," Brock said. When he pried off the lid, the first thing he noticed was the school letter Jimmy had been awarded for playing on the Bulldog junior varsity football team. Beneath it was the team photo the players received. There were also newspaper clippings from every one of Brighton High's football games, beginning with the year Jimmy was in the ninth grade. Along with the clippings was a note in Brock's handwriting, congratulating Jimmy on his great year of football. He gave one to all his young players to encourage them to keep up their grades and prepare for the next year.

They discovered photos and music disks further down in the box. Finally, at the bottom of the stack was a single photo in a frame. It was of Saphire with Jimmy cradled, as a baby, in her arms. Standing with them was a smiling, handsome black man with a military haircut. Brock assumed it was the boy's father. "Wonder what happened to him?" Brock said out loud. Did the man know of Saphire's death? And did he have any idea his son was living in Glory Grove?

"I think I need to go," Irene said. She was exhausted from the long day. After helping his mom down the stairs, Brock thanked the landlord and said he'd return the next day with a trailer to empty the apartment. He scribbled out a check for the month's rent, and they departed. He'd gotten to know Jimmy's situation a little better; he realized how tough life was for some of his football players. He vowed never to take them for granted again.

CHAPTER 15

ARTIST

THE FOLLOWING DAY, Brock left Irene at the hotel to recover from her exhaustion and rented the U-Haul trailer. Admittedly, the combination U-Haul and sedan looked like an odd match, but it would do the job. He returned to Jimmy's apartment and checked in with the landlord. It was early in the day, and it was apparent he'd awakened him. But the man was courteous and friendlier than the day before.

"Whatcha gonna do with the stuff in the apartment?" he asked.

"I'll just load up Jimmy's personal items. As for the furniture and beds, we don't need them. I'll take them to Goodwill."

"If you want, you can just leave it all here," the man said. "The next renters will probably need it. People 'round here don't have much, so they'd use whatever's there."

Brock nodded in agreement and went up to begin filling boxes. On each trip down the stairs, he'd unlock the trailer and then lock it again before returning to the apartment. Strangers were watching, and he didn't want to create any temptation to take what little there was. One middle-aged man came over to see what Brock was doing.

"I'm just picking up things for Jimmy Ivory," Brock said.

"Won't be the same 'round here without him," the man said. "We all thought someday he was going to be a great football player for the Brighton 'Dawgs. He was working hard to get there. Would have made this 'hood proud. But I hear his coach jumped ship. Damned shame."

Brock didn't confess to the stranger that he was the coach who'd left but let him know Jimmy was all right. "He's moved in with us over on the other side of the state. He'll probably play ball over there."

"Well, I guess that's better'n nothin'. Take care of him," the man said, his eyes downcast. "We're going to miss him. And Sassy too. The folks 'round here liked her a lot." Conversation over, he wandered off down the street.

By noon Brock was done. He took one last look around Jimmy's apartment and descended the stairs. He handed the key to the manager with a sincere thank you, got into his car and drove away slowly with fragments of Jimmy's sixteen years of life following in an orange trailer.

Brock and Irene planned on attending the special exhibit at the gallery scheduled for that evening. The event was important to Celia, and they wanted their surprise visit to be supportive. But first, Irene needed something to wear besides her oversized housedresses—something to make her feel comfortable in the high society scene. "Let's go shopping," Brock said.

At the store, she found a few dresses to try on and popped several times out of the dressing room like a teenager trying on a prom dress. Eventually, after much laughter between them, she found an attractive outfit they agreed would bulk up her tiny figure.

"What about you?" Irene asked. "Don't you need something to spruce up your wardrobe?" She wasn't kidding. Her son had never been particularly style-conscious.

He shrugged, like a schoolboy shopping for a back-to-school outfit. "You're right. I should try to upgrade a little."

At the men's store, it didn't take long to find some slacks and a matching shirt and tie to go with the blue blazer his mom had picked out for him. What he forgot to add to his outfit would have more impact on the evening than the items stuffed into the plastic shopping bags they left the store with. The work boots he'd been wearing on the farm and a pair of sneakers were all he'd brought on the trip. It would prove to be an embarrassing oversight.

The event started at seven p.m. When they arrived downtown, Brock was in a quandary. Pulling up to the gallery with a cargo trailer would be awkward. On the other hand, his mother didn't need to walk four blocks from the nearest parking lot. Risking odd stares he might receive, he pulled into the circular drive and waited for a valet to come to greet them. No one came. He stepped out of the car and motioned for an attendant.

"Can you find a place to park my car and trailer?" Brock asked.

"Sorry, sir, I thought you were making a delivery. I'll give it a try," he said and reached his hand out for a tip.

When Brock and his mom stepped into the gallery, they heard the string quartet playing a soulful composition by Beethoven. The deep resonant sounds of the cello mixed with the buzzing of the local celebrities who wanted to be seen at such social events. Most of them didn't know the sculptor but made sure to read up on him so they could praise his work.

The lobby was immense. Brock could see the signage Celia had prepared, with photos of the artist and descriptions of the sculptures they would find in the gallery. He admired her talent. This is what she loved to do.

They followed the formally dressed crowd down the hallway, and as they did, Brock became increasingly self-conscious of his footwear. He'd hoped no one would notice the worn boots he was wearing. Despite his efforts to clean and polish them with the hotel towel, he knew they weren't appropriate attire. He stuck his hands in his pockets and pushed his pants down as far as he could.

When they reached the ballroom, they saw the artwork that had attracted the crowd. In the center of the room was an immense bronze statue of a mythical creature juxtaposed with doe-eyed children staring up at it. Off to the side was another work, a Native American warrior atop a leaping whale. Further down the hall, a bronzed man hung suspended from a trapeze, his eyes forever frozen with the look of fear of falling. "It's a bit bizarre, but you have to admire the fellow's imagination," Brock joked to his mom.

"I don't get it," she said.

They were moving with the flow of the crowd when Brock caught sight of Celia, beautiful, as always, in a sleeveless, figure-hugging black dress. She was wearing a diamond necklace with matching earrings that hung nearly to her shoulders. She was in conversation with a man Brock hadn't seen before. He had dark hair to his shoulders and a four-day growth of beard to meet the current fashion trend.

Brock swallowed hard when he saw the man suddenly reach over and kiss Celia on her cheek. She didn't back away or seem startled but acted pleased by his affection. Irene was so intent on trying to interpret the sculptures she hadn't seen what had occurred.

"Mom, I see Celia over there; we need to go say hello."

"Of course we do. That's why we're here."

ARTIST

They made their way through the crowd avoiding the huddles closest to the art pieces. Brock's heart was beating faster than normal. They were nearly to Celia when she saw them approaching. The color went out of her cheeks. Her companion noticed her change in attitude.

"Who is this?" he said when Brock stepped up to him.

"Jovan, this is my husband, Brock Gallagher, and his mother, Irene," said Celia. "I didn't know they were coming, so I'm a bit surprised."

"Didn't want to miss your big day," Brock said, looking away from the man and directly into his wife's eyes. "It looks like you have a great turnout. The artist must have a big following."

"Brock, Jovan is the artist," Celia said, giving her husband a hard stare. "He's from New York and is known throughout the world for his work. Aren't they amazing?"

"They certainly are different," Irene said, trying to wedge into the conversation. "It must take a lot of imagination to come up with ideas like those. Do they sell?"

Celia was embarrassed. "Irene, do you see the one over there with the Native American warrior and the whale? A buyer just paid $250,000 for it. Some of the others might bring even more."

Irene didn't see how something looking that strange could bring so much money. She couldn't help herself. "We could buy a pretty nice piece of farm machinery for that."

"Perhaps you could excuse me," Jovan said, feeling there was an uncomfortable undercurrent taking place. "I must mingle with my fans," he said, glancing around the room.

Irene also excused herself to go to the lady's room, leaving the couple alone.

"You could have acted a bit more respectful," Celia said softly once Irene was out of earshot. Her lips were tight as she spoke. "Why didn't you let me know you were coming? I might have been more prepared for your entrance. And Brock, those boots?" She stared down at his feet.

"We thought it would be nice to surprise you," he said. "We should have called." He rocked back on his heels. "But why so chummy with your friend Jovan? What was that about?"

"It's what professionals in the art world do," she glanced across the room, following Jovan's movements. "He was being nice, that's all." She desperately wanted to change the subject. "Did you come all the way over here with your mom for this exhibit? That's a long trip in her condition, isn't it?"

"We came to see a specialist at the hospital about her cancer. But we wanted to surprise you since we were here already," he said. "I'm sorry if we spoiled your night. I guess we don't quite fit in here. But you might compliment Mom on her new dress. She was trying hard to look nice for you."

Celia hadn't meant to be so angry at her husband and certainly didn't want to disappoint Irene, but she'd been caught in an awkward moment.

"Where are you staying tonight?" she asked, hoping they'd already made arrangements since she was staying with Alan at his house.

"We have a hotel near the hospital," said Brock. "We're leaving early tomorrow morning, taking some of Jimmy's belongings to the farm. Why don't you circulate with your crowd? You need to do that. Maybe we can talk on the phone when all this settles down. By the way, you look beautiful, and your presentations look terrific. Proud of you," he said and kissed her softly on the mouth. "Sorry about the boots."

She squeezed his arm as he turned to walk away. "I'm sorry too, Brock," she said, not revealing to him Jovan was also staying at Alan's house.

CHAPTER 16

PARENT

BROCK AND IRENE WERE UP before dawn the next morning, anxious to get going—Irene to get back to the farm and Brock to flush memories of the museum debacle from his mind. They talked during the entire drive, stopping only twice for coffee and bathroom breaks. Irene didn't ask about his encounter with Celia. Her intuition told her it hadn't gone well. She hoped Brock's return home wasn't the cause.

Instead, the two talked about the farm. Was Uncle Richard doing well enough to keep it afloat? Were his partying and gambling under control? Irene assured him his uncle was living up to his side of the bargain. He was no Max Gallagher, but no one could be. The crops got planted and harvested on time, and he kept the machinery running. "He's a good man," she said.

But living up to his brother's reputation was a struggle for Richard. He blamed himself for Max's tragic death when he was accidentally overcome by the fumigant he was using to rid some stored grain of insects. Richard was supposed to have been there to help with the procedure that Saturday morning but had arrived late. When he found his brother motionless in the pile of wheat and dragged him from the bin, he had tried to resuscitate him, but it was too late. After Max's death, his drinking got worse. Irene reassured Richard it wasn't his fault and was glad he'd been there with Max at the end, struggling to save him as he took his final breaths.

It was time for a new subject. Brock drummed his fingers on the steering wheel. "Mom, what do you think about me coaching football at Glory Grove?" He'd been tossing around the idea again and needed advice. But the incident at the museum made the subject more complicated. Celia would never be happy on the farm; he knew that.

"I have the urge to coach again," Brock said. "That's what I'm good at. I feel empty without it, like a pilot without an airplane. But it wouldn't be easy. The kids would have to be committed. They'd have to buy in, or it would be a miserable couple of months being beaten up with no joy for the effort."

"It sounds like you have your speech ready. Maybe you've already made up your mind," Irene said. "Honestly, we don't have enough farm here for three men. Richard and Jimmy can keep it running. You need to stay busy. You can't watch over me every minute." She lay her head back on the headrest and closed her eyes. "But if it's only because of me that you are back in the Grove, you know I'd move to Seattle in a second if that's what it took for you and Celia to be happy."

"Mom, you won't have to leave the farm. Celia and I will work something out."

Heat was radiating off the tin roof of the barn as they pulled up the driveway to the farmhouse. Tim Palmer's pickup was parked next to the corral. Brock hadn't seen Tim since he'd come by to tell him about

Conrad Newton's exit. He was sitting on the front porch with Jimmy, a beer in his hand, his shirt unbuttoned to cool him from the summer heat. He barely looked up, as if he knew Brock and Irene would arrive at exactly this minute.

Jimmy was at the other end of the porch, casually tossing a dry willow stick in front of Sassy. She would limp a few steps on her fractured leg, pick up the stick and bring it back to drop into Jimmy's lap. Tim laughed when he saw the little U-Haul trailer behind the sedan. It looked like the mismatched Tonka toys he'd played with as a child.

"You men busy watching the sun move across the sky?" Brock asked. Sarcasm always worked with Tim. "All the work must be done if you two can't find something to do. Tim, don't you have a job?" Tim worked on the county road crew, but, of course, he had Sunday off.

"Good to see you, too, you pathetic schoolmarm. I've got news to share." He took a final swig from the aluminum can, then crushed it in his big bear paw.

"It must be important for you to drive out here on your day off," Brock said. "Let me open up the trailer so Jimmy can start unpacking his things, and then we can talk."

Jimmy began pulling boxes from the trailer as Brock and Tim walked out toward the barn and leaned on the fence Max had fashioned years ago from the pine poles he harvested from the ridge behind the house. The old mare came up to greet them. Tim stroked Dolly's mane and let his hand slide down her face to feel her soft muzzle.

"What's going on, Tim?" Brock asked, dropping the sarcasm. "It must be serious."

"Kind of," Tim said. "My ex has fallen off the wagon again."

"Peggy … can't stay sober, can she. That's too bad. Where is she now?"

Tim spit part of his chew into the corral. "In jail. Got caught driving drunk and with a suspended license. She's in big trouble this time. The cops are serious in Denver."

"Tough deal. What about Luke?" Brock asked. Tim's son was still in high school. "Who's taking care of him?"

"There's the problem. He doesn't get along with Peggy's sister, and the only other relatives he has are here in the Grove. Peggy says she has no other choice but to send him here. Her parents are too old to handle him. So, guess what? She wants me to take him in. I'm not sure I'm ready to parent a sixteen-year-old kid with a chip on his shoulder." Tim was staring into the horse's eyes as if looking for condolences.

"You don't have a choice, old friend. I wouldn't know, but I think when you sire a child, you should know they will get older and maybe cause you some problems. You're going to have to step up. Every boy needs a dad. It may be a bit late, but it might be the best thing that could happen to Luke."

"Well, Luke was an accident, you know. We weren't thinking ahead sixteen years; we were thinking how good it felt for sixteen minutes."

Tim was falling back on his usual crude humor. "I know what I have to do, just wanted to let you know what was going on and hoping I might be able to count on you for help. You've dealt with the sixteen-year-olds on your teams, so you know more about them than I do. Luke's a big kid and loves football. So, would you please throw your hat in the ring for this coaching job at the school? At least then he might have something to do if he comes here. I'd love to see you coaching my kid." He turned from the horse to look at Brock.

"Well, with Jimmy and Luke, we'd have at least two guys who want to play. That wouldn't be a bad start."

The two men went to help Jimmy finish cleaning out the trailer. Irene was napping, so Brock threw together some tuna fish sandwiches, and they sat at the kitchen table. Tim cracked another beer and began to chat up Jimmy about football, telling him about the year the Grizzlies played for the state championship. About how he and Brock had been oh-so-close to making history.

With football on his mind, Brock thought it was time for him to contact the school principal, Lester Colquit, to see if the football job was actually available. He'd heard Colquit didn't like sports. But what kind of man didn't like football? On Monday morning, he dialed the school, and it rang only once before a man on the other end picked up. The voice was tinny but professional.

"Glory Grove High School, may I help you?" It was Colquit.

Brock explained who he was and asked if he could come for a visit and that he was interested in the football position. There was silence on the line for a minute. "You might be a little premature," Colquit said. "No decision's been made yet on the subject." He was hoping to delay it so the board would postpone the season for another year. The public outcry had finally simmered down, and if he could hold off long enough, maybe the town would adjust permanently to life in the Grove without football. *Just let it die*, he thought.

It also was a personal matter to the principal—a situation closer to home. His son, Lester Jr. would be a freshman in the fall and wanted to play football. Like his sister, he was long and gangly, with little meat on his bones. But he loved competing and, much to his father's consternation, wanted to play every sport.

Colquit had bent a little and reluctantly allowed his daughter to play basketball and Lester Jr. to turn out for junior high basketball and baseball. Sports would be a passing fancy, he thought, thinking the allure would fade when the family gene pool displayed itself and the boy failed to succeed. But he didn't fail and, in fact, played as well as any of the other boys. Contrary to the principal's predictions, his son's grades improved with his participation.

But Lester Jr.'s dream of playing football was a step too far. Colquit couldn't get past his own humiliation at Les's age. The thought of his son trying to make the football team made his stomach churn. It was a wretched game played by wretched people. Besides, research was proving that contact sports could lead to permanent brain damage. What kind of father would allow his son to play?

Brock was patient. He persisted. "I understand there are some younger players who really want to play," he said. "And I've talked to parents who want the program. I think they'd throw their support behind reestablishing Grizzly football."

"I'm not so sure about that," Colquit said coldly. "There really wasn't much of an outcry over last year's decision to drop the program." It was a lie, but he continued. "None of the seniors wanted to play. And Coach Newton couldn't rally any support. What makes you think anything has changed? And what do you know of this community or of football for that matter?"

Brock told of his background growing up in Glory Grove, his success playing at the college level, and his ten years as coach at Brighton High.

"Oh, I see. Well, you certainly have the background, but coaching in a city school and coaching here are two very different animals. I'm not convinced there's enough interest here. I'll take it up with the school board, but I know their philosophy. Most of them agree with me that school is about academics and sports needs to take a back seat. Thanks for the call, Mr. Gallagher. If we decide to open the position, we'll let you know." He hung up the phone.

PARENT

Brock laid the receiver back in its cradle and gripped the pencil he'd been taking notes with. He scribbled the word *stonewalled* and set the pencil down gently, trying to cool his temper. It was clear. If he wanted to coach in Glory Grove, it was going to take some effort. He was insulted he could be denied an open position in his hometown with his background and knowledge. It was a setback. But Colquit's denial made him want the job now more than ever. He was going to go after it. He picked up the pencil, drummed it a couple of times on the table, then casually scratched through his writing.

CHAPTER 17

GALLERY

BROCK SENT OUT INVITATIONS for a get-together to talk about the future of football in Glory Grove. He invited Tim and his uncle, the old assistant coach Don Baker, a few men from the Methodist Church, and the parents of the boys he knew wanted to play. He hoped to have a friendly visit with the locals to measure how many loyal fans there were.

He'd rented the community art gallery, which had a small meeting room in the back. Renting the room was one way for the art folks to get people to visit the gallery and appreciate the talents of local artists.

Brock arrived early, carrying two dozen donuts, and flipped on all the light switches he could find. He brewed a pot of coffee and turned on the overhead fans to cool the old brick building. As he waited for others to arrive, he walked slowly through the gallery, studying the art and comparing it to the high-priced creations he'd seen in Celia's gallery. It had been days now, and he hadn't heard from his wife. He'd tried to reach her by phone to let her know he was thinking seriously about pursuing the football job, but she hadn't returned his calls. He hoped she might call after the exhibition was over.

Glory Grove art was simple yet beautiful, with scenes of familiar places—the waterfall below town where Cold Creek froze over during the winter. And the Wilson barn, a five-sided masterpiece of rural architecture built over one hundred years ago, now leaning precariously to the west. There was a watercolor painting of the old, abandoned union church, weathered and empty, surrounded by wildflowers. It was art Brock appreciated.

At the end of the row of paintings was one that caught his eye—a night scene of a clash of football teams on Sullivan Field. Overhead lights beamed down from their perch on the tall wooden poles brought down from the ridge, illuminating the green gridiron. Twenty-two young men were poised in perpetual readiness to charge with abandon across the line when the quarterback gave the signal. Referees stood hunched over with their puffy mid-sections covered in stripes. Another dozen young players stood along the sideline waiting for their turn in the action.

The painting showed the grandstand packed with parents and students dressed in red and white. Brock hadn't noticed when he was playing, but if the scene depicted reality, nearly every seat was full. It took him back to the drama he'd experienced on that field, the moments of despair and elation. He remembered the adulation he received from parents, fans, and the high school girls. The painting on the wall drew feelings that had been lingering in his mind, hidden away like a hibernating life form.

He searched for the artist's name, wondering who'd captured the scene so beautifully on canvas. He raised the tag attached to the bottom of the oak frame … *Veronica Jepson. Price– $75.*

Brock stood spellbound. Then he remembered notes she'd pass him in high school study hall with miniature figures sketched across the tiny pieces of paper. Ronnie would smile at him when he nodded his approval. He appreciated her drawings when he was seventeen, but now even more. She'd become a capable artist. He wanted to write a check for seventy-five dollars and take the painting from the stucco wall, carry it home to hang it in a special place in the farmhouse.

There was a sudden banging on the front door. It was Tim. "Where the hell is the beer and chips?" he hollered; he knew Brock had to be there somewhere.

"Quiet down, you old lizard. You're going to wake the sleeping artists," Brock shouted back with a laugh, having been pulled abruptly from his trance. "Nice of you to come; you may be the only one here."

"Oh, hell, half the town is probably going to show up." Tim was dressed as usual in his plaid shirt with a county road crew cap, the bill crunched up into a semi-circle, pushed back on his shiny head. "I've called everyone I know who gives a damn about football and told them to be here."

"Then you'd better go get more donuts."

For the next half hour, the little gallery filled with the men and women of Glory Grove. Most were fans of the high school game, but there were a handful of skeptics who doubted whether the sport could be brought back to life in the Grove. Brock introduced himself and proceeded to tell them why they'd been invited. "I thought it was time to find out if there is any interest left in putting a football team on the field." People wouldn't even let him finish before they jumped into the conversation.

"Of course, we want football. One year without a team is one too many," said a man wearing heavy work boots and a seed cap pulled down hard on his head. "That coach we had didn't make it fun for the boys. They didn't like him, so they all quit."

"Hell, in my day, most guys would have played for Jack the Ripper, just to get on the field. Since when is it about having fun?" argued another.

The night wore on with each person in the room having their say. The consensus was that they wanted football back … for their kids, the school, and the town. "It's an American tradition," said one middle-aged mom, summing up what all the others had meant to say.

Brock asked how he should approach the school about becoming the coach. That was where the unity fell apart. Most folks in the room were all for him. They knew of his high school and college successes and of his coaching accolades, but they weren't sure if he'd stay and build a program. They wondered what his agenda might be.

"Why shouldn't we pick someone who lives here and will be here for a long time? We all know in a couple of years you'll be gone, and we'll be back where we started."

"Who else then?" wondered the parent of an incoming freshman boy. "Name names."

"I know Cort Jepson wants the job," said a man in the back row. His statement silenced the crowd. "And I think he'd make a helluva coach. He wouldn't take shit off anybody, leastways that puny-assed principal. We need somebody who can turn this team into a hard-assed bunch like Glory Grove used to be. We didn't always win, but by gawd those other schools knew they'd been in a fight."

Brock remembered seeing the man hanging out with Cort at Derby Daze. But why would Cort think he could run a football program? *It's about Justin*, Brock thought. Cort wanted that boy to get a scholarship, and if he was running the ship, Justin would probably carry the ball on every play.

Few in the room thought Cort Jepson would make a good coach, but not everyone agreed that Brock would be the man for the job. Still, one thing was clear. Those who had come to the art gallery were ready to get behind the push to bring football back to the Grove. The five-member school board would soon be bombarded with calls. And the board meeting in two weeks was the focal point of the group's energy.

The hour was getting late. The crowd had eaten all the donuts, drunk all the coffee, and talked themselves out. They slowly dispersed, heading out into the heat of the summer night. Brock turned off the lights and, in the shadows of the gallery, looked one more time at Ronnie's painting. He stared at it in the semidarkness, absorbing the details. Without thinking, he ran the fingers of his right hand down the oak frame of the painting and stared at her name.

CHAPTER 18

LUKE

SIXTEEN-YEAR-OLD LUKE PALMER returned to Glory Grove on a bus from Denver at ten o'clock in the morning. He stepped down onto Main Street in front of the local convenience store, just down the street from the Cozy Corner drive-in and across from the police station. He hadn't been in the town since his mother packed their suitcases and took him with her to Denver when he was five years old. He didn't remember the place, except for a few horseback rides on his dad's lap and Christmas at his grandparents.

He wasn't happy to be here. His family life in Denver wasn't the best, watching his mother struggle with her alcohol addiction and him getting in fights with his aunt. But he liked the school—although he couldn't read very well and took mostly vocational and remedial classes—because it gave him what he really wanted … sports. He excelled at all of them. Football was his favorite because he could let out his anger on the opponents, knocking them bloody without fear of being criticized for it. But he also made the varsity basketball and baseball teams as the only sophomore on those squads. He was physically tough and played with a passion coaches rarely found in other players.

He couldn't believe his circumstances. A couple years older and he could make his own life choices, but at sixteen, either the parents or the courts would decide what he could do. He'd even asked his football coach if he could live with him in Denver until he graduated. But because of his attitude, he'd been rejected. The coach had a wife and young children and didn't need a troublemaker in the house despite what he could do for him on the football field.

So here he was in a one-horse town with a single stoplight and, from what he'd been told, a school with no football team. Maybe he should just walk away. The driver pulled his suitcase from the belly of the bus, dropped it on the sidewalk, and slammed the aluminum door shut. "There you go, big boy; I hope you enjoy Glory Grove." He hopped back into the driver's seat and throttled up with the four passengers who remained on board. Diesel fumes washed over Luke as the bus drove away.

Luke turned away, coughing, and looked up and down the street. No traffic. He felt abandoned in a bad zombie movie. Once inside the air-conditioned store, he sucked in the clean air. The cashier, a pretty girl with blond hair and blue eyes, maybe high school age, said hello.

"Looking for something to drink," Luke muttered. He was six feet three, a few stones over two hundred pounds, with muscles popping under his sleeveless white t-shirt. A large tattoo on his right bicep showed an eagle swooping from the sky. Sweat showed through the dark green gym shorts he was wearing.

The boy looked sinister to the young clerk who'd begun working at the store when school ended for the summer. His rusty-red hair was fashioned into a mohawk, and a large gold ring hung from his pierced right ear. "The drinks are back there in the cooler, or there are fountain drinks right behind you," she said. "Where'd you come from?" She was trying to stay composed and friendly.

"Denver. My dad was supposed to pick me up, but as usual, he's nowhere to be found."

"Who's your dad? Maybe I can call him. If he's from around here, I probably know him."

"Tim Palmer … works for the county road department."

"Sure, I know Tim," she said as she wiped the counter with a cloth. "The county crew comes in all the time for fuel. I like your dad. He's friendly. Doesn't complain like the other guys, you know what I mean … always complaining about the heat, or the cold, or the wet, or the dry. Sheesh, they get paid well enough, only work four days a week, and still find reason to whine. Your dad doesn't. How come you don't live with him?"

"Family problems. My mom took me to Denver when I was in kindergarten. I guess she couldn't get along with my dad, so I really don't know him. He calls a couple of times a year. But now I guess I have to live here until I graduate. Two years in this little hole-in-the-wall town should be about as exciting as watching my toenails grow. You go to school here?"

"I'll be a sophomore. My name is Ashley; what's yours?"

"Luke. Luke Skywalker." He paused for effect. "No, sorry, just kidding. It's Luke Palmer." He smiled for the first time since leaving Denver, even if it was at his own silly joke.

Ashley thought he had nice teeth and shook her head over the pun. "Want me to call your dad?"

"Not yet. I'll wait here for a while. He's bound to show up, isn't he? I mean, where else could he go in this little burg? You seem nice; maybe I'll just hang out with you."

Was he flirting? It made her uncomfortable. But their conversation was interrupted with the sound of squealing tires as a jacked-up, silver Dodge Ram pickup came sliding to a halt in front of the gas pumps outside the store. Tim, in an untucked cowboy shirt with snaps up the front, hopped out of the truck and loped into the building.

"Hey, Ashley," he began, wondering if she'd seen his son when he caught sight of his flesh and blood standing at the counter. "Luke?" he asked, not wanting to mistake someone else for his son. But he should have known. The boy, now nearly a man, was his likeness, plus the spiked hair and tattoo.

"Welcome home, son," he said, hoping his boy might still recognize him.

Aha, Ashley thought, *"Luke, I am your father."* Her mind circled back to the movie theme. She laughed at the coincidental reference as she observed the two men awkwardly checking each other out. She could picture Tim as the misunderstood villain and the new boy in town as Luke the reluctant hero. She would play the scene over in her head throughout the day.

"How was your trip?" Tim asked, pacing back and forth in front of the ice cream cooler.

"Long and sweaty."

"Well, you're here now, so let's get your things, and I'll show you the wonders of Glory Grove."

"Sure, whatever," Luke said. "That should take all of five minutes."

The boy followed his dad out of the building, but after a couple of steps toward the pickup, he turned around, opened the glass door, and winked at Ashley. "Nice to meet you, Ashley. I'll be seeing you at school," he said, flirting again.

She blushed. "Guess so. Welcome to the Grove."

LUKE

Tim gave Luke a tour of his new surroundings. First, they stopped by their home. Luke would have his own room upstairs in the smallish two-story house. It was larger than his room in Denver, and it raised his spirits. Later, after they'd eaten lunch—Tim made peanut butter and jelly sandwiches because he remembered that as a five-year-old, they were Luke's favorite—they got back in the pickup and cruised around town.

Tim showed Luke the two eating establishments, the art gallery, the drug store, the espresso stand at the edge of town, the fire station, and the five churches, although he hadn't been in one since he and Peggy had their hurry-up wedding seventeen years before at the Presbyterian Church. Tim wondered if they would even let him in the door now.

"So, what's with the name Glory Grove, anyway?" Luke asked. "Don't seem like there's much glory here."

Tim told Luke what he knew. How when the pioneers began to lay claim to the land back in the 1800s, traveling preachers moved among them, trying to gather converts into their ranks. Word would spread of the revival meetings, and the isolated newcomers would flock to the days-long outdoor gatherings as much for social interaction as for religious enthusiasm. Much of the area was devoid of trees, so a shaded spot along the creek became a place for a camp revival meeting. One area had a large grove of cottonwood trees arching over the shallow banks of Cold Creek. It was a favorite place to gather. Cynics said people went there "seeking the glory of heaven." Over time the spot became known as Glory Grove. The name stuck.

"And people here are still waiting for some kind of glory," Luke smirked. He stuck his big arm out the window of the pickup directing airflow toward his body.

Much of the tour was about the businesses that had once been in

Glory Grove but now were gone—the movie theater, three car dealerships, the hardware and jewelry stores, two drug stores, three service stations, and the bowling alley that had been converted to a second-hand junk store. "When I was growing up, this little town was humming," Tim said.

"Where'd it all go?" asked Luke, disheartened by all the empty buildings.

"To big box stores in the city, mostly," Tim said. "People can drive thirty miles and pay less money. And there aren't as many big families, so we don't need as many stores. It's a shame. But we still have the school, that's a big deal, 'cause some of these puny towns don't even have that," he said.

"Where's the school?" Luke asked, knowing he'd be spending a couple of years there unless they threw him out.

"Thought you'd never ask," Tim said. He wheeled the pickup around in front of the giant grain elevator that towered over the town with a faded Grizzly Bear painted on its side, turned south, drove six blocks past the park with the oak trees, and pulled up in front of the high school; a three-story sandstone building built just prior to the Great Depression when the community was flush with money. A large rectangular stone was placed over the front door, the date chiseled into its face, *Glory Grove High School, Established 1928*.

"Well, she ain't pretty, but she's seen a lot of kids pass through here."

"Any of them become rich or famous?"

"Well, my good friend Brock Gallagher was an All-League quarterback at the university and spent a bit of time in the NFL. That's the only one I know."

Luke wiped the perspiration from his forehead. "So, he's somewhere rolling in cash and living in a big house, glad to get out of this dead-end town?"

"No, right now he's living with his mother out on Kirby Road, just out of town a dozen miles—came home to help her on the farm."

"That doesn't sound like it ended all that well. He played football here?"

"We played on the same team and ended up undefeated until the state championship. Almost got us a championship ring. We had a helluva run."

"What happened?"

"Oh, one of our best players got hurt toward the end of the game. Started pointing fingers at us like it was our fault. Kind of ruined it for everybody. That and our coach had us so beat up by the final game we ran out of gas. But we went further than any other football team from the Grove. This town still hasn't won the big trophy." Tim opened his door and slid out of the pickup.

Luke followed his dad but kept talking. "I've heard they don't even have a team here now."

"We're working on that. Maybe this fall, things will change," Tim said, as he spit a wad of chewing tobacco into the empty pop can he was carrying. The pair skirted around the end of the high school, heading for the football field. They'd just rounded the corner when a voice brought them to a stop.

"Hold it. Can I help you, folks?" It was Principal Colquit. His tone was serious.

Tim's head jerked around like he'd been caught pulling one of his high school pranks. "Just wanted to show my son the football field," he said.

"And who are you?"

"Tim Palmer. I went to school here a long time ago and wanted to show my son where I played ball."

Colqit wasn't impressed. "The field is off-limits to the public. We have some liability issues with nonschool personnel using it."

"Luke's going to school here this fall, so he'll be playing on this field." Tim's voice turned gravelly.

"I'm not sure we will have a team," Colqit said, looking at the big teenage boy with spiked hair and tattoos. "But we never turn away a new student. What subjects do you like, young man?"

Luke wasn't ready for the town or the school and didn't like the principal with his nose in his business. "Mostly sports," he said, refusing to look the principal in the eye.

Those weren't the sentiments the principal wanted to hear. "Well, we might have to change that attitude if you're going to fit into my high school," Colqit said and turned to walk away.

"We're going to go look at the field now," Tim said, his voice raised so Colqit was sure to hear. "We promise not to sue the school if we stub a toe."

Luke liked his dad's attitude … not taking crap off anybody. He strode out, keeping pace with the older man, his head high and chest out. Even from a distance, you could tell they were father and son.

CHAPTER 19

BOARD

BROCK WAS FRUSTRATED. He wanted to talk to Celia, but she still hadn't returned his calls. He could feel a gap growing between them, so he gave it another try. This time she answered.

"Hi, hon," she said. "I've been meaning to call. I've just been so busy."

"I thought it was time we talked," he said. "How are you doing now that the exhibition is over? I assume it was all a great success."

"It was wonderful." Suddenly her voice was energized. "We had record attendance and some big financial contributions to the gallery. And we got great reviews in the newspapers. Jovan seemed to strike a chord with the people."

"So, what now? You coming back to the farm?" There was a moment of silence.

"Well, that's why I needed to talk to you. Jovan has another exhibit opening in Chicago and wants me to go with him to work on some presentations. He liked the way the exhibit was done here. I was hoping you'd understand. It's a big honor for me."

Brock closed his eyes and took a long deep breath. So, there it was. Celia wanted to move on to something more important. And she wanted to do it with a man his opposite—fashionable and cultured with the draw of celebrity. Brock was stunned. Celia's short time on the farm seemed to unsettle her. Perhaps it was difficult and uncomfortable, but it wasn't a prison sentence. The attraction she had for a New York artist and his lifestyle was something he had always feared. That someone in her world would pull her away from him,

He'd experienced the same sense of abandonment years ago when his father left, not from his own choosing, but from the accident. This was different, but the emptiness and longing he was feeling were the same—a desire to turn back a clock and return to a happier time.

"Celia, do you think that's the right thing to do?" he asked. He struggled to keep his emotions in check.

"I want you to understand what I'm feeling," she said. "I need freedom to live my life with the things that make me happy. Give me this one chance to try something I've always dreamed of. You have football. That's what makes you happy. I want to feel the same joy doing what I do."

Brock grasped the phone tighter in his hand. "And I have to confess; I'm applying for the football job here in the Grove. I hope you can understand. We seem to be heading in different directions, but I know we can work this out. Just be careful and come back to us as soon as you can."

He hung the phone back on the wall and, for a moment, felt lightheaded. If only he'd been more eloquent ... more compelling with his words. He'd wanted to deny her request but knew it might make things worse. His old home now seemed empty and cold.

BOARD

The Glory Grove School Board met on the third Thursday of every month. It was a gathering of the five board members along with the district administrators, including Lester Colquit. Business typically consisted of taking milk bids from area vendors and choosing between fuel distributors for heating fuel. Sometimes curriculum issues were discussed, although most of those decisions came down from the state capitol.

The one real power the local board had was the hiring and firing of personnel. The teachers union made it nearly impossible to dismiss a teacher, but the board had total control over the athletic coaches. And if there ever was a need for more seating at a board meeting, it was when there was discussion about a coach.

When the board canceled the football season the previous year, it drew the ire of the community. But since the decision came from a lack of student turnout, there'd been no rallying cry among the citizenry to pack the board room. However, the meeting on the third Thursday in July was different. Glory Grove wanted football back. They'd been embarrassed and ridiculed by their neighboring towns for being a school without a team. Was Glory Grove heading into the death spiral other small farm towns had succumbed to, no more than ghost towns along the highway?

It wasn't as though football was an economic driver. But it was an inspiration that could lift people up and give them pride when the young men representing their families and their history went to battle against neighboring teams.

That was the void people in the Grove felt, and they wanted it filled. The key was the board meeting. It would take a majority of the board, three members, to vote to reinstate the program. Many suspected Principal Colquit would do whatever he could to delay the decision.

And with the lateness of the process, any delay would mean another lost season of football.

"I'm calling the meeting to order," said the board chairman, Charles Wallingham, a small man with large glasses, as he pounded his gavel. "Since we have too many people for this room, we're all going to move to the cafeteria." He led the procession down the hall into a more spacious room without windows. It was stuffy.

Reassembled, the meeting began. Principal Colquit insisted that Wallingham stick with the agenda and deal with all the minutiae of school business first. The audience showed their patience as the board dealt with milk and fuel bids and the purchase of a new computer for the library. Following that was a report from the coordinator of the accelerated learning program. The meeting drug on and on, but the masses hung tough. They wanted to talk about football and weren't going to be denied.

Finally, at half-past nine o'clock, the last item on the agenda was read—the resignation of former teacher and coach Conrad Newton. Since the board couldn't speak of personnel issues in an open meeting, they left the room and went into an executive session for fifteen minutes, leaving the exasperated audience growing more impatient by the second.

"This whole thing sucks," said a woman sitting in the back row. She waved a newspaper under her chin to ward off the heat. The temperature had risen with each hour the large number of bodies huddled together in their folding chairs. "They're trying to duck the issue. Maybe it's time the whole board and administration is sent packing."

As the group grumbled their endorsement of the idea, the board returned to reconvene the meeting. "The resignation of Conrad Newton has been accepted," said Wallingham. "A position will be opened, and applications accepted for a teacher of history and world problems."

"What about a football coach?" The woman in the back row shouted. "Seems like the world problem we have here is we don't have a football coach."

"I have to ask the audience to remain silent unless you are called upon," Wallingham said, trying to maintain order. "In regard to reinstating football, we're up against a wall since the school year will begin soon, and we don't have a coach. It may be impossible to put something together that fast."

Tim Palmer slowly rose from his seat in the front row. He'd been silent throughout the evening but had heard enough. "What in God's name are you waiting for? You're all slower than a sow givin' birth to a litter of thirteen," he said. "You all know there's a guy in town who'd fill that role and do a helluva job. Just ask him. What are you all waiting for?"

"Silence, please," demanded the chairman. "We have to do this in an orderly fashion."

"Just take a vote," Tim said. His face was red from the heat and frustration. "What would it hurt?"

The school board was tired and frustrated with the crowd and more so with the principal who'd put them in this situation. "Okay, I can't see where it would hurt to find out where you all stand," said Wallingham. "How many of you here want to reestablish the football program?"

"Hold on," said Colquit. "That's not how this works. These people don't decide. The elected board makes that decision."

"Mr. Colquit, if you please." Wallingham hammered his gavel. "I run this meeting, not you. We will take a show of hands to let these people express their opinion."

"But that's not official." The principal snapped his big three-ring binder together.

"No, it isn't, but we're going to do it anyway. How many of you want to see football back in Glory Grove?" A roomful of hands shot up instantly.

"Okay, I think we know what the group wants," said Wallingham. "We have a lot of questions to answer, but we'll stay here all night if we have to."

Even though the board had yet to take a vote, Principal Colquit knew he'd lost. Despite his protests, he knew three members would vote for football. It was a lost cause for him. He didn't like where it was headed or what he would face at home with his own son. He felt once again like he was taped to the goal post, unable to break free. Right now, he hated the little town.

CHAPTER 20

SABOTAGE

AS A RESULT OF THE MARATHON MEETING, the school board concluded that if a coach could be found in the next few weeks and if twenty players signed a petition to play ball, Glory Grove would have a team. Justin Jepson heard the news the next day. He'd driven to the convenience store, which often heard rumors first, early in the morning from his family's home just outside of town to pick up some aspirin for his dad. Cort had stayed home from work complaining of a headache. Ashley told Justin the news as he was paying for the aspirin.

"Are you sure?" asked Justin. "You're not kidding, are you?"

"No. I heard it from the men who were at the meeting. They said maybe a guy named Brock Gallagher might be the new coach." She could see his excitement and thought he might come around the counter and give her a hug. Justin was considered the hottest boy in school, and she was thrilled to be the first one to tell him about the football decision.

Justin let out a whoop. More than anything in his life, he loved football and now might play again. All he'd have to do was find nineteen others. Ashley, caught up in the moment and wanting to share in the excitement, said if there was a football team she might try out for the cheer squad. Justin gave her a high five like he'd just scored a touchdown for the Grizzlies. She'd never touched him before, and her hand was tingling. She wouldn't wash her hands all day despite the sign in the bathroom demanding all employees do so.

"Thanks, Ashley," Justin said and bounced out the door heading for home. His dad was in a bad mood with a headache, and he didn't want to anger him by being late. But the news about the football team should cheer him up.

Cort was indeed pleased but bristled at the thought they might give the job to Brock. He'd gotten in Brock's face at the dance. Now, if Brock became coach of the Grizzlies, Justin might end up sitting on the bench. He didn't want his son or wife to have any relationship with his old teammate. His head throbbed.

I need to get people off the Brock Gallagher bandwagon, he thought. It was time to start some rumors. The people in town loved to gossip, and perhaps he could stir up a little dirt to give them something to talk about. If they turned away from Brock, they might reach out to him for a coach. If he were going to change minds, he'd have to move quickly.

On the farm, Brock waited for Tim Palmer, anxious to hear about the meeting. He'd purposely skipped it, letting the community send a message to the board without the appearance that he was behind it. When Tim came flying up the driveway at sunrise, Brock assumed it was big news one way or the other.

"Well, the freaking board finally got off their asses and made a decision," Tim said as he yanked open the kitchen door. "But we had to stay half the night before they finally got around to vote. They said yes but with a bunch of chicken shit strings attached."

"Like what?" Brock slid a chair over so Tim could sit.

"Oh, they have to have a list of at least twenty boys who say they'll play. And they want a coach hired as soon as possible."

"You think that'll be a problem?"

"We might have to shake the trees a little, but I think we can find twenty bodies. Are you ready to be their coach?"

Brock had decided. He wanted to coach again. He knew he'd have to tell Celia and didn't look forward to the conversation, but he was lost without football. And he needed to get his mind off her. "What about Newton's teaching position? Are they looking for a teacher?"

"You're not thinking about becoming a teacher again, are you?" Tim pushed his cap back on his head and narrowed his gaze.

"Just thinking out loud. Celia's going to Chicago to help with an art exhibit, and I need to get my mind off her. I need something to stay busy."

Tim hadn't heard about Celia leaving but knew she didn't like the farm. He'd always wondered how Brock kept her from straying, with her beauty and the body of a model. She probably had a lot of men chasing after her.

"Better get down to the school and check it out," Tim said. "It was clear last night that people want you to coach. Well, except Colquit, that turd. He'd rather hire someone who'd kill the football team once and for all."

The men's voices through the walls of her bedroom woke Irene. She quickly slipped on some clothes, combed her hair, and joined the conversation. "Good morning, Tim," she said when she popped into the kitchen. "You sound pretty chipper so early in the morning. You almost beat the sun up."

"Had to come and give Brock the good news about the football team we're going to have this fall. Get him pumped up to put on his coach's whistle again. And I thought maybe Jimmy would be excited about it too. Where is that kid?"

"In bed like most teenagers this time of morning. I'll go get him; he'll be excited. He'll probably run out and start lifting those weights as soon as he hears." She walked to the foot of the stairs and yelled up at Jimmy. He came stumbling down the steps, rubbing his eyes. When Tim told him about the football team, those eyes sparkled, and a smile spread across his face.

Irene fried some omelets while the men talked. Laughter and chatter competed with the sound of frying bacon and eggs. She absorbed the sounds and watched as sunlight peeked in through the kitchen window.

At his home, Cort was still trying to shake off the Friday morning hangover he'd acquired at the tavern the night before. He swallowed some aspirin and chased it down with tomato juice. His plan was coming together. He knew who the town gossips were. All he needed to do was plant the seed, and a rumor would spread like a summer stubble fire out in the wheat fields. What he decided on was a simple anecdote people could find believable yet unacceptable in their conservative community.

Cort stroked his goatee and smiled. The gossip mongers always looked at town happenings with a dark lens of suspicion. He would use that to his advantage. Some of the local doubters already had reservations about Brock, thinking perhaps he'd lost his job at Brighton for something unsavory—perhaps pilfering from the booster club funds or illegally recruiting top athletes from other schools. But Cort's rumor would top that. He'd hint that Brock might have been having a sexual liaison with a student. It was the kind of juicy gossip people would love to spread, made more believable since people had noticed that Brock's wife had suddenly left town and not returned.

    All Cort had to do was encourage people's mistrust. Once his head quit throbbing, he'd hit the Cozy Corner first, then the steak house, and finally go back to the Wild Horse Tavern where he'd spent his prior evening. By Saturday morning, everyone would be talking.

CHAPTER 21

FRIEND

TIM HAD LEFT LUKE in bed so he could first deliver the news to Brock. Now he headed home. It was still early in the morning, but he wanted his son to hear about the board's decision. He rushed into the house and hopped up the stairs, skipping every other one. "Hey Luke, wake up. I've got big news."

"What now, Pops?" Luke grumbled. He pulled the sheets down from his eyes.

"I went to the school board meeting last night, and it looks like we're going to have a football team this year. The Grizzlies are back."

"Sweet." Luke's eyes blinked wide open. "You must have some pull in this town," he said through a giant yawn. He was joking but wondered if his dad maybe did have some pull in the community.

"Well, it's not a done deal yet, but we're getting closer. All we need are twenty players and a coach."

"How hard can it be to round up twenty guys to play ball. In Denver, we had hundreds who wanted to play."

"Yeah, well, this ain't Denver, Son. Last year we couldn't even find eleven, so it's going to take some recruiting. But if you and Jimmy Ivory sign up, some of the other boys might see the light. And I know a kid named Justin Jepson wants to play. He's a good kid despite his asshole father. That only leaves seventeen more to round up."

"What about a coach? I heard you say he left town. We can't coach ourselves. And who is Jimmy Ivory?"

Tim caught his breath and slowed his speech. "Jimmy's a young black kid living with Brock Gallagher out on their farm. I told you about Brock; he's the guy who went on to play college ball and had a year in the pros. Well, he was a big-time high school coach over in Seattle, but he's back in town, and everyone wants him to coach the Grizzlies. He says he'll do it, but that little pip-squeak principal we met the other day might try to keep him off the field. Colquit knows if the team is any good, he won't be able to convince the board to cancel the program again."

Luke rolled out the side of the bed and sat there staring at his father. "So, what now?"

"Well, get out of bed. I want to take you out to the Gallagher farm so you can meet Jimmy and Brock. It's time you all got to know each other." Luke stood up with a groan and stumbled down the stairs wearing the same green shorts he'd worn on his trip from Denver. He used the bathroom, slapped water on his stubbled face, and put on some deodorant.

"Okay, I'm ready to go anywhere to find some excitement in this dead-end town," Luke said.

Tim looked at him and shook his head. "I guess if that's the best you can do. We'll stop at the convenience store for breakfast before we head out."

Luke stopped, remembering the pretty cashier at the store. "Hang on. Maybe I should clean up a little more. I'll be ready in a minute." He returned to the bathroom, shaved, stiffened up his mohawk, and brushed his teeth a second time. "Now I'm ready," he said.

Luke was disappointed when he saw the lady behind the cash register. She was in her sixties and didn't look a thing like Ashley, who was on her break and had gone home to check on her little brother. Luke had no way of knowing she was still tingling with excitement about her time spent with Justin Jepson.

The men scarfed down their microwaved egg and sausage muffins as Tim's pickup bounced down Kirby Road and around the right-angle corner with the steep embankment that dropped into the canyon. "Remember this corner if you ever come out here at night," Tim cautioned. "Even with the warning sign, it can sneak up on you. That ride wouldn't end well if you missed the turn."

"Understood, Pops."

When they pulled up to the farmhouse, Jimmy was sitting on the porch with Sassy, now nearly recovered from her surgery but still with a shaved leg from the procedure. Tim hurried around the pickup to make the introductions, and Jimmy stood to greet him, perspiring from the late morning sun.

"Hey, Jimmy, looks like your dog is doing better," Tim said, bending down to pat Sassy. "I brought my son, Luke, so you could get to know him. I think you two have something in common. You both want to play football."

"Yes sir," Jimmy said.

Luke walked over and took stock of the other sixteen-year-old.

He'd been told Jimmy was a football player, but he looked like he'd forgotten to grow. *Can't be much over five feet six*, Luke thought, towering over him. "What's up, Cuz?" He pounded Jimmy's fist.

Luke assumed Jimmy was like him, uncomfortable in this country environment. "What's a dude like you doing in a dead-end place like this?" he asked, ready to share tales of unhappiness at their predicament.

"It's my home now," Jimmy said. "I like it here. It's quiet. And I never had a dog before."

"Looks like your dog had an accident. Did somebody try to put her out of her misery?" Luke said, laughing.

"I ran over her on accident." Jimmy dropped his head.

"You were driving?"

"I was driving the hay truck and didn't know she was under the tire. Broke her leg, but me and Coach took her to the animal doctor. She fixed her up. Said she's going to be okay."

"Sorry, dude, I didn't know. Glad she's all right. Looks like a sweet little thing." He kneeled down and cautiously patted her on the head. He'd never had a pet of his own, living in the small house in Denver with his aunt. She didn't like animals.

"We have a horse too. You wanna see?"

"Sure. Let's go ride."

"I haven't ridden her yet. I think Coach needs to show me how first."

The two teenagers strolled out onto the gravel driveway, chatting furiously, looking comical with their contrasting appearances. One was a clean-cut undersized youth with close-cropped hair; the other was a muscular man-child with a punk hairdo, tattoos, and piercings. They were different. But each had come to the Grove from desperate situations and were similar in their need for safety.

The two men watched from the porch. "Looks like the boys may have hit it off," Brock said, gesturing to the teenagers standing at the corral fence, laughing, and petting the head of the old mare. "I hate to jinx this, but I can't wait to see them in football pads. I need to drive to town and talk to the principal again and get an application for the coaching position. He can't ignore me now that the board has made the decision to have a team. But Tim, how do we get eighteen other boys to sign up?"

Tim was ready for the question. "It's gonna take some recruiting." He ran his hand over his shaved scalp. "I think the linchpin might be Cort's son, Justin. He's the one boy in school everybody looks up to. But you can't get to him without going through his dad. And I know for a fact Cort doesn't want you anywhere around."

"Understood."

"This may sound crazy but hear me out. The fair is in a couple of months. A lot of the kids take swine projects to the fair. They auction off the pigs after the show, and the community turns out and pays big money for their animals. The purple ribbon winners, especially, can take home a thousand dollars or more."

"Come on Tim. Don't keep me in suspense. What's that got to do with football?"

"Hang on; I'm getting to it. Most of the kids get their pigs right here from your uncle. He has a Pig Pick day, and the kids come and choose the animal they want to buy. It'll happen soon. I know Justin comes, so I'm thinking we make sure Jimmy and Luke are here. Maybe they could pick too, and they could meet Justin and some of the other boys. Cort can't object to Justin being here, 'cause for one thing, they need the money his project brings in."

"You think Luke would want to raise an animal?" Brock stared out at the boys by the fence.

"Why not?" Tim rocked back in the chair he'd collapsed into. "He's always saying he's bored. It would give him something to do. If you'd let him keep the pig out here, he'd probably jump at the chance to get out of town to work with it. What do you think?"

"Great plans come from great minds," Brock joked. "It's a stretch, but it might work."

The door swung open behind the two men. It was Irene carrying a plate of cookies and a pitcher of lemonade. The July heat was cranking up. "Tim, you want to go see the principal with me this afternoon?" Brock asked. But Tim, remembering his altercations with Colquit, declined the invitation.

"You go on in," he said. "I'll stay here and eat Irene's cookies." He lifted a couple off the plate.

CHAPTER 22

TROPHIES

BROCK PARKED IN FRONT of the high school where he'd graduated eighteen years earlier. The two pine trees which once towered over the front walk had been removed, making the entrance seem less inviting, but the building itself looked the same. Large rectangular windows lit every classroom with their tall ceilings and waxed floors. Ivy still clung to the walls.

He loved his high school years. Being the star athlete had its benefits, and he enjoyed his classes. But it was the atmosphere he missed the most after graduating, the noisy passing in the hallway, the jostling with friends, the pep rallies, and the flirting. The school was as orderly and predictable as the bells that rang to dismiss class every fifty minutes. But there were anxious moments as well. He'd once followed Veronica O'Malley down the hall in this same building, visibly shaking as he worked up the courage to ask her to the homecoming dance.

TROPHIES

The door to the school was unlocked, so Brock stepped into the darkened hallway and smelled the familiar aroma of old linoleum, floor wax, and stained wood. In a few weeks, there would be the cafeteria smells that enticed the students' appetites.

As he made his way to the principal's office, he stopped at the trophy case. He was pleased to find his escapades still held some importance. They were now memories encased in glass. The leather football from the title game he played his senior year sat prominently front and center with the names of the players who'd participated. The final score still disappointed him.

Leaned up behind the football was a black and white team photo of the varsity players, flanked by Coach Sullivan and a younger-looking Coach Baker. In the front row, he and Tim stood side by side, grinning. Cort was at the end of the row, looking unhappy, as if angry about not being in the center of the lineup.

Time stood still as Brock was transported back to his youth. His focus was shattered when he heard rapid footsteps coming toward him. In the dimly lit hallway, Lester Colquit couldn't see Brock, but when he did, he jumped back, and his knees buckled.

"What the … mister, what are you doing here?" he said, rocking on his heels.

"Sorry to startle you, sir. I'm Brock Gallagher. We visited before on the telephone. I was just looking in the trophy case. It brings back memories. Seems like only a couple of years ago I was walking these halls as a student."

"So, are you just reminiscing, or are you here on business?"

"Business," Brock said. "I understand there has been a vote to reestablish a football program. I'd like to apply for the coaching job. And I hear there might be a teaching position open as well."

The principal shook his head. "Well, you may be getting the cart before the horse, Mr. Gallagher. We don't even know if there are enough boys to play football yet. And we won't know for a while. Why don't you just wait until we know about numbers before you hand in an application? Then we might look at your qualifications. And I think we already have a young man lined up for the teaching position."

Brock knew how a program worked, and this delay wasn't good. "Don't you think it might be too late by then? A coach will need to hire assistants, put together a schedule, and meet with his players."

"Well, sometimes we have to be patient with these things, Mr. Gallagher. And let the chips fall where they may." Colquit refused to meet Brock's gaze. "And by the way, I've received a couple of phone calls this afternoon. Seems there are rumors floating around about some professional misbehavior on your part. People want to know if you've been accused of wrongdoing in your previous employment. If we do go ahead with putting a team together, we'd have to do a thorough background check before we'd even consider you for a job here."

Brock was stunned. He'd never wandered outside the lines of professionalism. Was this idle gossip, or was there something deeper going on? He couldn't let talk like that linger. "Sir, I'd like to know where those rumors are coming from, so I can put a stop to them."

"Well, you know small towns, don't you? Everyone is talking. It'd be hard to find where it all started."

"Even so," Brock said, stepping closer to Colquit. "I'll have the principal and athletic director at Brighton give you a call. Better yet, I'll have them mail you a letter letting you know there's nothing in my background that I'm ashamed of. I'll do it today." Brock moved away from the trophy case into a shaft of sunlight streaming through a hallway window. "I'll stop by next week and get an application for the opening. In the meantime, I'm going to see about getting some football players rounded up. I think it's time for the Grizzlies to get back onto the football field."

"Patience, Mr. Gallagher," Colquit said. "Now, if you don't mind, I'm leaving, and I'm going to lock the door behind me. I doubt if you want to reminisce about your high school years all night in an empty school, so I suggest you leave with me." The two men walked side by side out the door. Brock kept walking as the principal turned to lock the door to Glory Grove High.

Brock was more than a bit angry and frustrated. He'd been slow to give in to the idea of coaching football in his hometown. But once he'd made that decision, he was ready to get started. It seemed now like he was jumping hurdles on a muddy track reaching for the finish line. His mother's cancer was on hold—that was a good thing. His marriage seemed on hold, and it was slowly breaking his heart. Now the one thing that could ease the hurt—coaching football—maybe wasn't going to happen.

He drove home with the windows down, breathing in the warm July air. The winter wheat was turning the golden shade of brown that makes farmers pick up their pace as they ready their equipment for the coming harvest. He could smell it, the scent of his youth. He'd had peaks and valleys growing up and mastered them with patience and hard work. He could do it again. He'd find a path and follow it, just as he'd always done.

Sunday morning, Richard came to the farmhouse. "So, Rocket, I heard you have a football team," he said. His grin was infectious. "Going to take the Grizzlies to the championship game like you did at Brighton?"

"Not if I can't get the job. Seems we have a roadblock."

"What now?"

"First we have to find twenty players. And then I have to get hired as their coach." Brock explained about the board meeting and his visiting the principal. Then he shared Tim's idea for getting the boys together at the Pig Pick.

Richard nodded his head. "It's scheduled for next week. We've got to get it behind us so we can get ready for harvest. We'll call it a Pig Pick and Pigskin Saturday, he joked. "We usually get twenty or thirty kids out here. Justin Jepson has always come and has done well with his pigs. It helps his family put food on the table."

Brock added one more thing. "Tim says Luke and Jimmy should also think about raising pigs for the fair. Have we got room to keep a couple of extras out here on the farm?"

"Sure, but they're going to need some training. I'm betting they won't know a sow from a boar. This could be fun to watch."

When the mail arrived at the school a few days later, Lester Colquit received two letters from Brighton High School. One from the principal and another from the school's athletic director. They confirmed Brock's claim that there had been nothing negative involving their former coach. They held him in their highest regard. Their only regret was he'd quit his job at Brighton to tend to his mother in Glory Grove. *You would be lucky to have him on your staff*, both letters said.

Colquit read each of the letters, put them back into their envelopes, and unceremoniously dropped them one by one into the trash can at the end of his desk.

CHAPTER 23

PICK

SATURDAY MORNING, early July, broke clear and hot with a breeze from the east, the kind of weather wheat farmers welcomed to help finish the ripening of their grain. It was also a good day for the Pig Pick out on the Gallagher farm.

Tim and Luke showed up early to help Richard and Jimmy sort the pigs.

"Wow, this pig stink is stiff," Luke said when they walked into the pen.

"It smells like money to the kids coming today," Richard said as he strolled out from the barn. He'd never been introduced to Luke but had to stifle a laugh when he saw his appearance. *I should get out the hog clippers and do a quick trim job on the mohawk*, he thought. A grin stretched wide on his face. "Why don't you help Jimmy get these hogs sorted out," he said.

Jimmy had been around the pigs enough to feel comfortable and tried giving instructions to Luke. But the big boy was sure he could push them around, even if they didn't want to go. "They might be smarter than you," Jimmy said as he watched Luke struggle.

"Yeah, watch this," Luke said. He stepped in behind a big sow and began pushing. But the massive six-hundred-pound pig whirled around and headed through his legs. She split them, knocking him off balance. Luke took three big staggering hops backward with the pig between his legs, neither riding nor walking. He was soon airborne. "Goddam it." The big youngster began reeling, his boots slipping in the mud. With a final teetering thrust, he lurched backward, falling flat into the manure and muck. He contorted his body, thrashing about to free himself.

Jimmy turned away, choking back his laughter. He helped Luke off the ground. "Now you smell like country," he said. "Welcome to farm life."

As the two were wrestling with the pigs, they didn't notice the old Chevrolet Impala pulled up beside the barn. Justin Jepson had gotten out and was watching all the activity. He tried not to laugh out loud at the two novices. "You fellows need a little help?"

"Crap, I was hoping no one saw that," Luke muttered. He had a sheepish grin on his mud-splattered face and was trying to shake off the muck from his backside. "Sure, dude, come on in and see if you can do any better," he challenged.

"Name's Justin," he said as he climbed over the fence. He began quietly moving the sows toward the shed, separating them from their offspring. "Who are you guys?"

The boys introduced themselves.

"I heard there were some new guys in town. Glad to finally meet you," Justin said. He walked away from the pigs to face the boys. "Also heard you like to play football. Let's hope you're better at pushing around people than you are at pushing around pigs." His face betrayed his sarcasm.

"I'll admit to that," Luke said. He reached over and shook Justin's hand. "So, they say we can't have a team unless we get twenty guys. Aren't there twenty guys in this town with enough balls to play football? Gawd, I can't believe you wouldn't play football last year. What the hell were you thinking?"

Justin stiffened. "Hey, my friends and I wanted to play, but a lot of guys didn't like our coach, and they were tired of losing. But my dad's team played for a state championship, and I'd like to think I could do that too."

Luke was quick to let Justin know his dad had played on the same team. "He's still mad about losing that game. But let's forget the old-timers and get our own trophy. You know the guys here; let's get them signed up. I don't want to live in this godforsaken place without playing ball."

The three young men agreed they'd do whatever it took to get twenty names on the sign-up sheet. "Even if I have to threaten them with this," Luke said, holding up his massive fist.

"Sure, that'd convince a few to run like scared rabbits," Justin said. "Let's go about it diplomatically, and then if that doesn't work, we can try it your way."

Pickup trucks pulling stock trailers began turning into the driveway, and Richard stood in the middle of the barn lot welcoming all the young people. As they arrived, he entertained them with his latest jokes. He was soon surrounded by kids. Laughter punctuated every punch line. Finally, he said, "It's time to pick pigs. But first, I want everyone to meet some new young men in our town. This is Luke and Jimmy," he pointed to each one in order, "and they'll be picking pigs today along with you. And they also might be trying to persuade some of you to sign up for football this fall. We want to see a team back on the field come September." He gave the message a few seconds to sink in before continuing.

"Now, you know how this is done. I've got numbers in a hat. Everyone picks a number, and that's the order of the draw. Who wants to go first? Step right up."

The youngsters lined up, and everyone could hear the groans or cheers with the drawing results. Jimmy and Luke drew last. Jimmy was satisfied with a late draw, not wanting to embarrass himself by picking a poor pig. Then Luke pulled his number—number one. "Wow," he said. "Finally, I win a freakin' drawing, and I don't know a pig from a penguin."

"I can help," Justin said. He gave a brief lesson on how to tell a good pig from a poor one, and Luke made his choice.

"I want the one with the big spot on its butt," Luke said. "It's shaped like a football, so it must be an omen." He looked at the young men in the crowd. "This town needs a football team, so you guys better get on board. We need twenty of you to sign up."

The youngsters from Glory Grove weren't sure what to make of the two new arrivals. They were different for sure, out of the mold. They created a stir, and everyone went home from the Pig Pick talking more about the new boys than about the pigs.

The following Monday, Justin, Luke, and Jimmy met at the convenience store for breakfast. They planned to drive around the county and make visits to potential teammates. Ashley was behind the counter when Luke and Jimmy walked in. "Good morning, Luke Skywalker," she said, glad to see him again. "Who's your friend?"

"Ashley, this is Lando," he said, referring back to the *Star Wars* characters. It made her smile and roll her eyes. "Actually, his name is Jimmy Ivory. We're heading out to recruit some football players for a team. I don't think you'll make the cut," he said, giving her an up and down look. "Maybe when you grow up, you can have a tryout."

Ashley was embarrassed but liked the attention. There were two new boys in town. Jimmy looked nice, and Justin was joining them. She wished she could ride along. "So, can you find enough guys to turn out? It'd be nice to have football again. The homecoming dance doesn't seem right without a football game."

Luke liked her attitude. *Maybe I should ask her to the homecoming dance*, he thought, since she was the only girl in town he knew. But it was too soon. And maybe there was some hottie out there who was more his style. Yet, he liked Ashley. He'd keep her in mind.

The door chime sounded as Justin walked into the store. The three boys took a booth and planned their strategy. Since Justin knew the potential candidates, they'd follow his direction, tour around town first, then head to the countryside to meet up with the farm boys before wheat harvest began. The trip would give Justin a chance to introduce Luke and Jimmy. He'd break the ice and then let the two new boys talk about how much they loved football and wanted to help Glory Grove rebuild the program.

"So, if we get enough guys to sign up, what's the deal with finding a coach?" Luke asked. He suggested they encourage the boys to support Brock Gallagher.

But Justin said he'd heard rumors. "They're saying he was run out of Brighton."

"Where the heck did you hear that?" Jimmy asked. He stopped nibbling at his sausage sandwich. "Man, why would anyone throw shade on Coach? That's why I came here, to be with Coach."

Luke chimed in. "My dad thinks he's the best coach in the state. One of his teams played for a state championship at Brighton. And in college, he won a ring for playing in the Copper Bowl. What kind of trouble are you talking about?"

"Beats me. But my dad said it would be a mistake to hire him. That he wouldn't stay for long anyway, with his wife taking off and leaving him."

Now Jimmy dropped his food. "I rode all the way from the city with her, and she didn't say nothing bad about him at all. Where you getting all this anyway?"

"Just repeating what my dad said," Justin said. "He seems to know a lot about it. Anyway, let's not talk about coaches until we have enough guys to play. Let's grab some drinks and chips for the trip and get going."

"How about some beer too?" Luke said. He shot a mischievous grin at his new partners.

"Sure, get busted for drinking before the season starts. Bad idea," Justin said.

Jimmy stood up from the table. "Thanks, but I'll stick with water. This is the only six-pack I need." He pulled up his white t-shirt to show his abs. "Strong, like a Grizzly."

CHAPTER 24

APPROVAL

THE SCHOOL BOARD'S next regularly scheduled meeting was Thursday, the third week of August. But the crowd pushing for the reinstatement of the football program knew time was running out. They asked for a special meeting one week earlier to deal with football. The board chairman, Charles Wallingham, considered the request and called Principal Colquit.

"Out of the question," he said. "We hold our meetings on the third Thursday; I see no reason to change the schedule."

"Lester, as board chairman I have the right to call a special meeting. I've polled the other members of the board, and they agree. We're going to meet next Thursday, whether you're there or not. We have to move on this football question."

"I guess there's nothing I can do about it, but I still object. We still require twenty names on a petition, or we won't have a team. I doubt if that happens. Besides, I'm getting phone calls about this Brock

Gallagher fellow. Seems he left in some kind of trouble at Brighton High. We don't want a coach like that in Glory Grove."

"We can deal with hiring a coach after we put a team together. Let's start there." What the chairman didn't tell the principal was he already knew the list of twenty had been completed. He'd seen what the three boys achieved in their recruiting efforts.

Colquit tried to stall the football decision until it was too late for the board to act. But to his consternation, they'd overridden his efforts. However, his attempt to sabotage Brock Gallagher could still play out. No one needed to know he'd received glowing reports from Brighton.

At the special meeting, supporters filed back into the boardroom before being ushered again into the cafeteria. "If you would take your seats, we'll get started," Wallingham said. Tim was scrunched into one of the cafeteria chairs, sitting in the front row, proud of Luke and his friends for gathering the twenty names they needed.

The board chairman addressed the others on the governing body. "I'm handing you the list of committed players so you can look it over. I believe it meets the requirements we set."

The principal, who'd not been privy to the list, scanned the text to make sure the names matched students in the school. As he read through it, he felt the breath go out of his body. Halfway down the page was his son's name.

"I must address the board," he said. His face was flushed, and he was drumming the table with his pen. "There is a name on here I cannot accept. It is the name of my son. He won't be playing. I won't allow it, nor will his mother. This list is invalid."

"Can I speak?" Tim's voice boomed from his front-row seat.

Wallingham nodded his approval, anticipating Tim's protest.

Tim cleared his throat. "You asked for twenty kids who said they wanted to play. Well, a couple of our boys worked hard to find them. Those kids put their signatures on that paper. That means they want to play; whether they have approval from their parents is another matter. They met the challenge. Let's don't f-ing blackball this because of some technicality."

The audience began to mumble. "Let 'em play."

"Silence, please," said the chairman. He pushed his glasses up on his nose. "The chair will entertain a motion to accept the list of players and approve the reestablishment of the Grizzly football program for this school year." A board member at the end of the table raised his hand and, with a husky voice, made the motion. Another seconded it, and it was voted on and passed before another word was spoken. The crowd clapped their approval—a long, loud applause.

"Now, what about a coach?" Tim hollered. "We need a coach, and the best coach in the state is ready to go if you'll give him a chance."

"I assume you're talking about Mr. Gallagher," Colquit said. He was ready to play his final card in his delay strategy. "I think many of you have heard the talk around the community about his sudden departure from his former employer. I think it would be unwise to consider him until we check into those concerns. That may take some time."

Tim interrupted. "I know for a fact you have letters clearing Brock of any negative crap over at Brighton. Maybe you just don't want anyone else to see them."

"Mr. Palmer, since you aren't a member of this board, you're out of order entering into this discussion," said Wallingham.

"Well, since I can't talk, maybe I can give you a copy of those letters. Brock had them send copies to him just in case someone happened to lose them. Here they are." He took three giant steps to the head table and slammed the documents down in front of Wallingham, who was gripping his gavel and staring angrily at Colquit over the top of his eyeglasses.

He read the letters out loud, one after the other, so the audience and the board could hear. When finished, he didn't bother to berate the principal for his careless handling of the letters but thanked Tim for making them available. "It sounds like Mr. Gallagher is well thought of at Brighton," he said. "We'll take his candidacy into consideration and make a decision at our regular meeting in one week." He hammered his gavel and adjourned the meeting.

The audience milled about for several minutes, and members of the group came to Tim and slapped him on the back for standing up to the board and the principal. "Maybe next term, you should run for the board," said one, loud enough for others to hear.

Tim laughed. "You never know. That would shake things up a bit. Trouble is, I'm not sure I'd vote for myself." The crowd filed out, vowing to come again in a week when the board would finally name a coach.

When Tim got home, Luke was sitting in front of the television, watching highlights of NFL games from the past. He grabbed the remote and hit the off button when he heard his dad open the door. "Did they like our list?" he asked.

"They sure did." Tim gave Luke a congratulatory slap on the back. "You did enough to get it passed. You should call your friends and let them know the good news. Then I'll call Brock and tell him he'd better get ready to coach. By the way, why did you put Les Colquit on that list? His dad crapped a brick when he saw his name."

Luke thought a minute, trying to figure out who Les Colquit was. "Oh, you mean the skinny kid that lives down past the park? I gotta say, he was more fired up than anyone else. He said he's going to turn out, no matter what his parents say. He needs some groceries, but he wants to get after it. He would have been pissed if we left him off the list."

"Good. Now call your friends."

CHAPTER 25

SECURED

THE SCHOOL POSTED the job opening the following morning. The only applicants were Brock Gallagher and Cort Jepson. Two days later, the men found themselves sitting in a classroom together, each waiting their turn to be called in for an interview. They didn't look at one another, and the room was silent except for the sound of barking dogs coming through the open window. Brock spoke first. "Good run you had in the Derby," he said.

Cort didn't raise his eyes. "Should have won. Fricking rainstorm ruined it."

"Maybe. But it was entertaining."

"I don't do it to entertain. I do it to win. Like I'll do when I get this coaching job."

The door to the hallway opened, and the school secretary stepped in. "Brock, if you're ready, they'll do the interview now," she said, smiling at them despite the chilly feel she was getting from the room. Brock stepped out quickly and walked down the hall to a conference room. He sat across from a five-person committee—two from the school board, the girls high school track coach, and two members of the community. For the next half hour, he was peppered with questions. When Brock was done, Cort was ushered in for his turn. They asked Brock to stay in case they had further questions for him.

When both men were finished, it was clear Brock had far greater knowledge and experience as a coach. And all the members of the interview committee knew Cort was a hot head and heavy drinker. A few had heard rumors he sometimes took his frustrations out on his wife, Veronica. However, they knew Cort had a passion for the game and would give as much energy as he could to make the team a winner. Sometimes the town could turn their eyes away and ignore vices if the results were favorable.

Regarding Brock Gallagher, there was reluctance to hire him by members of the panel who wondered how long he might be in town. They favored a candidate who could give them a long-term commitment. During deliberations, they agreed if the final vote went in Brock's favor, they'd request a caveat. They wanted more than a one-year commitment.

They called Brock back into the room and made their proposal. "I understand but can't make that promise," Brock said. Despite Celia's sudden fling with freedom, if she made him choose between the Grizzlies and their marriage, he would live up to his vows and comply with her request. He couldn't say it to the committee, but he said something else. "If you let me run this program for a year, I think I can create enough goodwill for the game that it will have a lasting impact. You've got good boys in this town, and they deserve a good coach … even if it's only for a season."

The board sent the two candidates home to be notified of the vote the following day. On the way to his car, Brock found Cort blocking the sidewalk by the front door. "So, Rocket, I guess it's down to me and you. If the board has any sense, they'll send you back to Brighton."

"It's in their hands now," Brock said, working his way past the man.

"I know you won't give my son a chance. You wouldn't let a boy with my last name have a shot. Big man. Hell, I don't care if you've coached in the Super Bowl; you don't belong in the Grove anymore."

Brock turned to face his old teammate. "Listen, Cort, I don't know what your problem is, but if I get the job, the only thing I'll try to do is build a winner. I'll treat all the players with respect, and that includes Justin. I've done that my whole career, and that's what I'll do here. If Justin's the best athlete, then he'll be front and center. You and Ronnie don't have to worry."

"Leave Ronnie out of this. And just so we have this straight, if I get the job, you might as well take that little black pet of yours and go back to Seattle. We don't need him here."

Brock stepped closer to his old teammate with a clenched fist. He didn't often lose his temper, but now he was angry. "That young man is as good-hearted as any kid in this town. He's become like a son to me. Don't ever talk about him like that again."

"Like a son? That figures. You're not man enough to sire a son of your own."

Brock stopped and turned back. Suddenly he was seventeen years old and back in a locker room. At halftime. In a state championship football game. The same anger he'd felt then overwhelmed him now. At seventeen, he'd dropped Cort Jepson with a blow to his stomach. But this time, he didn't swing low. Instead, his clenched fist struck a powerful blow to Cort's face, dropping him to his knees. Blood trickled from his nose. As Cort looked up, dazed and unable to gain his feet, Brock marched to his car. He slid in, punched the accelerator, and sped off.

"This ain't over," Cort bellowed as he staggered to his feet.

Inside the building, the selection committee was still deliberating on which of the two men was best suited to bring honor back to the Grove when they heard the yelling and the squeal of tires. "Darned kids hot-rodding in front of the school again," said one of the women. "Maybe we should call the police."

"I'm sure it's nothing," said Wallingham. "Let's make a decision."

On Friday morning, Irene was cleaning the dishes from breakfast as a cool breeze drifted through the room from the open kitchen window. She could smell the ripening wheat outside the fence behind the house and saw the swallows diving from the power line, snatching up insects hovering in the heat. Brock and Jimmy had left early to take salt to the cows up on the ridge. At eight o'clock, her reverie was interrupted when the phone rang. It was Charles Wallingham.

"Yes, Charlie, I'll have him call as soon as he gets back. It shouldn't be long unless the cows are out. You know how cows are. Did you make a decision on the coaching position?"

"We did, and I think it will please Brock, but I need to talk to him to make it official."

Irene was happy. Brock wanted the job. At the same time, she worried this move might make things harder for Celia when she returned from her trip. She hadn't called or written for weeks. The morning wore on, and Brock and Jimmy didn't return. Irene sat on the porch waiting, staring at her watch. Finally, the men came rambling up the driveway, dust spewing out behind the old pickup.

"What's going on, Mom?" Brock asked.

"I was about to go looking for you," she said. "Charlie Wallingham called and wants to visit with you about the football job. I think it might be good news."

"Does this mean we can get our team together and start practicing?" Jimmy asked. He was bouncing on both feet. "Brighton's been practicing all summer. We're way behind."

"Let me make the call, and if it's a sure thing, we'll get started," Brock said. "And don't worry, Jimmy, we won't be playing Brighton, but we do have a lot of catching up to do." Brock slipped into the house and called the chairman. Irene was right. They'd voted to give him the job, even if it was only for a year. He could hire one assistant and call his team together as soon as possible. The school was trying to put a schedule together.

What impressed Brock the most was the sudden urgency coming from the board. Perhaps it had something to do with their unhappiness with the principal over the letters from Brighton. Tim had told him about having to shove the letters of commendation into the chairman's face. As he sat alone inside the living room of his boyhood home, he studied the family photos hanging on the wall-papered walls. *I hope I can make you proud*, he thought. He could feel the rush of adrenaline that always came with a new football season.

He walked back out to join the others on the front porch, who were waiting for the good news. He winked at his mom and then turned to Jimmy. "Well, young man, what position do you want to play on your new football team?"

CHAPTER 26

PLAYERS

TWENTY-FIVE BOYS strode into the school cafeteria, anxious to meet their new coach. Twenty had signed the petition to play, but more showed up when word spread the football program was on again. Brock looked them over. At Brighton, the first meeting of the season would number well over one hundred, and almost all had been lifting weights all summer. The schoolboys at Glory Grove looked healthy but weren't ready to trot onto the gridiron.

"Thanks for coming," Brock said when all were seated. "If you don't know, my name is Brock Gallagher. Since you're here, I assume you want to play football for the Grizzlies. Boys your age have worked for that privilege since they started playing football in the Grove over one hundred years ago. Some good men have played here. Many of your fathers and grandfathers put on pads and laced up their cleats and played with passion to uphold the honor of our town. Now it's your turn. Forget last year. If you chose not to play, that's okay. But starting today, we're building a new future for this team."

The boys stared at him, their enthusiasm growing. "I left this town several years ago to chase my own football dream, so I don't know many of you. I'd like to go around the room and have you introduce yourself and say why you want to play football. Luke Palmer, why don't you start."

"You got it, Coach." Luke jumped to his feet and threw out his chest. "My name is Luke Palmer. I'm going to be a junior. I moved here from Denver this summer to live with my dad. At first, I thought this town sucked, but now I'm kind of excited to be here." The boys in the room whispered to one another and nodded.

Luke continued. "Football's my favorite sport. I got to meet some of you already, and y'all seem like good dudes. I don't care how big the town is. Football is a helluva lot of fun, so here I am." He sat down, and the others clapped.

"Jimmy, why don't you go next," Brock said.

"Yes sir, Coach." Jimmy was reluctant to lift his eyes and look into the curious faces. The boys in the back rows were straining to hear his voice. "My name is Jimmy Ivory, and I came to this town to visit Coach Gallagher. He was my coach at Brighton High in Seattle. He's a great coach. So, when my mom died (his voice cracked for a second) and I had nowhere to go, I came here. It's my home now, and I like it. I wanted to play at Brighton, but now I want to play here."

The rest of the players took their turns introducing themselves. The freshmen were nervous being in the same room with the bigger boys. When everyone was done, Brock asked them to stand and give themselves a round of applause for being there and getting to know their football family.

As they stood, Brock said, "Look around. These are the guys you will sweat with, hurt with, and try to win with. And they are the ones you will suffer with if we fail to win. But in the end, and most importantly, these are your new brothers." Brock saw some of the boys shift on their feet. "You will learn to respect the game of football. You will learn to play with enthusiasm and spirit. And you will learn to love the other boys in this room as family—because if this team is not like a family, it will not succeed."

The boys were silent yet excited at the same moment. They liked their new coach's passion for football. They'd never heard a speech like that from Conrad Newton. Then Brock got down to business, starting with his expectation that they be in the weight room every day. He laid out his plans for practice: two-a-days the week before school started, with early morning practices so farm boys could get home for harvest, then a late evening practice. He was replicating the routine he had in high school. The coming weeks would be full of exhaustion and pain. But after looking at this collection of boys, he knew there wasn't time to waste. They were a year behind their competitors and needed to get in shape fast.

"Okay, men. Let's put this team on the map," Brock said as he dismissed the boys. The room was full of excited chatter. It was a good beginning, but there were a few more things Brock needed to do. He hadn't drawn attention to young Lester Colquit Jr. during the introductions but wanted to reach out to him.

"Les, can I have a word with you?" Brock asked.

"Sure, Coach," the slender freshman said and boldly strode up to the podium.

"I understood from your dad that he wasn't going to let you play this year."

"Well, that's what he said, but I'm going to play." He clenched his jaw. "My parents can't stop me. They think I need to focus on my studies—want me to be a doctor—but I have a perfect grade point. And I told them I'll stop studying if they won't let me play."

"That's a novel approach." Brock chuckled. "Why do you want to play so badly if it creates friction with your parents?"

Les looked around to make sure none of the other boys were listening. "Truth? It's hard being the principal's son," he said. "I'm always being teased because my dad is constantly hovering over me. I want to prove I can play. I know I'm not big or strong, but I want to show I can be tough."

"That's exactly what we need on this team, Les," Brock said. "We're glad to have you if you can work something out with your parents."

"Thanks, Coach." There was a gleam in his eye. "They may not like it, but I'll be there, starting tomorrow in the weight room."

With the conversation ended, Brock turned to Justin Jepson, curious how the young man felt about him being chosen as the coach. He pulled him aside as everyone was leaving.

Before Brock could speak, Justin said, "Great speech." His head was nodding as if he were giving his approval. Brock had a hard time looking at the young man without thinking of his mother. The hazel eyes and high cheekbones were like hers, and even the way he smiled when he was speaking.

"So, you ready for another season?"

"I can't wait."

"Well, I'm counting on you to take a leadership role on this team. It seems all the boys look up to you. Starting a season without last year as a guidepost is going to be difficult. And it will be an interesting mix of personalities, with Luke and Jimmy being new. I hope you can help put it all together. Can I count on you?"

"Yes sir. I've been thinking about it a lot. I like these new guys, and we've become friends already. This is going to be a lot of fun."

Brock folded his arms across his chest and dropped his voice so no one else could hear. He didn't know if Justin knew of the confrontation between him and Cort. "Is your dad okay with me being the coach? I know he wanted the job."

Justin shifted his weight from side to side. "He's okay. And I'm glad you're my coach. You know how to coach for championships. That's what I really want."

"Well, we're a long way from that. Let's just get ready for the first game." Brock walked over to the light switch and turned them off. He followed Justin down the hallway, past the trophy case with all the memories. He wanted to bring those same amazing feelings to the twenty-five boys who'd gathered in the cafeteria. It would be a challenge, but he clung to the feeling that every sacrifice was worth it. He'd try to channel that belief into these youngsters—Justin and Les, Luke and Jimmy, and all the rest.

CHAPTER 27

PREP

"GET UP," Brock hollered up the stairs. "We need to get going." It was harvest season along Cold Creek, and each day started before the sun came up. Brock and Jimmy would have a quick breakfast and then race off to the school for team weightlifting and running. Irene had their food ready when they got to the kitchen.

"I don't want you running out of energy," she said as she filled their plates. Irene showed the strain from her treatments, but harvest was her favorite time of year.

At the school, sleepy-eyed boys met and descended into the darkness of the basement to lift weights. After lifting, there would be wind sprints in the cool morning air before the blast furnace heat of harvest descended on the valley.

While the boys prepared for football, a flurry of activity was happening on area farms. From the first evidence of sunlight in the morning until the flaming red ball sank on the western horizon, families toiled to bring in the small grains. They'd been nurturing those crops since the first seeds were dropped.

Richard and Brock agreed to employ Jimmy and Luke as field hands, to keep them out of trouble and put money in their pockets. The experience was new to them, but Brock had seen it all before. The routine felt natural to him, although with more modern machinery, it had changed since he was in high school. Richard gave him instructions, and he followed them like he'd done as a youth.

To fill out the crew, Richard invited a retired neighbor—Herman Jones, a man with years of harvest experience—to join them. Herman and the two boys would drive the trucks from the field to their grain bins at the home place, where the bushels would be augered into steel bins, including the one where Brock's father had lost his life. It was a reminder of the hazards of farming. "Recognize danger," the men preached to the boys. Jimmy was already on edge, having experienced the trauma with Sassy. She'd be tied each day, so there wasn't a repeat of the accident.

In the morning, while the football players were in town lifting weights, the men fueled the combines and greased the wear points. The tasks were time-consuming but had to be done each day for the machines to make it through the season without a breakdown or a fire.

"Fire in a harvest field is an absolute nightmare," Richard told the youngsters. "It can destroy a crop in minutes," he said, "and can ruin machinery and threaten the people in the field. If you smell smoke, let someone know immediately. Neighbors will come to help fight a fire, and we do the same for them."

Once the Gallagher's combines rolled into the field, with Richard and Brock at the controls, the crew didn't stop working until the day's final load of wheat was augered into the bin. As the shadows began to stretch out from the ridge above the valley, the dusty machines were driven back to their staging area. Lumbering like circus elephants, they jockeyed into a spot by the fuel truck so the routine could repeat the following day.

"You better go for a run before supper," Brock told the boys when everything was put away. "Your opponents are out running as we speak." Luke looked at Jimmy and sprinted down the field road, slipping and sliding on the wheat straw packed down by the truck tires.

"Come on, you little running back," he yelled over his shoulder. "Race you to the house. See if you can catch this big linebacker."

Brock could hear them laughing as he climbed into the pickup with Richard and Herman. "They're still having fun," Brock said as he slammed the door shut on the truck. "Let's see if they're still laughing once practice starts."

Luke had moved into the spare bedroom in the Gallagher home when harvest started. It gave Brock a chance to get to know him better. "What offense did you run when you played in Denver?" Brock asked Luke when they sat down for dinner. He liked to pick Luke's brain whenever he could. The questions were continuous, popping up throughout the day whenever there was a break in the action. And while they talked, Jimmy soaked in the details, knowing it would also make him a better player.

Midway through harvest, football practice began. Richard and Herman agreed they could have the combines ready in the morning if everyone could be back to the field by eight o'clock. And they could put everything away at the end of the day so Brock and the boys could go to late practice. Catering to the football players would slow harvest down by a day or two, but the weather forecast looked favorable. With luck, they could wrap it up before the fall rains came. It was a risk Brock and Richard knew they had to face if the team was to be ready for their first game in less than two weeks.

As the boys gathered for their first practice, the sun was barely visible in the morning sky. Brock took a head count. All twenty-five boys, including Les Colquit, were there. They came in better shape than Brock had predicted. They'd taken his challenge to heart. "Take a lap," he ordered. The boys took off, and Brock could quickly make out those who were most motivated.

Jimmy and Justin led the group, with the rest trying to keep pace. Luke was in the middle of the pack, barking orders at anyone falling behind. "Step it up, losers," he yelled.

Brock was attempting to make speedy evaluations of the players to match their skills with the needs of the team. He was so focused on the boys he hadn't noticed a man walking along the edge of the field behind him.

"Pretty rough-looking bunch you got there." It was Brock's old high school assistant coach, Don Baker. He'd startled Brock, who welcomed the intrusion.

"I think we're going to be okay. But it will take time to sort it out. You know these kids; do you want to help me do some evaluating?"

"Thought you'd never ask. If you have a clipboard and a pencil, I can start right now. But I know one thing, those new boys you inherited are going to give your team a boost."

"I hope so. The first game is only ten practices from now. We need twenty. And most of these boys are working in harvest too." Brock took his eyes from the players to look at the old silver-haired gentleman. "Say, I still have a position open as a paid assistant. I know it's been a while since you've coached, but would you be interested?"

"Heck yes. I'd do it for nothing. I love this game as much as you do. I can give you all the time you need. When can I start?"

"Well, officially not until you sign a contract and get a background check. But unofficially, you started about five minutes ago. Let's see what we can do." Brock placed his favorite silver whistle to his lips—the same one he used for ten years at Brighton—and blew hard.

The boys sprinted over and gathered around him, breathless from their run. Brock waited for them to settle in, then held up his hand. "This is a great day, gentlemen," he said. His voice was strong. "First, I want to introduce our new assistant coach, Don Baker." He put his hand on Don's shoulder. "He knows a lot about football and will help you become better football players. He is going to be a big part of this family. Because, starting today, this family, called Grizzly football, is back and ready to fight and claw and scrap to win football games. Are you ready to go to work to make it happen?"

CHAPTER 28

BURNED

IT WAS LATE EVENING, and Brock was exhausted, ready to fall into bed after another long day, when the phone rang. It was the call he'd been waiting for … from Celia. She'd finished her work with the art exhibit in Chicago and, to Brock's surprise, traveled with Jovan to New York to visit his studio and meet his friends. Without giving him time to respond, Celia quizzed him. "You didn't take that coaching job in Glory Grove, did you?"

"I did."

"How long will that last?"

"Until the season is over. I hope you can understand. The boys here need a coach, and I'm going to be here until mom's situation is stable. She gets sick from the chemo. She shouldn't be alone."

"I get it. But since you were staying there, I didn't think you'd mind me spending a little more time with the art business. New York is exciting. There are so many interesting people, and the social scene is amazing."

Brock tried not to imagine his beautiful wife mingling with her new friends and Jovan, the sculptor, at cocktail parties or lingering over a candlelight dinner high atop some New York skyscraper. He was jealous, not of her surroundings—because he preferred the countryside to the craziness of the city—but of another man enjoying the company of his wife.

"I don't like where this is headed," he said. "I wish you were here. I think about you all the time, and I miss you. Try to come back as soon as you can." He paused for one last thought. "Be careful, that lifestyle can change you, and I love you the way you are."

"I'll be fine," she said. "Enjoy coaching your little team." She hung up the phone.

Little team hung in the air like a gray cloud. She had ridiculed his passion. He was more determined now to make his "little team" something special. But even if they won a state title, he knew Celia wouldn't be impressed.

Harvest was speeding to its conclusion, and the first football game was just days away. Everyone was getting weary and irritable from the grind. One late afternoon, Jimmy was driving his empty International truck back from the grain bins, climbing a slight rise toward the two combines. Luke was parked in the middle of the stubble, waiting for a command to move his vehicle to receive a combine's tank full of grain. His back was toward the sun to give him relief from the searing heat. He didn't see the slight puff of smoke trailing behind Jimmy.

As Brock completed his pass, gathering the grain into the combine header, he swung out to make the corner and stiffened behind the wheel. He could see smoke. Small flames licked at the undercarriage of Jimmy's truck. "Fire!" he yelled into his CB radio. But Jimmy had his earbuds in, listening to his favorite hip-hop group.

Luke heard Brock's alert on the radio and sprung from his truck. The fire spread rapidly into the chaff and residue left in the field behind the combines. A breeze pushed it, fueling the flames, making them leap into the air.

"Christ, Jimmy, get out of there," Luke yelled, sprinting toward his friend. But Jimmy was still unaware until he saw Luke waving his hands wildly. He yanked the earbuds off his head and could hear the crackling of the fire.

"Oh God," Jimmy groaned. He slammed on the brakes and jumped out of the driver's seat. He grabbed the fire extinguisher mounted on the truck's rack and swung it to the ground, his fingers trembling as he searched for the pin to release the handle. "Come on, come on," he yelled at the device. But with every second he fumbled, the fire rose in intensity. It was now boiling up under the vehicle licking at the rubber tires and creeping toward him.

"Jimmy, get the hell out of there," Luke yelled, rushing toward his friend.

"We have to put it out," pleaded Jimmy over the roar of the fire. "We can't let it burn."

"It's too late. Get away from the truck." Luke grabbed the smaller boy, intent on dragging him away. But while he wrestled with Jimmy, a flame licked at the frayed cuff of his blue jeans and quickly crawled up his leg. "Holy shit, now I'm on fire," he screamed.

Jimmy recoiled at the scene … horrified. His big friend who'd come to save him was being burned. His heart raced as he dragged the metal container of fire suppressant upright and pointed the nozzle at Luke. "Come on, dammit, work," he shouted. He yanked on the handle, and a blast of water shot out directly at Luke, who was jumping and slapping at his ankle. Jimmy juggled the extinguisher, soaking the fire on his friend's leg as the two boys hobbled away from the inferno.

They reached Luke's truck and crawled into the cab. Despite the nasty burns to his leg and the water dripping from his clothes, Luke was able to engage the clutch, slam it into gear and race away from the blaze.

"You guys okay?" Brock shouted over the radio.

"I got burned," Luke said, cradling the plastic microphone in his blackened fingers. "Hurts like hell."

"Get that truck out of the field, go to the house and have Mom check it out. And have her call the fire department."

As they were talking, Herman, who'd been back at the bins, came rolling into the field driving the farm's big tractor, pulling a disk. He'd seen the smoke and, with his years of experience, knew what to do. He began plowing a path around the fire, driving dangerously close to the flames between the fire and the combines. Minutes later, another tractor and disk, manned by the next-door neighbor, came flying down the driveway.

Pickup trucks, carrying portable water tanks and filled with farmhands from neighboring farms—many of them high school kids, some of them football players —wheeled in, ready to join the battle.

Luke and Jimmy spilled out of the truck and ran to the house. Luke showed Irene his leg, with some of his pant leg missing, and told her to call the fire department. But when she did, they learned the firefighters were already on their way.

"What happened?" Irene asked.

"Something caught on fire under Jimmy's truck, and it spread fast. I think the truck's a goner. Jimmy tried to save it, but it was too late."

Jimmy shook his head and stared at Luke's leg. "I'm sorry, Irene," he said. He looked up at the woman who had taken care of him for the past months. His shoulders were slumped, and his head bowed. "What are we going to do without that truck?"

"Jimmy," she said, lifting his chin with her weathered fingers, "things happen in this business. The truck can be replaced, but we can't replace you. Now stand up straight and go see if you can help put out that fire. With everyone working together, it will be under control soon. Then we can pick up the pieces. And Luke, you and I are going to the emergency room to see about that burn."

Luke groaned his displeasure at missing the excitement, but the pain made him realize she was right. He needed to heal fast for the first football game. It was mere days away.

In less than an hour, firefighting came to a halt. The pickups with their water pumps drove slowly along the fire's blackened edges to make sure there were no sparks that would reignite. Another was spraying water on what remained of Jimmy's truck. It was now just a blackened hulk. And the two big tractors with their disks sat in the middle of the burned stubble, engines idling, in case they needed to race to another flare-up.

"I think we've got it under control," Brock said to Richard as he was wrapping the hose back into the farm pickup. "Good thing the wind wasn't blowing hard, or we would've lost the whole field."

"And maybe a combine or two."

The harvest crews and firefighters began to assemble around the Gallagher pickup. Men handed out pop and beer from their coolers and began to visit. After days of solitary toil, the gathering became a social event. They talked about the fire. They compared their crop yields and which outfits were done with harvest, and who was lagging. And naturally, since Brock was the new coach, they wanted to talk about football.

Brock circulated through the group and thanked everyone. They were all curious about how the fire started and agreed it was probably chaff on the exhaust of the old gas-powered truck that had dropped sparks.

"Who was driving?" quizzed one of the neighbors.

"It was the young man living with us, Jimmy Ivory," Brock said. As he spoke, he could see Jimmy hiking slowly over the hill to join them. When he was within earshot, Brock hollered, "Jimmy, hurry up and come over here; these men want to meet you."

Jimmy hesitated, afraid Brock was going to condemn him for starting the fire. He considered running away but forced himself to continue walking toward them.

"Fellows, this is Jimmy Ivory, our truck driver. He did everything he could to save that old truck. And he kept our other driver from getting burned up in the fire. He's a pretty good shot with a fire extinguisher."

Jimmy stood perfectly still, catching his breath, aware of all the men looking at him. He knew he was at fault for not noticing the fire and for leaving his headphones on in the field. Yet, to his relief, Brock was defending him. If he had enough money saved up, he'd buy the Gallagher family a new truck. He would make it up to them somehow.

"Oh, and by the way, guys," Brock said, pointing at Jimmy, "this fine young man will be the starting running back in our first football game. You all need to come out and watch him run."

CHAPTER 29

STARTERS

A SCHEDULE OF GAMES WAS ARRANGED for the football team. It didn't bode well. Since they'd defaulted on their games the previous year and hadn't approved the program in time to join their old league, the Grizzlies were considered an independent. To find the necessary nine games, several had to be scheduled with opponents several hours away. Other games were with teams in upper divisions. The Grizzlies only avenue to make the playoffs was a one-game play-in with the champion of their former league at the end of the season. But it was available only if they tallied a winning record in their nine games.

"We may be in over our heads this year," Brock confided to Don Baker. "But we need to decide on a starting lineup."

Baker knew the kids. "Simple for the most part. Jepson at quarterback, Palmer at fullback, and Ivory at wing. I'd put the Simpson brothers at guard and tackle on the weak side and Tommy Anthony and Matt Peterson on the strong side. Anthony and Peterson are seniors, and they're still miffed they didn't get to play last year."

"What about center?"

"Augustine Swenson's got good hands. Those Swensons are a pioneer family, and Augie is fifth generation. The whole family has played football."

Brock agreed with everything Don said but needed more. "That leaves a tailback and two receiver spots to fill. Got any suggestions?"

"We're going to have to start a couple of young guys, maybe even a freshman."

"What about Derek Baker, the sophomore at tailback, he's got speed, and he's pretty tough?"

Don looked up from his clipboard. "You're not saying that because he's my grandson, are you?"

"No. You've got an eye for talent, even if it's your own. He's the best we've got. Now, what about the two ends?"

Don's brow furrowed with the question. It wasn't an easy one to answer. "Well, I think that big farm boy, George Olson, who lives down the road from you, can handle the tight end spot. He's a freshman, but he'll get better after he gets some game experience. And I know this may sound crazy, but we might have to put Les Colquit at the receiver position. He's got good hands and gives 110 percent on every play. It'll probably bring the wrath of God down on our shoulders from his dad, but I could see him in that role."

Brock accepted the idea of using Olson as tight end but hesitated to throw the young Colquit boy into the fire. He needed time to grow. "Let's go with Wally Thompson," Brock said. "He's a junior and will be less intimidated. Les and the others need time to mature."

"Okay, boss." Baker was glad they'd settled on a starting lineup for the offense. They'd figure out the defense later.

But even before the season began, the plan, as good as it looked on paper, began to unravel. Luke wasn't cleared to play. The second-degree burn on his leg was serious, and the doctor feared it would get infected if he played so soon after the injury. "Give it a week of rest. Then we'll see," the doctor said.

Luke couldn't believe his luck. He'd done a good deed saving Jimmy from the fire, and look where it got him. He was promised nine games, but only if he stayed eligible with his grades. Now the first game was taken away. It put him back in the same foul mood as when he arrived in the Grove. He was lying at home on the couch when the doorbell rang.

"Pop, can you get it? I don't want to get up."

Tim opened the door. It was Brock. "Hey, Rocket, you out looking for trouble?"

"Nope, just came to say hi to Luke and let him know we finished harvest. Of course, we didn't have as much wheat to cut since the fire did some of that for us. Anyway, I brought some friends over to cheer up the big guy. Can we come in?"

"Sure, if you don't mind the mess."

Brock stepped outside and signaled the others to join him. Justin, Jimmy, and the rest of the starting lineup walked up the crumbling sidewalk. Luke had been riding them for two weeks to practice harder; now, they could accuse him, in a good-natured way, of course, of lying down on the job.

They carried Luke's game jersey to make him feel a part of the team, and Jimmy had a six-pack of Luke's favorite sports drink. Trailing the boys, carrying a large pizza fresh from the convenience store, was Ashley. When Justin mentioned where they were going, she asked if she could tag along.

The boys pulled chairs around Luke, and they all inspected the nasty burn covered with antibiotic cream. They'd only met the young man a few weeks before but going through two-a-day practices with him had already made him one of the team leaders. Some turned away from the gooey redness on his massive leg while others couldn't keep from staring. They wondered how it could heal enough to play in two weeks.

Ashley laid her hand on his arm and peered down at the wound. She patted him. "I'm sorry," she said. It was the first compassion he'd been shown by a female, aside from Irene, since moving to the Grove. He loved the attention and liked the smell of her perfume.

While the teenagers were visiting, Brock motioned Tim into the kitchen so they could talk privately. "What do you do on Fridays and Saturdays when you're not working?" he asked.

"Odd jobs. To earn a little extra money to feed that boy in there. He eats enough for three men. Other than that, nothin' much, why?"

"I need help. Do you suppose you could man the booth above the field at our games and give me some perspective? I need another set of eyes. Over at Brighton, I had twelve coaches on my staff. Now I have Don Baker, and he's great, but I feel a bit lonely."

"You got it, Rocket. You better believe I'll do that. I don't have to wear a tie, or nothin' do I?"

"Nobody would know you if you did. But you can't swear into my headset. I won't let the kids swear, and the same goes for you. We're on the road Saturday for a game with St. Michaels if you can come. It's that private school up in Centerville. They've brought in some good athletes with their tuition scholarship program, so it will be a good test for us right out of the gate."

Brock could hear the boys in the living room starting to get restless, so he wrapped up his talk with Tim. "Try to come around this week after work and get to know the players. By the way, I can't pay you anything, but I'll buy you dinner at the steak house when we get home."

"Cripe, that'll cost you plenty. I'll work up a damned big appetite callin' plays. After a year with no Grizzly football, me helping with this team is like cracking the first can in a cold six-pack on a Friday night."

Spectators began to appear in the grandstand in the days just prior to the first game. Farmers who'd finished their harvest were there, relaxed after an exhausting season in the field. They came to make their own evaluations of the team and to check out the coaching of their famous favorite son.

Once, Brock observed Cort and Ronnie watching their son going through his paces. Cort's arm was tight around her waist, even in the afternoon warmth. Brock had once held her close on the same field.

The Grizzlies were working hard to learn the offense Brock had brought from Brighton. It was keyed by the play of Justin at quarterback and Jimmy at the wing. Jimmy, who was new to the position, at first had trouble securing the ball, so he and Justin stayed late working on their handoffs. Justin also spent time throwing the ball to Wally, Les, and George. It seemed for every pass they caught, two went off their fingertips.

With Luke recovering from his burns, the coaches moved Wally to fullback. It meant Les Colquit would start at the wide receiver spot. Before the game with St. Michaels, Brock stepped into the principal's office to break the news. Colquit was seated behind his metal desk, dressed in his black suit and brown tie. He looked annoyed by the intrusion.

"Mr. Colquit, may I have a minute of your time?" Brock asked.

"Go ahead, Mr. Gallagher. Is this about football?" He crossed his arms and leaned back in his chair.

"Yes sir, and it's about your son, Les."

"I suppose you're going to cut him from the team already. I knew we shouldn't have let him turn out."

"No sir, quite the opposite." Brock slid into the chair across from the principal's desk. "I wanted to let you know Les has earned a starting position on the team. I know he's young, but he's worked his tail off to be ready for the game. He's better than anyone else we have at that position."

"What?" It took a few long seconds for Colquit to compose himself. "I didn't want him to turn out for the team. You know that. And I still don't want him to play. Just leave him on the sidelines with the other subs. He's only a freshman and doesn't weigh 150 pounds. Find someone else. His mother and I don't want to see him get hurt."

"We don't want anyone to get hurt. But it is a game of collisions. There are risks, and occasionally, there are injuries. Boys take that chance when they put on the uniform. But your son loves football. He's one of the leaders on the team, even as a freshman. The others respect his courage and need him to play. We're going to put him out there, and if he fails, we'll make a change. But unless that happens, he will play. And Lester, I hope you come watch him. Les needs to see you there."

"We'll see." Colquit maintained a professional posture as he sat up in his chair. He let the coach's words sink in. He had tried to kill football at Glory Grove and failed. But the following Saturday, he would travel to watch the team play St. Michaels. It would be the first game of Grizzly football he'd ever watch. He wouldn't go to support the team as the principal. And although he was frightened for his son, he would go to support his son as a father.

CHAPTER 30

OPENER

THE MOMENT HAD ARRIVED. Brock and his assistants and all twenty-five players loaded into a yellow school bus and headed north. It was a three-hour journey for their game with St. Michaels. Some of the boys on the team had played varsity football before the year hiatus, but it had been a long time since they felt the adrenaline and nerves that come with a game.

Brock had done his scouting and knew the Patriots had good athletes. Some of them, not good enough for a large public school, found their way to the little private school to showcase their talents. When the bus rolled into the St. Michaels parking lot, Brock faced his new reality. *Okay, this isn't Seattle, but it's still football,* he counseled himself. At Brighton in Seattle, his teams played in expensive stadiums with field turf, press boxes, and security staff. In contrast, the St. Michaels field was bordered by three sets of aluminum bleachers, enough for a few dozen fans. Other onlookers would have to stand. The announcer's booth was a rickety box that hung above the field suspended from four used power poles. Brock hoped the ladder would hold Tim as he climbed skyward.

Before the players got off the bus, Brock had a word. He stood at the front row and motioned for them to be quiet. "This is what you've all been working for. The folks in Glory Grove chose to have a football team again. You need to make them proud. Win or lose, give your best effort. Now let's go."

The boys headed for the locker room. Some were trembling with anxiety, breathing hard from the excitement. As Brock followed, his eyes were drawn to the cars lined up at the entrance to the field. Many were from the Grove. Their fans were showing up. They weren't going to miss the Grizzlies' first game. Richard brought Irene, and the Jepsons were there to watch Justin. Brock wondered if the principal would show.

As the clock counted down to kickoff, the men in striped shirts gestured to the Grove captains. "Gentlemen, line up and walk with me to meet your opponent," the head referee said. Brock's team had voted Justin, Jimmy, and Luke to lead them. On his signal, the boys marched hand in hand to center field to meet the St. Michaels captains. Jimmy and Justin carried their helmets and wore eye black. Luke, sporting his stiffened mohawk, was in jeans and his game jersey. As he limped along with his friends, he was an intimidating figure.

The Grove fans cheered when the Grizzlies won the coin toss and chose to kickoff. The ball rotated through the air off the foot of Justin Jepson. Filled with first game enthusiasm, the boys wearing the red jerseys of Glory Grove sprinted like wild men toward the receiver and hammered him to the turf.

"Did you see that, Brock?" Tim yelled into his headset. "We're going to pound those little shits."

OPENER

Brock was determined to stay relaxed even though he shared Tim's enthusiasm. "Calm down, partner. There's a lot of game left. And watch your language, please."

The first series of downs for the Patriots set the tone for the game. Dressed in their green and yellow uniforms, matching the tree-lined field, they ran a ball-control offense to push the Grove boys back three or four yards on each play. Burning time off the clock, it took five minutes to get within ten yards of the Grizzlies' end zone. But four plays later, thanks to the stiffened defense of the interior line led by the Simpson brothers, the Patriots were held on downs and turned the ball over to the Grizzlies.

"Justin, we need to move it away from the end zone," Brock told his quarterback. "Run a pitch-sweep to Jimmy." It was time for the Grizzlies to see if they were ready for the challenge. Justin stepped up behind Augie and called his signals.

"Red, 43. Red, 43," Justin called in a strong, confident voice. "Hut." The ball sailed into his hands. He faked the dive to Wally Thompson, his fullback, then pulled it back into his own chest before pitching it to Jimmy. Jimmy secured the ball for an instant, then took a ferocious hit from a Patriot linebacker, snapping his head back and spinning him like a top. A second tackler raced in, yanked the ball from his hands, and sprinted into the end zone. Glory Grove had run one play and handed a touchdown to the other team.

Brock could hear Cort Jepson in the stands screaming his displeasure.

"Jesus," Tim mumbled through the headphones.

"Not a good start," Brock said. "Still, lots of time left. They have to get the jitters out." He gathered the team around him. "Okay. You gave them a gift. They think they own you, and they'll relax, and we'll take advantage. We're okay, just play your game." He patted Jimmy on the helmet. "You'll be fine. Let the game come to you. Remember, you're the best runner on the field."

The Patriots lined up for the kickoff filled with confidence. Some were laughing. Things were going their way, and they knew Glory Grove hadn't played ball for a year. It could be a runaway victory. The kicker jogged to the ball and sent it soaring high into the fading afternoon sunshine. Jimmy was nervous. He ran under it, arms outstretched, but it fell to the ground onto the freshly cut turf. The Patriots converged.

"Just fall on it," Tim said into his headphones. Brock said the same thing under his breath.

But Jimmy frantically struggled to pick it up and dropped it a second time before finally bringing it into his hands. Three boys in green and yellow dove at him, but he spun away and broke free, sprinting down the sideline. Everyone gave chase. Perhaps he was running from the city and from the tragedies he'd lived through. Or from the mistakes he'd made on the farm. His mind was clear and blissful. He ran for Brock and Irene and his friends and the little dog that had kept him company throughout the summer. He ran the length of the field and into the end zone, where he was tackled by his ecstatic teammates.

"I think Jimmy may have just put his name into the Grizzly record books," Brock said, trying to hold back his emotions.

The rest of the game was filled with big plays and the missteps of a season opener. Justin threw two touchdown passes, and Jimmy ran for his second score. Late in the fourth quarter, Glory Grove was leading 28–21. But St. Michaels marched to the fifteen-yard line with less than a minute left showing on the clock. On first down, they powered through the Grizzly line, now wearing down from the late afternoon heat, for an eight-yard gain. From the seven-yard line, a second-down play gained no yardage. It was third down with two yards to go and only seconds left on the clock. "Come on, fellas, we can do this. Suck it up. This is our game," Justin yelled to his teammates, many with their hands on their hips trying to catch their wind.

The Patriot quarterback, a big boy with strong legs, stepped in behind his center and took the snap. Everyone expected him to power his way through the middle of the line for the tying touchdown to send the game into overtime. But instead, he faked a handoff to his fullback and bootlegged his way around the corner. Only Les Colquitt, the little freshman, stood between him and the end zone.

It was a mismatch, and Brock was already preparing mentally for how they would approach the impending overtime. The senior quarterback took a quick look at the scrawny teenager in his path and got ready to drive him into the end zone. But Les Colquit didn't move. He widened his stance and focused on the big man's belly button. When the two met, Les sprung with all the power he could muster from his wiry frame. He didn't stop the quarterback, but his helmet hit square on the end of the football, jarring it from the runner's grip. It spun to the ground, wobbling across the turf like a drunken groundhog. Three boys in red and white gave frantic chase and surrounded it.

"I got it. I got it," Derek Baker yelled.

The referee stood over the prone sophomore and said, "Yes, you do, son. Now give me the ball." He cradled it against his striped shirt and pointed in a direction away from the end zone. "Grizzly ball." The Grove fans erupted with cheers when they saw the referee pointing.

Tim Palmer was in Brock's ear. "It's our ball. Holy crap, that skinny little son of a gun knocked it free. We've done it, Brock."

Only those on the field heard the referee's call, but everyone watching knew from his signal what it meant. With a couple of kneel-downs, the victory belonged to Glory Grove. The fans who drove for three hours to watch the boys' first football game were jumping up and down in celebration, and shouts could be heard echoing off the metal bleachers.

Richard and Irene slapped their hands together in a gentle high five. Lester Colquit, although still opposed to football, beamed with pride over his son's dramatic play. And Cort and Ronnie made a beeline for their son. Cort couldn't wait to read the headlines of his son's terrific performance; sure the victory was all because of Justin.

The team had met their first test, and it was a happy ride home to Glory Grove.

CHAPTER 31

SCHOOL

SCHOOL STARTED THE NEXT MONDAY. Jimmy got out of bed early to do his chores (including feeding Luke's pig) and to have breakfast with Irene. "You'll be the most handsome boy there," she teased.

When the school bus that crisscrossed the county picking up rural students arrived, Jimmy was the first one to board, so he sat up close to the driver, a middle-aged woman with a warm smile. "Welcome, Jimmy," she said as he slid into his seat. "Are you ready for your first day of school?"

Jimmy was nervous about going to a new school but being a part of the football team helped. The friendly greeting from the gray-haired woman eased his anxiety.

"I heard you had a great game last Saturday. I wish I could have gone. Everyone said it was an exciting finish. My husband and I are glad we have football back, so we'll be there Friday night to watch you play. You're going to win, right?" She didn't pause between sentences.

Jimmy nodded and smiled. He liked her. She did all the talking, and that suited him. As the other kids piled into the bus, he relaxed. Most were younger and were either friendly or oblivious to his presence, caught up in their own first-day-of-school excitement. When the bus, filled to its capacity, crawled to a stop in front of the school, the place was swarming with students. Principal Colquit stood by the door in his usual black suit but now sporting a red tie.

"Hey, Ivory, you ready for our big day?" Jimmy jerked his head around. It was Luke, shuffling up the street from his house.

"Ready as you are," Jimmy said, happy to see his big friend. They stood together staring at the little high school. "At least we shouldn't get lost in there," Jimmy said, looking up at the old block building.

"Ivory, we're not in Denver or Seattle anymore," Luke said, shaking his head. He grabbed Jimmy by the shoulders. "But now you're a town hero, with the touchdowns you scored. They might roll out a red carpet."

"I doubt that. Just one game, but it felt good playing again. If you would've played, it wouldn't have been close." He and Luke followed the others into the building through the main entrance, under the slab of rock chiseled with the school's name.

"The bell's about to ring; come on inside." Colquit motioned to the students. "Everyone into the auditorium. Palmer and Ivory, I'll need to see you in my office since you're new here." They followed him down the hall with the handful of other new students, then through the open door with Colquit's name stenciled on the window.

"I've received transcripts from your former schools," the principal said. "Both of you will be entering here as juniors. That means English, biology, history, and two electives—either music, publications, or shop."

SCHOOL

After making their selections, the boys were handed their schedules and thanked their principal. Luke shook Colquit's hand, trying to get back on his good side … for the sake of football.

As they walked from the office, they heard a commotion coming from the auditorium. Young voices were cheering and laughing, the sound echoing down the empty hallway. They eased open the door to the auditorium and peered inside. The music teacher, not much older than the students, stood on the stage, leading the classes in competitive cheers. Luke and Jimmy spied Ashley motioning them over to the empty seats beside her. They slipped in and sat down.

"Were you sent to the principal's office already?" she whispered into Luke's ear.

He could feel her breath on his face. "Yup. We're in deep trouble, and he wants to send us home," he teased. "Naw, actually, he wanted to welcome us. Said we're the best thing to happen to this school."

She rolled her eyes. "I can't believe anything you say. How's your leg?"

"Ready to kick ass in our next game."

"You'd better play. We're home against a team from the Big North League, the Prairie Panthers. They were division champions last year and only graduated three seniors. Last Friday they won 34–0. You guys better be ready."

"Holy cow, what are you, some kind of football geek?" He nudged her with his elbow.

"Just thought you needed to know," she said, slapping at his arm. She didn't admit how she'd learned all the details from the men at the store.

As the two were whispering, neither heard the band teacher call on the new students to stand up and be recognized. Luke felt Jimmy tugging at his sleeve to get him up. He stood and saw every eye in the room staring at him and the other newbies.

"Let's give our new students a warm welcome," the bandleader said, starting the applause. He was a favorite among the kids for his quirky behavior and musical talents. He'd bemoaned the lack of football the previous year because he loved leading the pep band at the games. "Let's start the year off by singing the Grizzly fight song," he said. All the students joined in.

It was a nice introduction to their new school. The day was a whirlwind of activity, meeting new people and being introduced to new subjects. The food in the lunchroom was okay, certainly not as good as Irene's cooking.

After the last bell of the day rang, Luke headed to the doctor's office to get his leg inspected. If Ashley was right, the team was going to need him. The clinic knew he was coming, and a nurse directed him to an exam room. Soon the doctor entered. "Hello, Luke, good to see you. Let's take a look at that leg. I'll bet you're hoping to get cleared to play football this Friday."

"Dang right. I can't wait until Friday. Want to lay the hammer on those boys."

Luke pulled down his jeans, exposing his lower leg. It was still red, but the swelling had gone down, and the flesh was healing. "It's still a little sore, isn't it?" the doctor asked.

"No, it feels great," Luke said, trying to sound sincere when in fact, it bothered him to walk. "Sure as heck ready to play football."

The doctor took a seat on the stool next to the exam table and looked up into the boy's face. "Listen, young man; I know how anxious you are to get back on the field. But if I turn you loose, that flesh you see that's all red will tear open; then it will be another two or three weeks

SCHOOL

for it to heal again. Or even worse, it could get infected, and you might lose the whole season. I'm sorry, but I can't release you yet."

"Please, doctor," Luke said. "I'll bandage it up, and nobody will touch it. My teammates are going to need me Friday. I have to play." Luke was pulling his pants up as he talked, as if by covering the injury, he could make the doctor forget it.

"I wish I could say yes, but there are a lot of games left in the season. I can almost promise by next week, if you keep treating that burn properly, you'll be good to go. Keep using that antiseptic cream and keep it elevated. Then when you get on the field, you'll be healthy enough to play. And I'll be there cheering for you."

The doctor gave Luke a pat on the back. He felt bad for the boy. Some of his own best memories in life were playing football for the Grizzlies. He'd get Luke back on the field as soon as it was safe.

"Thanks, Doc," Luke said in a hushed voice. "I'll go tell the coach." He hobbled out of the room with disappointment showing on his face. The nurse noticed and knew it wasn't good news.

Luke went straight to the field to tell Brock. It was a blow to any chance the Grizzlies had of beating the Panthers. By agreement, coaches in the state exchanged game films from the previous week, so Brock had watched the film and realized the Prairie Panthers were way ahead of the boys from the Grove. The only hope the Grizzlies had was to put pressure on the opposing quarterback with the size and speed of Luke Palmer. Now it wasn't an option.

CHAPTER 32

LOSERS

THE COACHES, STILL AT PRACTICE, were disheartened with the news from Luke but carried on with game preparations. "We'll try to get it done without you," Brock told him. "You'd better get off that leg and give it time to heal. Head on home and treat it like the doctor said."

Luke sat in the bleachers and watched the team go through their exercises. Across the field, he saw a group of girls trying out for the cheerleading squad. Ashley was among them. They were going through their routines. Ashley did well for a sophomore, but the older hopefuls were clearly more practiced. When they finished, the girls huddled around their coach, then scattered as they were dismissed. They detoured around the end zone to avoid the football players.

Luke edged his way to the sideline and walked beside Ashley. "Hi," he said cautiously. "Are you a cheerleader now?"

"I didn't get picked." There was a slight quiver in her voice.

"I watched. Thought you did great."

"The coach picked the older girls. Told the rest of us to try again when basketball season starts."

Luke dropped his voice. "I'm sorry. I guess we're both losers. I can't play football again this week. The doctor won't clear me."

"Maybe we should give up." She shrugged.

"No way. Our time will come; we need to be patient. Hey, you want to come hang out at my house?"

"No." She glanced over at the other girls who were watching them. "Why not?"

"Because people will see us going into your house alone, and by tomorrow morning, the church ladies will have me pregnant. Gossip travels fast here."

"Good point. Let's drive out to the Gallagher farm. I have a pig I'm taking to the fair, and I've been too busy to get out there. Jimmy's been doin' all the work. Wanna go?"

"All right. But I have to be home in time to fix dinner for my brother."

They jumped into the Palmer's pickup, Ashley sitting next to Luke on the cushioned bench seat. As they drove, they left the windows down, enjoying the breeze on the warm September afternoon. Luke dialed the radio to a country station and turned up the volume.

"Do you like country music?" Ashley was surprised a city boy would choose country.

"Didn't use to, but it's all my dad plays, and it's grown on me. Like this town, it's kind of slow and laid back." He casually laid his hand on her thigh, covered with cut-off blue jeans. His heart beat a little faster. She grasped his fingers but left them on her leg and closed her eyes, trying to forget her disappointment from the cheerleading tryouts. Luke drove slowly and crept around the sharp gravel corners.

At the farm, they parked by the pig barn. Each animal was now nearly three hundred pounds, approaching the weight Richard said they needed to compete at the fair in two weeks. Irene, who'd been sitting on the porch brushing Sassy, saw them drive in and sauntered across the driveway to say hello. She'd been alone most of the day and was glad to see company.

"Hi, kids, what are you doing here so early in the day?" she asked.

"Doc says I can't play football till next week, so I'm goin' to show Ashley my prize hog. She thinks I'm still a city boy, so I wanna show her how country I've become."

"Okay, then get in the pen and show this nice young lady how to exhibit a pig," she challenged.

"Come on, Mrs. Gallagher," Luke said, embarrassed. "I'm no hog expert. But I can learn. How hard can it be?"

"Let me show you," Irene said as she opened the gate into the pen. "First, take this little whip and see if you can make old Football Butt there move where you want him to go. Do it without using your hands. Use the whip to guide him. Don't push him with your legs, especially the one with the burn."

"So, I need to show him who's boss?"

Irene shook her head. "No, pigs are smart, way smarter than sheep or cows. They won't be bossed. You must form a partnership. Move together around the ring but make him think you are doing it together. Keep him moving by tapping on his hocks, but don't use force, or he'll become stubborn, like some people I know." Irene winked at Ashley.

The women watched Luke as he got acquainted with his pig. "Come on, Football Butt," Luke said, tapping the hog on his heel. He'd jumped on the name Irene had given his pig. He was now officially Football

Butt. As they practiced, he became more adept at making the hog move around the ring.

The sun was beginning to set, but it was still warm. Irene was growing weak, so she excused herself and walked Sassy to the house. Luke watched Irene leave, then stopped moving with his hog. "I should get off my leg," he said. "Let's sit down for a while." He and Ashley stepped into the barn, out of the sun, and sat on a bale of straw.

"Do you like it here?" she asked, remembering when he'd first arrived in the Grove and how angry he acted.

"I'm starting to," he said. "I like you."

Ashley turned away and stroked the barn cat that had crawled up in her lap.

Luke leaned against her. "This is kind of romantic, isn't it, sitting in an old barn, with the smell of pigs drifting through the door?" He hesitated, then asked, "Can I kiss you?"

She turned toward him. "Just once maybe. I don't want you to get the wrong idea."

He leaned over, put his arm around her, and, in a motion witnessed only by the two hogs and the barn cat, placed his mouth on hers. Her lips were soft, and he could taste her lip gloss. She opened her mouth slightly but seconds later put her hand on his chest. "I probably need to get home."

"Got it." He pulled back and looked into her eyes. "That was special, wasn't it?"

"Very special."

They said good-bye to Football Butt and honked at Irene, who stood in her doorway waving. For the moment, they were free of cheerleading and football. Ashley leaned her head on Luke's shoulder as they listened to a country song about a farmer and his tractor in a place that reminded them of Glory Grove.

The first home game fell on a humid evening, alternating between rain showers and swirling gusts of wind. Farmers in the crowd were pleased, anxious for a good rain to soak the ground so they could start seeding their winter wheat. They sat among the large crowd, from all corners of the county, who had come for their reintroduction to Grizzly football.

The band instructor was in a jubilant mood, directing the pep band through their warm-up songs while the public address announcer, Jerry Glenn, known as the voice of the Grizzlies, was busy testing his equipment to make sure the year layoff hadn't caused any problems.

"I think we're ready," he told his booth mate, who did color commentary on the local radio station which reached ten miles into the country.

The maintenance staff had the field perfectly manicured. The lines on the turf were chalked by the math teacher, who prided himself on straight lines and precise angles. At the end of the field, children gathered behind the east goal post. Aspiring grade school athletes spun miniature footballs to their buddies. Between showers, the erratic breeze moved the aroma of hot chocolate, pretzels, and popcorn through the grandstand.

The Prairie Panthers arrived in two busloads, twice the number of local boys. As they formed *en masse* at the end of the field, Brock got a sick feeling in his stomach. The Panther players looked huge in their mint green and gold uniforms with white helmets bearing a panther's claw on the side. In a column of four abreast, they marched onto the field, chanting in unison. "Play hard, play to win. Play hard, play to win." Their rhythmic intonation could be heard over the noise from the crowd.

Coaching at Brighton, Brock had been in several mismatches, but usually it was his teams that overwhelmed the opponents. Tonight, he was on the other end of the scale. His players weren't ready for what was about to take place.

The coaches huddled before the game. "I don't like the looks of this," Brock said. "We're clearly outmanned. Best thing we can do is keep the ball on the ground and keep the clock running. We won't put the ball in the air unless we have to. If we're lucky, we can keep it close and get out of this without scaring the wits out of our young kids or losing someone to injury."

Grove fans were primed for some fast action. The win at St. Michaels had them hoping for more of the same. When the Grizzlies received the ball on the opening kickoff, they ran three dive plays to Wally Thompson before punting the ball back to the Panthers. With the wind at their back, the visitors used a series of short passes to march down the field for a quick score. The crowd went silent, but the band jumped in with a snappy number to lift their spirits.

A long kickoff return by Jimmy got the locals on their feet, but again the offense couldn't muster a first down, and the Panthers quickly put up another score. Cort Jepson was seething as he sat with his wife and buddies. The men had primed themselves earlier with beer and were ready to cheer for Cort's son. But Justin had thrown only a couple of passes. Why would any college scout be interested in a high school quarterback who never threw the ball?

One of Cort's friends picked up his vibes and began yelling. "Throw the ball, Gallagher!" His angry tone caught the attention of those in the bleachers, but Brock had his back to the grandstand and didn't hear the edict.

Again, the man hollered. "Throw the ball!" This time it was in full throat. Still, Brock did not respond. But others in the audience turned to stare at Cort's group. When the final invective was hurled at Brock, several stood up, ready to make their way up into the crowd.

"Throw the fucking ball, Gallagher, you dumb ass," shouted the man seated next to Cort, opposite Veronica. She turned pale with embarrassment.

Tim heard the yelling and trotted out of the press box, jumping two stairs at a time to reach the guilty party. But he was headed off by Lester Colquit, who was determined to preserve a proper decorum on school property. Colquit leaned his skinny frame into the man. "Sir, I must ask you to leave this game now. Your language won't be tolerated here." The fans nearby applauded his courage. They knew the drunk man could easily throw their little principal down the two dozen steps he'd climbed. But they also saw, behind Colquit, Tim Palmer ready to fight.

"I ain't goin' nowhere." The burly man was enjoying the confrontation.

"Cort, tell him to stop," pleaded Veronica as she squeezed her husband's arm.

Cort nodded to the man. "You'd better leave. These assholes will probably call security if you don't. You ain't going to miss anything in this game anyway, not the way Gallagher is waving his white flag. Christ, I've never seen anything more pitiful."

"Maybe you should go too," said Tim over Colquit's shoulder.

"I ain't leaving, and if you make me, my son's coming with me."

Ronnie grabbed her husband's arm. "Cort, please. Settle down. You're not helping."

"Shut up, Ronnie." Cort turned away and refused to look at her. "I can handle this." He motioned his friend to leave.

"Thank you, Mr. Jepson," said Colquit. "We won't allow another outburst like that, or you'll be suspended from these games for the rest of the year." He backed away, and he and Tim cautiously returned to their business, looking back occasionally to make sure the instigator was leaving the stands.

Brock was so focused on the game he'd barely heard the ruckus. Even if he had, he wouldn't have changed his tactics. He was going to spare his team from a massacre. The only things keeping the game from being a total humiliation were the intermittent rain, which caused several Panther fumbles, and the opposing coach's good sportsmanship, sending in his second-string players to keep the score from being too lopsided.

The hometown fans had hoped for a win. But their boys were playing against an overpowering opponent. No one was surprised by the outcome. Still, they expected to see more excitement from the new players and their hometown coach. With the loss, any thought of a miraculous upset had been washed away with the rain squalls. Still, there were more home games left on the schedule. Perhaps the team would improve with time.

CHAPTER 33

ASHLEY

DON BAKER WENT EARLY to open the Cozy Corner drive-in, as he did each morning, to share coffee and gossip with friends. After the game with Prairie, there was plenty to discuss. Each of the men at the table had an opinion about the loss. It would have been a tough game to win, but they were surprised by the poor showing by their Grizzlies. Their team only made a few first downs and didn't score until the Panther coach put in his third string. The loss was embarrassing for the community, and the men questioned their earlier assumption that Brock could bring a new winning tradition to the football program.

"There will be more wins in the future," Baker reassured his friends but reminded them the Grove players had some catching up to do after their year off. He even hinted that Luke Palmer would be cleared to play soon, and with him in the lineup, the offense would improve significantly. Most of the men remembered Luke's dad, Tim, and how he played with reckless abandon. He was a key to that remarkable season a generation ago when the Grizzlies nearly brought home a state championship.

Still, throughout the community, people were beginning to question whether Brock could repeat his success at Brighton at their small school. Maybe he didn't know how to coach with such limited resources.

On the other end of town, Justin Jepson had more serious things on his mind. He woke early, stiff and sore, hurting from the game the night before. His shoulder throbbed, but it wasn't from overuse. He'd only thrown a couple of passes in the game with the Panthers. The pain came from a blindside hit he took from one of their linebackers.

But the bigger hurt wasn't physical; it was emotional, from a confrontation with his father after the game—an argument that had turned ugly. As a result, he tossed and turned all night and then left the house before his dad woke. At first light, he drove to the convenience store hoping to find something to quiet his stomach. Ashley was behind the counter.

"Morning," he said softly. "Looks like you're here alone." His eyes were barely open.

"People sleep in on Saturday. They won't start coming for a while." She was surprised to see Justin there early after the game the night before. She tried to be pleasant to the handsome young quarterback but noticed he didn't exhibit his usual friendliness. "You look like you need somebody to cheer you up. You want to talk?" She had already done all the prepping of the store for another day's business.

"Sure," he said as he slid into a booth near the door, put his head in his hands, and waited for her to join him. "I had a rough night."

"Yep. I saw the game. Didn't turn out like everybody hoped. But you played well."

"I didn't throw any interceptions, did I." He shook his head and tried to force a smile.

"That might be the talk of the town this morning. Why didn't they let you throw the ball more?"

"Coach had a plan."

"Well, I'm sure next week will be better. Are you all right? You look sad."

"You probably wouldn't understand. It's a family problem. My dad can be a hothead."

"Yep, I saw the thing in the stands last night. He seemed pretty angry. Who was he mad at anyway?"

Justin turned to stare out the window. "Mostly the coach, but me and Mom too. He came home and started yelling about how they should fire Coach Gallagher. Mom told him to calm down, but that made him even madder. Then he got after me for not telling the coach what I thought of his game plan."

"Geez, that's not good."

"That wasn't the end. I told him to quit yelling at Mom … to leave it alone. That Gallagher is a good coach and knows what he's doing. That's when he got in my face, but mom stepped in between us. He shoved her down and didn't help her up, just glared at her. And told me to go to my room, like I was a little kid."

"Your mom wasn't hurt, I hope. She's one of the nicest people in town."

Justin shook his head. "She's all right, but it's not good. For some reason, football brings out the worst in my dad. I love the game, but sometimes it's not worth it."

Ashley knew people would start coming in the door at any minute but wanted to do something to make Justin feel better. She risked making a fool of herself and reached across the vinyl table and grasped his hands that were covered with bruises from the game.

The gesture startled him, but he didn't pull back. Instead, he looked into her eyes and noticed for the first time how pretty she was.

"I'm sorry," she said. "I wish I could help."

"That's okay. I'll be all right."

She looked at him without blinking. "If you ever need someone to talk to, come see me. I'm a good listener. Maybe you need to stay away from your dad for a while. Let him cool down. He wants you to be a star football player, and you are. Everyone sees that. But maybe you need to play the game for yourself. To heck with the parents."

He liked how warm and soft her hands were. "How much are you going to charge for the therapy session?" He forced a grin.

"Sorry," she said, embarrassed. "I don't know what I'm talking about." She suddenly felt dizzy from the whole encounter. He was, after all, Justin Jepson.

"No, Ashley. I'm serious. I needed to talk to somebody this morning. I appreciate you listening."

The door chimed, marking the arrival of a customer. As he came through the door, the couple dropped their hands, and Ashley jumped up to do her job. The intrusion had come at just the right moment because her heart was beating too fast.

CHAPTER 34

BANK

IRENE HAD CHECKS to deposit at the local bank. But on Monday morning, she was feeling ill. She asked Brock to take care of it for her. "Veronica O'Malley works there; she can help you," she said matter-of-factly.

"You mean Ronnie Jepson, don't you?"

"Of course. She's worked there for a long time and is the assistant manager now."

Ronnie had always done well in school, and Brock wasn't surprised she'd be good at whatever occupation she chose. This was a chance to see her without Cort looking over his shoulder.

He cleaned up after doing chores and drove to town, thinking of the things he might say if he had the chance. However, when he entered the bank with its floor-to-ceiling windows, carpeted lobby, and computer music playing, any idea of a personal conversation seemed unlikely. He made his way to one of the three tellers and asked to deposit some checks for Irene.

"Yes sir," said the young girl. "We can do that for you."

Brock hadn't noticed Ronnie in her office. But she'd spied him walking in the door. As a grown man, he'd matured but still possessed the rugged good looks he'd had as a teenager. She took a deep breath, stepped outside her office door, and motioned to the teller. "Cindy, would you please ask Mr. Gallagher to step into my office for a minute when he's done there. I need to talk to him about his mother's farm account."

"Sure thing," the teller responded.

Brock spun around and saw his old girlfriend standing in the doorway to her office. He'd seen her at the Derby Daze dance and at the demolition derby, but now she was dignified looking, wearing a gray blazer over a black skirt. The heels of her mid-calf boots made her appear taller than he remembered. Her auburn curls fell to her shoulders and framed her face, still as perfect as porcelain. She'd been an adorable teenager. Now she was a beautiful woman.

"Hello again," he said as he stepped into her office.

"Come in and close the door," she said politely. Her office, with its glass walls, was fully visible to all the other employees, and they didn't need to hear what she was about to say. "How are you, Brock?" she said in a much softer tone.

"Good, thanks. I guess you want to talk business. Is there a problem with our farm account?"

"Your account is fine. Your mom does a good job of keeping the farm in healthy financial shape. I asked you to come in so I could talk to you on a personal level. There are a lot of things I'd like to say, but with the young ladies out there watching, I'll keep this short."

"I understand," he said.

"First, I want to thank you for being so good to Justin. He likes you, and I'm relieved his dad isn't coaching him. I want to apologize for the way Cort and his friends acted at the game Friday."

"Not a problem. Coaches get yelled at all the time. I didn't even hear it. But I'm sorry if it upset you. Justin's a good athlete, and he'll get his chance to show his talent. He's got Cort's ability on the field, but his character reminds me a lot of his mother." Brock paused to let the words sink in. "I'm sorry his dad is putting so much pressure on him."

Ronnie spun a pen in her hand. "It's been hard. We had a little family blowup after the game. Justin and his dad almost came to blows. Cort still has a bad temper, and it's been worse since, well, since you came home."

"I'm sorry. Anything I can do except stay away?"

"No, but I want you to understand if Justin seems troubled."

"How about you? Are you all right?"

"Not really," she said. Suddenly her demeanor changed, and she looked hurt and vulnerable. She turned and stared out the window at a passing car. She no longer seemed like an assistant bank manager but quickly sat up in her chair and regained her composure. "It would take longer than we have now to explain."

Brock tried to reassure her. "You've been married for a long time. We all have rough patches to work through. I'm sure you and Cort will get through this."

"Yes, Justin deserves two parents. We'll work it out for him, but it won't be easy."

Brock didn't know if he should feel guilty for making Ronnie's life more difficult by returning to his hometown or be happy that she was confiding in him. If they weren't being watched, he wondered if he would have gone behind the desk and put his arms around her.

Time was running out on their staged banker-client meeting. But neither wanted it to end without closure. "Ronnie, you know if you're ever in trouble, you can call me," Brock offered.

"I can't be seen talking to you. Even this meeting might cause problems. But someday, it would be nice if we could sit and talk. We had some good times in high school, didn't we? But never really had a chance to say good-bye."

"I know. Maybe when we're old and gray, we can get together and reminisce."

"I hope we don't have to wait that long." Her voice was trembling. For weeks, her dreams had been filled with images of Brock. In her fantasy, she'd go for a late-night walk in the rain while Cort went drinking with his friends at the Wild Horse Tavern. Brock would appear out of the darkness, and they'd stroll together through the mist. The dream seemed exciting and dangerous.

The sudden pause in their conversation seemed awkward, so Brock broke the silence. It was as if he'd read her mind. "Sometimes it's better not to make life too complicated. We both have our own lives to lead. But Ronnie, you'll always be a favorite part of mine. Thanks for the visit." He stood up to go. "I'll see you at the football field. We were always at our best there, anyway," he said. "I'll watch out for your boy, that I can promise."

"Good-bye, Mr. Gallagher," she said as she stood up. She extended her hand so the others in the bank could see.

"Good-bye, Mrs. Jepson." It was the first time Brock had felt her touch in a very long time, and he held her hand perhaps a second or two too long. The girls, who were watching out of the corners of their eyes, noticed the lengthy handshake and concluded it must have been a profoundly serious meeting.

Later in the day, Brock watched film on the next opponent, the Galesburg Coyotes. He concluded the third game of the season was winnable, not easy, but there was a chance. Galesburg was the second straight opponent from the larger classification, but they weren't highly ranked. He particularly noticed the inexperience in their secondary. "If Justin has a good night, we can exploit that," he told Don and Tim. "And if we get Luke back to give Justin protection, he'll be able to find his receivers." The good news came Monday afternoon. Luke went to the doctor and was cleared to play.

The team spent the week polishing their passing game, the one they hadn't used against the Prairie Panthers. Luke was like a man possessed all week. The coaches made him throttle back so he wouldn't hurt his own teammates. On Friday, he couldn't sit still in class and paced around the classroom. He hadn't played since his final game with his Denver team the previous season. Now, he didn't care if this was football in a one-horse town. He was itching to play.

Before the game, some of the fans debated whether a single player on a football team could change the nature of their performance. But against Galesburg, the Grove fans watched as Luke Palmer made a difference. From his linebacker position, he terrorized the opponent, sacking the quarterback repeatedly and hounding their running backs. On offense, he gave Justin time enough to find Jimmy and the freshman receivers, Les and George, for big gains. They didn't catch every pass but corralled enough to put the Grizzlies on the board for a halftime score of 21–21. Justin threw for over two hundred and fifty yards in the two quarters.

In the visitors grandstand, Cort Jepson was ecstatic. "I guess Gallagher got my message," he said, loud enough for the fans around him to hear. "The dumb fool could have won last week if Justin had thrown the ball."

The third quarter was a standoff, but late in the fourth, the Coyotes pushed across for a touchdown, tacked on the extra point, and led 28–21.

"Luke's wearing down," Tim said from the press box. "He's starting to limp on his bad leg." It had been Luke's energy that kept the Grizzlies in the game with the big-league opponent.

Brock gave him some rest on the next series, but without the big fullback, Justin was under heavy pressure. Brock shifted his strategy and directed Justin to throw quick swing passes to Jimmy, who could use his quickness to get around the defensive ends. It worked. With the clock running down, Justin completed a series of short throws to Jimmy, and each time, Jimmy managed to gain yardage and then step out of bounds and stop the clock.

With the score clock about to reach double zeroes, Brock reinserted Luke. From the five-yard line, instead of using him as a blocker, Justin stuck the ball in Luke's stomach. Now refreshed, he powered through four would-be tacklers and dove over the goal line for a score. The Grove fans erupted with cheers, and Tim screamed so loud over his headset Brock temporarily pulled them off his ears. "Whooee, that's my boy. Great play. Way to go."

Now Brock was faced with the decision. Kick the extra point for the tie and overtime or go for two and win the game. "What do you want to do?" Brock asked his team as they gathered around him.

"Let's win this sucker right now," Luke's husky voice overshadowed the rest, but they all yelled their approval.

"I agree," Brock said. "We've worked on the fake dive play all week. Let's use it now. Les, are you ready to make the catch?"

"Yessir, Coach. I've got this."

The play called for Justin to fake the handoff to Luke, mirroring the play they'd run for the touchdown. Anticipating the Grizzlies would use the big man to crash into the end zone, the defense would be drawn to him. Meanwhile, the slender Les Colquit would slip into the corner of the end zone. If the deception worked, Les would be open for the catch.

Justin huddled his teammates around him. He was confident. "This game is ours to win. Let's do it and go home." As he barked out the snap count, his teammates were ready for the upcoming jubilation of a winning play. Augie's center exchange was perfect, and Justin secured the ball. Luke moved like a machine, seeming to grab the ball and plunge into the line. The entire Coyote defense instinctively converged on him, intent on denying him the score.

At the same time, Les Colquit casually loped into the end zone, acting indifferent to the action. He stood, waiting patiently … alone. Justin took two quick steps back, spun the ball so his fingers were on the laces, focused on his freshman receiver, aimed, and zipped the ball to his open target. An easy throw would yield a winning tally. The ball spiraled toward Les; however, it didn't land in his outstretched fingers. Despite the young receiver's desperate leap skyward, it sailed over his fingertips, fell harmlessly to the turf, and lay in the corner of the end zone like a deflated party balloon.

Grizzly players were in disbelief. Devastated, some fell to their knees in exhaustion and disappointment. Justin shook his head and stared into the starlit sky. Luke slapped his thighs and howled his angst. The game was another frustrating loss.

"Shit," Tim muttered to no one through his microphone.

"It's okay," Brock said. "We gave it a try. Better console them. They played a hell of a game and are getting better each week. Luke was outstanding. Remember to tell him that."

"I know, but dammit, I hate losing," Tim said.

"And that's why we try so hard to win."

The teams filed past one another, shaking hands. There was mutual admiration since either team could have won. The Coyote coach pulled Brock aside and congratulated him. "That's a hell of a team you have," he said. "The rest of the schools on your schedule better be ready, 'cause you're going to win some ball games."

"Thanks, Coach," Brock said. And he believed it. In the visitors grandstand, Cort couldn't believe his son had failed. "Wait till he gets home," he said. "Me and him are going to have a little talk."

Ronnie shuddered.

CHAPTER 35

FAIR

FAIR WEEKEND COINCIDED with the Grizzlies' fourth game. The players were juggling their time, preparing their fair entries, and getting ready for football. Jimmy and Luke hurried to the farm from practice each night to train their pigs, coaxing them around the barnyard to get them ready for the show ring.

Both newcomers to the high school were enrolled in an agricultural class. The FFA was an optional component. The teacher let them know they had to be members of the organization to show their swine projects. The boys agreed, although they were clueless as to what the organization was all about.

"You'll need official jackets to wear," the man said and took their measurements. Days later, the package arrived. They ripped open the box and slipped on the blue corduroy jackets. Their names were embroidered on the front in gold. They weren't sure whether to laugh at the idea of joining the organization or to delight in being members of a bigger group.

"I've heard you might have some winning hogs out there at the Gallagher farm," the teacher said. "Are you ready to drive them into the winner's circle? The grand champion gets a pretty big paycheck."

"You bet. My pig is named Football Butt," Luke said. "Looks like a champion to me."

"Can't wait to see him, but I have a word of advice. The man judging the show is a bit old school. You might want to tone down your appearance. It's up to you, but you want to give yourself the best chance to come out on top. It's like a sport. You need to do everything you can to win, right?"

Luke didn't say it, but he'd grown weary of the angry rebel look anyway. He dressed that way in Denver to stand out—projecting an angry image so no one would cross him. But in this school, people didn't care what his hair looked like or how big his earring was. They liked him as a big, fun guy and a hard-nosed football player.

Before leaving the class, the boys hurried to the nearest washroom with its giant mirror. They stood, looking at themselves with their stiff new jackets zipped to the top. "Ivory, what do you think?" Luke asked.

"Straight fire," Jimmy said, twisting his body back and forth to check his profile. "I'll impress those farm girls coming to see my pig at the fair."

"Could be, but not as much as I'll impress the ladies coming to the fair to see me."

While the boys were admiring their jackets, Brock was at home on the phone with Celia. She was back from her travels with Jovan. It had been weeks since she and Brock had last spoken.

"How are you doing?" Brock asked, trying to remain calm. "How was your trip?" He asked but hoped she'd spare him the details.

"It was the most exciting thing I have ever done," she said. There was joy in her voice. "I met so many interesting people and went to some great parties. There is so much to do in New York."

"Sounds fun."

"I wish I didn't have to come home, but the exhibit closed, and there wasn't anything left for me to do. But Jovan promised when there is another show, he'll want me to help."

"I was hoping you'd call more often. I like knowing what you're up to."

"I didn't want to bother you. I know how you are during football season. But I'm coming over in a couple of days."

"That's good. It's a busy time of year with the fair happening and a big football game Friday night." He heard his own words and was embarrassed thinking of the comparison she must be making between Glory Grove and New York City. Busy for him meant a football game and the fair. It wouldn't mean much to a cosmopolitan like Celia.

On Wednesday, shortly after noon, Celia arrived at the farm. Brock watched her drive in, but when she pulled herself out of the SUV, she looked different. Her blond, shoulder-length hair was cut short, and a heart-shaped tattoo on her arm peeked out from her blouse. There were dark bags under her eyes despite the heavy makeup. Brock met her at the door.

"Welcome back," he said, shocked by her appearance but sincerely pleased to have her home.

"Hi, Brock. Boy, that drive gets longer every time."

"Come in and relax. You look different."

"Jovan thought I needed a little makeover to fit in with the New York crowd. What do you think?"

Brock hesitated. "It's fine…good. I'll get used to it. Do you need something to eat?"

"I am hungry. Where's your mom?"

"Out with Richard checking on the cows. She can fix a big dinner tonight if you want. For now, I can make you a sandwich or soup. And we can talk about your trip. But first I need a hug."

"Sure." She shuffled closer and held out her arms. "It's been a while." The gesture felt contrived. "I can fix soup for myself, I'm sure you have other things to do, but I would appreciate it if you would get my luggage out of the car. After I eat, I'm going to nap a little; I'm exhausted."

Brock was disappointed she didn't invite him to the bedroom. It had been too many weeks without the warmth of a woman's body. He walked out, opened the trunk, and lifted her baggage with New York airline tags hanging from the handles. The sight of those tags bothered him. He and Celia had always traveled together. An unwritten pact was broken. He lugged the suitcases up to the bedroom and returned to the kitchen. He found Celia with a look of disgust on her face. She was frustrated, trying to open a soup can with the old hand-crank opener.

"Let me help," Brock offered.

"I don't know how to work this thing, I guess," she said. "This place is like an antique store."

Brock said, "Sorry for that." He worked the device and handed her the opened can. He took a deep breath before speaking again. "I think I'd better be going. We can visit after your nap." He walked out of the house, not letting the screen door make a sound. He wanted to slam it hard but resisted. He pulled himself into the pickup, drove to the ridge high above the canyon, and sat there, looking down at the ribbon of water coursing through the valley. His wife was back with him, but he felt very alone.

Next to the Derby Daze event in June, the mid-September fair was the area's biggest celebration. The fairgrounds burst at the seams with people. Hundreds of individuals entered their handiwork. The six buildings that comprised the fairgrounds were filled with vegetables, flowers, photography, and paintings. Farm machinery was displayed on the lawns outside. The barns were filled with livestock including nearly one hundred pigs. Food was sold by local service clubs. There was a dunking booth where local politicians and teachers sat precariously positioned over a tank of cold water, ready to be immersed and embarrassed while helping raise money for a good cause.

"You throw like a little girl," a male teacher hollered just before being submerged into the cold bath. Children screamed their approval.

There were lawnmower races for teenagers and chicken scrambles for the youngsters. And the grand finale of the three-day event was the sale of 4-H and FFA livestock. Individuals and businesses would surround the auction arena, ready to compete to see who could be the most generous in supporting the local youth.

However, before all that excitement of the fair could begin, there was a Grizzly football game on Friday night. If the boys pulled out a victory, everyone at the fair would be in a good mood. The boys wanted to even their win-loss record. The home game against the West Hill Warriors provided the perfect opportunity. The Grizzlies were finally facing a team from a school their own size. The Warriors were a good squad, but there were weaknesses in their defense that Brock planned on exploiting.

When the sun set on Friday night, the weather was perfect. A huge local crowd assembled for the game. People were in a festive mood. Irene and Richard were seated with Celia on the top row of the bleachers. They tried to keep Celia interested in the game, but after halftime, it was clear her mind was elsewhere. As they marveled at the performance of their home team, Celia continually scrolled through photos on her phone and feigned excitement only when they pointed out a great run by Jimmy.

When the contest was over, with a definitive 41–14 shellacking of the visitors, the parents and fans gathered on the field with the football players in a happy celebration. Brock searched among them for his wife. But as he scanned the surroundings, he saw the taillights of her red SUV leaving the parking lot.

CHAPTER 36

SHOW

BROCK CLIMBED INTO BED with Celia when he got home from the game. She was already asleep. He put his arms around her and held her close, but she didn't wake. "I still love you," he whispered. She didn't hear, but he said it for himself to reaffirm she was still his wife, and he'd be patient with her. He kissed her cheek, then rolled over and stared at the stars shining through the window. Finally, early in the morning, he drifted off to sleep.

Most of the fair events took place Saturday. Jimmy and Luke would show their pigs at one o'clock. Irene and Richard were anxious to take in the entire day, so Brock rolled out of bed early and left Celia sleeping. He tiptoed downstairs and found Irene in the kitchen preparing breakfast for the family. Jimmy was outside gathering the supplies he needed for the show.

"You coached a great game last night," Irene said. She set his coffee in front of him. Even though her son was a man, she reveled in his success.

"It's good to get a win for the hometown. The team is coming together. If we don't have any catastrophes, we could make a successful run, knock on wood." He reached over and tapped on the door frame. "Did Celia enjoy the game? I didn't get a chance to talk to her afterward."

"I think she was still just a little tired," Irene said.

"I'll take some coffee up to the room and see if I can get her moving. She'll want to watch the boys and their pigs." He grabbed a cup from the cupboard and poured it full. His mom had fried potato donuts and covered them with sugar. It was a tradition for fair weekend. Sugar donuts and the fair somehow went together perfectly. Brock wrapped two in a napkin and climbed the stairs to the bedroom.

"Celia, I have coffee for you," he said, trying to wake her gently.

"Oh Brock, you're a good man," she murmured into her pillow, then rolled over to face him. "I don't deserve you. But I'll take the coffee."

"I brought Mom's donuts too. They're fresh from the fryer."

"Your mom has many talents." She pried her eyes open, rubbed them, and sat up on the side of the bed. The loose-fitting nightgown exposed her thin frame. "I didn't hear you come in last night. I was pretty unconscious, I guess."

"That's okay. I was tired too. But it takes me a while to unwind after a game. Still, it's easier to fall asleep after a win."

She stretched her arms and yawned. "It looks like you're a winner, just like you were at Brighton. Not quite the same, though, is it? With the little crowds and only a handful of players."

"You know, a win still feels the same. In fact, in some ways, it's more exciting here because the town has the team in its heart. Everyone here has watched these boys since they started walking. Well, except for Jimmy and Luke, I guess, but people here have really taken them in. Doesn't Jimmy seem happy to you?"

"I suppose."

"Well, today we're going to watch them show their pigs. It's something you won't see in any of the cities you've been visiting."

"When in the Grove, do as the Grove people do, I always say." She struggled to get to her feet.

"Come down when you're ready. Mom's got more breakfast on the stove."

After picking at her breakfast, Celia put on her makeup and found an outfit to wear. Brock took note of her mesh leggings and opened-toed sandals. They'd look out of place in the livestock barn, but he didn't say anything. Everyone climbed into Richard's pickup. Jimmy and Celia were in the back seat together. Jimmy was glad to see her again but wondered why she'd changed her appearance. She was still pretty but harsh looking with her short hair and painted eyebrows.

On foot, they wove through the early arriving fairgoers, past the food booths that were lifting their shades. Several people noticed Brock and shouted their "congratulations" on the great football game the night before.

"You're pretty popular this morning," Celia said.

"Last week after our loss, it was just the opposite," Brock countered. "You have to win in this business to be loved."

"Kind of a shallow way to win people's affection, don't you think?"

"You need to take love where you can find it," Brock said, avoiding his wife's sudden stare.

As the crowds started to build, more and more people stopped Brock to talk about the team and game. Celia rocked back and forth, impatient to be moving on. "I want to go look at the art exhibit," she said finally. "See if there are any great artists in this town."

"Okay, you go on," Brock said and patted her arm. "We'll go to the barns to see if the boys need any help." When they arrived at the building labeled The Pig Castle, it was a tornado of sound and fury. Hogs squealed, and the kids shouted over the squeals. Feed pans were filled, and the wash rack was full of pigs and their handlers. Water flew in a frenzy of pig sanitizing and pampering.

From the end of the barn, the adults watched all this activity. "Our boys have really taken to this," Irene said, seeing how well they were responding to their new surroundings. "It's good seeing them working together." Luke was wearing a dirty ball cap with a Denver Broncos team logo. And Jimmy had on a worn lopsided cowboy hat. Both boys were covered with water and soap suds.

When he reached them, Brock reminded the boys to get their FFA jackets so they could wear them while showing. "Also, take off your hats and spit out your gum when you go into the ring." When he finished speaking, Luke whipped off his cap and exposed his shaved head. The mohawk was gone. "Wow, that looks a lot better," Brock said. But he realized he was also a bit disappointed he'd lost the intimidation factor his team had when he sent his football captains to meet the opponents on Friday nights.

Brock ignored his instincts. "Looks great, Luke. Starting a new image?"

"My ag teacher told me if I want to win, I need to look more civilized. I hope it's worth the sacrifice." He rubbed his hand over his slick scalp.

"Gotta look your best to do your best. But remember, only one can win it all."

"Got it, Coach. And ol' Football Butt will do his best."

There were eight flights of ten hogs each. Only the top two animals from each flight would return to compete for the overall championship and the right to sell first in the sale the next day.

A large crowd crammed into the wooden bleachers. They were in the shade, but the heat from the afternoon sun shining on the corrugated roof made the enclosure like an oven. No one moved. As the show progressed, Brock kept watching for Celia, but she hadn't appeared when Jimmy entered the ring in class four.

Jimmy, despite never having shown before, did a good job controlling his animal as Richard and Irene had taught him, presenting side and rear views for the judge. His barrow, a late pick out of Richard's sale, was one of the two selected to come back out for the championship. When the announcement was made, Jimmy's smile lit up the arena, and the audience applauded his efforts. Irene clapped the loudest.

Jimmy passed Luke on the way back to the holding pen. "Hey, I made the finals. Maybe I know more about picking a pig than you do."

"We'll see about that," Luke said, patting his spotted hog on the rump. "Wait till this big boy gets his chance." When it was Luke's turn to show, it didn't take long for the judge to reach the verdict. "The barrow with the big spot on his rump easily makes my top two," he said. Luke had expected to make the finals and was thankful Justin helped him make his selection months ago.

In the next flight, Justin's hog was also selected to come back for the final run. While the boys waited for the two remaining flights, they sat together on the short fences that held the animals and talked. The conversation steered away from livestock and focused on football and girls. They compared aches and pains from the game the night before and talked about the homecoming game scheduled with Pine City in a week. None of the boys had dates for the dance and agreed before the weekend was over, they needed to remedy that situation.

As the boys were talking, Brock saw Celia picking her way through the crowd, being careful not to bump into any of the spectators. She spotted them and carefully climbed the steps and squeezed in between him and Irene. "You almost missed the show," Brock said.

"Sorry, I guess I lost track of time."

"What have you been doing?"

"I looked at the artwork, but I was sleepy, so I went back to the pickup and took a nap," she said. "I'm not used to getting up so early."

Brock had never known his wife to need so much sleep but figured it was from all her travel. "Well, anyway, now you can watch the finals. The boys are coming back out to show for grand champion."

"Boy, it's hot and smelly in here," Celia said, covering her face with a handkerchief. "How long will this take?"

"Not long. You'll want to see how Jimmy does? It's his first time showing a hog."

"Sure, but I could do without the flies."

The sixteen hogs making the final round entered the ring. It was getting late in the afternoon, and the animals were getting cranky. Fights broke out between some of the more aggressive barrows, but ring men with plywood shields quickly interceded to separate them. The boys and girls in the competition were also getting tired, and sweat could be seen dripping from their faces. There was serious determination to do their best to win the grand prize.

One by one, the judge signaled the pigs to exit the ring, weeding out the inferior animals, leaving those still in contention circling the arena. When only six remained, Jimmy, Luke, and Justin were still in the running. The judge commented on each animal, one at a time, praising each of them. But some were a bit too light in weight. Others didn't carry enough meat in the hams or over their back. Finally, he was ready to make his choice.

"I will select my grand champion first," said the judge, a husky man with a booming voice. "And then, I will pick a reserve champion." He slowly paced the ring; looked again at every one of the six pigs, building up the suspense. Jimmy was dizzy with the heat and excitement. Luke thought he had a good chance of winning. Justin was anxious, knowing how being selected as champion would help with his family's finances.

Finally, the judge held out the big purple rosette ribbon. With a grand gesture and a handshake, he handed it to a young blond girl with pink cheeks showing a pure white pig. Most everyone in the audience knew she'd been showing since she was nine years old and came from a well-connected family. Luke and Jimmy looked at each other, their eyes expressing their shared disappointment.

"This is a terrific pig with all the right pieces and parts," the judge said. "And little lady, you've done a remarkable job showing your animal. You should be proud." He returned to the podium and picked up the reserve champion ribbon. "And now for my reserve champion animal," he spun around and stared at Luke, "I'm going with this powerful barrow with the big spot on his rump. Young man, you and your pig make quite a team. With a little more practice, you'll soon be competing for the top prize. Great effort on your part; you and your pig look terrific today."

Luke always wanted to act like a tough guy, but he was tired and hot and sore from the game the night before. And for just a moment, he got emotional. He saw his dad smiling in the crowd and Brock and Irene clapping. He blinked a couple of times and was surprised at the lump in his throat.

Except for Cort Jepson, who claimed Justin had been robbed, the audience was happy with the result and relieved they could leave the heat of the arena. Celia quickly stepped down from the bleachers and away from the crowd. She didn't think she could ever understand this place or the kind of people who'd sit all afternoon in the sweltering heat to watch a bunch of sweaty kids and squealing pigs. She missed the city. She would stay a few more days to say she'd tried, but she planned to leave as soon as possible.

CHAPTER 37

DRAMA

ON SUNDAY AFTERNOON, the project animals were sold. Luke wasn't the first to sell; that honor went to the owner of the grand champion. But, as reserve champion, he was second in the ring. Folks told him Football Butt would command a high price, so he was curious how much money he'd make. He'd never had a pet before and was surprised how attached he'd become to the big pig.

When they entered the sale ring together, the barrow shied away from the men calling out the bids. He was frightened, making grunting noises and crowded up against Luke's leg. Luke didn't want to think of the pig hanging in a meat locker. To put it out of his mind, he listened to the auctioneer chanting out numbers. His words were staccato sounding and undecipherable to the untrained ear. But finally, he understood the closing sentence. "Okay, folks, this is your reserve champion … shown by Luke Palmer, one of those great Grizzly football players. I'll bet, young man, you could pick up that pig and carry it out of here."

DRAMA

Luke grinned up at the man and shook his head no.

"This is the second-best hog in the show. He's worth the money. Let's put some cash in Luke's pocket. We're going to close the bid. $6.00 is the bid. Going once, twice, sold for $6.00 per pound. What are you going to do with the money, Luke?"

"Pay my feed bill," Luke hollered back.

"For you or the hog?" The audience laughed. A cameraman climbed over the fence into the ring and took a photo of Luke and Football Butt with the buyer, the local implement dealer.

"Okay, bring in the next animal," said the auctioneer.

Luke guided his pig into the sale pen, where the hogs would be picked up for transport to the meat processing plant. He patted him between the ears and mumbled a quiet good-bye.

"Kind of sad the first time, but it gets easier every year." The voice startled Luke. It was Justin who'd come up behind him. "You got a nice price for him. It helps when the buyer likes football, and you had a great game Friday."

"I can use the money," Luke said, turning his eyes away from the hog.

Justin changed the subject. "Hey, I got a date for homecoming. Have you asked anyone yet?"

"Not yet. Who's the lucky girl?"

"Ashley, your friend down at the convenience store."

Luke felt like he'd been kicked in the stomach. At first, he thought Justin must be kidding. But he wasn't. He'd planned on asking Ashley but had waited too long. "I didn't know you liked her."

"Oh, we had a good talk the other day, and I got to know her better. She's down to earth. The other girls always get silly when I'm around them. Anyway, she said yes, so I won't have to go alone."

Luke was angry. Justin knew he liked Ashley. He'd seen them together. He shouldn't have come bragging about asking her to homecoming. "Well, congratulations. I hope you have a good time." He slammed the gate to the pigpen, rattling the fence. He turned and walked away, thinking he liked his old pig more than he liked Justin.

Despite his disappointment, Luke found a date for the dance. She was a senior cheerleader named Bernice, who'd made it known she wanted to go with one of the football captains. She was loud and brash, not too smart but attracted a lot of attention with her tight-fitting outfits. It looked to everyone like the perfect match. But Luke kicked himself all week for being slow with an invitation to Ashley.

The game with the Pine City Mustangs was scheduled, as are most homecoming games, with the assumption the home team would win and make the celebration a happy time for everyone. When the Mustangs took the field, Brock was confident things would turn out well if the boys weren't too worn out from all the homecoming week activities. During the week, Brock could tell there was something wrong between his key players, but no one wanted to talk about it.

In practice, Luke tried to obliterate anyone who got in his way. He had a scowl on his face but said nothing before the game and had none of his usual pregame histrionics. He wouldn't look at Justin during warm-up drills. When the game began, he assumed his position and played with fierce intensity. When he carried the ball, it took four Mustangs to bring him down. But when Justin was tackled, he'd walk past without a hand to help him up. His anger energized him.

At halftime, the team gathered in the end zone to talk over the first half. Brock didn't ask what was going on. Whatever it was, he would let it play out. Despite the unhappiness, it was working to the advantage of his team. "Keep it up," he told the boys, "and we walk away with a victory."

As the scoring margin grew for the Grizzlies in the second half, Brock planned on bringing in the underclass substitutes in the fourth quarter. But late in the third, as Justin dropped back to pass, a blitzing linebacker came off the corner and hammered him to the ground. His helmet bounced off the hard turf. For a second, he lay motionless but quickly scrambled to his feet and shook his head to clear away the cobwebs.

Brock jogged to his side. "You okay, Justin?"

"I'm fine."

"Look into my eyes," Brock commanded. He studied his face and decided Justin had played long enough. The margin of points was enough already to secure the victory. "Jimmy, you take over at quarterback."

In the stands, Cort Jepson and Ronnie were watching intently. "What the hell?" Cort said under his breath.

"I think he's hurt," Ronnie said.

"He was only down for a second; he's all right. He needs more time to build his stats. For cripes' sake, leave him in there."

Ronnie didn't care about numbers in a stat book. She cared about her son and was relieved when Brock pulled him out of the game.

For the rest of the contest, Jimmy handed the ball to Luke or threw short passes to his receivers. Jimmy didn't have the arm strength of Justin, but he could throw an accurate spiral. He was thrilled to be playing quarterback. "Let's take this game home for Justin," he said as he faced the other ten boys in the huddle.

"Serves him right," Luke mumbled as he kicked at the ground.

"Shut up, Luke," Jimmy said. He gave his friend an irritated stare.

He'd never raised his voice before to anyone on the team, but he was now the quarterback in charge, and he wasn't going to let some stupid grievance ruin the moment. "Just play ball."

"Yes sir," Luke said in mock sarcasm. "Just give me the rock."

When the game was over, the Grizzlies had done what was expected, winning, 44–7. They now had a winning record and a realistic shot at a playoff spot. They only needed two more wins for an opportunity to take on the champion of their old league.

The homecoming dance on Saturday night wasn't a glamorous dress-up affair like the prom, but it was one of the top social events of the school year. Brock and Celia agreed to chaperone, and she'd been called on to help dress Jimmy—he'd gotten a date with one of the other students new to the school—and Luke. Celia was thrilled to venture away from the farm on a shopping excursion to the closest city mall. She found dress slacks, shirts, and sport coats for the two boys.

When the night arrived, the boys went to Tim's house to dress. When they exited the bedroom, Tim whistled. "Ooee, look at them pretty boys."

"Easy, Pop. What do you think? Too fancy?"

"Hell no. You guys will sweep them young things right off their feet. Now you better get goin' if you want to dance."

Brock had volunteered his car to Jimmy and Luke to help make the evening special. So, he and Celia drove to the dance in the farm pickup. "Pretty classy, don't you think?" he teased when Celia slid in beside him.

"We appear to be lowering our standards," she said with a half-smile. "Do you think we are dressed okay?" She hadn't been to a high school dance since her own teenage years.

"Trust me; those teenagers won't be looking at us." He thought back to his senior homecoming dance with Ronnie on his arm. She'd been stunning, wearing all black with a yellow ribbon in her hair.

The kids straggled in slowly. The disc jockey attempted to fire them up with modern rock but had few takers. They milled around, talking quietly while waiting for the more popular couples to make their entrance. When Justin and Ashley strolled in together, the only sound in the room was the music as everyone stopped talking to stare. No one knew they were dating, and a buzz went through the small crowd, especially among the girls wondering how little Ashley had pulled it off.

She was in a dream world. When Justin asked her to the dance, she suspected he was kidding. But he was serious. She'd only told a few of her closest friends, still afraid he'd call it off. But when he didn't, she splurged and spent her paycheck on a special dress for the occasion.

But along with her excitement, she knew Luke's feelings were hurt. After their trip to the farm, she assumed he'd ask her to the dance. She waited, but the invitation never came. And now, even if she had the option of turning down the hottest boy in school for a date with Luke, she didn't know if she could do that. After all, this was the boy all the girls dreamed about.

Some of the kids ventured onto the dance floor. Justin led Ashley to the center of the group, put his arms around her waist, and began moving very slowly back and forth. They laughed as they attempted to coordinate their swaying. "I'm pretty bad at this," she said.

"We're fine. And just so you know, you look great tonight. I think you're the prettiest girl in the room."

She punched him softly on his shoulder. "And I think you're full of it, but I like it anyway," she said.

Brock and Celia were watching from the corner when Luke and Jimmy ambled in with their dates. Brock did a double take. "Wow, you pulled a little magic on those two ruffians," he said. He looked over at his wife, and she was beaming at her successful fashion undertaking.

"Maybe I overdid it," she said.

"No way. That is the best those boys have ever looked."

Soon the cafeteria was filled with students. As Ashley was dancing with Justin, she saw Luke out of the corner of her eye. He was more handsome than she thought he could ever be. His hair was short, and he was neatly shaved. His clothes fit him perfectly. She was suddenly very jealous of the well-endowed cheerleader hanging on his arm, flirting with him. Once she caught Luke staring at her. Their eyes met, and she smiled at him, but he didn't smile back.

Justin was aware of the rift he had caused with Luke and knew the big guy was still angry. They'd been friends, and he needed to ease the tension with his teammate. "Ashley, would you mind trading partners with Luke and Bernice for one dance?"

She thought Justin had read her mind but casually agreed, trying not to seem too eager. They approached the other couple. "We wondered if you two would like to trade dance partners for one song?" Justin asked.

"Sure, whatever," Luke said rather coldly. He knew Bernice would jump at the chance to be with Justin; he dropped her hand while simultaneously reaching out to Ashley. The couples followed each other to the dance floor. It was a slow song. Luke put his arms around Ashley but didn't talk at first, just stared off into space as they moved with the music.

Ashley finally broke the ice. "Are you having fun?"

"Sure."

"Good," she said. "You look nice, all fancy and handsome."

"I had help. How about you and Mr. Dreamy?"

"He's nice." She looked over at Justin, who was laughing at something the cheerleader had said.

"Are you going to let him kiss you?"

"Yes, if he asks."

"And anything else?"

"No. You know me."

"I was going to ask you to homecoming, you know." He pulled her in a little closer.

"I was waiting, but you never called."

"Sorry. I'm slow. Will you go out with me sometime?"

"Of course." She smiled up at him.

"Will you go with me to the prom?" He inhaled hard.

"That's in April," she said, and her eyes almost crinkled closed in amusement.

"I don't want to be late next time." Luke turned serious. "So, how about it?"

"Yes, I'll go with you to the prom. I can't wait. But right now, we'd better get back to our dates." The music had ended, and everyone else had left the dance floor. Justin and the cheerleader were standing back, watching them. Ashley reached up and patted Luke's cheek. "You be careful with Bernice, okay?"

The couples walked back across the floor and stood together, laughing and smiling as if nothing had ever been wrong.

"Seems like everything is going well," Brock said to Celia.

"There's a lot of drama going on out there," Celia said. She'd been watching the couples.

"There's always drama between men and women." Brock stared down at the punch he was swirling in his cup.

"Do you want to talk about it?" she asked.

"I have a feeling you aren't staying here with me," he said over the din of the music.

"At the dance?" She ran her fingers down his arm, stopping at his wrist.

"You know what I mean. You're going back to Seattle, aren't you?"

She dropped her head. "I'm so sorry. I just can't fit in here. I know you're happy in the Grove, but I'm not. And I know you need to stay with your mom, and I can understand that. But when it's over, you need to come back so it can be like it used to be."

The music stopped abruptly in the middle of her sentence, and a few students overheard what she said. It didn't take long for the word to spread that Coach Gallagher's wife wanted him to leave the Grove. They could see the pain in his face and knew there was some adult drama happening.

CHAPTER 38

MELTDOWN

CELIA AND BROCK danced to a couple of slow songs at homecoming, and later that night, they made love for the first time since she'd arrived. But to Brock, it seemed she was just going through the motions. When they finished, she rolled onto her side, away from him, and pretended she was asleep. In the morning, she prepared to leave the farm.

"I wish you didn't have to go," Irene said as she fixed her daughter-in-law some yogurt with strawberries and a cup of coffee. But Celia said she needed to get back to Seattle, while insisting she'd enjoyed the visit. Irene appreciated the white lie.

Brock walked Celia to the door and gave her a hug. "When will I see you again?" he asked.

"Maybe when your football season is over or whenever, you know…" she nodded to Irene, still in the kitchen.

"Understood. Well, be safe on the road. You seem tired all the time. I don't want you falling asleep at the wheel."

She kissed his cheek and climbed into her car. The vanity plate reading ILUVART disappeared behind the road dust as she maneuvered down the driveway. He could feel her slipping away at this moment and in their marriage. "I'm losing her," he said softly to himself, although Sassy heard and stared up at him.

He and the dog walked slowly down the drive, following the dust until she was out of sight. He stood by the road, waiting for his mind to clear. He told himself he had to move on without her … at least for now. He turned and walked back toward the house, purposely shifting his mind back to the football team. The Grizzlies now had a 3–2 record, and two more wins in the next four games would be enough to get them into a mini playoff. There was a chance. That thought eased his pain.

The Thomasville Titans were next on the schedule, and from the film Brock watched, it was the team most closely matched in every category to his own. Thankfully, Luke and Justin had stopped their feuding, and the trip to Thomasville was a short drive, so the boys would be fresh and ready to go.

Brock's only concern was the reputation of the opposing coach. He was known for working over the referees to sway their decision-making. It was the wild card. The officials in the first five games had been honest and capable, but Brock hadn't met the crew for the Thomasville game and would have to wait to see how they handled the situation on Friday.

That concern quickly became a meaningless footnote on Wednesday morning when Don Baker's wife called. "They flew Don to the metropolitan hospital last night. They're pretty sure he's suffered a minor heart attack, and he'll be there for at least a couple of days while they do some testing."

Don had been Brock's right-hand man for every practice and game, and now it was as if someone had tied his right arm behind his back. He called Tim and told him the news. "Would you coach on the sideline with me on Friday night? You could call the defenses. My uncle has agreed to man the headset up in the booth."

"I can't freakin' wait," Tim said. His voice seemed to burst from the telephone. "I'm sorry 'bout Don. Hope he's all right. But man, I can't wait till Friday."

When the ball was teed up on the Thomasville field, there was an October bite to the air. A sizable crowd showed up. Many of the Grizzly fans had made the short drive, and since the Titans were on a winning streak, hundreds of their fans were stacked into their old wooden bleachers.

Justin was on his game early, connecting with his receivers. Jimmy snagged four before halftime, and Les and George each had a couple of catches. However, when the team got into the red zone, the Titan defense stiffened and held their ground. Several scoring opportunities were negated by yellow flags thrown by the referees, especially the white hat umpire, who seemed to be listening to the Titans coach more than he was watching the action. Fortunately, Luke scored on a simple dive play early in the game, but those were the only numbers on the board. Glory Grove led 7–0 at halftime.

Tim, up close to the action, was disturbed by what he was seeing. "Brock, those refs have it out for us," he said as they walked to the dressing room. "Somethin' stinks like rotten cow guts here."

"Nothing we can do about it," Brock said. "We'll have to beat them on the field. We can't win with the referees."

"You're right, but I'm gettin' mighty pissed at that white hat."

"Just focus on the defense, Tim. We won't win this game by complaining about the officials."

The Titans took the second-half kickoff straight to the end zone for a touchdown. Tim and the Grizzly fans could see why.

"Dammit, ref; there was a block in the back right in front of you. Get that flag out of your pocket," Tim screamed. "How could you not see that?"

"Back off, Coach," said the ref. "I didn't see anything."

Brock hurried down the line in front of his players and put his hand on Tim's shoulder. "Let it go. They won't change their minds. Quit worrying about the officials."

But Tim was caught up in the action and the calls the referees were making, whether they were intentional or out of incompetence. When he'd been in the booth, he could scream into Brock's ear, but on the sideline, close to the action, his emotions were edging up on the anger meter.

When the Titans came out to tack on the extra point and tie the game at 7–7, Tim was too wound up to notice the Thomasville quarterback was the holder on the kick. He should have warned his players of a possible fake extra point. But he was still jawing at the referee when the ball was snapped. When the Grizzly defense swarmed forward trying to block the kick, the quarterback stood up, dropped back three steps, and fired a pass to a receiver open in the corner of the end zone. The two-point conversion was good, and the Titans led, 8–7.

"Are you happy now, ref?" Tim hollered as the official jogged by with his head down, purposely ignoring Tim's outburst.

There was no further scoring late into the fourth quarter. It appeared neither team might score again. But the Grizzlies took possession of the ball with over two minutes left on the clock and enough time for one final drive. With a combination of Luke's dive plays and quick out-routes to Jimmy, the boys from the Grove methodically marched to the ten-yard line with three seconds left on the clock.

MELTDOWN

Brock was convinced Justin could kick a short field goal, and his team could leave Thomasville with a victory. He sent in the play, and Justin and his holder lined up for an all-but-sure field goal. The Grove fans were abuzz in anticipation of the winning play. The snap was perfect. The placement by Les was good. Justin took two steps and casually sent the ball spinning through the uprights, then raised his arms as if he'd just made a perfect toss in a carnival arcade for a giant stuffed animal.

The Glory Grove players and fans were ecstatic. They were so busy celebrating that they failed to see the yellow flag lying on the ground in the middle of the field, thrown by the referee in the white hat.

"Holding," he said, grasping his left wrist with his right hand.

On the Grizzlies sidelines, there was a sickening silence. But Brock seemed unruffled. He knew Justin could still kick the game winner, even with the ball placed ten yards further back. But Tim, who'd reached his boiling point, was outraged, not thinking rationally or strategically.

"You son of a bitch," he screamed at the ref. "Why don't you just give 'em the game ball. You've been trying to give them the win all night. How much did their coach pay you?"

Tim's son, Luke, and his Grove teammates were watching the meltdown, shocked by the adult's behavior and wondering if there would be repercussions. It didn't take long to find out. Another yellow flag went flying.

"Penalty for unsportsmanlike conduct on the Glory Grove bench," the referee said, glaring at Tim. "That will be fifteen yards."

With the mark-off, the ball was moved back out of field goal range. There were still three seconds left to try a long pass to the end zone, but the Titan defense knew what was coming and blanketed the Grove receivers. They easily batted down the pass. The game was over, and the Grizzlies had their third loss of the season.

Tim went silent. He stared at the ground and couldn't look at Brock or Luke. He'd cost the team a win. He swore under his breath, but this time his profanity was aimed at himself.

CHAPTER 39

ORATOR

MONDAY, AFTER THE THOMASVILLE GAME, Brock scurried around to finish the farm chores before heading to town. He'd grudgingly agreed to be the guest speaker at the monthly luncheon meeting of the local Grove Givers Service Club. The members prided themselves in doing public service, and at each meeting, they'd invite a special guest to deliver an upbeat message.

Brock had planned to share good news about the resurgence of Grizzly football. But the meltdown at Thomasville didn't fit the script. It wasn't the steppingstone he needed to launch a winning speech. Speaking was his least favorite part of coaching football. Even at Brighton, where he was treated as a celebrity, he dreaded the days he'd have to entertain a crowd with his wit and inside information.

This, he thought, *might be his toughest crowd... locals who knew him personally and some who might not wish him well.* When he pulled into town, Brock noticed there were a lot of cars and pickups parked along

Main Street. There must be something special going on downtown. He parked his car three blocks away, and as he strolled up the street, it hit him ... all those people were in the steak house.

Conrad Newton, who had headed the Grizzly team for the last seven years, always refused to speak at these meetings. So, when the public found out Brock was obliging the Service Club, and they had a chance to gather and talk about the Grizzlies, they turned out in force. It was the biggest crowd the club had seen since the governor made a brief whistle-stop tour there a decade earlier, and the crowd had responded out of civic responsibility.

"Thanks for coming, Brock." It was the club's president, an always happy man, who greeted him at the door. "People are anxious to hear your speech," he said, slapping Brock on the back. As they made their way into the dining area, Brock could feel every eye turn their way. The crowd was eating and laughing, hurrying through their meal. As Brock sat and picked at his hot-beef sandwich, a knot was growing in his stomach. He hadn't expected such a large crowd.

When he took the podium, the crowd quieted. He began. "As you know, my name is Brock Gallagher, and I used to play football here in Glory Grove." The audience surprised Brock by applauding. "And I'm very pleased to be back in town to coach the young men of this community. I hoped I could come here today with my team sporting a winning record. Unfortunately, we have as many losses as we do wins. We've had our ups and downs and a few close calls, but I think the future looks bright."

Brock talked about some of his players and what the remaining schedule looked like. He'd spoken for about fifteen minutes when he noticed a few of the older citizens in the crowd starting to doze off. *It was time*, he thought, *to open it up to questions*. But once he did, he regretted it. As the questions rolled out, they became more personal and biting.

"Don't you think you might be more successful if you ran the offense like your old Coach Sullivan?" quizzed the first man to begin the questioning. "It seems like your players might be a little soft."

Another sympathized with the team's loss of Don Baker from the previous game. "We know Don's in the hospital. Maybe you could ask for volunteers to help you out. It seems your friend Tim can't handle that responsibility by himself."

One of Cort's allies stood and angrily accused Brock of holding back the talents of the quarterback, Justin Jepson. "That boy is capable of winning every game if you'd just throw the ball a little more. You should be throwing the ball forty times a game."

Each of the questions elevated the desire for others to speak their mind. The town's seed dealer said, "We have all noticed your offense centers on some of the students new to the Grove. Do you think they should be taking the place of the local boys?"

Brock was patient, trying to handle each of the queries diplomatically. But the last question he fielded bothered him more than the others. It suggested part of the reason the boys were losing games was their sense that their new coach might only be there one season. "Can you expect them to give one hundred percent if they think you might not be here long?" Brock couldn't decide whether to be angry or frustrated with the level of suspicion and disrespect. He could defend his players all day long, and he knew he was a good coach. There probably wasn't anyone in the state who could have done better with the situation he'd been handed. Finally, he'd taken enough second-guessing.

"Well," his fingers strummed the podium, "I see the town has as many opinions as it did when I left eighteen years ago. I'm glad that hasn't changed. Your questions show you all care. You've asked good ones, and they don't have easy answers. But I can assure you the boys are trying their hardest. And I'm doing my best to help them. Don't give up on us. The boys aren't giving up … and you shouldn't either."

The club president stepped in and addressed the crowd. "I think we should all be happy with the job Coach Gallagher is doing. It was a long year without Friday night football. We might be a bit pushy wanting to get this program back on track, but I think we all understand it can't happen overnight. I personally want to thank Brock for accepting this job. It's not easy, but if anyone can do it, it will be Coach Gallagher. Now, if you would, let's give him a round of applause for coming here today."

As the audience rose to their feet and applauded, Brock bowed his head for a moment to let it soak in, then looked up and said thank you several times. He made eye contact with as many people as he could. He hadn't completely won over the crowd, but he'd shown enough courage to take on his hometown.

Don Baker was back on Monday, looking as spry as ever. "False alarm," he said, waving off their concern. "They put me through every test you can imagine and determined I was over-caffeinated. Told me to avoid stress and to stop drinking so much coffee. So, it'll be decaf every morning at the Cozy Corner." He shook his head at the thought. "Sorry for putting you in that situation against Thomasville. You can count on me being on the sideline for Liberty," he said.

The boys were shaken by how their game against Thomasville had unraveled at the end. They'd lost two games they should have won and now were 3–3, with the chance of making the playoffs slipping away. But their next game with the Liberty Hawks could put them back on a winning track. The week of practice was intense. Luke, more than anyone else, was giving extra effort. If it hadn't been for his dad's temper, the team would have won the game with Thomasville. If they could get a victory Friday, people might forgive his dad.

Liberty was a private school, a member of their old league. They'd only lost one game in the season, running a wing-T offense, keeping the ball on the ground, controlling the clock, and limiting the opponents' offensive opportunities. Brock focused his practices on defense, teaching the boys how to key on certain players to determine where the ball was and where it was going. By the middle of the week, he felt they were ready. Thursday night practice would be a simple walk-through.

Before the team left the locker room, Augie Swenson came running to Brock. "Coach, I left my football cleats at home. Can I go get them?" Brock knew where Augie lived, on the farm six miles south of town.

"Augie, it's a walk-through. Practice in your sneakers." But Augie was embarrassed and said he could be at practice on time if he hurried.

"Okay, but don't drive fast."

Augie sprinted from the locker room toward the parking lot, churning his thick stump-like legs. Brock suddenly regretted his decision to let him go. He didn't like nervous teenagers driving fast on country gravel roads.

When practice began, Augie hadn't returned. After warm-ups, the coaches started the walk-through. Augie was one of his most reliable players, so Brock assumed he'd been delayed somehow. Then he heard the sirens. First the wailing of the fire engine, followed by the high-pitched shriek of an ambulance.

Word traveled fast in the little town. Soon, a messenger from the school came to the field with the news; Augie had been in an accident. It was serious. Brock clenched the football he'd been holding and looked across the field at the other young men in his charge. He'd told Augie he could leave. But why? It was only a walk-through. He could have practiced in his sneakers. Now, what if he'd been killed. He dropped the football to the ground.

CHAPTER 40

AUGIE

BROCK CANCELED the rest of practice. Before he dismissed the team, he gathered them together, told them what he knew, and suggested they say a prayer for Augie. And then he told them to get their minds ready for a game with Liberty. He wouldn't let himself or the team think about the worst-case scenario.

The players gathered around fellow sophomore Derek Baker, Augie's best friend, who, despite being visibly shaken, led his teammates in prayer. A tear trickled down his face as he finished. Brock always thought Derek looked childlike, with his chubby cheeks and round eyes. Now he resembled a sad old man, worried and worn.

When Derek finished, Brock waved his players off the field and jogged to his car. He hurried to the police station, his heart pounding.

"They've airlifted him to the regional hospital," the dispatcher said. "He's in bad shape with multiple injuries. They won't know more until they get him there. The officer said it was pretty ugly."

"Was he speeding?" Brock clenched his jaw … sure of the answer.

"They don't know. Said he just drove off the side of the road into an embankment, and the car rolled. It could have killed him, but he had his seatbelt on. They think maybe he was on his phone."

Brock's guilt eased, but not enough to make him feel any better. He'd been the last one to talk to Augie. He shouldn't have let him go. Now he needed to get to the hospital to be with the Swenson family. It was an hour's drive, and Brock spent most of it second-guessing himself. For his entire tenure as a head coach, he'd dreaded the day one of his players might die, whether on the field or off. Could he find enough courage to perform as a coach under those circumstances?

Brock knew the Swenson family well. They were the first ones to host the traditional Thursday night team dinner. They were a close-knit group, supportive of Augie and the Grizzlies and would be strong whatever the outcome of this tragedy.

When Brock walked into the hospital, he noticed its sanitized smell and gleaming fixtures. Miracles happened in these places with modern medicine and therapy. He slipped into the elevator and pushed a button for the intensive care unit on the third floor. He found the family sitting in the waiting room and approached slowly, trying not to impose if he wasn't wanted.

"Thanks for coming, Brock." Augie's mother was the first to speak when she saw him coming through the door. A strong woman with erect posture, her round face was lined with worry wrinkles.

"How is he?" asked Brock, fearing the worst.

"A lot of internal injuries, they said, but they don't think there is any damage to his head. We can be thankful for that."

"It's my fault," Brock said. "I let him go home to get his cleats. I shouldn't have let him go."

"Don't even think that. It was an accident, that's all. And if anyone is at fault, it's me. He was talking to me on his phone, wanting me to get his shoes out so he could hurry back to practice. He loves football. And you as his coach." Her lips quivered. "We've told him a hundred times to stay off his phone when he's driving. He knew better. But I know he'll fight with everything he's got to get back on the football field. Maybe not this year, but someday." She forced a smile.

"Yes ma'am. I know so."

Brock stayed in the waiting room with the Swenson family throughout the long night. No one slept. They talked about Augie and the team. And of the generations of Swensons who had played ball for Glory Grove. Augie lived through the night, and when the doctor came to consult with them early in the morning, he said with each passing hour, the boy's chances of survival were better.

Upon hearing the news, Augie's dad took Brock by the arm. "Go home, Coach. Your team has a game to play, and they need you. The best news Augie could hear was that you met Liberty and came home with a win."

"We'll do our best," Brock said. "Thanks for letting me sit with you. We're going to miss Augie tonight. I'll have the boys say a prayer for him before the game. He'll be in our hearts."

Brock filled a thermos full of coffee from the hospital cafeteria and began the long drive home. His eyes drooped, but with each passing milepost, his mind filled with thoughts of the Swensons and the love they had for their boy.

As the sun rose in the mid-October sky, streaks of crimson and gold broke over the mountaintops signaling the beginning of a crisp autumn day. Brock shielded his eyes and focused on the white line running down the highway. Football, once the top priority in his life, suddenly didn't seem all that important.

Brock slept a few restless hours, then woke and got Don Baker on the phone. They needed to decide, not about whether to play the game—the Swenson family had insisted—but who would take Augie's place at center. It was the key to the contest, particularly against a ball-control team like Liberty. A few turnovers and the contest could easily get away from the Grizzlies. They decided to put Wally Thompson, a junior, in Augie's place.

Before the boys loaded the bus for the trip to Liberty, Wally practiced snapping the ball into Justin's hands. It looked simple, but without practice, it wasn't. The mechanics were slow and tentative. Eventually, after dozens of attempts, the actions improved.

As the team gathered in the visitor's locker room before the game, Brock asked the boys for silence. "Fellas, you all know Augie is hurt, and he's fighting for his life. If you remember, I told you when we first met that we had to become like a family for this team to succeed. Now one of our brothers is in trouble. You know how much Augie loves football. I want you all to give every ounce of effort you can find within yourselves to win this game, for the team, for Glory Grove, and especially for your friend and teammate. You know he's here in spirit. Now, let's say a silent prayer and then get out there and win this game."

The team bowed their heads, each boy saying his own version of "Please, God, make Augie well." Wally Thompson added a postscript to his prayer, saying, "And help me get the ball into Justin's hands."

Luke broke the silence. "Let's win this frickin' game for Augie," he yelled. The boys, relieved to be free of the emotion of the moment, all screamed at once and hustled out the door.

The pregame high soon wore off. The Hawks took the opening kickoff and, using their ball-control plays, succeeded in using up most of the first-quarter clock with a long-sustained drive into the end zone.

That was followed by an early fumble on the center exchange between Wally and Justin. Again, the Liberty team put together a long drive resulting in a second touchdown.

"We need to hold onto the ball," Brock scolded the team as they prepared for the kickoff. At first, it seemed as if they responded. Jimmy returned the kickoff to midfield, and Justin went to work. Unlike the time-consuming drive of the Hawks, the Grizzlies moved down the field quickly. They were ready to cash in from the five-yard line when Augie's absence made itself known again.

Justin readied himself behind Wally, ready to run a simple quarterback sneak for the touchdown. He'd noticed the Hawks anticipating his snap count, so he changed it to "go on two." But Wally, new to the position, nervously snapped the football early. It dropped between Justin's legs, and in the ensuing scrum, a Hawk linebacker pulled it under his belly as he lay on the ground. The scoring opportunity yielded no points. When the half ended the Grizzlies trailed 14–0.

As the Glory Grove coaches walked together to the locker room, Brock asked Don and Tim for their opinions.

"I can't stand that ball-control crap," Tim grumbled. He shook his head as he kept pace with Brock. "I wish they'd just play football." Tim was desperate for a Grizzly win so people would forget how he'd cost them the game against the Thomasville Titans.

"It's not the most exciting offense in the world, but they're sure good at it," Don said. "It works especially well when we keep turning the ball over. If we can clean that up, maybe we have a chance. You can't blame Wally. We're asking a lot of him, and at this point, we can't replace him."

But things didn't get any better in the second half. The Grizzlies had spotted the Hawks too many points. Despite their efforts, the boys from Glory Grove, their energy fueled with thoughts of Augie, couldn't work their way out of their predicament.

When it was over, they walked off the field with their heads hanging. They'd let down their friend who was miles away fighting for his life. Why couldn't the game have had a fairy tale ending? Their prayers for a victory had not been answered. But they should have considered something more important. The prayers for Augie Swenson seemed to have made a difference. He was still alive.

CHAPTER 41

CHILL

IRENE'S DOCTORS were keeping a close eye on her lab results. Her most recent readings showed her bile duct cancer was again spreading. Surgery was deemed necessary, and it needed to be done immediately. The news was a blow to the family. They'd hoped the dangerous procedure could be avoided.

"Might as well get this over with," Irene said. She was disappointed but, in her heart, had assumed surgery would eventually be needed.

Brock was so focused on Augie's accident he'd almost put his mother's situation out of mind. Once again, it was front and center. He'd returned to Glory Grove for this reason … to help his mom through these tough times. Now it meant dividing his attention between his job as a football coach and being a good son.

The surgery was scheduled for Wednesday, following the team's home game with the Willitas Chiefs, in the same hospital where Augie was making his recovery. Willitas was a small school from the neighboring Indian Reservation. They were known for their successful basketball teams, but in all sports, they were notorious for their tenaciousness. But late into the football season, their minds would often turn to the hardwood, where they frequently hung championship banners in their high school gymnasium. Brock hoped Willitas was in a basketball mood. After his team's back-to-back losses, their postseason hopes hinged on this game.

The week leading up to the contest tested both the players and the coaches. Brock was constantly thinking about his mom and Augie. Or he was downhearted over his wife leaving him to go back to the city.

His friend, Tim, was despondent. He'd cost his son's team a victory in the game against Thomasville, and until the Grizzlies could put a win on the board, he couldn't rest. He began taking afternoons off work and showing up at practice. When Tim was in high school, he'd been coached by Coach Sullivan, a tough guy who'd push his players to exhaustion. Now, Tim was beginning to act like the old coach.

Don Baker, who'd backed off his caffeine consumption to regulate his heart, was experiencing withdrawal headaches. It made the afternoons on the field torturous. The pain was exacerbated by his attempts to remedy the turnover problem that plagued the team.

The players were also out of sorts. Justin was beginning to buckle under the pressure from his dad, who constantly berated Coach Gallagher for the losses. Luke, meanwhile, was notified by his teachers that the nine-week grading period was almost over, and he needed to pick up the pace, or he'd be ineligible for the last games of the football season.

Jimmy hurried home from practice each night to be with Irene. He was sick with worry over the upcoming surgery facing the woman he'd come to love. And the entire team was depressed over the absence of Augie Swenson. They'd tried to win a game for him but couldn't deliver.

Wintry winds blew down from the ridge over Glory Grove, as if icy fingers were wrapping around the soul of the team. The chill seemed to signal an end to the joy and contentment of early fall football as the autumn colors disappeared from the landscape. It was a message to the players that from here on, it would be the kind of grind only champion caliber teams would embrace.

With the turmoil playing on everyone's nerves, practice turned into bickering and scuffles. The usual camaraderie among the boys was disintegrating. When Luke hollered at a teammate, he'd be met with condemnation of his effort.

The sour emotions channeled into sloppy play. Jimmy couldn't hang onto the football, even in the simplest drills. And the receivers, faced with the new challenge of attempting to catch a spiral with icy fingers, often let the ball hit the turf.

Brock needed to bring his team back together. A Thursday night team dinner held at the home of the Simpson brothers offered the opportunity. When the boys all gathered to fill their plates with the offerings of Mrs. Simpson, a soft-spoken rotund woman known for her talents in the kitchen, Brock said he wanted to say a few words.

"It's been a rough week," he said. "We all have things going on in our lives that make us a little uneasy. I have some problems of my own. My mother, Irene, is our team's biggest fan. But this Friday may be the last game she'll be able to watch this season. She's having surgery next week to try to stop her cancer." He swallowed hard, pausing to catch his emotions and steady his voice. "It's a dangerous operation, and it will take a long time for her to recover.

"I know many of you are thinking about Augie and his struggles. The good news, from what I've heard, is he has every chance of making a full recovery. But he won't play football again this year."

Brock strode across the room toward Luke and Justin. "I'm aware some of you are facing difficulties of your own. But you need to recognize that this is also part of life. We all have challenges. Life is going to throw some roadblocks in front of you to test your will. But it's the true champions in life who can meet those challenges. Don't fear them but let them make you tougher and more determined. I think this group is as tough a bunch of boys as I've ever coached. I know from your character you won't disappoint me."

Brock could see some of the boys nodding their heads and noticed Mrs. Simpson wiping her eyes. He'd made his point but wanted to end his talk in a positive way. "Starting tomorrow, we're going to turn this emotion we've been feeling into passion on the field. The only way we can feel better about ourselves is to go out and play the best football we've played all year. We're going to do it right here at home for our fans. They've been patient, waiting for us to show them how good this team can be."

He motioned to the table overflowing with food. "Now, fill your plates and sit down like a family because that's what we are. And get ready for tomorrow." There was a hushed silence in the room. Brock was afraid he'd been too dramatic with his talk. But suddenly the Simpson brothers, the two linemen who protected Justin's blind side and were hosting the dinner, rose from their chairs. Neither was boisterous in school or on the football field, but they were hard workers, never complaining.

"Coach," the older brother began in a soft voice, "my mom and dad wanted me to say how pleased we are to share our home with you." His words came out deliberately, as if he were reading off a script. "It's a great honor for us to have you come here to our house. And my brother and I want to say how much we enjoy being with you all, even when things aren't going so well. It's been a bad couple of weeks, and we don't like losing, but we think we can do better. It's just taken us a while to come together after last year, and we've been playing a weird schedule. But we think now is the time."

He let out a sigh, relieved to have finished, then turned to his younger brother and asked if there was anything he wanted to add. The boy blushed but slowly stood up to speak. "I think you will like the barbecued ribs my mom made. She's a pretty good cook. That's all," he said and sat down.

Everyone chuckled at his awkwardness, then got up out of their chairs, forming a line to fill their plates. They ate until all the food was gone and then sat and talked for another hour before wandering off to get some rest before the Friday game.

The cold weather that plagued the team all week kept its grip on the town as the teams took the field for the game. Still, the Glory Grove fans showed up in large numbers. Their hometown boys had a chance to even their season record at 4–4, and it had been three weeks since they'd played a home game. The town knew of Augie Swenson's accident and his struggles to recover. And word had spread around the community, via the church ladies, of the upcoming surgery for Irene. But hard times bound this community together like gauze on a wound. In shared concern, they rallied to support one another.

"Let's go make it happen," Brock hollered at the players as they jogged out of the locker room, their cleats clacking across the concrete floor. After the opening whistle, it wasn't long before it became clear the boys from Glory Grove were ready to play. The turnover mistakes they made in the game with Liberty were rectified. On offense, the team moved with flawless precision. Justin was on target with almost every pass, whether a thirty-yard bomb to Jimmy or a short crossing route to Les or George. The receivers, despite their cold, numb hands, were making the catches look easy.

Luke, now fully recovered from his leg injury, elicited oohs and aahs from the fans with his punishing blasts into the middle of the line as a fullback and crushing tackles on defense from his linebacker position. The one outstanding player for the Chiefs, a stout, two-hundred-pound Native American boy sporting a braided ponytail hanging to the middle of his back, challenged Luke with a violent level of play throughout the first half of the contest. The two young men verbally jousted with one another early, raising the level of physicality after each encounter. But by the second half, the Willitas boy had begun avoiding contact whenever he could. He'd had enough of the big man from Denver and was thinking ahead to basketball.

The coaches were almost silent on the sidelines, recognizing something special was happening. Tim, in the booth above the grandstand, made a point of speaking on the headphones only when Brock asked him a question. He, too, could see the boys taking control of the game and didn't want to spoil it.

Midway through the fourth quarter, Tim finally spoke. "Hey Brock, do you know the school record for passing yards for Glory Grove?"

Brock knew the answer because he was sure he still held the mark … 526 yards from a game his senior year. "What's up?" he asked out of curiosity.

"The stat girl up here says Justin is way over 500 yards and wondered if it might be a record."

"Okay, let me know when he is over 550, and we'll have Jerry announce it to the crowd over the PA system."

"Good as done. The kid deserves the moment. He's played a heck of a game."

"They all have," Brock said.

After three more passes were completed, the announcement was made. "Justin Jepson has just set a school record for passing yards, eclipsing the record set by Grizzly coach Gallagher many years ago," said Jerry Glenn. "Let's give the young man a round of applause."

The audience stood and clapped, acknowledging they'd witnessed something special from their quarterback. Justin's dad, Cort, in a fog from the flask he and his friends were passing around, stood and faced the crowd, whistling and cheering, to draw attention to himself as the father of the quarterback.

"Way to go, Justin. You're the man," he shouted. Ronnie clapped politely.

When the final horn sounded, the Grizzlies had rung up forty-seven points and given up only a single touchdown. Cheers and laughter rang out from the crowd as the twenty-four boys in uniform huddled on the field. Forming a circle with hands joined, they bowed their heads. This time it was Jimmy who spoke. "Thank you, Lord, for keeping us safe tonight and for letting us play so good. Please help Augie get well soon and take good care of Coach Gallagher's mom, Irene. We know you'll be with them. Amen."

"Amen," said the other boys.

"Grizzlies on three," Luke shouted. And the boys, at the top of their lungs, repeated their team's name and broke ranks, rushing to the sideline, anxious to be with their family and friends.

The happiness was infectious. The chill wind had quieted. There was a new warmth on the field. Moms and dads hugged their sons. Cameras clicked. Little boys hung on the legs of their heroes. Lester

Colquit, who'd once been despised by the citizens of Glory Grove and had now become a fixture at football games in his bright red winter coat, embraced his son, who was surprised by the gesture.

Brock sought out his mother standing at the foot of the grandstand. She smiled up at him, her blue eyes sparkling. "If this is the last game I see for a while, it was a great finish," she said, patting Brock on his arm.

"You better plan on coming back," Brock said. "We finally have a team that's ready to play. You're not going to want to miss this." He wouldn't admit to himself; it really could be her last game. That thought would spoil the night.

The moment of reflection was broken by his uncle, who strolled up to join the pair, a big grin on his face. "Sorry about you losing your passing record," he joked. "I guess you're just a little footnote in the record books now."

"He deserved it," Brock said. "I'm glad to relinquish the honor." He waved his arm in a forward circle, imitating the gesture of a nobleman. As he finished the act, Cort Jepson grabbed his shoulder from behind.

"He's a helluva lot better quarterback than you ever were," he said with slurred words. "Nice that you finally let him show it. He could have done it all season long if you'd have let him."

Politely but to the point, Irene said, "Mr. Jepson, would you please just enjoy the moment. Your son was terrific. Maybe you should try being more like him."

"Quiet down, old woman," Cort shot back. "Stay out of it. This has got nothin' to do with you."

Ronnie, who had been talking with friends in the grandstand, saw what was happening. She hurried down the stairs and grabbed her husband's arm. "We're leaving now," she said to Cort. "Let's go congratulate Justin. It's his big night."

"I'll go when I damned well please," Cort said, glaring at his wife.

"I think you should go," Brock said. He squared his shoulders. "And don't ever speak to my mother like that again. You know what can happen."

"Anytime, shit head," Cort said, raising his voice so those on the field could hear. He spun around, breaking free of his wife as he pushed her out in front of him. "Let's get away from these people before we catch some kind of disease," he said.

As she stumbled away, with Cort's hand on her back, Ronnie turned and looked at Irene. "I'm so sorry," she said.

"Me too," Brock said under his breath. "Me too."

CHAPTER 42

SURVIVAL

THE HEADLINE on the Saturday morning sports page told of Justin Jepson's passing record. But Brock wasn't concerned about the newspaper. He had more serious things on his mind. On Wednesday, his mother was having surgery. And he couldn't get his confrontations with Cort Jepson out of his mind. He'd tried his best to avoid the man since coming home to the Grove, but they continued to butt heads. Now, Cort's disrespect for his mother had him angrier than ever. He needed to vent, so he called Tim.

"Sure. Let me bring my horse, and we'll go riding," Tim said. "I'll be there in an hour."

Brock threw a saddle on Babe while Jimmy was playing catch with Sassy. Irene was busy in the kitchen.

"You all right, Coach?" Jimmy asked. "You should be happy 'bout our game last night. I thought we played a great game."

"Especially you," Brock said, giving a quick wink to his running back. "I don't think you let a single pass hit the ground. Helped Justin set a school record. You and Les and George … like you all had glue on your hands. If you guys keep it up, you never know how far we might go."

As he finished the sentence, Brock could hear the rumble of Tim's Dodge pickup turning at the mailbox. "Tim and I are going for a ride," he told Jimmy. "We need to clear our minds a little. Why don't you go keep Mom company? I'll be back pretty soon."

Tim rolled in, unloaded his horse, and the two men headed for the piney ridge at a slow trot. The air was still chilled, but the winds had settled down, so the ride was peaceful and exhilarating in the morning air. The scent of the pine forest was fresh, and dew made the bromegrass shimmer in the morning sun.

As they slowed their horses to climb the steep incline, the sunshine and heat radiating off the animals warmed the men. When they reached the summit, they dismounted and found an old log where they could sit—not too close—but a comfortable manly distance from one another. Tim poured coffee from a thermos he pulled from his saddlebag and passed a cup to Brock.

"Okay, what's up, Rocket?" Tim asked. He'd noticed Brock's downcast appearance. "You have a problem?"

Brock was silent for a time. He shook his head and stared straight ahead. Finally, he admitted, "I don't know what to do about Cort."

"I know what I'd like to do with that son of a bitch."

"No one knows, but he and I already came to blows right before the season started," Brock admitted. "I lost my temper and smacked him in the face. Knocked him down. I'm probably lucky he didn't press charges."

"Yup, but I'm pretty sure he wouldn't admit to anyone that you got the best of him," Tim said.

"But last night, he got in my face again—insulted my mom. I'd had enough but knew it would look bad—a head coach getting in a fight with the father of his quarterback after a game. But, Tim, he's making his son miserable. And he's awfully rough on Ronnie. I wish I could do something, but I don't want to set him off. What's his problem anyway?"

"Aw, he's had a burr under his saddle for a long time. Drinks too much. And spends a lot of time feeling sorry for himself. Not a good combination. But he has a strong dislike for you, that's for sure. Hell, it started clear back in high school. Jealous of you, I guess. And that time in the championship game keeps haunting him. Wasn't your fault he got hurt." Tim picked up a stone and spun it hard off the cliff, listening to it ricochet down the canyon wall.

"I'm not so sure, Tim. We needed to score, but I knew calling that play, sending him across the middle against their stud linebacker, was dangerous. But I'd heard enough of his lip and wasn't happy with him hanging around my girlfriend. Maybe down deep, I wanted to see him get hurt. I don't know."

"Cripe, everybody gets hurt eventually, playing the game. But everybody else mans up and goes on. He's living in the past, and now he's trying to live in the future through his boy. But somebody sure as hell needs to put him in his place. Maybe I need to have a little man-to-man with our old friend."

Brock was silent again. "Let's try to get through the next few games. I'll stay out of his way and encourage Justin to try to ignore all the nonsense he's getting at home. Maybe after the season, Cort will cool off a bit."

Tim turned to face his friend. "I think you're dreaming. He's not going to stop. But I'll do whatever you say; you're the boss … at least until the season is over. Maybe then it'll be my turn to flatten his nose."

The two friends sat for a time listening to the sound of the wind through the trees as if it were a song calming their anxiety. Finally, Brock stirred. "Let's head back," he said. "I've got a few things to do before I take Mom to the hospital on Wednesday. I'm counting on you and Don to cover practice for me until I get back. We have a big game coming up. If we get our fifth win on Friday against Brookside, we'll earn a ticket to a play-in game with our old league champion. I think it's within reach if we can get past all the distractions."

"Then we'll be ridin' high," Tim laughed as he swung his big frame into the saddle.

Early Wednesday morning, Brock drove Irene to the hospital. The procedure would remove the tumors from her liver before they could spread. It was a serious operation, especially for someone of Irene's age. But the doctors said many of the patients who'd undergone the operation made sufficient recovery to resume a normal life for a time. However, there was no guarantee the cancer wouldn't return.

Brock got his mom checked in and sat with her as she filled out paperwork and went through preliminary testing. There were enough breaks in the protocol for them to talk. They visited about the farm and what would happen to it if she failed to survive the operation. Could Richard run the farm?

The conversation eventually veered away and touched on the personal. Irene wanted to know about Celia. Would Brock go back to her in Seattle? How was he going to deal with Cort? And how would he feel about leaving the football team after only one season?

Brock smiled and patted her arm, making sure not to disturb the papers she was holding. "Mom, with all these issues, I think it'd be better if you just make it through this operation, so you can help us work these things out."

"Okay, if that's what it's going to take, I'll do my best," she said. Tears were welling up in her eyes, but she managed a smile.

Soon the attendant was there with a gurney. "Are you ready to go, Mrs. Gallagher?" he asked. Irene gave a thumbs-up, squeezed Brock's hand, and without missing a beat, began chatting with the young aide … asking about his life.

Knowing the operation on his mom would take a couple of hours and wanting to get his mind off the seriousness of the procedure, Brock took the elevator up to the third floor and found Augie Swenson. He knocked on the open door and stepped in. "Hello, Augie," Brock said.

The boy jerked his head around from the paper he was reading, and a grin spread across his freckled face. "Oh, hi, Coach," he said, surprised to see Brock at his bedside. "Thanks for coming. Heard the team had a great game Friday. Wish I could have been there."

"The guys were thinking of you, Augie. It's been a struggle without you hiking the ball. But we're getting better. We have to be ready for Brookside."

"You'll get 'em easy, Coach, no problem. Sorry I got everybody all worried about me," Augie said, straining for breath. "That was stupid, me driving into the ditch. I missed out on Justin's record. Doctor says I won't get to play for a while, but he says I should be okay; just going to take some time."

"Don't worry about it. Just try to get healthy and be ready for next year," Brock said. But he already felt guilty knowing he might not be around to coach for another year. Because two floors below, under the glare of the operating room lights, the doctors had begun the tedious process of separating the cancerous tumors from his mother's liver. The results of the surgery would dictate the future.

CHAPTER 43

WRECKAGE

THE BROOKSIDE BOMBERS, another team vying for a playoff position, would sport a winning record when they came to visit. Brock knew they were well coached but also recognized they were using a lot of underclassmen in their starting lineup. He knew his Grizzlies would be able to wear them down physically. "We'll use Luke to run the ball down their throat," he told his assistants. But he'd heard rumors Luke might be struggling with his grades, so he made a call to the school.

"Mr. Colquit, sorry to bother you, but I wanted to make sure none of my players are in trouble because of grades."

"Trust me, Mr. Gallagher, I've been monitoring the situation very carefully. We have another week before the quarter grades come out, and Luke is the only one I worry about. But he's been working hard to catch up in history class. He isn't a good student but puts in the time. Truthfully, the man we hired to replace Conrad Newton isn't a very good teacher. You might think about applying for the job next year if he decides not to come back."

There was a long silence. The offer caught Brock off guard. Colquit had put a roadblock in front of him all summer. Now he was inviting him into the school. It seemed being the father of a football player had somehow changed the principal's attitude.

"Thank you, sir. I'll keep that in mind. By the way, your son has really helped our team. I think you know that. He's a good athlete. Is your wife coming to grips with him playing ball?"

"Not yet. She's still nervous, but I'm going to try to get her to the game Friday. She needs to see Les in action. I think she'd be proud. I know I am. Coach, you've done a good job with the boys. I want to thank you for helping our son. He's never seemed this happy. And his grades are still good."

When Friday night rolled around, the last weekend in October, Lester Colquit was there with his wife. She looked as if she was headed to an execution. The weather seemed fitting for the Halloween season, chilly with a full moon and no wind. The home crowd was anxious to see if their boys could match their performance from a week earlier.

Brock's strategy of pounding the interior of the defense with Luke worked as planned. Each time he carried the ball, he chewed up big yardage. At the end of the first quarter, the Grizzlies had notched a 14–0 lead. But the Bomber coach, a savvy veteran, adjusted his defense, stacking the box, daring the Grizzlies to throw the ball.

"They're loading up the middle," Tim relayed down to Brock. So, Justin was quickly green-lighted to showcase his arm again. A play-action pass to Jimmy was good for a fifty-yard touchdown. And on the next series, short tosses to Les and George added more yards. Each time Les caught the ball, the principal nudged his wife, and she'd look to the field and clap her trembling hands, even though she hadn't seen the play. But she pulled herself more erect each time she heard her son's name announced on the PA system.

Fans, seeing the shift in strategy on the field, were ready for Justin to set another passing record. But in the third quarter, the Bombers recovered a fumble near the Grizzlies' goal line and ran it in for a score. They were creeping back into the contest. The Grizzlies were the better team, but with another break or two, the Bombers had a chance to steal a win.

Still, leading 21–7, another score by the Grizzlies would put an end to any challenge the Bombers might make. Justin's protection had been good all game, and he began holding the ball a second or two longer than he should have to give his receivers a chance to break. "Black formation, 340 streak," Justin called in the huddle, a simple play that sent all three of his receivers sprinting straight down the field. He could pick the one most open to put up a quick score.

Wally Thompson, the center, snapped the ball from a shotgun formation. Justin surveyed the field, fully focused on his receivers, especially Jimmy, who had created separation from the cornerback. With his attention on the receivers, Justin failed to see the safety coming on a blitz. At the last second, he caught sight of him and ducked, but too late. The safety lowered his head, and the two helmets met, sounding like a muted cannon.

Justin dropped to the ground as if he'd been shot. "Oh shit, Brock, he's not moving," Tim said on the headset. The fans didn't make a sound. But to everyone's relief, the quarterback rolled to his stomach, pushed himself off the ground, and staggered to his feet. He wobbled to the huddle, wanting to call another play.

Brock quickly jogged to his signal caller. "Look at me, Justin," he commanded while holding Justin by the shoulder pads. "What's your name, and where are you?"

"Justin, and I'm playing football."

"Who are we playing?"

"Willitas Chiefs."

"Who snaps the ball to you?"

Justin hesitated and looked around. "Augie Swenson?"

Brock had enough training to know Justin had received a head injury. He didn't know how serious but wasn't going to take any chances. Even if it meant losing the game, Justin was going to sit out the remainder of the contest. "Jimmy, take over," he said and led Justin to the sidelines.

"He's doing it again," grumbled Cort, sitting in the stands with his friends. "Justin falls down, and he yanks him." He crumpled up his program and threw it down.

"Cort, he's hurt, can't you see that?" Ronnie said. "Brock's protecting him."

Cort didn't want to hear that name. "He just doesn't want Justin to set another record. Watch, he's going to put in his little black pet to run the show. His adopted kid from the ghetto. Glory Grove doesn't need him here."

Jimmy couldn't hear the remarks. And he wouldn't let the opportunity to play quarterback pass him by. After Brookside pushed across another score to trail by a single touchdown 21–14, Jimmy settled in behind the center and directed the offense like a veteran.

He was quicker than Justin, and with the change of pace, the Bomber defense struggled to contain him as he scrambled out of the pocket. They chased him around the backfield like they were chasing a shadow, unable to bring him down. Then, when it looked like they might catch him, he'd throw a quick pass to Les. In fewer than a dozen plays, Jimmy had the ball in the end zone, and the Bombers no longer threatened to pull the upset.

The home fans were thrilled with the new dimension to their team's offense. The week before, they'd fawned over Justin Jepson and his passing skills. Now they were just as enamored with Jimmy Ivory.

The more the crowd cheered for Jimmy, the more disgusted Cort Jepson became. When the final horn sounded, he stormed to the sideline and headed for a confrontation with Brock. Tim, anticipating trouble, bulled his way through the fans and got to the sideline just as Cort reached Brock.

"Stop right there," Tim yelled as he caught up to Cort. "Nobody talks to the coach until he's met with the team."

"Says who?"

"Says me. Nobody talks to the coach until he's met with his players, period. Now cool down, or I'll get the sheriff. He's standing right over there." Tim waved his hand at the uniformed officer.

Cort turned and saw the sheriff staring at him as if waiting for a signal. "He can't hide from me forever," Cort said. "He's going to hear me out. He can't treat my son like that."

"Justin was hurt," Tim countered.

Cort raised his index finger and thrust it into the air at Tim's face. "Bullshit!" he screamed. "He's trying to keep him from becoming more famous than him. That's it, plain and simple. There's nothin' wrong with Justin. You haven't heard the last of this." Cort wheeled around and headed back into the stands to find his wife. But she was gone. Too angry to spend time looking for her, Cort grabbed one of his friends. "Let's get out of here," he hollered.

Gravel flew as the dented Chevrolet spun its wheels leaving the parking lot, almost striking an elderly couple walking behind the car. Tim watched them go. *We haven't seen the last of him,* he thought.

Cort wasn't satisfied. He'd tried to confront his son's coach on the football field. But he'd been thwarted by Brock's friend, Tim, the same person who'd sided against him those many years ago when they'd all been on the field playing for a state championship. The memories burned in his mind like hot embers. Now he had to watch the same two men interrupt the dreams he had for his son. With them holding Justin back, there might never be a college scholarship or a chance for stardom.

Retreating to the Wild Horse Tavern, on the other end of town, Cort and his friends mixed beer and bluster. When Cort complained about the coaching his son was receiving, his friends encouraged his anger. It just wasn't right, they said, especially pulling Justin for some black kid from the streets.

A noisy crowd soon filled the tavern, everyone talking over the events they'd witnessed on Sullivan Field. Cort could overhear them gushing over the way the little backup quarterback had pulled the game out of the fire. They didn't think they'd seen that kind of elusiveness before in a Grizzly uniform.

Cort couldn't keep the lid on his anger any longer. "To hell with all of you," he shouted. "The best player on that team is Justin Jepson. Any idiot can see that. But he has a dumb-ass coach pulling him out of games. Well, I've had enough." He slammed his hand down, spilling beer on the wooden table and knocking one long-necked bottle to the floor. He picked up the bottle and smashed it against the wall. Glass flew. "I'm gonna fix Brock Gallagher right now." The room suddenly hushed as people watched him stagger to the door.

Two of Cort's tipsy friends tried to block his path, but he pushed them aside and burst out of the entrance. Within seconds, they could hear his old Chevy roar to life and tires spinning out of the parking lot.

The town of Glory Grove had gone to sleep. The night was silent, and other than the cars parked at the Wild Horse, the streets were deserted. No one witnessed Cort's car careening down Main Street and turning north on Kirby Road. If they had, they'd have wondered why the driver was taking the gravel road at such a breakneck rate of speed.

The man behind the wheel knew where he was going. And why. Brock Gallagher had stood in his way one time too many. He would let him know what he really thought about his coaching and the treatment of his son. And about his flirting with Veronica. And finally, about the play he'd called in that fateful championship game that cost him his own football career. Brock had gone on to stardom and a life of celebrity. He'd left Cort stuck in this little hole called Glory Grove, married to a woman who never really loved him.

The auto was flying, and Cort felt the adrenaline high of speed and anger. Then for a brief moment, with the waxing moon in front of him sliding behind the horizon, he relaxed his grip on the wheel. It was in the middle of his break from turmoil and descent into self-pity when Cort remembered the corner—that bend in Kirby Road which threatened even a sober driver. His heart raced, and he instinctively slammed on the brakes. "No, no, no," he gasped as he realized a skid would send him over the embankment. Panicking, he stomped the accelerator to the floor, trying to power through the hairpin turn. In a cloud of dust, the car fishtailed wildly away from the edge, only to whip back again. The rear wheels pawed at the soft shoulder like a desperate animal trying to avoid a fall, then finally slipped over the edge.

The sound of destruction broke the stillness and echoed off the ravine walls. Red-tailed hawks, perched in the old cottonwood tree along the tiny creek in the canyon's bottom, flapped their wings. And the coyotes, a mother and her pups, stopped their howling and scurried back to their den.

When Brock's neighbor spotted the wreckage early the next morning, it was poised against a tree, grill down, and the trunk lid open, suspended in the air like an aircraft that had fallen from the sky. The sheriff estimated the car had flipped at least three times before reaching the bottom. Those who saw the wreckage could only imagine the terror Cort must have felt during those summersaults.

Authorities tried contacting Veronica, but she'd left the football game angry at her husband. Instead of returning home, she'd taken Justin, woozy from his concussion, to her mother's house for the night. So, there was no one at the Jepson home to realize Cort hadn't returned. Instead, he was alone at the canyon bottom, lying amidst the crushed remains of the old automobile. He lay there, unconscious, barely breathing, curled in a fetal position, covered with blood and gravel.

Word spread fast in town. Neighbors checked Veronica's mother's house and found her and Justin. At the same time, Tim Palmer heard it on his police scanner and called Brock. They all converged on the scene, arriving simultaneously. The ambulance crew was already at the foot of the drop-off, working to free Cort from the auto. Brock and Tim started down to help.

"I'm going with you," Justin said, fighting back tears.

"You'd better stay here with your mom," Tim said. "It ain't going to be pretty."

"We're all going down," Ronnie said flatly, void of any emotion.

The trip to the bottom, nearly four hundred feet below, was a nearly vertical descent on soft dirt and small stones. The four of them held onto one another as they made their way down, with Veronica holding tight to Brock, slipping and sliding, trying not to fall. When they reached the bottom, the ambulance crew was preparing to lift Cort's body from the car.

"He's still breathing," one of the EMTs said to Veronica. "It's a miracle he survived, but he's hurt bad and unconscious. We're going to carry him out of here and get him to the hospital."

They laid Cort on a backboard and strapped him down. Justin watched, feeling sorry for his dad, a once strong, combative man, now looking helpless. A rope was attached to the front of the gurney. The ambulance crew, along with Brock and Tim, grabbed sections of the rope and began the ascent.

With Justin's help, Veronica followed close behind, staring blankly at her husband on the gurney and the procession caring for him. A darkness hung over her, and despite the warmth of the morning, a chill passed through her body.

CHAPTER 44

UPSET

IRENE HEARD THE ROTORS of the helicopter carrying Cort's unconscious body as it settled onto the hospital's landing pad. She was sitting up in her hospital bed reading a newspaper story about the Grizzlies' game with Brookside. Her incision was causing pain, but she held the sports page at arm's length and kept reading. When she finally set the paper down, she was thrilled with the news of the team's win and Jimmy's stellar performance.

Two floors below, Augie was hungry, anxious for lunch. He was feeling better, but his frustration grew each passing day he couldn't be a part of the Grizzly team. His mother told him of the victory over Brookside, and the news cheered him despite his pain. His teammates were now set to battle in a one-game play-in contest to try to advance into the state's playoffs.

As the two patients rested, they listened as the whirring blades of the helicopter slowly came to a stop. Attendants rushed to carry the new patient to a waiting crisis team. It would be another hour before Ronnie and Justin reached the hospital in the car they'd borrowed from Ronnie's mom. Brock and Jimmy weren't far behind.

It was a miracle Cort was alive. However, his condition was still undetermined. He clearly had numerous broken bones and lacerations, but it was the head trauma that needed diagnosis. Monitors beeped and tubes dripped while Cort lay motionless, eyes closed, and teeth clenched. When Ronnie got to the hospital, she hurried to the intensive care unit. She was told she and Justin could sit by her husband's bedside after the doctors finished their initial evaluation.

Brock planned on following the Jepsons but first went to his mother's room. She was surprised to see him there so early in the day.

"The winners are up and at 'em early this morning," she joked. "Sounds like it was a good game last night."

"It was a great game," Brock said. "Puts us in a playoff with our old rival, Ralston. It will be fun knocking heads with them again."

Irene nodded in agreement. "The Raiders are always good. Seems like no one's challenged them since Glory Grove quit putting out a good team."

"Mom, I have other news. Cort Jepson is here in the hospital. He wrecked his car last night in the canyon. He's unconscious." He watched her eyes widen.

"Oh no. What happened?"

"No one knows. Ronnie and Justin were staying at her mom's house. But his friends said he was drunk when he left the Wildhorse … thought he might be looking for me."

"Good Lord, that's awful. How's Ronnie?"

"She's here with him, kind of in a state of shock."

"Poor girl. She deserves better." Irene reached for her water glass and gingerly raised it to her lips. "This may sound cold, but it isn't good news for your team, is it?"

"Justin won't play next week anyway. He got a concussion in the game, and I'm betting the doctor will make him sit out. It's just as well with his family in crisis. But I think the boys will rally. It's been a complicated season, but somehow our team keeps getting better. We'll just have to see how we do without Justin. Now you better rest. The doctor says you're doing good. Says you're a tough old bird."

"Great. That's what I want to be … an old bird." She smiled, trying not to laugh because of the pain from her incision.

Jimmy had been outside the room, letting Brock have some time alone with his mom, but came in at Brock's invitation. He was relieved to see Irene looking so peaceful. He pulled a chair up next to her bed as Brock left to join Ronnie and Justin.

After getting directions from the nurse at the reception desk, Brock made his way down the corridor and found them sitting in the waiting room. Ronnie motioned him into the hall so they could talk privately.

"Rough day," Brock said. "I'm so sorry."

Ronnie's face tightened. "It didn't have to happen. I'm as angry as I am sad. What was he doing out there on that road anyway? What am I supposed to do now?" A tear trickled down her cheek leaving a trail through the traces of dust left on her face from the morning's trek into the canyon.

Brock struggled for words as he gently wiped the tear from her cheek. "Just remember, you're not alone. Everyone in the Grove is with you. Lean on Justin; he's a strong young man. Someday things will sort themselves out. You know we all love you." Brock hadn't spoken of love to Ronnie since the day he left Glory Grove for the university, but now it seemed right.

The three families at the hospital, the Swensons, the Jepsons, and the Gallaghers, spent the weekend with their loved ones. But on Monday, Justin was back in school. He had an appointment with the local doctor to run through the mandated concussion protocol the state required for football players after a head injury. The headaches and nausea had subsided, but he was still experiencing short-term memory loss. The doctor insisted he sit out of any contact sport for at least one week.

Brock had been strategizing, expecting the result. The team's ranks had become dangerously thin. Forced once again to juggle players to fill the holes, they would try to use Jimmy's speed to their advantage.

"We'd better score early against the Raiders 'cause our kids will be out of gas by the fourth quarter," Don said.

Brock agreed. "Yes, but they haven't met a team like ours this year. They'll be prepping to stop Justin's passing game and won't find out until later he's not playing. But they'll still be feeling confident. That team is always on top, and they expect to stay there. We're an underdog, but maybe we can shake things up a little."

Since the Grizzlies were the challenger, they had to travel to Ralston, a thirty-minute bus ride away. They wouldn't have a home-field advantage, but there were plenty of Grove fans who would make the trip. Their team hadn't been near the playoffs in over a decade, and they weren't going to miss a chance to witness an upset, if there was one.

In Ralston, football was serious business. Their field was the envy of every coach in the small school ranks. It was manicured to perfection, grass trimmed like a billiard table. A new set of bleachers was covered with a massive awning to keep the home fans comfortable in late fall weather when the Raiders routinely made their playoff run. Their scoreboard was the latest in high-tech wizardry, and the sound system boomed out rock music for the audience when the school's well-practiced pep band wasn't entertaining the fans.

The field wasn't the only state-of-the-art *accoutrement*. A press box stretched along the top of the seating area with rooms for announcers, video crews, statisticians, and guests. In keeping with the high-profile program, all seven Ralston coaches were dressed in matching gear donated by a sporting goods company. Behind them, facing the crowd, a full squad of cheerleaders showed off their aerial stunts and precision dance moves.

Glory Grove was down to just over twenty players, many of whom were underclassmen, while the Ralston sideline was crowded with over three dozen extras anxious to take their turn on the field. If the Grizzlies were to steal a victory, Brock knew it would take a special effort by his boys and more than a little luck.

"Let's go, captains," the referee said and motioned them to take the field. Luke and Jimmy clasped hands with Justin, who was dressed in street clothes, and moved to the fifty-yard line. Justin was clearly distraught over his father's accident and his own injury. As he walked forward, he alternately stared into the night sky and then the grassy field surface, trying to hold back his emotions.

An early November chill had settled over the field as the home crowd for the Raiders filled the bleachers. They cheered as their team won the coin toss and chose to kick off to the Grizzlies. The kicker boomed the ball end-over-end to the one-yard line. Jimmy waited patiently for it to settle in his arms. When he finally secured it, he saw a blur of blue and white uniforms streaking toward him.

Be patient, he told himself. He hesitated, waiting for them to converge, made a quick lateral move, then shot forward with more speed than the Raiders had seen at any time in their season. Three of them were suddenly grasping at thin air, and Jimmy was off to the races. The Raiders, in their confident enthusiasm, had overrun their lane assignments, and once Jimmy had escaped the gunners, the rest of the team became pursuers, like desperate lions chasing a gazelle. Quickly, they realized they had no hope of catching their prey, and the Grizzlies had the game's first score.

"Good start," Tim said calmly on the headset to Brock.

The Raiders and their fans were stunned. They hadn't trailed in a game all season. Now they'd given up a quick score to their town's oldest rival. Still, the fans and coaches weren't especially worried. The squad across the field had lost four games during the season, and they looked rather pathetic with so few players and only two coaches.

When the Raiders took the field and tried to run their option offense, they were stymied by Luke's strength and speed at linebacker. If they tried to run their end sweep, Luke would be waiting. And if they chose to run their power up the middle, he would crush the back before he could get started.

Neither team had mustered much offense through the first three quarters, and when the fourth quarter began, the early touchdown by the Grizzlies was still the only score. The temperature had dropped below freezing, and receivers from both teams were having trouble fielding the ball. The Raiders, accustomed to having built a big lead by this time in the game, were becoming desperate. Their coaches could be seen arguing with one another over how to deal with the pesky players from their neighboring town. At one point, the head coach shoved his quarterback onto the field, yelling at him for lack of courage.

Brock had Tim in his ear. "They're starting to lose it down there. We'll have them on the ropes if we can stick another score on the board."

"Okay, next time we get them backed up on their end of the field, we'll go with an all-out blitz, see if we can force a fumble. It's a gamble, but in this cold weather, it might work."

With four minutes left in the game, the Grizzly offense bogged down at midfield, and Brock sent word to punt the ball. Luke boomed a tight spiral high into the night sky. The Raider punt return man signaled for a fair catch at the fifteen-yard line.

"Don, we're going with a full blitz right now," Brock said.

"Got it, boss," said the old coach, knowing Brock was rolling the dice. A more conservative approach would try to hold off the Raiders by playing base defense for four minutes.

The Raider quarterback wasn't prepared for a blitz. He dropped back in his usual rhythm but instantly found three linebackers and a safety in his face. Panicked, he saw his tight end curling behind the rushing line, and in desperation, he floated the ball over the Grizzlies. Brock swallowed hard. If the tight end made the catch, it could end in an eighty-five-yard score. Don Baker clutched his chest as if he expected to suffer a real heart attack. But Les Colquit, the freshman who'd forced his way around his parents and onto the team, recognized what was happening.

The ball hung in the air a split second too long—long enough for Les to sprint to the spot where he and the receiver met simultaneously. Both players leapt for the ball, but Les timed his jump perfectly and wrestled the ball away from the bigger boy. He crashed to the ground, still clutching the ball for the interception.

In the visitors stands, Lester Colquit was holding back his emotions. His wife raised her head to see what the cheering was about and sprung enough tears for both her and her husband. Her skinny, overprotected son was a hero. The game wasn't over yet, but with Brock calling the plays and Luke blasting through the holes made by the senior linemen,

Matt Peterson and Tommy Anthony, a second Grizzly touchdown was soon in the books. The Grizzlies would head home assured of a spot in the playoffs.

Ralston fans wandered through the stands in disbelief, unable to fathom the reality of the unexpected defeat. The year before, Glory Grove couldn't field a team. Now they'd denied the Raiders a spot in the playoffs. The losing players were on their knees in tears, and a few angry parents were making their way onto the field to have frank discussions with their team's coach.

Brock paused for a moment to take in the scene and witness the joy on his players' faces. He lived for moments like this. The thrill of winning this game after a tough week was the sliver of bliss he craved as a coach. It was like a very powerful drug. He inhaled it.

CHAPTER 45

QUARTERFINALS

WITH THE WIN OVER RALSTON, the Grizzly team became the conference representative in the playoffs. Their opponent, the Crawfordville Tigers, would travel to the Grove for a quarterfinal contest. The town hadn't hosted a playoff game since Brock, Tim, and Cort squared off in a similar contest nearly twenty years before.

Justin spent the weekend with his mother in a hotel near the medical center. His father remained motionless in his hospital bed. On Monday morning, the young quarterback checked in with the family's doctor and got released to play football. At least for a time, he could take his mind off the family crisis and think about the sport he loved. He didn't want to miss the excitement bubbling up in the school and community.

Augie also received good news. He was released from the hospital and arrived home early in the week, still confined to a wheelchair and on a strict regimen of antibiotics. "I want to go to football practice," he told his parents. They agreed it might be good to let him see his friends.

Tuesday, on the field, Brock called the team together. "I have a surprise for you," he said. He motioned to Augie's father in the van alongside the practice field, and the doors of the vehicle slowly opened. Augie rolled his chair down the ramp onto the field to the cheers of his teammates.

Augie had a huge smile on his freckled face and, never at a loss for words, carefully raised his arms to get his teammates to quiet down. "I want to say I'm sorry for screwing up and missing practice and the games. But I'm glad you found someone else who can spin a ball backward between his legs," he said and pointed a finger at Wally Thompson, who waved and grinned as if to say no problem.

Augie continued. "I won't be suiting up for a while, but I'll be on the sidelines with you from here on out. All the way to the City Dome for the state championship." His voice rose to a high pitch to put a finish to his thoughts.

If the team lacked inspiration, they found it with Augie's return. They surrounded him, and each one, in turn, patted him gently on his shoulders.

Luke hollered. "That's it, boys. We're going all the way for Augie. We've missed you, Swenson, but you'd better keep those little wheels on your chair lubed up, so you'll be ready for the ride, 'cause we're going all the way."

"Augie on three," Justin commanded. "One, two, three."

"Augie," the team responded as one.

While Augie had returned to the Grove, Irene remained in the hospital. Brock visited as often as he could, but the demands of prepping for the Crawfordsville game and helping Richard on the farm pulled him in a dozen different directions. And hanging like a cloud over the entire situation was the disconnect between him and his wife and a

QUARTERFINALS

creeping guilt that he didn't miss her more. To avoid the labyrinth of emotions, Brock forced himself to focus on the upcoming game.

He'd been determined to resurrect a program on the verge of elimination, to rebuild a passion among the boys for the game he loved. When the season began, he hadn't dared to think a team patched together with holdovers, misfits, and freshmen could reach the highest rung of achievement. But now, they were only two wins away from playing in the City Dome. Brock wanted it as much as the townspeople and the players themselves. He ached for the high that came with running onto the field as coach of a championship contender, to feel the tingle of excitement and the rush of emotion that comes with playing for the big prize.

The game with Crawfordsville was scheduled for Saturday afternoon on Sullivan Field behind the high school. Local farmers patched the wooden grandstands and trimmed the shrubbery encircling the field, trying to put a good face on the facility that the year before had been used only for phys-ed classes. Students put fresh paint on the team's name alongside the logo on the end of the concession stand.

On Saturday morning, there wasn't a cloud in the sky. It was unusually warm for a mid-November weekend. The locals who parked just outside the fence by the school were barbecuing burgers and hot dogs. The tantalizing smell of charcoaled meat drifted toward the grandstand as the smoke rose high into the air. Willow trees alongside the creek next to the field were refusing to drop their brilliant yellow leaves until after the game, insisting on making the perfect backdrop for the event.

The home bleachers began filling early, and laughter and chatter could be heard blocks away. "It's been a long time since people have been this fired up for a football game," one of the old farmers in the crowd commented. The people were in a celebratory mood—that is, until Ronnie walked past the ticket booth and headed into the stands. The bubbling roar of the crowd softened, and conversations stopped as people turned to stare. She walked with dignity; her head held high—a serene smile on her face. Auburn curls fell from under her black ball cap onto her gray overcoat.

As she made her way into the stands toward the place where she and Cort always sat with his tavern buddies, she turned away from them and continued to climb higher. When she reached the top row, she stepped toward Richard Gallagher, bent down, and in a soft voice asked, "Do you mind if I sit with you?"

"Please do. I could use the company. You can have Irene's seat. She would love for you to sit in for her." Richard usually had a joke or laugh for anyone near him, but this time he felt a twinge of sadness over the absence of the two Grizzly fans, Irene and Cort, who weren't there.

"Is Justin ready for the game?" he asked.

"I've never seen him quite this excited," Ronnie said. She unrolled the game program she held in her hand and stared at the cover. "He's been dreaming about playoff football his whole life. I think he's going to have a good game."

As the team came onto the field for the opening ceremonies, the crowd came to its feet when the three Grizzly captains wheeled their injured friend, Augie, onto the field. Luke grabbed the handles of the wheelchair, and the four friends moved slowly to the referees for the coin toss.

"You call it, young man," the referee said, looking down sympathetically at the boy in the chair. Augie, his teeth clenched to ward off his discomfort, made his call and watched the referee spin the silver dollar into the blue autumn sky. After the routine was complete, the players returned to the sideline, and the band played their rendition of the national anthem.

QUARTERFINALS

Ashley, who'd asked for the day off at the convenience store, lowered her clarinet and blew a kiss to Luke, who looked particularly threatening with gobs of black face paint smeared under his eyes. "For luck," she mouthed the words. He patted his cheek to acknowledge the gesture.

Once the game began, the significance of this day to the athletes and community overwhelmed the Tigers. Jimmy, who'd done an admirable job at quarterback in the game against Ralston, was back at his slot position. His speed in the open field was too much for the Tigers. They found themselves chasing him into the end zone four times before the first half ended.

Justin was now clearheaded from the week's rest and directed the team like a master conductor, connecting with his favorite receivers and handing the ball to Luke for big gains.

By halftime, it was clear the Grizzlies would be moving into the semifinals. The second half was a relaxing celebration of their dominance. No one said it out loud, but the absence of Cort Jepson jawing from the stands was a pleasant respite, although the hurt his accident had caused Veronica and Justin was felt by the community. This team victory helped ease the pain.

When the final gun sounded, every player on the Grizzly team, including the freshmen who got to play in the game because of its lopsided nature, raised their fists in the air and raced to midfield to join the team's mosh pit, jumping and yelling without restraint. Then, before meeting the other team in the traditional single-file congratulations, the Grove players passed by Augie, who doled out high-fives. He beamed as if he'd made the winning play.

In the grandstands, Ronnie stood to leave and smiled as she patted Richard's arm. "Tell Brock congratulations. He's made my son a very happy boy."

CHAPTER 46

QUESTIONS

A REGIONAL NEWSPAPER made a call to the school Monday morning. They were doing a feature on the little school in farm country, which had gone from having no football program one year to nailing down a spot in the state semifinals. Principal Colquit took their call and answered their questions. He praised Coach Gallagher, never mentioning he'd done everything in his power to derail Brock's efforts to restart the program.

"This town's excited about our team ... follow them wherever they play," he said, searching for the right words so they could be used in the paper. "We stumbled a bit last year when some students chose not to play but were lucky to hire one of the top coaches in the state. With some talented players new to the school and a couple of freshmen who've stepped up, we've become a strong team."

Colquit dropped the suggestion of the team's talented freshmen, hoping the reporter would pick up on the idea and maybe get his son's name in the paper. But the scribe didn't bite.

"We'll run someone over to your town tomorrow to get some quotes and photos if that would be okay," the newsman said.

"Wonderful. We'll look forward to meeting your reporter."

The semifinal game would be played on a neutral site, midway between the opposing schools. The stadium had artificial turf, so Brock assumed the faster surface could be an advantage for Jimmy. But after watching film of the opponent, the Loki Lake Eagles, he realized the game might turn into a track meet. The Eagles featured twin brothers, both with sprinter speed. Brock knew they'd attack his team's cornerbacks—Les Colquit and Derek Baker. If the Eagles got around the outside linebackers into open space, Les and Derek weren't fast enough to keep up.

The championship game was within reach, and Brock could feel the excitement starting to kick in. He told himself it was for the boys, but he wanted the drama of being in the championship game for himself as well. He'd been there as a player in high school and as a coach at Brighton. He wanted to share that feeling with this team.

The young reporter came at Brock with his leadoff question. "How did you manage to turn this team into a playoff contender in such a short time?" Brock hadn't had to answer many reporter's questions since he left Brighton. He hadn't missed them.

"Well, we weren't very good at first," Brock admitted. "But the kids have bought into what we're doing and are anxious to succeed. We have some good leaders, starting with our quarterback, Justin Jepson."

"I've heard about him," the reporter said. "People think with his arm, he might have a shot at playing at the next level." He jotted notes on a yellow pad as he spoke. The young man, in an obvious attempt to look more mature, had sprouted a wispy mustache and feigned a deep voice.

"Too early to tell," Brock said respectfully. "He's only a junior, so he'll have next year to prove what he can do. But he has all the tools."

"How did you recruit some of your other players? I understand a couple of the boys came from bigger programs." He twirled the pen in his hand.

Brock could sense the reporter was fishing. He answered quickly with authority. "We don't recruit. Our fullback, Luke Palmer, came from Denver to live with his dad, who resides here. And our running back, Jimmy Ivory, moved here with me from Brighton. His mother passed away, and he had no family left in Seattle. He was here even before the board reinstated football this fall."

The reporter pivoted. "I've heard talk there might be some college scouts at the game on Saturday looking at some of your players. Do you think it will affect their play?"

"No."

"Glory Grove hasn't been to the championship game in over a decade. What do you think your chances are?"

"If we stay focused and play hard, we should be okay." Brock fell back on his coach-speak habits from Brighton. "But no matter how this ends, it's been a privilege to coach back in my hometown. The economy has been a little tough here the last few years, but the people don't change. They are good folks with a toughness you might not find anywhere else."

With that, Brock excused himself to let the reporter interview some of the players. He urged the newsman to select the seniors to reward them for their efforts. After coaching at Brighton, Brock knew how petty jealousies could grow from attention being paid to certain star

QUESTIONS

players. But he wasn't worried about his boys. They were excited to be receiving any attention.

The following morning, Brock stopped at the convenience store on the way to the school and picked up the morning's newspaper. When he read the article on his team, he was disappointed. He'd hoped the paper would treat his players better. Instead, he was troubled to read the headline: *Big-Time Coach Makes Silk Out of Sow's Ear*. It was printed over a less than flattering picture of Jimmy and Luke.

The article dropped a subtle hint at the impact the *recruited* players had on the Grizzlies' success and cast some doubt on whether there could be a fairy tale ending for the boys. The final paragraph questioned whether the school could keep Brock in the fold for another year.

Brock headed to the locker room and tried to think of what to say to his players. He needed the boys to focus on their next game, and this was the kind of outside distraction they didn't need. But when the first of his players came in the door, he was pleasantly surprised.

"Hey, Coach, we got the front page in the sports section," said the older Simpson brother as he plopped down on the bench in front of his locker. "They called us silk. What do you think of that? Sounds like a great new nickname. *The Silk Merchants*." He waved his arms as he drew the words out for effect. "And that goofy picture of Luke and Jimmy, pretty sweet, don't you think?"

Soon, other players walked in jabbering about making the big-time paper, teasing about the photo and the quotes they'd given the reporter. So what if the newsman called them a sow's ear? So what if he'd suggested they'd recruited their best players? None of it mattered. The Grizzlies had arrived, and now everyone was talking about them.

Brock had underestimated the team. They'd come together for many individual reasons but now had one goal in mind—a state championship. He couldn't wait to get on the field.

The practices during the week were spirited. After the decisive victory over Crawfordsville and the media attention, the players were beginning to think they were invincible. After the walk-through on Friday night, as the sun was slipping over the trees at the end of the field and the lights had begun casting shadows, Brock gathered the players around him at center field and leveled with them.

"This is going to be the hardest test you've faced all year. Loki Lake is a great team. They have talent at every position. They have speed and are well coached. It will take every ounce of energy and desire you have to come out on top. But I've seen you grow up over the past three months. I know you're ready for the challenge." Brock moved his gaze to look into the eyes of every player. "So, go shower and get home early. Sleep well tonight. Dream about the victory you are chasing. Then let's meet tomorrow morning, ready to ride. It will be a three-hour trip to get your minds right and then show the world what the Grizzlies can do."

As he dismissed the players, Brock noticed a solitary figure sitting in the stands. Dozens of fans had come to watch the team practice, but as the evening cooled, almost all had drifted off. All but Ronnie Jepson, sitting with her collar turned up against the chilly wind.

Brock followed his players part of the way off the field, then turned at the grandstand and slowly climbed to where she was sitting.

"They look ready," Ronnie said, smiling up at Brock.

"I hope so."

"Justin can't wait. It's taken his mind off his dad. I think this game is a blessing."

"How is Cort?" Brock sat down beside her.

QUESTIONS

"The same, still in a coma. The doctors say he is in the twilight of consciousness. They don't know if he'll ever wake up."

"I'm sorry."

"I was going to leave him, you know." She bit her lip and inhaled.

"When?"

"The night of the accident. I watched you take care of Justin when he got the concussion. Cort wanted you to keep him on the field to add to his statistics. It was wrong, and I was sick about it. I went to stay with my mom and decided I was going to file for a divorce."

"And then he had the accident." Brock said quietly.

"People say he was on his way to try to hurt you. We'll never know how that would have ended. When he was drunk and angry, he could get ugly. Somebody upstairs was looking out for you, I think."

"What now?"

"I don't know. I'll take care of Justin the best I can and see what the future might bring. I stayed married to Cort because I thought he loved Justin like I did. But toward the end, I think he just wanted the glory for himself."

The groundskeeper walked around the corner of the concession stand and saw Brock sitting with Veronica.

"Sorry, boss, I've gotta turn out the lights. You know, board policy and all. Hope you don't mind."

"Not a problem," Brock answered. "We'll be gone soon."

Ronnie turned her back to the wind. "You have time for a walk?" she asked as the eight banks of lights shut down, one after the other like a slow-motion countdown, leaving the two in near darkness.

"Sure, where to?"

"Out there," Ronnie gestured toward the field. "I want to ask you something."

Brock followed along beside her until they reached the center of the 50-yard line. The sun was gone, and they were immersed only in the light from a crescent moon and the distant stars. She stopped and turned to face him. Her hair was blowing gently in the evening breeze… the moonlight reflecting off her curls.

"You okay? "Brock asked. He reached up and brushed a strand of hair from her face. Despite the darkness he could feel her gaze, looking into his eyes—a curious expression on her face.

"Do you remember the night before you graduated?" she asked, waiting for her words to sink in. "It was a beautiful warm night. We sat right here, staring up at the stars. You made a promise you'd wait for me, and I believed you. I've always wondered how long it took for you to forget me?" She stood poised, ready for whatever answer he night give.

"I never forgot." Brock didn't say more. But he knew how often he thought of her, even after college and into his adult years. Too painful to confess to a schoolboy heartache.

There was a long silence. "But you didn't call or write."

"I did call, but your mother always said you were out. And we did exchange letters at first, but I'm not good at expressing my feelings on paper. And later you never answered my letters. Maybe your mom was trying to help you forget about me. I missed you a lot. I was in over my head at school. Coming from this little town, the university was overwhelming…football and all. My studies were hard, and the coach was pushing me to get ready for varsity."

I sound like I'm making excuses, Brock thought, but he continued. "I wanted it all. The excitement and celebrity of being on a college team. It was addicting. But I thought of you all the time. Then some of my friends said you were hanging out with Cort, that maybe you'd moved on."

QUESTIONS

"Cort was here, and you were gone. It's as if you'd disappeared from my life."

Brock could see the tears in her eyes. She was beginning to shiver, so he moved closer and calmly cradled her hands. "I was only seventeen, but I meant it. I really planned on coming back to you," he said. "But when I heard about you and Cort, I think my pride got in the way. I couldn't get past the thought of him and you together. I was jealous, and I guess I got stubborn and just walked away…to focus on the game. I thought maybe we'd get back together during the summer, but by then you were…"

"Pregnant with Justin," Ronnie said, finishing his sentence. News of it years ago had collapsed on Brock's world like a tidal wave of hurt.

"Yes, that ended any thought I had of keeping my promise." He looked away.

"You want to know how that happened?" She squeezed his hands.

He turned back toward her, shook his head and inhaled deeply. "I don't need to know the details."

She kept on. "Cort brought wine to the prom and afterwards he wanted me to try it. I said no, but he kept pestering me, so I gave in. I'd never had alcohol before, and it made me feel kind of warm and free. Then he started coming after me and wouldn't stop when I told him to." She rocked back and forth on her heels as she remembered the night.

Brock held her hands tighter. "I'm so sorry." He felt angry and sick.

"It sounds awful now talking about it. I tried to hold him off, but I couldn't. I was so young. You know who I was." She paused to catch her breath. "I didn't want it to happen. He took my innocence from me. Afterwards, he said he loved me, but I was scared." A tear ran down her cheek.

"And then you got pregnant," Brock said, almost in a whisper.

"Yes. One time and just like that I was pregnant. I didn't tell my mom right away, afraid she would disown me or something. And I wasn't going to give up the baby. Cort said we should get married, that he'd take care of me. I didn't know what else to do. I wanted to call you but was too ashamed and embarrassed."

"I would have listened. I wish you had called. That's a rough way to start a marriage."

"I know. There was never any love, other than for Justin. We got along okay when he was a baby, but Cort was never happy. He knew I didn't love him. That I only married him because I had to. He drank more and always seemed bitter and angry at life. When you came back in June, it seemed to push him over the edge."

Brock reached up and gently ran the back of his hand down her cheek. "I'm sorry if I made life worse for you. I just came for my mom. But I'm glad to be here with you again. What can I do now to make it better?"

"I don't know. Say you're sorry for leaving me. Or for coming home. Or don't say anything at all. I just wanted to get it off my chest. I know you've had this perfect, wonderful life. And you have a gorgeous wife. And you're famous and all. But I wanted to tell you how I felt." She paused and looking squarely into his eyes, in a sincere tone, said, "and I wanted you to know I'm glad you came home."

Brock's mind drifted back to that night under the stars on the football field. He remembered what a teenage crush he had on a pretty young girl and realized he could have been happy to stay forever in Glory Grove. But he also understood he would have missed all the wonderful things that happened in his life. They couldn't change the past. They couldn't go back in time.

QUESTIONS

But now, Brock felt tears welling up in his own eyes. "Dammit, Ronnie, I said I'd always love you, and in my heart I have. But we were just kids. Life is complicated. We made some wrong turns along the way."

I wish I could wrap my arms around her and promise her my love, like I did back on this field so many years ago, Brock thought. But he wouldn't. He couldn't. Not now. Celia was his wife and Cort was clinging to life in a hospital bed.

"I'm really sorry that I hurt you and for what you're going through now," he finally said.

"I know," Ronnie said. She dropped her hands. "Thanks for coming out here after all these years. I was so happy on this field back then. And I'm happy again now, knowing you care." She slowly slid her hands up his arms and put them around his neck. She reached up, balancing on her toes, and kissed him gently on the lips. Memories from their teenage years enveloped them, yet they both understood they might never share such a moment again. "Good luck coach. I'll be cheering for you," she said.

She wheeled around and walked away.

Brock watched her as she disappeared into the darkness. He stood for several more minutes in the middle of the field with his hands tucked into his pockets, breathing in the cool evening air. He was thankful for the moment, it had been a long time coming. *So ironic,* he thought. *Here on the 50-yard line, the crucial center point in any football game. A team moves forward from here toward happiness and joy…or is pushed back on their heels, trying to hold on and hold back failure. Life and love on a straight white line.*

He lifted his eyes and began to slowly walk from the field. He told himself he needed to think of his team. He was their coach. He would lead, be structured, organized, disciplined, and unemotional. He would have to put away his personal feelings. He needed to stay focused. Tomorrow was the Grizzlies' big day.

CHAPTER 47

ELEMENTS

THE OLD-TIMERS around Glory Grove knew three straight days of east wind would bring in a storm. They weren't surprised when they awoke early Saturday morning to find four inches of snow on the ground. As the players gathered at the school to board their bus, they shivered in the cold. Brock had warned them early in the season how playoff football meant a struggle against the elements. Now they understood.

After a slow journey on icy roads, the team reached the giant stadium with seating for thousands of fans. But because of the road conditions, they were already late for warm-ups, and the players scurried to their locker room. The stadium was like an icebox. Fans huddled under layers of blankets. When the teams were announced, there was only the muffled flop-flop of gloved hands slapping together.

Everything Brock had seen on the film of Loki Lake proved to be true. The Eagles were even faster in person, and momentum quickly turned in their favor. After the coin toss, the Grizzlies kicked off and the twins, wearing numbers 12 and 21, were back to receive the kick. Number 12 took the ball cleanly with the Grizzlies in hot pursuit. But as the Grove players converged on him, he met his twin running the opposite direction on a reverse and pitched the ball for a long return. A few plays later, the Eagles were in the end zone. Only minutes into the game and the Grizzly players were shaking their heads in disbelief. It was too early for despair, but the action took away some of their bravado.

"We're okay," Brock yelled. "Lots of time left. Now get your heads straight."

Everyone knew the Grizzly offense could score points. With their trio of scorers, they quickly answered the Eagle touchdown with one of their own. So, the stage was set. Neither team could stop the other from sustaining a drive. Luke could defend anything inside, but the quickness of the Loki Lake twins and their quarterback made it impossible to shut down their offense completely. It was an exciting game for the cold-numbed fans to watch. Frequent moments of celebration were shortened by the desire of those in attendance to quickly cover up under their blankets to ward off the chill.

Halftime came, and the teams headed to their heated locker rooms to thaw out. Twenty-four minutes had been played, and neither team had the advantage with the score knotted 26–26. Brock and his two assistants let the players warm up while they discussed their strategy for the second half.

Brock proposed his plan. "We'll shadow those twins … stick Jimmy on whichever one is playing the strong side. Then we zone the rest of their receivers and rely on Luke to disrupt their quarterback. We're bigger up front than they are, and with the cold, they might be wearing down. This game belongs to whoever wants it the most."

By the start of the second half, the temperature had dropped to single digits. The water boy was having trouble keeping the water in the containers from freezing. Tiny icicles clung to his gloved hands. The youngest players along the sideline, knowing full well they probably weren't going to play, huddled around propane heaters like moths around a flame.

Luke had played in conditions like this in Denver. As he headed to the field for the second half, he stripped off his elbow protectors and rolled up his sleeves. "Perfect weather for a Grizzly Bear," he yelled at the top of his lungs. "Follow me, boys; we need to rip apart some Eagles."

The Grizzly players responded and came out fired up and ready to play. The Eagles kicked the ball away from Jimmy, but it spiraled so high that Jimmy had time to field it at the twenty-yard line. He hesitated for a second, and then with his patented double move, shook off the Eagle defenders and sprinted straight into the end zone. The scoring duel was off and running again.

Brock's defensive strategy slowed down the Eagles as Jimmy was able to collar one of the twins. But the other boy found holes in the zone defense. Still, as the fourth quarter was winding down, the Grizzlies were holding a single touchdown lead, 44–37. And the boys from the Grove had the Eagles pinned inside their own twenty-yard line. There was less than a minute left on the clock.

"What do you think, Tim, an all-out blitz?" Brock asked his friend in the booth.

"Well, it worked two weeks ago. If we stop them here, the game is over."

It was third down with three yards to go for the Eagles, and Brock guessed they would keep it on the ground to get their first down. But he didn't know the Eagle coach. The man wasn't afraid to gamble. When the ball was snapped and the Grizzly defenders came blitzing into the backfield, the quarterback lobbed a little crossing route screen pass to twin number 21, who never looked back.

"Gutsy call," Brock muttered. If the Eagles gambled again on a two-point conversion try and succeeded, Loki Lake would have a 45–44 lead with little time left. When they lined up for the try, the Eagles had four receivers spread across the field. It was a formation the Grizzlies hadn't seen before. Brock quickly called a time-out to school his defensive backs on how to react.

But when the Eagles returned to the field, they went back to a kicking formation, and the kicker easily pushed the ball through the uprights. Score 44–44. Many of the fans pulled their blankets tighter, realizing the Eagle coach had chosen to play for overtime on this bone-chilling evening.

With a minute left on the clock, Brock knew the outcome of the game would ride on Justin's passing skills. On first down from the twenty-yard line, a simple sideline pass delivered to George Olson bounced harmlessly off his frozen fingers. Without the threat of a running play, the defenders were now lying-in wait. On second down, a seam route to Jimmy was tipped away at the last second. But on third down, a crossing pattern to Les secured a first down. Without a time-out, the clock continued to move. It ticked down to thirty seconds.

Brock knew they had to throw the ball, but a poorly thrown pass, intercepted by one of the twins, could end the game even before overtime could be played. He didn't like gadget plays. They often backfired, but they'd practiced a few. And with Jimmy's experience as a passer, Brock decided to gamble. It was time to give his opponent a different look.

"Strong side, double pass," Brock signaled to Justin. His quarterback nodded, settled in under center, and began his count. "Red

43. Red 43," he repeated a second time. Then the count. "Hut. Hut."

The ball snapped into his fingers, now throbbing from the cold. He looped a pass to Jimmy, who was to his right in the slot position. Jimmy took two steps forward as if he were going to run, but not beyond the line of scrimmage. The defense converged, knowing Jimmy could take the ball to the end zone given enough head start. But instead, Jimmy took a step back, surveyed the field, and found Les running as fast as his freshman legs would carry him.

The pass was a tight spiral that almost didn't have enough velocity to reach Les, but he adjusted, and the ball dropped softly into his hands. There wasn't a single green-clad Eagle within twenty yards as he jogged into the end zone.

The Grizzly fans broke into a frenzy, waving their blankets and jumping up and down like polar bears at a polka party. Brock had out-coached a credible foe. And his players had responded. With only a few seconds left, the outcome was obvious. For only the second time in school history, the Grizzlies were headed to the Dome to play for a state championship. Their coach had been there before, and now they would follow him in search of their own glory.

CHAPTER 48

NEMESIS

BROCK AND JIMMY ARRIVED back at the Gallagher farm late Saturday night after the game. Brock built a fire in the woodstove to take off the chill and made hot chocolate for himself and his star running back. Jimmy was still euphoric with their victory over Loki Lake and wanted to relive every moment of the game. It was almost midnight before they turned off the lights and headed to bed. The night was quiet, and the snow that had fallen on Saturday morning made a perfect white blanket over the farmstead. Happiness filled the old home.

They were deep in slumber when the ringing of the phone made Brock sit straight up in bed. He'd been in a dream world of football and hospitals and Ronnie jumbled together in a complicated drama. He quickly threw off the covers and stumbled down the stairs.

"Hello."

"Hi, Brock, it's Celia."

"Hi, what time is it?"

"I don't know. Sometime after midnight, I think. We just got home, and I thought I'd call my dear sweet husband."

"Um, thanks. I was asleep, so I'm a little groggy."

"You been out chasing pigs or something?" she giggled. Her words were slurred, and Brock suspected she'd been drinking.

"Honey, we had a game yesterday," he said. "You know, I'm still coaching a football team." Brock settled into the office chair, almost awake now.

"Oh sure, I knew that. Did you win?"

"Yes, we won. We'll play for the state championship next week."

"Oh, back on top. Just like always. Congratulations."

"Celia, are you all right? You don't sound too good."

She didn't hesitate. "No, I'm good. Still just a bit wound up from the party."

"What's the celebration?"

"Friday." She laughed again. "We were just celebrating Friday."

Brock now knew his wife was inebriated. "Celia, what's going on? It sounds like you're drunk."

"Oh, Brock, we just had a few drinks. Maybe it's the pills. They make me talk a little funny. Don't worry. I'm fine." She changed the subject. "How's your mom?"

"She's still in the hospital."

"Why, what happened?"

"She had surgery for cancer … two weeks ago."

"Why didn't you tell me?"

"Celia, we haven't talked since the fair. It's been two months," Brock said, trying to hold back his anger at her.

"I'm sorry, I just seem to have lost track of time. I went back to New York to help Jovan again. I thought I told you. Anyway, I hope your mom is going to be okay."

Brock was wide awake now. He could feel his heart pounding in his chest. He took a deep breath to calm his voice. "I'll be in Seattle for the game next weekend with the team. We play on Saturday in the Dome. It sounds like you and I need to get together and talk about our marriage. I'll touch base when we get there. You'd better get some sleep and try to sober up a bit."

"Okay, Mr. Grumpy, if that's the way you want it. I was just trying to have a little fun. Sorry I woke you."

"Sure," Brock said. "Sure. Good night." He laid the phone in its cradle and rotated his mom's office chair so he could look out the window at the farmstead. The stars were brilliant in the cold night sky. Not a single snowflake moved. It seemed peaceful and pure, the opposite of what he was feeling. He wanted his life to be like that. So, he kept staring out the window until his mind calmed.

He turned and saw his mom's crucifix hanging on the wall above her desk. He knew it was time to ask for help. He needed someone stronger and wiser to watch over his mother. And a steady hand to guide Celia off the path she was on. Then Brock asked God to be with Cort in his blackness and with Ronnie in her sadness.

Feeling guilty for laying so much on the good Lord at one time, Brock shifted his mind to give thanks for the good things in his life—the football team—Jimmy, Luke, Justin, Augie, Les, and all the others who had followed his lead. Finally, he thanked God for his friend Tim, Uncle Richard, Don Baker, and even Lester Colquit, whom he'd come to value as a reluctant supporter.

Suddenly, the worry left his mind. He stood, walked to the window, and looked up at the heavens. He felt relieved. He knew every one of his problems could be worked out somehow. He smiled to himself, thinking that life was a bit like a football game, hard and complicated.

But if he let the answers come to him, he could eventually call the right play. He added a log to the fire and slowly climbed the stairs to his bedroom. He lay down, pulled the covers up tight around his chin, and was soon in a deep sleep.

The following week was chaos, planning for transportation and lodging for the team and boosters. It had been so long since Glory Grove had played for the state championship that there was no protocol to follow. But Principal Colquit was determined to make the trip seamless and trouble free. He arranged for a rooter's bus to carry the band and its enthusiastic director to the game along with any other student who wanted to go.

Don Baker claimed he liked being around teenagers, kept him feeling young, so he volunteered to travel with the team. Brock and Tim would drive over in Brock's car since he would need the vehicle if he were going to see Celia over the weekend.

"I think the whole damn town is going," Tim said after practice on Wednesday night. "Even the sheriff, so the outlaws might have a field day while we're all gone."

"I imagine the outlaws are Grizzly fans too," Brock said.

The biggest news of the week came on Wednesday night when Brock got home from practice. His mom called and said she was being released from the hospital, with the stipulation that she was to take it easy and get lots of rest.

"I'm going to the game," she said flatly, barely into the conversation.

"That's probably not a good idea, Mom," Brock countered. "You'd better stay home; we can get someone to come and take care of you."

"Son, if I die next week, I'll have ended my life having watched you coach the Glory Grove team in the state championship. I'll drive that old pickup over the mountains myself if I have to."

"God, Mom, you're stubborn. Let me see what I can do," he said.

So, Brock and Richard rented a van with a couch where Irene could lie down. Richard would drive, and they'd hire one of the local EMTs to ride with them. They would get Irene to the game as comfortably as possible.

The team and staff were all leaving on Friday so they could spend the night in the city and be ready for their scheduled Saturday championship game which kicked off at four o'clock pm. Their game was sandwiched between the 3-A and 4-A games. The 4-A game was the main event of the championship weekend. Brock had experienced those bright lights and television cameras when his Brighton team was making waves.

The most complicated part of the weekend for Brock was making time to visit Celia. They needed to talk. To repair hurt feelings. To plan for their future. Had the months apart destroyed the trust they had for one another? It would take time, but he didn't want his personal life interfering with his team's one big chance at bringing home the giant trophy.

When the boys were dismissed from school, they headed for the bus. The cheerleaders and students of all ages formed two lines for the team to parade through. There was cheering and high fives for all twenty-four boys, and they were plastered with confetti as they made their way through the crowd. As Luke passed by, Ashley pulled him aside and whispered in his ear. He laughed as she blushed. Jimmy gave Luke a good-natured push from behind. "Keep your mind on the game," he scolded.

When the bus departed, the sheriff, in his patrol car, led them down Main Street with his siren blaring. The players felt like community heroes and wondered how much better it could get if they won the game.

Brock and Tim left town shortly after the bus. It was a chance to reminisce about their own time playing for a state championship. "It was the best moment of my life until we ended up on the wrong end of the score," Tim said as the car sped through the deserted flatland of the state. "And you know what, even though we lost, it's still probably the best moment of my life. Just being there, playing for the whole freakin' enchilada."

"Mine too, really," Brock said.

"Oh, come on, Rocket. You played college ball and were the MVP of the Copper Bowl. Oh, and had a chance at the NFL. And you're telling me playing for Glory Grove was the best moment in your football career?"

"I think so. It just means so much more at that age. There is something about the passion. The energy is different. You aren't old enough to understand the realities of life like you do in college and the pros. In high school, you're playing for yourself and your friends and your school. It's more innocent. And that's why when you lose, it hurts so bad. And when you win, you're on top of the world."

Brock saw Tim nodding his head out of the corner of his eye. "You saw those boys loading the bus this morning. There is pure joy in a moment like that. Hopefully, for this team, it ends well tomorrow, and it won't sour someone for life like it did for Cort."

Tim sat up erect in his seat. "Do you remember that halftime blowup he had?" He asked knowing Brock couldn't have forgotten it. "Still makes me wonder what happened. I think the pressure got to him, and he snapped. He was getting manhandled by their defense, and I think any confidence he had before the game had gone to hell by halftime. Then Coach Sullivan came into the locker room screaming at him … called him a wuss for getting pushed around. Cort tried to blame you for holding the ball too long and scrambling around in the pocket. Lost his frickin' mind."

Tim carefully spit chew into the empty pop can he was holding. "Chucked his water bottle in your face and called you an asshole. That's when you threw that punch. Hit him right in the gut. Doubled him over like a rag doll and left him sucking for air. He deserved it. Everyone on the team knew he had it coming."

"I shouldn't have lost my temper," Brock said. "The biggest moment in our lives, and I blew it. I should have walked away. But down deep, I couldn't stand his loudmouth and him hanging around Ronnie all the time. In the end, I guess he won that battle. Anyway, I feel sorry for him now. Wish it could have been different."

"What do you suppose will happen to him?" Tim asked.

"Doctors say he could stay in a coma for a long time. Might recover some but will never be the same. Or he could just pass on. Only time will tell. Hey, let's talk about something more pleasant. Like how we're going to beat Northfork." Brock drummed his fingers on the steering wheel. "Ironic, isn't it? Same school we played nineteen years ago. This is our chance for redemption. Been a long time coming. Of course, since then, they've won half a dozen championships, including last year."

The two men spent the rest of their long commute planning … trying to find a way to turn the tables on their long-ago nemesis, the Northfork Loggers.

CHAPTER 49

CRISIS

IN THE EVENING, after the team got settled into their hotel, Brock met with them and made clear his expectations—to represent the school and community with class. He then ran through Saturday's schedule: a team breakfast, a walk-through in the park across from the hotel, and their departure for the Dome.

After he dismissed the team, Brock asked Don if he'd check in on the boys from time to time to make sure they were behaving themselves, while he arranged to meet with Celia. He pulled his phone from his pocket and dialed.

"Celia, it's Brock. I'm in town. Do you want to get together?"

"Sure. I've been expecting your call. Where do you want to meet?"

"We're staying at the Crystal Hotel downtown. You want to come here for dinner?"

"I'm not really hungry, but I'll meet you for drinks. I'll get a taxi and be there in a couple of hours." She hung up the phone. As soon as she did, Brock was sorry he'd suggested the hotel. Half his town and all his players were there. But he needed to stay close to monitor some of the team's activity. After all, they were teenage boys away from home. That could certainly mean the potential for mischief.

When Celia walked into the lobby, Brock hardly recognized her. Her hair was close-cropped and dyed black with silver streaks. Her weight loss made her almost unrecognizable to anyone who'd known her even six months ago. She spotted Brock and smiled as she ambled toward where he was sitting.

"Good to see you, Brock," she said, but her eyes were having trouble focusing.

"Celia, nice to see you too. Are you all right?"

"Of course. What, don't I look all right?" She was raising her voice, and Brock was afraid others in the lobby could hear.

"You just look different, that's all. Let's go sit down somewhere we can talk in private," he said, trying to usher her out of the lobby.

"Good idea," she agreed.

When they found a booth in the lounge, away from everyone else, he asked if she wanted coffee or maybe some dessert.

"I'd like scotch on the rocks," she said without hesitation.

"Okay." Brock was surprised. He had never known her to drink scotch. He motioned for the waitress and ordered Celia's drink and a coffee for himself.

"Celia, why have you lost so much weight? You look a little thin."

"Oh, I don't know. Just not so hungry anymore," she said.

Brock knew he'd better change the subject before the conversation turned sour. "How are things at the gallery?" he asked. "Is everything good living with Alan?"

"Oh, I don't work there anymore," she replied, staring out the window of the lounge to the city skyline. "And I don't live with Alan."

"Okay, tell me what happened."

"Alan thought I was taking too much time with Jovan. And he says I've become unreliable because of my lifestyle. You know that's not true, don't you?"

"So, where do you live?"

"With some people Jovan introduced me to. They're nice. Don't charge much rent."

"Celia, honey, I think Alan might be right. You aren't yourself anymore. I think we need to get you some help. It's my fault for letting you run off with a stranger."

"Jovan is no stranger. He's shown me the excitement I've been missing in life. He's introduced me to some talented people, and I've been able to visit some incredible places."

"At what cost, Celia?" Brock set down his coffee. "Look at what this has cost you. Your job, your health, and maybe your marriage." He reached out his hand, but she pushed it away.

"What do you mean? We're still married."

"Honey, not unless you get yourself straightened out. I don't know what's going on. Whatever it is, it's changing the person I married. I won't give up on you. After the game tomorrow, I'll come by, and we can make a plan."

Celia's eyes were suddenly filled with anger. Brock had never seen that look before. "I don't have a problem, and I don't need your help. Just go back to your football team." She tipped her glass of scotch and downed the rest of the drink. "Good-bye," she said as she sprang to her feet, turned, and weaved her way through the tables, heading back to the lobby.

Brock wanted to stop her but didn't want to make a scene in front of the other guests. He followed behind at a distance and watched as she hailed a cab. *At least she isn't driving*, he thought. He went back to the table in the lounge and lay down some cash to pay for the drinks. He swallowed the last of his coffee and pondered what had just happened. He was on shaky ground. His most secure moments in life were on a field marked off in perfect lines, exact and precise, where success was simply determined by the ability to move a ten-yard chain from one end of a rectangle to the other—inches and yards measured by men in striped shirts, who demanded movement within predetermined parameters. It was a world of aggression and emotion but contained within a straightforward set of rules.

He wished the rest of life were so simple. It was as if the boundaries and rules and measurements in his life had all suddenly been ripped away. The chain had been broken. Celia's actions made him feel as if he'd lost the most important game of his life. He was the man who always called the plays. What could he have done differently for a successful outcome? Why wasn't he better prepared? He struggled with his own guilt for not doing more to keep his wife by his side.

He was deep in thought when Tim burst into the room. *What now*, Brock wondered.

"Thank gawd I found you," Tim said. "We've got a problem."

Brock knew it couldn't be worse than what he had just been a part of.

"Jimmy is at the police station. He may be in serious trouble."

"What the hell?" Brock pushed up out of his chair. "The players were supposed to be in their rooms resting?"

"The other boys said he was meeting some of his old friends from Brighton. Now there's been some kind of gang shooting. Luckily, Jimmy had one call and was smart enough to call the hotel. The police are questioning the kids who were at the incident to see what happened."

"Let's go. Don can do a bed check on the others at eleven o'clock. We don't want anybody else messing up."

"Already done, Brock. Don is in charge. You and I better go before they lock that kid up and throw away the key. It would ruin any chance we have tomorrow against Northfork."

When they got to the police station in Jimmy's old neighborhood, Brock recalled the day he and Irene had collected Jimmy's belongings from his old apartment. He was glad Jimmy chose to stay in the Grove but was angry at him now for leaving the hotel and heading to his old neighborhood, especially on the night before the big game.

Brock spoke to the man behind the counter. "Officer, we got a call from a relative of mine, Jimmy Ivory. We think he's here. Can we see him?"

"He was one of the kids involved in a gang shooting," the elderly black man said. He didn't seem especially alarmed.

"That's what I understand. He is here, isn't he?"

"Yessir, he's here. Let me talk to the detective and see what's going on." He spun around and walked through an interior door and was gone a few minutes before returning.

"The detective says they have a few more questions, and then he can go."

"Thank God," Brock said and let out a sigh.

"Who are you?" the officer asked. "You don't quite look like a relative."

"He lives with me on the other side of the state. We're here for the football championships tomorrow."

"He's a player?"

"Yes, and a good one. He needs to be at the hotel in bed."

"You're right about that. What's he doing hanging out with these gang bangers?" Now the man seemed genuinely interested.

"He grew up here … probably wanted to see some of his old friends. Was anybody hurt?"

"No, someone was nearly killed. Young guy. Seventeen years old. They had some kind of argument, not showing the right respect, you know. Makes you sick. Seventeen years old. He'll be lucky if he survives."

As he finished the sentence, the door opened, and another policeman escorted Jimmy into the lobby. "You're free to go," the officer said to Jimmy. "If we need more information, we'll be in touch. You have someone to come and get you?"

"My coaches are here," Jimmy said, gesturing toward Brock and Tim.

"Okay, kid, stay out of trouble." The officer nodded at Brock and Tim then turned and walked back into the interior of the station.

Brock had never seen Jimmy so upset. Even after his mother's death, he'd stayed composed. But this time, he looked anxious and frightened.

"Coach, I'm so sorry," he stuttered, voice shaking. "I just wanted to see my old friends, and somebody got shot. I was right next to him when he fell. He was spittin' blood and moaning. Everybody was screamin' and runnin' around. I was scared."

"It's over now, Jimmy. Let's get you out of here. You weren't at fault, were you?"

"No sir, my friends said we was goin' to a party. That's all. One of them had a gun and got into an argument with this other guy and shot him. I shouldn't have been there. Can we just go back home to the Grove?"

"Not yet. Not until after the game." Brock spoke calmly, trying to quiet the young man. "You shouldn't have left without telling me. You know that. But we have a game tomorrow, and your team needs you. I know it's hard, but you're going to have to try to put this behind you, at least for one day."

They climbed into the car, and Brock drove back to the hotel, slowly, as if he were carrying a precious cargo of fine china. *Ironic,* Brock thought. *Despite the crisis, Jimmy would be back at the hotel before the eleven o'clock bed check.*

CHAPTER 50

DISTRACTIONS

EVEN THOUGH SATURDAY'S GAME wasn't until four o'clock, Brock woke before dawn and went to the hotel coffee shop. When he entered the dining area, he wasn't surprised to see Tim and Don already sitting at one of the tables.

"You guys are early risers," Brock said as he slid into the booth.

"When you work for the road department, you're always the first guy out of bed," Tim said, a sleepy smile on his face.

Don chimed in, "And I'm the guy who opens the door at the Cozy Corner, so it's kind of my routine."

"Well, I guess that makes me the slowpoke here," Brock said as he motioned to the waitress to bring him coffee.

"How do you think Jimmy slept?" Tim asked.

"Probably not at all, would be my guess," Brock said. "And you can't blame him. That incident is going to stay with him for a while. But we need to get him squared away before kickoff."

DISTRACTIONS

"Kids are resilient," Tim said. "Hopefully, he can put that crap behind him by four o'clock. Wouldn't you know, he leaves the hotel and two hours later is in police custody. Welcome back to the freakin' city, huh?"

Brock's phone suddenly chimed. It startled him, and he patted three pockets before finding it. Without cell service on the farm, he'd stopped carrying it with him. He looked down at the screen and recognized the number … Brighton High School. "Hello," he said, wondering who might be calling so early from Brighton.

"Just wanted to tell you congratulations," said the man on the other end of the connection. It was Bill Buchanon, his former athletic director. "Another shot at a state championship. I'm not surprised. I wish it were Brighton, but I'm happy for you."

"Thanks," Brock said. "Nice of you to call. How are things?"

"I'm great, but the football team … not so hot. You probably saw we barely had a winning season. Folks here are a little unhappy right now with the direction the team is headed. I'm taking some heat." He paused, as if working up the courage to broach the next subject. "If you have time today, maybe we could get together and talk. I don't know what your situation is over there with your mom and all, but I'd like to talk about your future."

Brock was intrigued. It sounded like his old boss was hinting at something. "I might have a minute or two at the Dome before the game. It can get hectic, but if you want to meet in the coaches suite at one o'clock, it'd be nice to get together and catch up."

Brock ended the call and took a sip of his coffee. Since he'd been involved with the championship weekend before, he was prepared for all the distractions. But he'd already gotten off to a bad start with Celia and Jimmy on Friday night. He needed to stay calm in front of his players so they wouldn't be overwhelmed by the moment. And soon, he'd have to deal with the parents and boosters. Even his mom and Richard were already on the road headed his way. Many of the town's fans would arrive around noon and check in at the hotel before leaving for the Dome. Those who were already there would soon be filtering down for breakfast.

At their booth, the three coaches began again to go over their strategy for dealing with Northfork. They'd watched their film and knew they were in for a tough afternoon. As they worked on their plan, Brock tried to block out all the other voices in his head and focus on the game. He thought they could win. It wouldn't be easy, but all the pieces were in place to make a run at the prize.

Before the coaches finished their discussion, fans began to stream into the hotel, and the men were inundated with well wishes and congratulations. Lester Colquit was shaking hands with everyone he saw, subtly claiming part of the credit for the success of the football program. The machinery dealer pulled Brock aside, handed him a check, and told him to put it to use … maybe buy new uniforms or a better score clock for the field at home. The band director bounded into the room, slapped Brock on the back, and thanked him for giving his kids a chance to play on the big stage.

Richard and Irene showed up at the hotel earlier than Brock had anticipated. "Your mom insisted we leave before the sun came up," Richard said, rubbing his eyes. "We would've got here earlier, but we had to stop twice to let Sassy out to relieve herself."

Brock didn't know the little dog was coming along but, seizing the opportunity, quickly sent for Jimmy, knowing what a calming effect Sassy had on the boy. It might be just the thing to take his mind off the awful experience the night before.

DISTRACTIONS

Ronnie had ridden over with a group of employees from the bank. When she walked into the hotel lobby, she stood out from the rest of the other employees, who were all wearing the red and white colors of the school. Ronnie was in gray, in deference to her husband. But even in the muted colors, she possessed beauty that shone through. She gave Brock a small wave, and he nodded in response. The hotel was alive with nervous cheerfulness. Brock hoped everyone would still be as happy when the game was over.

A quick lunch in a hotel suite was planned for the team after their walk-through in the park across from the hotel. Then they'd board the bus for the Dome. When they sat down for lunch, some of the players were so nervous they barely touched their food. Brock took note, stood up, and asked everyone in the room to be silent for a moment.

"Listen up, fellas. I know this is a big day for you," he said. "And I could tell you that this is like any other day. That the game you are playing at four o'clock is just another game. But that'd be a lie. This is a very special day. A day you'll remember for the rest of your lives. But win or lose, you need to take it all in as a team. We've been like a family ever since we met together last summer. We've gone through a lot together. It's been a great run and a special season. And what made it special are the guys around you. You'll remember these teammates forever. And I hope you'll look back on this day with fond memories because of the great times you've had with these football brothers."

Brock paused and shifted his eyes. "See Coach Tim standing back there by the wall? He and I became best friends twenty years ago. We have a bond because we had the privilege of playing in this game together, along with Justin's dad, Cort. So, go out and make today a day to remember, especially for those around you and all the people who've come to watch you play."

Brock lifted his water glass as if giving a toast. "Now, throw away your nervousness and lean on your brothers and our fans. We'll do this together. Then I promise you everything will work out." He raised his glass high in the air and asked his players to do the same. "Here's to victory," he said.

"To victory," the players shouted, then quickly devoured their lunch.

When the team filed into the City Dome, many of the Grove players were overwhelmed. Most had never been there before and were taken back by the size of the place. The facility could hold over sixty thousand people, nearly five times the population of their county. The Grizzly fans wouldn't fill one section of the place.

An enormous jumbotron video screen in one end zone was playing highlights from the 2-A game played the day before in the two-day football extravaganza. And down below, on the field, the one hundred or so players assembled for the scheduled 3-A game at one o'clock were going through their pregame warm-ups.

Brock had purposely brought his team early, so they could adjust to the environment and witness the game as played by the bigger high schools. By the time the Grizzlies would take the field, all the nervousness should have disappeared. He stayed with the boys until they found a place to sit, then left them so they could spend time with the kids from the band bus.

He headed for the hospitality suite to meet with his former athletic director. As he strode down the hallway, he noticed a woman walking toward him, studying his face. She looked familiar, but he couldn't place her.

"Brock Gallagher?" she asked with a whimsical smile.

"Yes ma'am," Brock said, still not able to put a name with her face.

"You don't remember me, do you?" she laughed.

DISTRACTIONS

"Sorry, you got me."

"Well, here's a hint. We both spent a night in the canyon by Cold Creek with a friend of yours."

It was Peggy, Tim Palmer's ex-wife.

"Oh my gosh, Peggy. I'm glad to see you. How are you doing?" Brock asked, embarrassed by his inability to recognize an old friend. He put his arms around her in a friendly embrace.

"Sober," she said with a laugh, answering a question she knew would eventually be asked. "Been that way for five months now."

"And here to watch Luke play for a state championship."

"I couldn't miss it. Flew up from Denver this morning. Just got here. I'm so excited for him. This is a dream come true. Playing in the Dome for the state championship, just like you and Tim did. I think we made the right decision sending Luke to live with his dad."

"He's been great for the football team, that's for sure," Brock said. "We've all learned to love Luke. It took a little while, but he fits in well now, acting like a country boy. And it's been good for his dad too. Tim's had to mature a little with Luke living at home. Although I don't think Tim will ever completely grow up, if you know what I mean."

"I definitely know what you mean." She shook her head with a small smile. "So, I'm sure you have a million things to do right now. I don't want to get in your way, but I need to ask. I'd like to see Luke but wondered what you thought. Maybe I should wait until after the game so I don't mess with his focus. What do you think?"

Brock appreciated her thoughtfulness. It made him remember her good qualities and why Tim had chosen her for his wife. But this moment called for a snap decision on his part, and he was struggling for an answer. Her appearance might not only rattle Luke's ability to concentrate but could also throw Tim for a loop. Brock needed to count on Tim when game time came.

"Peggy, I'm not going to tell you what to do, but Tim and Luke have a lot to think about this afternoon. So, if it's possible, it might be best if you wait until after the game to reconnect. Hopefully, then we can all celebrate together."

Brock thought for a moment. "You know what? My mom will be over in the handicapped section. She'd love to see you, and that would keep you out of sight for a while if you don't mind."

"Brock, you always had all the right answers. I'm so glad to see you. And even if you can't recognize me anymore, I still like you." She gave him another hug. "See you after the game."

Brock was impressed. From what Tim had said, he'd pictured Peggy wandering around in a drunken stupor or locked away in a jail cell. Now it seemed she'd gotten her act back together. He felt good about his decision to seat her with his mom. It was just one of many decisions he'd have to make this afternoon.

CHAPTER 51

INSPIRATION

"WE WANT YOU BACK AT BRIGHTON." Those were the first words out of the mouth of Bill Buchanon. He explained that the Bulldog's new coach had alienated his players and boosters and wouldn't be offered a new contract. There was no hurry to decide, but the position would close after the first of the year. Buchanon wanted a new coach signed as quickly as possible to start preparing the team for the next season.

Brock thanked him, they chatted briefly, and then he excused himself. He immediately put the proposal out of his mind. He needed to focus on the game and nothing else. He'd deal with Brighton later.

The one o'clock game for the 3-A championship pitted two traditional rivals against one another. Structured to resemble college programs, the teams had multiple coaches, some sporting credentials from their time in the professional ranks. Rumors always circulated around these schools, suggesting illegal recruiting and grade manipulation to skirt high school rules. At Brighton, Brock occasionally found his own team under scrutiny but always ran a clean program. As he watched the game, he was amused by the difference between these big schools and the program he was running.

At halftime, Brock signaled for his team to head down to the locker room. "Let's go get ready," he commanded. He watched as players pulled themselves away from the other students, receiving well wishes—and in the case of Luke and Ashley, a quick kiss for good luck.

The boys, anxious to take the stage, moved together like a pack of dogs, gazing around cautiously as they confronted their environment. When they entered the darkened bowels of the facility, they found their expansive locker room with plenty of space to arrange their gear and stretch their limbs. Brock let them take their time, knowing teenage joking and laughter would ease their nerves.

As they were dressing, Brock felt compelled to talk with some of the players individually. He called Jimmy into the adjoining room and asked him to sit. "Did you get any sleep last night?" he asked.

"Slept good, Coach. I thought about the farm. Whenever I wanna relax, I try to think about the pasture behind the house and how Sassy'd chase me back and forth when she was a pup. I kept that in my head and went right to sleep. Still, woke up early thinking 'bout the poor guy that got shot. Hope he's going to make it."

"Did you get a chance to see Mom and Sassy this morning?"

"Yes sir. Thought maybe I'd try to smuggle Sassy into the game but knew she wouldn't stop wiggling if I put her in a bag. She's still in the van."

"Good choice. So, you're ready to go?"

"Yessir, Coach. Like you said, this team is family. Nobody here's going to shoot each other. The Grove has been good to me, so I'm going to do my best for you all."

INSPIRATION

Brock slapped Jimmy's thigh. "That's what I expected. Now, please send Luke in; I need a few words with him." As Jimmy walked out the door, Brock's eyes followed him, and he was struck by his stature, even wearing all his pads. He was just a small boy but had done so much for the Grizzly team with his big heart. He needed to produce one more great game.

As he was reflecting on Jimmy's contribution, Luke stuck his head in the door. He hadn't painted his face yet, so he looked slightly boyish in a man's body.

"Coach, you want to see me?"

"Hey, Luke. I just wanted to tell you before this final game, whether we win or lose, you've had a terrific season. I appreciate how hard you've worked and what a leader you've become. After the game, I want to see you and your dad for a minute before everybody runs off."

"Coach, is this about my mom being here?" Luke cocked his head to one side and smiled.

"So, you met up with her?"

"No, I saw her walking down the hall but kind of ducked away. Didn't want to get all sappy-like before a big game. But it's cool she came all that way to be here. I'll talk to her afterward. But please don't tell my dad she's here. Who knows how he's going to act? You need him to chill. You know my dad." Luke rolled his eyes as if to say, 'Remember the Titan game?'

The boy was measuring the moment and trying to balance it the best he knew how. His head was in exactly the right place before the biggest game of his life.

As the minutes ticked down toward the moment they would run out of the tunnel, Brock caught himself thinking back to his own emotions when he took the field nineteen years prior. He and Tim had led their team onto the field, waving a giant Grizzly flag, each with a hand on the staff. Cort followed behind, barking at the others. They were a talented group of athletes who should have won the crown. All they lacked was the cohesiveness this Grizzly team possessed. Brock knew that's why they'd fallen short.

He was stirred from his reminiscences by a knock on the door. "Coach, you got a second?" It was Justin.

"Sure, Justin, what's up?"

"I just wanted to say thanks for what you've done for our team. It means a lot to me. And I'm sorry how my dad acted toward you."

Brock rocked back in his chair. "Don't worry about it. Your dad and I go back a long way. We were good teammates once but somehow got our wires crossed up a bit. This year has been hard on him. He wanted you to succeed and got a little carried away with it. That doesn't mean I don't feel terrible for the condition he's in. I pray for him every day."

"I'm going to try to make him proud today even if he isn't here," Justin said, nervously swinging the helmet hanging from his hand. "And my mom too. I don't know how I could keep going if it weren't for her." His eyes widened, and he chewed on his lower lip.

"Justin, don't put too much weight on your shoulders. You have twenty-three other guys on the team that'll help you get where you want to go. Play for the joy of the game. Just relax. You're the best high school quarterback I've ever coached. You have special talents. Use those skills, and things will turn out just fine. Now get ready to lead this team to a championship."

Moments later, the boys were racing onto the field to the cheers of their fans. Brock trailed behind, taking in the scene. He'd allow himself this moment because once the game started, he wouldn't take his eyes off the field. At the other end of the arena, he could see the players from

INSPIRATION

Northfork. There were a lot of them, dwarfing his squad in numbers. The Loggers had been to the Dome before and were going about their warm-ups, business as usual.

Brock and his coaches strolled among the rows of their players as they stretched, acting like parents guarding over their children. The younger players, Les Colquit and George Olson, were understandably nervous.

With ten minutes left on the warm-up clock, both teams headed to their locker rooms. The younger of the two Simpson brothers jogged straight to a toilet to vomit. He'd been holding back his nervous stomach and was happy to release the butterflies circling around inside of him.

Brock waited for the boys to settle in, then asked for their attention. He'd made a speech at breakfast and would be doing a lot of talking at halftime, so he called on Tim to say a few words. The request caught Tim off guard for a second, and he stumbled with his thoughts but quickly caught his balance. "I'm not a very good speech giver," he said as he twirled a roll of adhesive tape in his hands. "And I have a little trouble talking without mixing in a few four-letter words, so excuse me if I break Coach's cussing rule."

The players laughed and looked at Brock, but Tim continued. "But dammit, fellas, this is where every high school football player in the country wants to be on the last day of the football season. You're going out there to play for the state championship … a frickin' state championship. You've worked your tails off for this. Don't let any joker tell you it's just a game. It's a helluva lot more than that. It's a way to make a name for yourself and for your school and for your town. You'll be the first ones from the Grove to do it. You'll make history."

Tim's face was slowly turning a darker shade of crimson as he continued, his voice rising to a crescendo. "This isn't a game for sissies.

It's tough. It can hurt. And if you give it everything you've got, you'll be so damned exhausted by the end of the fourth quarter you'll feel like you're gonna die. But if you win … I should say when you win, and the final gun goes off, you will never have a sweeter moment in your life."

As he concluded, his voice softened and cracked with emotion. "Don't let this chance pass you by. For forty-eight minutes, forget everything else in your life and make every play count. By gawd, this is your time. You've earned it. Now go bring that trophy home."

CHAPTER 52

GAME TIME

A REFEREE'S WHISTLE SIGNALED the start of the game at exactly four o'clock. A sizable crowd was on hand including spectators from the 3-A game staying over to watch some of the next contest. Immediately they were rewarded with action on the field. Justin's kickoff was returned by a Northfork player who broke a couple of tackles by the over-eager Grizzlies and nearly took it to the house. Two plays later, the Loggers were on the board 7–0.

The Grove fans weren't disheartened. They'd seen their team recover from bad situations before and knew they'd hang tough. Their faith was vindicated when the Grizzlies methodically worked their way down the field. Brock was mixing his plays, keeping the Loggers off balance.

"Justin's on his game," Don said. Brock nodded in agreement and pursed his lips, holding back a way-too-early smile. The quarterback was throwing the ball accurately, finding his receivers for good yardage. And the receivers, happy to be indoors with warm fingers, were making nearly every catch. Luke was giving Justin all the time he needed to find them.

When the Northfork coach began dropping his linebackers into coverage, Brock responded by sending Luke pounding up the middle for sizable gains. The long-sustained Grizzly drive ended in a touchdown as Luke powered through from the two-yard line for a score. Justin added the extra point kick, and the game was tied.

Up in the booth, Tim's voice crackled with enthusiasm. "They're pounding each other down there," he hollered into his headset.

The teams were holding nothing back. A hard tackle by Luke sent a Logger running back limping to the sideline. Later, a massive pileup of bodies on a Grizzly third-down running play forced Tommy Anthony to the bench holding his left arm. It seemed the play might end the senior's career. He sat sobbing on the bench clutching his arm as Don Baker knelt in front of him, examining the injury and trying to console the big boy.

As the first half drew to a close, Jimmy put on a running display that would later make the highlight reel on the local news. Threatening to score from the fifteen-yard line, Justin threw a swing pass to Jimmy in his slot position. When he found himself bottled up by the Logger defense, he reversed his track and, against any coach's advice, ran the opposite way. He met another tackler, spun around, and found a crease in the middle, twisting and turning until, after covering about thirty yards, he leaped headfirst into the end zone. He was mobbed by his teammates.

Brock's eyes searched for a yellow flag. Seeing none, he joined in the jubilation on the sideline. The 21–14 score in favor of the Grizzlies would hold until halftime. The boys from the Grove jogged to their locker room, convinced a victory and a championship ring were within their grasp.

"Settle down," Brock hollered as he entered the room. "We won the first half. That's all. You have another twenty-four minutes of hard-nosed football ahead of you. That team knows how to win. They're not going to quit just because they're behind at halftime."

In the stands, the Grove fans were as proud as they could be. The Grizzlies had proven in the first half they belonged, going toe-to-toe with the premier team at their level. Another half of football like the first, and they'd take home their first-ever championship trophy.

Richard kept his eye on Irene. She was weak from her surgery but was enjoying every minute of the spectacle. And with Peggy Palmer at her side, she had another woman to share it with. Irene had always liked Peggy and had been heartbroken when Peggy couldn't fight off the demons that had destroyed her marriage.

As they watched the game, Peggy quietly talked about how she'd finally gotten her life together. Her honesty gave Irene hope that Peggy might have turned things around for good. Irene wasn't one to give up on the weak ones—animals or people. She always held out hope there might be better things just around the corner.

Throughout the first half, Ronnie, surrounded by her friends from the bank, cheered as loud as she thought appropriate for a woman saddened by the condition of her husband. She was on her feet with the rest of the Grove fans any time there was a good play. She enjoyed the freeing nature of the moment, being able to cheer for the entire team, not just for her boy as it was when Cort was by her side. She felt a twinge of guilt that Cort hadn't seen Justin's spectacular first-half performance.

The excitement of the contest kept many of the previous game's spectators from leaving the Dome. And now, others were starting to gather for the 4-A game that would follow. Altogether, it was a large crowd for a game between tiny schools. But the boys on the field didn't notice the crowd. Both teams were determined to put their opponent away.

The Loggers knew better than to kick to Jimmy to start the half and pooched the ball to the up-back. Wally Thompson ran forward, caught the ball, and then rather than drop to the ground, which would have given the Grove good field position, took off stumbling forward. He was met by a wall of tacklers, and the collision sent the ball flying. A Logger yanked it out of the air.

"Ah shit," Tim muttered into the headset.

Brock didn't respond. There was nothing to say. With short field position, the Loggers tacked on another touchdown to even the score. Brock feared the sudden turn of events might break the will of his boys and tried to rally them one more time.

"We're okay, Coach," Justin answered. "We'll get it back. Don't worry."

Brock was impressed by the calm demeanor of his quarterback, so unlike his father, who'd come completely unwound during his own chance at a championship.

Back on offense, the Grizzlies now faced a big challenge. They had bogged down at midfield. Brock, always reluctant to use gadget plays, thought this might be the right moment. "Run the hook-and-ladder," he said to Les, who was relaying plays to the quarterback.

When Justin got the word, he nodded in agreement. They'd practiced the play all season but had never used it. It was a quick down-and-out pass to the sure-handed George Olson, who in turn would pitch the ball back to a sprinting Jimmy. If all went as planned, Jimmy would glide into the end zone.

"Red 43, Red 43, hut, hut," Justin called out. The ball came into his hands—Augie Swenson, sitting in his wheelchair on the sideline, held his breath as he did on every center-quarterback exchange—and Justin took a three-step drop. He rifled the ball to George, who secured it, waited a split second then offered the perfect lateral to an already-galloping Jimmy Ivory. No one could catch him. The entire stadium crowd, excluding the Northfork fans, roared with delight. The underdog Grizzlies once again had the lead, and the throng began to get fully behind the Cinderella squad.

The announcers in the booth high above the field all agreed this was the most entertaining game of the entire weekend. But next door in the coach's booth, Tim was beyond the need for entertainment.

"Good call. Now let's pad this score a little and get some breathing room. Don may have a real heart attack if we can't put this thing away. And I may be lying there with him."

The Grizzlies held a fragile 28–21 lead when the fourth quarter started. Their fans were nearly hoarse from cheering. Principal Colquit, his high thin voice naturally weak, had trouble even making a sound, but he continued to clap and stomp his feet. His little wife assumed the cheerleader role.

To the dismay of the Grove fans and the happiness of the Logger loyalists, the boys from the west side managed another score late in the quarter and smelling the opportunity to put the Grizzlies away for good, went for the two-point conversion.

The Grizzly linemen had put up a tremendous battle all game. But now, with the muggy heat of the indoor arena causing cramping problems, they were wearing down. The loss of Tommy Anthony at right tackle was becoming especially troublesome for the Grizzly defense. When the Loggers lined up with the linemen tight together and all three backs behind the quarterback, it was raw power over will. The Loggers won out. Now the Grizzlies trailed 29–28 with just under five minutes left to play.

"We have plenty of time to win this thing," Brock assured the team as they huddled around him. But he was beginning to doubt if such success would ever come to him. He'd failed to win when he played in this game a generation ago. And he'd been beaten in the championship as coach of the Brighton Bulldogs. But the boys playing for him now couldn't see his doubts. They knew they had just enough time to march down the field and secure the victory.

Justin took control of his team. There was no arguing. There was no finger pointing. Justin was the leader, and Luke had his back. Brock would call the plays, and they would execute. It was that simple.

Brock wanted to use all five minutes so the Loggers wouldn't have time to respond. Neither team had a time-out left, having used them in the flurry of activity earlier in the third quarter. A touchdown or field goal with a couple of double zeroes on the clock would be perfect. So, starting at the twenty-yard line, the Grizzlies began their drive. Luke was going to carry the load. Straight dive plays into the heart of the Logger defense.

First down ... Luke carries for five yards.

Second down ... Luke for four yards.

Third down ... Justin on a quarterback sneak for another first down.

Just under four minutes left. Grove fans are all standing, wringing their hands. Members of the band, including Ashley, are bouncing on their toes. The ball is on the thirty-three-yard line.

First down ... Luke for four yards. The big man gets stronger with every carry.

Second down ... Justin, from a shotgun formation, hits Les for a thirteen-yard gain and another first down. Ball is on the fifty-yard line.

Less than three minutes left ... Luke runs straight ahead for five yards.

Second down ... Justin hits Jimmy with a swing pass for eight yards and another first down. He's on the thirty-seven-yard line and goes out of bounds to stop the clock with just over two minutes left. The Loggers are gasping for breath, looks of panic on their once-confident faces.

The Glory Grove fans and those from Northfork are on their feet screaming. Irene is squeezing Peggy Palmer's hand so hard her fingers are starting to tingle. Richard is feeling dizzy, so he sits down, thinking he probably needs a stiff drink. In the middle of the crowd, Ronnie stands completely still. She unexpectedly feels a sense of calm and serenity, while four hundred miles away, the nurses in the hospital notice Cort Jepson is beginning to kick his legs ever so slightly and mutter incoherently.

First down ... Jimmy follows Luke on an off-tackle play behind the Simpson brothers on the left side and gains five yards. But a holding call negates the play and moves the ball back to the forty-seven-yard line with under two minutes left on the clock.

It's first down and twenty. Brock knows they still have time for another running play. Once again, he runs Luke off-tackle, this time behind the blocking of Matt Peterson and Tommy Anthony, who has returned to the field of play, despite his injury. After swallowing a half dozen ibuprofens, he grits his teeth and reenters the game. His arm is now wrapped in a giant white pad. The hole the linemen create is big enough for Jimmy to squirt through, and he gains twelve yards.

Second down and eight yards to go for a first down, ball on the thirty-five-yard line. There is a minute and twenty seconds left on the clock, and it is running. Brock knows another first down will temporarily stop the clock and signals for a sweep to the outside with Jimmy carrying the ball. He wiggles his way for seven yards but can't get out of bounds, and the clock continues to run.

Third down and the Grizzlies need a yard for a first down. The clock ticks under a minute, and Brock senses the Loggers might bring full pressure. He calls for a little screen pass across the middle to Les, knowing that even if it's incomplete, it will stop the clock and still leave them with one more play. Or if Les makes the catch, a first down will also stop the clock.

Justin calls the signals with just forty-five ticks left on the clock. Brock has guessed right. The Loggers come with a blitz—both safeties and the outside linebackers. Justin waits for the oncoming defensive rush to nearly reach him before looping the ball to Les. If Les can get past the middle linebacker, he can easily get the first down or even more. It's the perfect call.

In the stands, the principal and his wife are hugging each other in anticipation of the big moment. But as the ball lands in Les's long fingers, the Logger linebacker levels his head and plants his helmet between the boy's numbers. The skinny freshman, who has been indestructible all year long, is flung backward with his arms flailing at his side. He lies writhing on the ground, the wind completely gone from his lungs. His parents continue to hug, only this time in sheer terror, thinking their son has suffered a mortal wound.

Les is on the ground, the ball ten yards behind him. But next to the ball is a yellow flag, thrown by the umpire. "Personal foul for a player leading with his helmet against a defenseless player," he says. The Logger coaches are storming up and down the sidelines in front of their players, arguing the call but to no avail.

Trainers rush to the freshman to determine the extent of Les's injury, but as they arrive, he sits up, trying to take in as much oxygen as he can. He rises slowly and jogs to the sidelines to the applause of the crowd and the relief of his parents. The principal and his wife slump onto the bleacher seats, overcome by emotions. The principal's wife has her head buried in her husband's coat.

GAME TIME

With the fifteen-yard penalty, the Grizzlies have a first down, but the clock shows just twenty seconds. The ball is placed on the left hash mark near the thirteen-yard line. Brock thinks a quick running play to center the ball for a straight-on field goal attempt might be his best call. He signals in the play, and Luke quickly powers through the Logger line for three yards.

The ball is now centered perfectly in the middle of the field. But the umpire, who has taken the worst of the verbal abuse from the Northfork coaches, throws his yellow hanky high in the air.

"Holy crap," Tim says in his headset. "What the hell are they calling this time?"

"Holding," the referee says deliberately into his microphone as if answering Tim's question. The entire arena hears the words echo throughout the building. "That's a ten-yard penalty from the line of scrimmage."

The Grove fans are hit with the negative turn. Some boo. Others scream at the referee. But Brock must make a quick decision.

The ball is now on the twenty-third-yard line… just on the edge of Justin's range for a field goal. Brock doesn't want to lose the game on a kicker's missed attempt. They will win it or lose it on the backs of the entire team.

"We'll throw the ball," Brock says to himself and Tim up in the booth. "We'll run a corner route to Jimmy in the back of the end zone. I think he can outjump their little defensive back."

"Give 'em hell, boss," Tim says. "Let's do it."

Suddenly the crowd grows silent. In a dream-like moment, Justin gathers his players around him and calls the play. For the first time in his high school career, he feels perfectly calm, as if someone has laid a hand on his shoulder.

"This is it, boys," he says. "Everybody do your job. We've been getting ready for this all our lives; make it count."

The team scurries to the line—a bunch of individuals—some too young, some from another part of the country, and some who thought they'd never get the chance to play the game. Like Tim had told them, they were so exhausted they almost felt like death, except at this moment, they seemed incredibly alive.

From the shotgun position, Justin calmly calls the snap count. Luke, his face paint now just a sweaty stream of black goo spread from his eyes to his chin, leans forward on his big hand, ready for one last play. Wally Thompson, who'd taken over for Augie halfway through the season, grasps the laces of the ball, ready to make the most important snap of his young career. Jimmy looks downfield at the young back he will try to beat to the corner of the end zone.

"Red, 43. Red, 43. Hut. Hut." Justin's count can be heard over the din of the stadium. Twenty-two bodies reach to find the last bit of energy they can muster. Justin has the ball in his hands and spins it so his fingers match perfectly with the laces. He bounces deliberately on his toes behind Luke, looking straight at Les Colquit, trying to draw the defensive safety a bit closer and away from Jimmy. But the young Logger defensive back isn't fooled and anticipates what is about to happen. It now becomes a foot race between him and Jimmy. It's a twenty-three-yard sprint to jubilation or despair.

Brock holds his breath. This is it, the final play in a season unlike any other… one of the best rides of his life.

Justin unloads the ball, his arm like a cannon, as Jimmy breaks for the corner. The ball is perfectly thrown, and some of the college scouts who have arrived early to take in the 4-A championship game, with their highly recruited quarterbacks, start scribbling notes about this junior quarterback from farm country. The leather pigskin spins in a laser-like spiral toward its target.

Jimmy and his counterpart sprint toward the corner of the end zone, each boy growling and gasping for air. The players, now intertwined like the strands of a rope, leap as one, reaching back, their eyes searching for the ball. It seems suspended in the air for an eternity. Finally, it comes within reach of two sets of strong, determined hands.

CHAPTER 53

CONSEQUENCES

ACROSS TOWN, Celia woke. Her head throbbed with a dull, never-ending pain, and her stomach churned. She tried to focus, slowly shaking her head, looking to see the clock on the wall. It read six o'clock, but morning or night? She wasn't sure.

"You feeling okay?" asked the middle-aged nurse as she stepped into the room.

"Where am I?"

"You're at Memorial Hospital. You overdosed. They brought you in a couple of hours ago," the nurse said as she checked Celia's pulse.

Celia was angry when she left Brock at the hotel on Friday night and went back to the house she shared with friends. Throughout the following day she seethed, thinking of the altercation. When one of the housemates suggested she relax and handed her a syringe, Celia agreed, thinking it would help her calm her nerves. But unlike the many other soothing moments she'd had with the drug, which left her in a state of ecstasy, her breathing slowed until it was almost imperceptible. She fell into unconsciousness. Her friend tried to rouse her, but she wouldn't wake.

Even in his own debilitated condition, the man with Celia could recognize a disaster unfolding. He dialed 911. Emergency personnel arrived quickly, in time to administer a dose of Narcan. Celia's breathing immediately returned to normal. But knowing Narcan had only temporary effects, the EMTs rushed her to the hospital.

Celia found herself in a flimsy cotton hospital gown, lying on an adjustable hospital bed. The room was sterile and smelled of antiseptic. Brock's words kept playing over and over in her head.

"Celia, I think you need some help. Whatever you're taking has cost you your job, your health, and maybe our marriage."

But she also remembered his pledge to help.

Frightened and depressed, Celia suddenly wanted to be loved again. She'd call Brock to apologize for what she'd become. To ask his forgiveness. She asked the nurse for her phone and dialed his number. 'Please, Brock, pick up,' she prayed, but he didn't answer. It was just after six o'clock pm. Outside the hospital window, the sun had long since set over the western horizon.

Brock had his cell phone tucked securely in his front pocket in case he needed to call someone at halftime or after the game. But as the crowd was buzzing over the contest's final play, he didn't hear or feel the incoming call from Celia. His focus was on Jimmy's fight for the ball.

Justin had thrown a perfect corner fade. Both young players had struggled for control, but Jimmy, as he had often done all season, leapt to high point the ball, tipping it away from his opponent and reeling it into his hands. Once he'd secured it, he raised the ball high over his head in front of the official to showcase the feat. On the sideline, Brock waited for the referee to raise his arms.

The fans from Glory Grove were delirious. The band leader quickly struck up the Grizzly fight song. Their boys had done the impossible, bringing home a state championship one year after not even putting a team on the field. Still, there was no signal from the men in striped shirts.

"What's going on, Tim?" Brock asked as he gazed up into the glassed-off booth overhead.

"Jeezus, I don't know. There is no flag, so it's gotta be a question of whether his feet were in bounds. It sure looked to me like he was in."

"I couldn't tell from here," Brock said, now starting to worry.

In the video crew's booth, high above the field, the men behind the cameras were rewinding the tape, although in high school football there would be no instant replay. "This is one time where it would be nice if we could signal down our opinion," said one man to the other, "because from what I can see, his feet were at least a couple inches inside the white line."

"They better not screw this up," Tim said, "but refs don't go against the favorites, and we're the underdog. My gut's starting to tell me we might get shafted."

Finally, after the five officials had huddled for several minutes, the head man ran to the center of the field, flicked the toggle switch to address the crowd and announced the verdict. "It has been determined the receiver's toes were outside the field of play. Therefore, there is no touchdown. The game is over."

Grove fans were devastated. The players were exhausted and heartbroken, particularly the seniors, who knew their only chance at a state championship came up empty.

The people in the stands, caught up in the David versus Goliath saga, were stunned by the referee's call, thinking they'd made a terrible blunder.

"Dammit to hell, Brock, this just isn't right," Tim said. But Brock had already removed his headset, handed it to the team manager, and headed onto the field.

"Heck of a game," was all Brock said as he walked out to console his players and try to convince them it wasn't the end of the world.

Jimmy rushed over and planted himself in front of Brock. "I was in, Coach," he pleaded. "I know I was in. It was a touchdown."

"You did all you could. It was a great catch, but it won't help to argue with the officials. We know we won, and that's going to have to be enough," Brock said, his arm cradling the boy's head, trying to ease the hurt for the one player who'd been with him the longest. Despite his calming words, he realized in a year or two, only the people in Glory Grove would remember just how close they'd come. They would be reminded each time they passed by the trophy case in the high school where a black-and-white photo leaned up against the second-place trophy from the championship game. The photo by a Seattle sports photographer showed Jimmy's catch in the end zone, his two feet clearly inside the white lines.

Parents and fans started to wander close to the sidelines to offer words of sympathy and congratulations to their boys. Principal Colquit and his wife were there, each one embracing their son, glad for his safety and proud of his accomplishments. Ronnie had Justin's face in her hands, cheering him as best she could. She knew his tears were about more than the game. He missed his dad, even though she suspected that if Cort were there, he would be chasing down the referee.

As the players began to settle down, Brock looked for his mother and saw her still seated in the handicapped section. Peggy was with her, and next to Peggy stood Tim.

Formalities followed. The runner-up trophy was handed to the boys from the Grove. As the team gathered for a photo, some kneeling while others stood, several boys wiped away their tears and forced smiles, wanting to look presentable for an image that would soon reside in the school's trophy case … next to the one with Brock, Tim, and Cort.

CHAPTER 54

TOGETHER

MANY OF THE DISAPPOINTED Grizzly fans left the city immediately after the game. Others planned to stay over and strike out after breakfast. Brock and the team would spend the night in the hotel recovering from their aches and pains.

Brock eventually noticed Celia's call on his phone and dialed her number, thinking it odd she would call during the game. When she answered and told him where she was, he hurried to her side. They spent the evening letting out their feelings and trying to plan some kind of future for themselves. They both agreed she needed help.

Before leaving the hospital, Brock, despite his weariness, was able to have a conversation with a doctor, who recommended a local rehabilitation facility. It would mean time secluded from her friends and family. And the doctor warned that rehab wasn't always successful on the first attempt. But they agreed it was her best option. Brock made arrangements for her immediate enrollment.

It was nearly two o'clock in the morning when Brock left the hospital. As he stepped out onto the darkened street, he was drained from the emotions of the day. He needed sleep badly and hurried back to the hotel. When he stepped into the lobby, it was empty except for the woman curled up by the fireplace. Ronnie, head down as if she were napping.

Brock nudged her gently. "Ronnie, what are you doing up at this hour?"

She raised her head. Her eyes were red and swollen. Brock wasn't surprised she'd still be upset about how the game ended.

"Cort passed," she said, with a tremor in her voice. "The hospital called a couple of hours ago. He's gone."

Brock sunk into the couch beside her and closed his eyes. Despite Cort's disagreeable character, the thought of losing someone who'd been a part of his life hit him hard. "I'm so sorry, Ronnie. Does Justin know?"

"Not yet. He was already in bed. I thought I'd wait until morning to tell him, let him get some sleep while he could."

"Was it peaceful?" Brock asked, hoping Cort hadn't suffered.

"They said he became restless in the late afternoon, tried talking some, and then all his vital signs crashed. They tried to help but couldn't bring him back. I feel terrible that he was alone."

Brock slid over closer to her. "Being here for Justin was the right thing to do. He needed you. It was amazing, how he led the team. Cort would have been so proud of him. I'm just sorry we couldn't pull it off."

"I was with the boys for dinner. They wondered where you were. They were all disappointed with how the season ended but already talking about next year. They're hoping you'll still be their coach."

"I feel bad I wasn't there for them. I had a family emergency. Celia was taken to the hospital, and I had to deal with some issues. As for football, next year is a long time from now. I have a lot to think about before then."

Ronnie stared over at Brock, then closed her eyes and laid her head back on the oversized couch. The fire in the fireplace cast a glow on her face. "I hope it's nothing serious with Celia. It sounds like you and I both have problems. It's been a rough day."

"And we'll find a way to deal with everything … starting tomorrow," Brock said. "I suppose you need to get home right away. Tim and I are leaving after lunch. You're welcome to ride with us if you want."

"Maybe. My bank friends want to stay over another couple of days and go shopping. Some of the girls have never been here before. But I'd better check to see what Justin wants to do."

Brock took Ronnie by the hand and lifted her off the couch. "Let's talk about it in the morning. We'll get something figured out. I'll walk you to your room."

They made their way up the stairs and down the deserted hallway, both drained from their exhaustion and personal turmoil. When they reached her door, Ronnie looked up at Brock. "Thanks for being here for me," she whispered. She pressed her head up against his chest. He could feel her tremble as she inhaled. He smelled the fragrance of her hair and wanted to be invited into her room. Instead, he slowly pulled away.

Filled with her own mixture of desire and guilt, she put her hand on his chest so neither of them could draw close together again.

"Call me tomorrow," she said, blinking away tears. She slipped the key card in the slot and saw the light turn green. She pushed open the door, stepped in, and then let it close behind her.

Tim called in the morning. "You awake yet?"

Brock exhaled into the phone. "I've been up for an hour. Couldn't sleep past five o'clock. It's been a rough night."

"Yep, tough loss."

"More than that," Brock said. He told Tim about Cort's passing and Celia being in the hospital with an overdose and their plans for moving her to rehab.

"Cripe, Brock, a whole load of crap fallin' on you in one day."

"Yes, but we couldn't have asked for more from the team. They gave it everything they had. Can you believe they almost won it all?"

"They played a helluva game. And they're already chomping at the bit thinking about next year."

"That's good ... that helps heal the hurt."

"Hey, Brock, my Peggy came up from Denver to watch the game. Says she'd like to visit the Grove for a couple of days. Suppose she could ride back with us?"

"Of course. I saw her. She looks good. We have room in the car, and Ronnie might need to ride back with us too. She needs to start planning a funeral. The four of us together. Who could have seen that coming?"

Minutes later, Veronica called to see if the offer for a ride was still on. After letting Justin know about his dad, he still wanted to ride home and finish the season with his friends. "I think he'd mentally prepared himself for Cort's passing long before the game. He played his heart out to honor his dad and is ready to move on."

"He's an amazing young man," Brock said. "If I'd ever had a son, I would hope he would have been half as good."

Brock spent the morning getting Celia checked into rehab. Both he and Celia shed tears as he walked out of the door. Then the four old friends gathered in the hotel, loaded Brock's car, and headed home. They had six hours to reminisce about old times and to acknowledge the mistakes they'd made in their lives since they'd gone their separate ways. Peggy and Tim sat in the back, and occasionally, Brock would catch a glimpse of them in the rearview mirror, looking at each other, almost like he remembered them in high school.

Ronnie was subdued for much of the ride, staring out the window at the passing scenery and closing her eyes from time to time, preparing for the sadness the next few days would hold.

CHAPTER 55

MEMORIAL

CORT'S FUNERAL was held the following Friday in the Methodist Church. It was a rainy day, and low gray clouds bumped along across the sky, skimming the top of the steeple. Ronnie chose Cort's tavern friends for pallbearers. She and Justin would have preferred Brock and Tim but respected what they knew would be Cort's wishes.

The football team attended the service wearing their letterman jackets. Most of the players only knew Cort as the hothead dad who was usually griping from the grandstand, but they were there out of respect for their quarterback. Ashley, one of the few girls from the school at the service, sat between Luke and Jimmy. It was a short service, sparsely attended, but there were still tears. It was a passing of a generation, and Brock found himself fighting to control his emotions, thinking of his times with Cort and contemplating his own mortality.

Peggy and Tim came to the service together, clearly at ease with one another. People were beginning to notice how Peggy seemed to be reconnecting with Tim and Luke. It drew special attention from the church ladies, who'd once condemned Peggy for her behavior but were ready to forgive—all Christian women would—if she had really straightened out her life.

Irene had slept for two days, exhausted from the long trip to Seattle, but felt strong enough to attend the funeral. She liked being back in the church, and Jimmy claimed he'd take her anytime she wanted to go. After returning from the game and the harrowing experience he'd had with the boys from Brighton, Jimmy had taken an interest in his mother's Bible.

When the ceremony ended, people milled around outside the church, making small talk. As the rain sprinkled down in tiny droplets, there were hushed conversations concerning Ronnie and Justin and about football and the future of the team. The finality of the moment had put some closure on the season and the drama they'd all witnessed.

The next Monday, Brock called his mom's doctor and asked about the chances for her recovery. "I'm sorry, Brock, but the prognosis isn't good. Realistically, Irene probably has months, not years, left to live, although I appreciate what a fighter your mom is."

Basketball practice also started the Monday following the funeral, and their coach was gushing over the future of his team with Jimmy at the point guard position. In fact, most of the two dozen boys who'd played football were now hitting the hardwood, although, they each admitted they would rather still be knocking people down on the football field.

Brock frequently called on Ronnie and Justin to make sure they were doing okay. Justin, as he had done when Brock first arrived in town, began pressuring Brock to lead the team for another year. "We all think we have another good shot at winning the champion's trophy," he said. "It should have been ours anyway." He added with a smile, "Just so you know, Augie is passing around a petition asking for you to coach us again."

Principal Colquit phoned during the week and asked Brock to come in and discuss the teaching position that might open on the faculty.

In somewhat of a surprise, the members of the state football coaches' association voted Brock Coach of the Year for the small-school division, despite the Grizzlies' four losses. "The boys on our team made me look good," Brock told the local paper. "It's an honor I share with the whole team."

Celia was always on Brock's mind. He'd been told, in the first days of her stay in rehab, he wasn't allowed to visit but called the head of the center to find out how she was doing.

"I'm sorry, Mr. Gallagher. I'm afraid she checked herself out a couple of days ago. She insisted we weren't to call you. Some friends came and picked her up. We tried to convince her to stay, but she was sure she could break her dependency on her own. I'm sorry to say almost no one can do that. She's probably going to find herself right back here pretty soon. My advice to you would be to try to convince her to come back in if you think you can."

The news was devastating. For the last several months, in these moments of conflict, his mind was quieted by the thoughts and preparations for the next football game. But now, the season was over. This wasn't a game. This was life, and he had to face it. He had to deal with Celia and his mother, the farm, and Grizzly football. And there was Ronnie. She needed him, and so did her son, who would soon be getting calls from college recruiters. In the frenzy of a football game, he could see the whole picture and make quick, precise decisions based on all the variables … pursuing a perfect outcome. But in life, there were no easy answers.

He hung up the phone and walked out of the house to the pile of wood stacked beside the barn for the winter. Sassy was at his side. Dolly watched from the corral as he grabbed an ax and began splitting wood. Wood chips flew. The November wind should have chilled him, but he continued to swing the tool until sweat poured down his face and drenched his torso. Again and again, he pounded with all his strength, grunting with every stroke of the ax. For over an hour, the pile of wood grew, and blisters formed on his hands.

CHAPTER 56

PARTING

WHEN THE CALENDAR FLIPPED to December, Brock knew it was time to return to Seattle and try to persuade Celia to return to rehab. While there, he'd also meet with Bill Buchanon, the athletic director at Brighton High. Perhaps if he removed himself from the influences at Glory Grove, he might realize a return to his old life in the city was best for everyone. But before he left, he wanted to talk with Ronnie one more time—alone, without the distractions of football, friends, or family.

She welcomed his invitation to the farm and arrived on a clear, crisp afternoon. With temperatures in the twenties, frost clung to the shady side of the farm buildings. Irene and Jimmy had hung Christmas lights on the front porch and along the old hog-wire fence around the yard. When Ronnie got out of her car, she was smiling as if she were a child seeing her first Christmas tree. It reminded Brock of the innocent happiness she'd possessed when they were in their teens.

PARTING

As he stepped out of the front door to greet her, she blushed like a schoolgirl on her first date. She hurried up the walkway. With the woolen mittens she was wearing, she struggled to open the little metal gate with two dog-eared latches. "Help, Brock, I can't find the combination," she said, dancing on her toes.

"Always something coming between us, isn't there," he said as he lifted the latch and swung the gate open.

She stepped through and threw herself into his arms, exaggerating the movement. She squeezed him tightly for several seconds. "Thank you, kind prince, for letting me in."

"You're most welcome." He bowed like an English gentleman. "Would you like to accompany me on a ride up to the piney ridge? I've prepared hot chocolate."

She slapped her mittens together to shake off the frost from the gate and feigned an awkward curtsy. "Yes, please, I love hot chocolate, and it seems a marvelous day for a drive."

They jumped into the farm pickup, and Ronnie, without hesitation, slid in close beside him like she'd always done when they were in high school. She fiddled with the radio and eventually found a station with Christmas music. She cranked up the volume, and they hummed along to the familiar tunes like school children on a winter hayride.

Reaching a turnout, Brock parked the pickup, and they stepped out into the midafternoon sunshine where they could look down into the canyon and see Cold Creek. It glistened like silver tinsel as it wound its way through the pine trees, where years ago, they first experienced teenage love. There was a skiff of snow on the tree boughs, and chickadees bounded from limb to limb chattering at the human visitors. Without asking, Brock took Ronnie's hand, and they walked along the trail without talking. Ronnie's cheeks turned pink, and her hazel eyes were sparkling. The cold turned their breath into vapor as they climbed high up the steep hill.

When they finally stopped to catch their breath, Ronnie broke the silence. "Where are we going?"

"Just a ways further. There is a nice view on the point of the ridge," he said.

Ronnie was silent for a moment as if reluctant to say the words. "No, I mean, where are you and I going—in our lives?"

Brock inhaled, pulling in the cold air. "Ronnie, it's not that simple," he said, looking off to the horizon. "I have a wife."

"Are you going back to her? Is that why you brought me here today? To tell me good-bye?"

Brock pulled the collar of his coat up around his neck. "I just wanted to be near you. Just to look at you. And hold your hand again. Honestly, I'm not sure what I'm doing." He turned to face her and saw she was starting to shiver. He unbuttoned his heavy wool coat, wrapped it around her, and pulled her close. The warmth of her body felt good in the cold air. When she looked up at him, he instinctively bent down and kissed her, gently at first but harder as he felt her lips pressing against his.

"I don't want you to go," she said softly as she turned away, gazing into the canyon hundreds of feet below. "But if you go, I'll understand. I'm just happy we had you back for a little while. But it's not fair. We all fell in love with you again."

"I never planned on coming back for good," he said. "I was just keeping a promise to my mom. But now …" He didn't finish the sentence, just shook his head.

"Does your wife love you?"

"Not enough, it seems." He didn't want to explain how she'd run off with a New York artist. "But she's in trouble, and I need to help."

PARTING

"I wish you weren't such a good man," Ronnie said. She looked down at the ground, kicked a rock, and listened to it clattering down the face of the cliff. Then she pushed him away, turned, and continued up the steep trail, leaving Brock to watch her move away from him once again.

As her footsteps receded, another sound echoed from deep in the canyon, the crashing of timber as a bull elk and two cows suddenly burst from the pine trees. The racket echoed through the canyon. *Perhaps*, he thought, *the same bull which had greeted him on his return to the Grove six months earlier.* It was December. The mating season was over, but he wished he could hear the bugling of that bull again, beginning with a slow growl and progressing to a high-pitched, repetitive scream … slow, methodical, and beautiful.

With Christmas just weeks away, Brock retrieved the mail from the mailbox at the end of the driveway. Tucked inside the daily newspaper were some Christmas cards for his mom, a few magazines, and a single letter in a plain white envelope addressed to him. He recognized Celia's handwriting, so he took out his pocketknife, slit the envelope, and pulled the lined paper from it. He began to read.

"My darlin, Brock, as you already know, I could not face the burdens placed on me in the rehabilitation facility and chose to leave. I know that's a disappointment to you, but feel it is the best way for me to work through my problems. Due in part to my travels to New York and Chicago, some of the cash reserves we accumulated over the years are gone. So, I don't think we can afford the treatment. Also, I have moved out of the house I was sharing with friends and have taken a small apartment close to the gallery. Alan has agreed to take me back as an employee part-time if I can straighten out my life. We both know I took a wrong turn. However, I can't deny the fact

I loved the experiences and the people I was exposed to with Jovan. I want to return to that life—without the drugs, of course. It's clear you are enjoying life back in your hometown, and I'm happy for you. But I would never be happy there. Because of this, and the guilt I feel over my infidelity in our marriage, I think it best if I try to deal with my situation alone. Please don't worry. I will be fine."

Celia

Brock fell back into the seat of the pickup. Through the last few months, he'd grown to resent his wife's absence … felt he'd been abandoned by someone he loved, painfully similar to the angst he experienced when his father departed. But he never considered his marriage would end like this. He'd thought that when things settled down, somehow he could put all the pieces back together. Had he failed his wife? Or had she failed him?

CHAPTER 57

RETURN

TWO WEEKS BEFORE CHRISTMAS, Brock left for Seattle to settle things with Celia. And he would go talk to Bill Buchanon at Brighton High, who suggested there might be a sizable monetary incentive if he returned to coach the Bulldogs. The money would be important if he could convince Celia to return to rehab.

As he headed west on the interstate, he realized it had only been six months since he'd left Brighton High and traveled east to Glory Grove. With the car radio turned off, the episodes of his life in the Grove ran through his mind like a movie on a never-ending loop. Drawing closer to the millions of urban inhabitants, he felt the knot in his stomach which always came with the frenzy of the city. He already missed the relaxed pace of his hometown.

He'd been on the road for four hours, almost reaching the summit of the mountain range that separated the state—east from west. A mix of rain and snow had been falling throughout the drive, coming down hard, settling on the black asphalt. The slush splattered up alongside his door.

When the car began to swerve and vibrate, Brock thought he'd hit a big puddle. But the thumping sound under the chassis told him it was more than rain. "No, not now," he said out loud. He'd been tormented by the conflicts in his mind but now faced the physical discomfort of changing a tire.

He pulled onto a wide spot on the shoulder, turned his car away from the traffic, and climbed out into the drizzle. With his jacket collar pulled up around his neck, he knelt beside the rear tire. He lifted the car with the screw jack and began to remove the lug nuts. Wet snow was pelting his face and running from his forehead into his eyes. He strained to focus and began to shiver as the wind drove the cold into his clothes.

His mind was numb. He'd suppressed a lot of emotion in the last few weeks; at times, he felt he might crumble. Now nature seemed to break something free inside him. His tears began to fall, mixing with raindrops as they ran down his cheeks. Putting his head in his hands, he waited for the moment to pass.

Finally, he forced himself to breathe and put the spare tire onto the axle hub. He quickly stored away his tools, climbed back into the driver's seat, and with a tissue from the glove compartment dried his face. Still shaking from the cold, he fastened his seatbelt, put the car in gear and slowly moved to face the highway. He looked both ways; there was no traffic in sight. But he didn't move. Instead, he sat. The wipers swiped the moisture from his windshield, and the sound propelled the images racing through his mind.

Suddenly, an eighteen-wheel semi roared around the corner, blasting his car with slush. His shaking amplified. Still, he didn't move, like a confused animal seeking a path to safety. He knew he should continue

RETURN

on to the city. Celia, despite her rejection of him, still needed his help. And there was the promise of a big paycheck if he returned to Brighton. He'd be welcomed by Bulldog fans—a hero's welcome and a chance to lead the big school to a championship.

He still hesitated. Why? If he returned to Glory Grove, keeping the family farm alive would take a lot of work, especially when his mother passed. The town, like all small farming communities in the region, would continue to struggle to survive. And the football team, even if he went back there, might only have one good year left. Without Jimmy, Justin, and Luke, they would be hard-pressed to be competitive.

Yet, somehow, he was drawn to the place where hard work and seasonal challenges brought folks together with a spirit and love unknown to city dwellers. He thought of the boys. How, at Augie's urging, they scribbled their names on a petition asking him to return to lead the Grizzlies in their quest to claim the elusive state championship. He'd left his team at Brighton and disappointed his players. Could he do the same to the boys from the Grove? He imagined the joy on their faces if they were able to hoist the coveted trophy, especially Jimmy, who had become part of his family. He thought of Justin without a father and Ronnie, whose very presence stirred emotions long ago buried by circumstance.

As he sat, his fingers seemed paralyzed on the turn signal, a mechanical appendage engineered to be intuitive to a casual driver. But now it wasn't. He fidgeted with it for a few seconds, then flicked it up … to finish his journey to Seattle. The staccato clicking made his forehead moist and matched the pounding of his heart. He wiped his brow again.

More seconds passed. But now, the storm was beginning to subside, and a bit of blue inched into the cloudy sky in the east. The rain turned to a mist, slowly ascending from the ground skyward. Like a veiled curtain, blue and silver, it sparkled and shimmered in the emerging sun. As Brock turned his head to witness the change, he saw an image—real or imagined, he wasn't sure—in the trees to the right. A bull elk, regal in its pose, stared at him for a fraction of a second, then raised its head, wheeled around, and darted into the forest.

With its disappearance, the crescendo of Brock's emotions eased. His shaking stopped, and his heart rate slowed as he grasped the turn signal again, pulling it down and holding it there. He let out a long sigh as he spun the steering wheel to the left, pressed his foot on the accelerator, and eased into the eastbound lane. The frown disappeared from his face. He was going home.

ACKNOWLEDGMENTS

A SHORT PHONE call from a high school friend led me to join a writer's group—Dawn, Cam, Cosy, Lillian, Fred, Sanford, and Tom. They started me on the journey to *Glory Grove*.

Thanks also to Bobby Haas, a great editor, who helped polish my writing and to Kiki Ringer, who led me through the publication process.

ABOUT THE AUTHOR

GARY BYE lives in rural eastern Washington state. When not writing, he can be found driving tractor or feeding cows with his son on the family wheat farm. With a background as a magazine editor and award-winning photographer for farm publications, Gary understands life in small towns. His formative years were spent as a high school teacher and coach, but he also spent several years working as a journalist in the nation's capital and as a freelance writer for various magazines. Previously published books include a two-volume set recounting a century of local small-town football—*From the First Whistle and To the Final Gun*.

He and his wife are active in the lives of their three grown sons and a passel of little grandchildren. In his spare time, Gary can be found downhill skiing, attending cattle shows, or helping lead a local church.

Made in United States
Troutdale, OR
01/20/2025